SHIFTING SANDS RESORT OMNIBUS

VOLUME 1

ELVA BIRCH

ZOE CHANT

PO Box 82851

Fairbanks Alaska 99708

ISBN 978-1-933603-67-4

For Layla, who convinced me to try.

CONTENTS

SHIFTING SANDS RESORT

Sun, surf, shifters, and secrets!

Escape to a shifters-only resort on a hot tropical island full of secrets and sizzling romance.

Shifting Sands Resort is a complete paranormal romance series with self-standing novels that interconnect in an intriguing mystery.

This omnibus edition is in the author's preferred reading order and includes:

Tropical Tiger Spy (book 1)
Other Duties as Assigned (short story)
Locked (short story)
Tropical Wounded Wolf (book 2)
Unlocked (short story)
Tropical Bartender Bear (book 3)
Tex's Cocktail Recipes

TROPICAL TIGER SPY

PROLOGUE

Snow flew beneath running tiger paws; the time for stealth was long past and Tony flat out ran, the precious drive carefully held between his teeth.

Behind him, there was distant shouting in Russian and a spatter of gunfire. Bullets struck stone around him.

Tony zigzagged a few paces, then sprang for the nearest wall. It would have been an impossible jump as a man, nearly nine feet in the air, but as a tiger he cleared it easily and landed in the deep snowbank beyond with an explosion of snow.

See, his tiger said smugly. *We got out easily!*

Concentrate on staying *free*, Tony reminded him. *Gloat later.*

Running through loose powder was harder than using the cleared road, but his pursuers would have considerably more trouble following him off-road. Down the mountain they ran, springing through the snow straight for the forest below.

Keen tiger ears heard the roar of snowmobiles starting pursuit from the compound; his lead was not a comfortable one.

Tigers were not built for marathon running, but just as Tony's inner tiger gave his human form certain advantages of strength and perception, his human could give his tiger endurance. Together, they were able to make it down into the cover of the trees before the machines could close the distance behind them.

Don't bite down, don't bite down, Tony reminded himself in a loop, trying not to drool too badly around the drive as he leaped over fallen logs and sprinted for the helicopter coordinates.

Please be undiscovered, he begged briefly.

But he had no such luck. The pilot was gone, and a handful of guards were milling about the snowy clearing. Tony spat the drive out; he'd need his teeth for this.

Teegr? A guard was saying in Russian into a staticky radio with confusion.

Their warning was too late.

Tony slammed into the man, driving him face-first into the packed snow. The impact knocked him out and Tony spun to face the others. One dropped his gun in alarm and sank to his knees, and two of them simply fled. Tony charged the only guard who remained armed and wrestled the gun from his hands with teeth and claws.

The snarling surprise attack was enough to drive them from the clearing but Tony knew it wouldn't be long before they regrouped and reinforcements from the mountain compound joined them. He shifted back to human and fished around in the snow desperately for the drive, naked and shivering.

He frowned when he finally found it; he'd managed to put divots in the casing with his teeth, but they weren't deep. Hopefully the moisture from the snow and saliva wouldn't damage the information.

He tossed the drive into the seat of the helicopter and began the process of spooling up the engines, pulling a frigid insulated coverall over his freezing body.

The blades began to turn, and Tony crammed his numb feet into stiff boots that were a size too small and as cold as the coveralls. His hands were too cramped and painful to tie them, so he didn't bother, closing the helicopter door and pulling the headset over his head. His frozen ears protested and he turned the radio on and dialed it to the right frequency.

"Tiger One, this is Tiger One to Castle," he said.

The blades were almost up to speed, and the trees around the clearing were beginning to whip around in their draft, snow whirling.

"Tiger One, this is Castle, what's your status?"

Rick's voice had never sounded so welcome.

"My status is really fucking cold," Tony said sharply, blowing on his tingling fingers. "Leaving Base One now. I've got the Prize." He eyed the drive and hoped again that his teeth hadn't damaged it beyond repair.

A shot left a round dimple on the windshield surrounded by a spiderweb.

"Okay, make that hot," Tony amended. He fingered the controls and the helicopter rose rapidly into the air as more shots followed. "Mind if I put you on hold while I'm being shot at?"

The forest shrank beneath him as the machine lifted into the air and Tony piloted away down the valley. He didn't dare breathe until the clearing was behind him, and the forest itself was a model train vista dusted with fake snow. None of the shots seemed to have caused major damage; the helicopter remained responsive and the fuel levels looked good. He swung towards the looming Siberian mountains in the south and thumbed the radio back on.

"Everything grrrreeeeeat?" Rick casually asked.

Through his chattering teeth, Tony managed to say, "Except for the impending hypothermia and the frostbit fingers."

"If Rochelle gets the information off that drive that we think is there, it will be worth a few fingers," Rick assured him.

"I hope it helps," Tony agreed, searching for mittens in the emergency gear. "But promise me one thing."

"Anything you want," Rick said confidently.

"The next assignment is somewhere *warm*. Somewhere I can have testicles again." The coveralls hadn't warmed up much and every inch of his skin was protesting the cold contact.

Rick laughed. "I've got just the job. You're going to love it."

CHAPTER 1

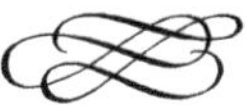

Amber Allen leaned out the open window of the resort van and drew in a breath of the fragrant jungle air. She could identify most of the plants by sight, but scents couldn't be conveyed in textbooks.

"Mr. Big owns the whole island," Jimmy, the scruffy man who had met her at the airport, shouted over the sound of the engine and crashing waves. "About a quarter of it was developed for the resort in the eighties, and his estate takes up another quarter of it. If you're lucky, you might get a tour."

He gave Amber a sleazy smile over his shoulder, suggesting that he personally could get her just such a treat. "The rest is left natural jungle, except the airstrip you came in on."

Amber wanted to ask if the island owner's name was really Mr. Big, but loathed the idea of encouraging Jimmy to keep talking. She had already made the mistake of mentioning her love of plants in a conversational way, and Jimmy had taken it as if she had batted her eyelashes and asked him to tell her *everything*.

He made another hairpin turn around a switchback with a steep cliff on one side, barely shrouded in trailing greenery, and a rocky plunge to the ocean on the other. The road was scarcely wide enough for the rusty van and had potholes large enough to swallow a bus.

"Scarlet took over the resort about three years back," Jimmy continued, as if Amber weren't studiously ignoring him to concentrate on staying in her seat. "She cleaned up the old cottages right nice and made it a shifters-only haven. We get animal folk from all over now. We've got a British boar couple, and a chinchilla from Singapore. There's a Siberian tiger, but I'd guess he's from the East Coast by his accent, not Siberia. Russian name, though."

Amber flinched despite herself and looked up in alarm. She wasn't sure she could get used to the idea of a place where she could speak freely about being a shifter.

"You didn't say what kind of shifter you were," Jimmy said invitingly, meeting her eyes in the mirror.

"A cat," Amber said vaguely, glad when he had to break their eye contact to navigate the narrow, bumpy road.

"Here kitty, kitty," Jimmy laughed, and Amber forced a smile, though she found it nothing but creepy. "How'd you hear about us?"

"I found out about it from my roommate," Amber said reluctantly, clinging to her armrest and her bag as the van whipped around another blind corner. None of the seat belts worked, and she was beginning to wish that she had more strenuously resisted her roommate Alice's suggestion that a tropical vacation was just what she needed. At least she should have insisted on something more traditional when her friend had encouraged this rather peculiar destination.

"That's usually how it is," Jimmy said sagely. "Can't exactly take an ad out in an airline magazine, you know, but word of mouth serves us well."

Miraculously, the road straightened, widened, and then opened out into a gorgeous verdant lawn, with lush landscaping peppered with low walls of dark volcanic rock and brilliantly flowering bushes. A tasteful sign announced, "Shifting Sands Island Resort." Below, it emphasized, "Private Property. Residents Only. No trespassing. No hunting."

"Here we go!" Jimmy pulled up to a wall that Amber realized

after a moment was actually a building, with a tile roof almost completely hidden in thick greenery.

There was no actual door into the building, just an open arch that went down a few steps into a little covered porch, which in turn opened into a charming little courtyard with a fountain and pots of plants everywhere. Amber couldn't stop herself from carefully touching spiky blossoms and stroking the green pitchers. There were orchids and hydrangeas and passion flowers. She paused at a brilliant red flower and frowned at its colorful leaves.

"The courtyard is the only place we will grow this kind of ginger," a voice behind her said. "It's a very popular ornamental on the mainland, but is very invasive and is choking out the native ginger strain there. Even in pots, we protect it from the wind to keep it from seeding out."

"I've read about the problems they're having with it in Hawaii," Amber said, turning to face the voice.

"You'd have to talk to our gardener, Graham, about that," the woman said dismissively. "I'm Scarlet."

She had hair as vivid as the ginger back in a neat bun, a shade that was more likely to be dyed than natural, but it matched her coloring perfectly. Her skin was unexpectedly pale for the latitude, and her eyes were flinty emerald green. Amber couldn't decide if she was very old, or very young—she could have been either. She wore tailored khaki pants and a spotless white blouse. Everything about her said 'no nonsense,' right down to her perfectly shaped nails, showing just a hint of subtle shine.

"Do you have more bags, Ms. Allen?" Scarlet asked.

"Ah, no," Amber said, keenly aware of her travel-wrinkled clothes and the chips in the bright nail polish she had impulsively applied before leaving home. "I decided to travel with just carry-ons."

That earned her a brief smile of approval. "A wise decision," Scarlet said mildly, turning to lead Amber through another archway. "Shifting Sands supplies the finest in all the consumables you should need, we have complete laundry facilities, and the clothing-optional setting means you need very little. Please don't hesitate to let the staff know if you find that there is anything you need."

The room Amber was led into was clearly an office, with an actual door, and a desk and a tidy bookcase. Windows beyond the desk looked down over the jungle, and Amber caught a glimpse of ocean before sitting in the chair she was gestured to.

"There are a few ground rules I need to clarify with you," Scarlet said, and Amber felt as if she had just been called into the principal's office. "Our first rule is no predation."

Amber blinked. "Excuse me?"

"There is no hunting permitted anywhere on the grounds. We have shifters of all types, and the island is home to several native endangered species. This restriction includes rodents, lizards, and birds, as well as larger mammals. Do you agree to these terms?" Scarlet's green eyes drilled into Amber.

"I, ah, yes, of course."

"If you would like to go fishing, we have equipment that can be checked out at the beachhouse, and expeditions can be arranged if there is enough interest. You are also welcome to fish in animal form." Scarlet opened a folder. Amber recognized the paperwork she had nervously filled out online. "We can skip the grazing restrictions, of course."

"As long as there are no catnip beds I need to stay out of," Amber giggled then stilled at Scarlet's withering stare. "Of course," she said contritely.

"You didn't specify what kind of cat you are," Scarlet said, pen poised over the paper. "Domestic, or...?"

Amber swallowed. "Andean mountain cat."

Scarlet raised one eyebrow. "I've never met one of those before," she said thoughtfully.

The tiny hope that Amber had been trying not to nurse turned to ash in her chest.

Apparently not noticing, Scarlet wrote neatly on the form, then turned it to Amber. "Please initial."

Amber did, numbly.

Scarlet took the form back. "There is no food storage in your cottage. We are in the tropics, and insects and other pests are quickly attracted to any unattended food and trash. You are welcome to eat at the dining hall buffet at any time of day, and there is a limited menu available at the bar during their open hours as well."

Scarlet passed a contract over the desk. "Please sign here to indicate your agreement with our rules."

Amber obediently signed two copies of that, and four more similar forms regarding medical care, liability, a draconian privacy policy, and a contract for payment.

Then Scarlet was all polite smiles, rising and giving Amber a firm handshake. "Your application suggested that you would prefer privacy over beach immediacy, so I've assigned you cottage twenty-seven in the upper ring." She handed Amber a glossy pamphlet that unfolded to a map, and circled the cottage in question, well away from any neighbors, and gave her the key.

"That looks great," Amber said with a nod.

"This is the dining hall." Scarlet pointed to the long building just below the office. "Though the drinks and buffet are available at all times, meal times are well worth making the effort to attend; our chef is incomparable. Massages and grooming services can be scheduled at the spa. There are yoga, dance, and meditation sessions daily at the event hall. We have a semi-formal dance on Saturday evening, you are welcome to attend."

Scarlet showed Amber where the schedules were printed in the pamphlet, pointed out a few of the other features, and gave her copies of the paperwork with a clear air of dismissal. "*Pura vida,*" she said off-handedly.

Pure life was the motto of Costa Rica, and seemed to be used as hello and goodbye, as well.

Amber stood for a long moment outside of Scarlet's door, clutching her carry-ons. Then she oriented her map and found her way out of the courtyard and down into the gleaming resort.

CHAPTER 2

Tony Lukin was not good at pretending to relax, and he was beginning to regret his request to Rick for a warm assignment without specifying 'and also not incredibly tedious.'

He scowled across the beach to the ocean, waiting for it to do anything but splash on the shore in regular intervals.

The most exciting thing it had done in the hour he'd been out here was attract a few birds, which had circled him hoping for food and then left. The miniature crabs that dug little holes and scuttled around moving sand piles had entertained him for about a minute on the first day. Beach-combing had turned up a lot of broken shells and lackluster pebbles.

He'd tried three different books of varying fluff, he'd tried closing his eyes for a nap, he'd even gone for a swim, in both human and tiger form.

And the sum of it was, vacation bored him.

Vacation that was just a sham bored him even more.

He wanted to be doing *something*, and it grated on his nerves that he wasn't. He'd been at Shifting Sands for a full week by now, and he was no closer to uncovering what he'd come to find than he had been when he stepped off the plane.

Tony growled, and rolled out of the beach chair, wrapping the towel around his waist. He'd become used to walking around without any covering, and it certainly simplified shifting, but he was still more than a little concerned about sunburning his more delicate parts.

There was an easy set of stairs up to the pool, where tables with umbrellas and lounge chairs were about a quarter full of guests in various stages of allowing sun on their skin.

He dropped himself easily beside a woman sunbathing alone in a generous spotted bikini that left acres of skin exposed. She spilled out over her lounge chair, and it groaned beneath her weight as she shifted to look at Tony. The gaze she gave him over her sunglasses suggested breezy confidence and amusement.

"Hello, Handsome," she trilled at him. "I've seen you talking with all the guests and was beginning to feel a little left out."

Tony had considered his efforts to get information out of the other guests and staff subtle, and was left a little dumbfounded by her odd mix of forward and flirtatious.

"I'm Magnolia," she said, extending one hand just a little.

Tony reached forward to shake it obediently, finding unexpected strength in her thick fingers. Her nails, he noted, were perfectly manicured, and she was wearing several sparkling rings.

"I'm looking for someone who knew Angelica Grayman, a guest here about three months ago who went missing. I understand you've been here that long?" Tony wondered if he sounded to her as much as if they were on opposite sides of an interview table as he did to himself.

"Honey, I've been here for more than a year," Magnolia said expansively. "I thought I was coming for a short vacation, but Shifting Sands will get under your skin like sand in your shoes if you let it."

Tony refrained from arguing against the appeal, but found himself feeling hopeful that possibly he had finally met someone who could help him find answers. The staff had been close-lipped across the board, and the owner was the worst of them. The other guests were largely short-term: happy to gossip but not useful.

"Did you know Angelica?"

"She was a shy thing," Magnolia confirmed. "Kept to herself, took meals early. She was a gorgeous Borneo bay cat, if I recall. Kind, but a little distant. I remember the search when she went missing, everyone was very concerned, but no body was ever found. Was she in some kind of trouble?"

Tony wished he knew, but gave the same brush-off that he answered other curiosity with: "I'm just trying to find out if she might have gone somewhere from here. Did she ever mention another possible destination after Shifting Sands?"

Magnolia rolled one shoulder in a shrug. "Not to me, she didn't. Sorry I can't be of more help, *cher*."

Tony believed her. "Thank you anyway," he said gruffly.

Magnolia smiled at him, and he realized that she was one of the most unsettlingly beautiful people that he'd ever met, every inch of her generous flesh glowing with self-confidence and sincerity. He felt somehow *better* after talking with her, even so briefly.

He looked up to see Jimmy, one of the handymen who worked for Scarlet, coming out of the pool mechanical and laundry rooms. Any peaceful feeling that Magnolia had left him with vanished into irritation at the thought of Scarlet.

He got up abruptly, muttered a polite farewell, and walked past the pool to head for his cottage. It was time to stop pussy-footing around and get some answers from Scarlet.

But first, he'd put on clothes.

CHAPTER 3

The resort was laid out in a crescent, with tiers of cottages along one side. There were grassy lawns and tidy white gravel footpaths throughout, with beautifully groomed bushes providing privacy for each of the cottages. The large dining hall and recreation buildings were in the center of the layout, with a hotel building and several private-looking residences on the other side overlooking cliffs.

All Amber could see of them from here were the gleaming tile roofs. Beyond those, she could see the glint of the pool area, the beach just past it, and then the incredible stretch of blue ocean. She could just hear the pound of the distant surf over the sound of the wind ruffling the tropical plant leaves.

As she walked along the winding path towards her own personal mark on the map, she marveled at the beautiful landscaping—it was all the perfect blend of tame and wild, and she was so busy admiring the array of flowers that she nearly walked into a gardener who was trimming back some wild brush.

He was wearing a long-sleeved shirt with the resort logo and full-length pants, but neither did much to hide the fact that he was incredibly ripped beneath them; arms as thick as her legs were wielding huge cutters as if they weighed nothing.

"Sorry," Amber said breathlessly, juggling her carry-ons. It was a shame that the staff didn't partake in the clothing optional portion of the resort, she thought with a sudden streak of mischief.

The gardener did nothing but glare at her accusingly, as if she had deliberately interrupted a personal moment. Finally, he grunted a grudging apology and moved his wheelbarrow out of her way.

Amber had to rip her eyes away and walk forward. She smiled to herself as she went. Maybe she could indulge a little vacation fantasy of hers while she was here and find a hot shifter for a roll in the sheets. One-night stands weren't her sort of thing, but on vacation, one didn't have to act entirely in character.

Amber giggled to herself, remembering Scarlet's rule against predation. Did men count?

She glanced back at the gardener, who was chopping down branches angrily. Someone a little friendlier would be nice.

The path wandered past several cottages that were far, far too grand for Amber's mental picture of a cottage. Amber had booked one of the budget options that the resort offered, and even that felt like a ridiculous luxury; she wondered what the prices were on these larger cousins, with their sprawling floorplans, stained-glass windows, and shrouded private porches.

Her own cottage was the perfect size—a charming little fairy-tale house with a vine-covered entrance and a little outdoor shower. She entered with a flutter of anticipation.

The front room had a comfortable bent-wicker couch and matching chairs, upholstered in tropical florals, and an antique looking writing desk with an anachronistically modern office chair. A steamer chest acted as the coffee table, and there were brightly painted wooden masks along most of the walls.

The downhill side of the room was a row of glass siding doors with screens that opened onto a narrow covered porch. A table and two chairs were off to one side on the deck, where she could just see down to the ocean through the jungle trees.

Amber stepped into the bedroom and gave the king-sized bed an experimental bounce. It was an exceptionally good mattress and a tall dresser with a matching vanity promised room for an entire closet of clothing. Amber dumped the contents of her carry-ons into two of the drawers, where they looked tiny and insignificant and untidy.

Amber thought about heading down to the beach or the dining hall, but the peace and quiet let all of her travel exhaustion catch up with her. After the endless drone of the flight from San Jose, and the bumpy road with Jimmy-who-wouldn't-shut-up, it was so lovely to be alone and still for a while.

She thought about how warm and muggy it was, about purring contentedly, and then she was stepping out of loose clothing in her mountain cat form and leaping up onto the big bed for a delicious nap.

CHAPTER 4

The resort manager, Scarlet, was not in her office when Tony got there.

Jimmy, the sharp-faced man who apparently did all manner of odd jobs, was hauling an impressive collection of matched luggage out of the resort van.

"Scarlet is probably down at the pool lounge," Jimmy said with a shrug. "We lost our bartender last week, and she's had to stand in."

"Lost your bartender?" Tony asked—too intensely, he realized belatedly.

"Moved back to Minnesota to take care of a sick mother or something," Jimmy said, dropping a gigantic suitcase on its side and wrestled it back upright.

Tony used a foot to stop the suitcase from rolling down the slight incline, and let Jimmy grab its handle.

"I could use a drink," he tried to say casually. He was supposed to be just another rich shifter on vacation, he reminded himself.

"You and me both," Jimmy said jovially. "That's my first stop after I deliver these. There's this hot new cat shifter that's just arrived, and I'm hoping she'll be the *social* type."

Tony had no interest in chasing tail, no matter how literal that phrase was here, and left Jimmy with a grunt to stomp down the trail to the bar at the pool. By this point, the sun had set over the ocean, and twilight was making a brief stay before full night took hold.

Scarlet was indeed at the bar, pouring and delivering drinks for a few tables of groups and couples who were laughing together.

"What can I get you?" she asked stiffly, with a scowl that Tony recognized from the mirror. She was no more suited to the social aspects of bartending than Tony was to relaxing on vacation.

Voice down, with a glance at the nearest table of revelers, Tony suggested, "You can get me the information I requested days ago. I'm sure you've had time to check my credentials by now."

Tony had not suspected that Scarlet's face could get colder, but it did.

"I haven't had time to spit in a pot," she said sharply. "If you haven't noticed, I'm a little shorthanded right now."

"I *need* that information," Tony growled at her.

"And I need to protect my guests' privacy," Scarlet answered just as fiercely. "You'll get your answers when I have *proper* assurance that you are who you say you are."

Keeping his temper had never been a strong point, and everything about Scarlet rubbed Tony wrong. "I've been very nice about asking," he said through bared teeth. "I could get the records myself."

Scarlet did not appear to be in the slightest bit intimidated. "I doubt you could," she said scathingly. Tony couldn't decide from her tone if she was dubious about his ability to force her to turn them over, or his ability to manage the most basic of alphabetic filing systems.

Tony might have answered more heatedly, but Magnolia's voice from a far table called, "Scarlet, darling! Another margarita for me!"

Scarlet waved back, and asked Tony through gritted teeth. "Can I get you a *drink*? Or would you like to continue monopolizing my time for something I won't give you?"

"A beer," Tony conceded. "And a shot of whiskey."

If he wasn't going to be able to conduct any business, there was no point in acting business-like. Besides, it kept up his cover of being on vacation.

He turned on his stool and let her get to work behind the bar while he analyzed the other occupants of the bar. Magnolia sat with a trio of well-dressed men and they were laughing together like old friends. The next table looked like an escaped troupe of actors from the set of a bad Hollywood western, complete with cigars and cowboy hats. They were playing cards, very enthusiastically.

A boy who looked too young to even be in the bar was hitting on a table of middle-aged women wearing terrible jewelry who were giggling at him indulgently. An elderly couple was sitting further out onto the deck, looking out over the pool and nursing glasses of wine.

Jimmy had apparently delivered the recalcitrant luggage, and was lingering near the self-serve snacks that were opposite the back entrance to the bar.

"Your drinks," Scarlet said, putting them in front of him with a little more force than necessary before swishing off to take orders from the table of card players.

Tony turned to take the shot of whiskey just as a new figure appeared in the doorway and paused to look around.

She was petite and curvy, with a curtain of black hair and medium-toned skin. She wore simple khaki shorts and a collared shirt, and she filled them up absolutely perfectly. The shirt was unbuttoned a tantalizing way, showing more than a hint of the curves of her breasts. Somehow, that was even sexier than the fully nude women who pranced around the resort in their heels. Her short, straight nose was the center of a round face, and her big, thickly-lashed eyes looked golden from this distance.

Pretty girls didn't usually turn Tony's head, and he certainly hadn't come to Shifting Sands looking for companionship, but something about the figure woke his tiger. If he had been in that form, his ears would be perked in her direction.

He realized he was staring just as her gaze swept the room and caught his. He downed the shot of whiskey in a moment of wild confusion and the next several seconds were a heated haze of pain as the fiery shifter-strength liquid went down the wrong pipe and he had to cough himself back to breathing. When his eyes had stopped watering enough to look around again, the gorgeous woman was right next to him, smiling invitingly. “Buy you a drink?” she offered.

“You do know that this is an all-inclusive resort?” Tony had to ask, looking around as if to make sure that it was, because between the burning whiskey and her proximity, nothing made sense.

That's ***her***, his tiger and all of his instincts were telling him, but after years of waiting to meet his one mate, Tony couldn't believe either his amazing luck or his awful sense of timing.

It didn't matter that he was at the resort on business, and potentially unfortunate business at that. It didn't matter that he hadn't given much thought to settling down. One look at this woman's light brown eyes, and he was hopelessly, entirely lost in her.

All of his vague ideas about what a mate meant went straight out the window. This wasn't about lust, or at least, not only lust. He knew this woman to the bottom of his soul, and she was everything he'd ever wanted in another person, all wrapped up in what was easily the sexiest package he'd ever seen.

CHAPTER 5

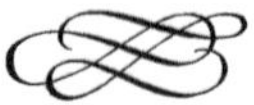

Amber lingered outside the entrance to the pool bar, agonizing over how many buttons to leave open on her shirt, and finally went in.

She had just decided she liked how much cleavage was showing when she caught sight of Jimmy, that odious chatterbox from the resort van, and it was everything she could do not to button her shirt up to her chin. A quick assessment of the room showed that everyone else there was with someone, except for a big, broad-shouldered man who was leaning on the bar itself.

Perfect!

He turned away from her approach to take a shot of alcohol from the counter, then coughed and sputtered ungracefully as Amber shimmied herself over to his elbow with the transparent excuse of getting a drink from the bar.

"Can I buy you a drink?" she blurted, hoping she looked sexy and not just desperate.

The man was even dreamier up close. He had beautifully-muscled arms, and a square jaw straight out of a superhero comic. He had brown eyes and dark brown hair, barely long enough to show some wave, and a smoldering look that unsettled Amber to her toes. It was like he had been lifted, word for word, out of her teenage dream diary.

She had never had such an immediate, physical attraction to someone and she felt oddly as if he was meant entirely for her.

But that was idiotic.

Much like she was.

"You do know that this is an all-inclusive resort?" he asked her, glancing around.

He was probably looking for an escape route.

Amber felt her face heat, and blessed her unknown progenitors for giving her skin that would mostly hide her blush. "Oh, ah, yes," she stammered, then chose honesty as her best path from there. "I'm sorry, I just didn't want to get caught alone with *him*."

She tried to subtly raise her eyebrows in Jimmy's direction, and probably only looked like she was having some kind of seizure.

"Who, Jimmy?" He looked around to the far side of the bar, and made no effort to keep his voice down. Fortunately, a rowdy group of shifters playing cards had a timely moment of noisy celebration and woe.

Failing to actually sink into her barstool and die, Amber said between clenched teeth, "Very subtle. Do you work undercover often?"

That made him nearly fall off his own barstool with a start. "I beg your pardon?"

Surprised by his reaction, Amber put up innocent hands. "It's just... that wasn't very slick. Okay, you know what, let's try this again." She put out a hand. "I'm Amber. I'll just order a drink and go if you'd like."

"Tony," he said, taking her hand and clinging to it like a drowning man. "Please don't go."

Gratified and surprised by his reaction, Amber gave his hand a shake that was a little more lingering than polite. "Okay," she said with a little laugh.

Scarlet had the beautiful timing to return from handing out drinks and ask brusquely, "What can I get you?"

"Something fruity," Amber said. "With an umbrella. I'm not picky."

She caught a glimpse of Jimmy out of the corner of one eye trying to catch her gaze and made a point of pretending not to see him. It wasn't a hardship to gaze at Tony as if he had all of her attention. He was probably the most masculine thing that Amber had ever had an excuse to talk to, all rippling muscles and jaw, and he had an amazingly expressive mouth.

Scarlet frowned and went to the other end of the bar to make her drink.

"Have you been here long?" Amber asked. "At the resort, I mean? Not the bar. Of course."

"A *week*," Tony said.

The way he said it made it sound like a finals week, or a week of torture, not a vacation at an upscale beach resort with all the gourmet food and fine alcohol you could want.

"I've got a week here, too," Amber volunteered. "It would have been nice to stay longer, especially after such a long plane ride to get here, but it's hard to get time off of work."

"Oh? Where do you work?" Tony asked.

"Just a little local garden store in Lakefield," Amber said with a shrug. "But I'm the only employee other than the owner and his wife, and they lean on me to do a lot of the day-to-day work."

"I don't have a green thumb," Tony said, as if it were a great confession. "I killed a jade plant once."

"They're surprisingly easy to over-water if you don't give them good drainage," Amber said understandingly. "How about you? Where do you work?"

"I work for an... er... in construction. *Management.* In, uh, construction."

Amber wondered where he really worked, but didn't press the issue. If he wanted to elevate himself to management to impress someone at a resort bar, she could understand why. After all, she was the one wearing her shirt one more button open than usual, and she was loving the way his eyes couldn't entirely keep from straying from her face as they spoke. Did that make her a floozy?

The idea alarmed her until she reminded herself that she was on vacation, and had come determined to live outside of her comfortable little box of wholesomeness for the week. She would probably never see this guy again. That idea gave her an unexpected pang of bone-deep regret, which she squashed as quickly as she could. Her cat gave an unexpected growl of disagreement.

This one is ours, her cat said, but didn't explain the cryptic idea.

Scarlet arrived with a brilliantly colored drink sporting not only an umbrella, but several pieces of fruit on a plastic cocktail sword. Amber gave a delighted "Ooo!" as she picked it up, but Scarlet didn't linger to appreciate her reaction.

"I wonder what her animal is," Amber said wryly, taking a long sip of her technicolor drink. It definitely met her requirements for being fruity, and it had a delightful kick that promised plenty of alcohol and went straight to her head. "It's funny that she knows that about every one of us, and we don't know a thing about her."

"She's probably a wolverine," Tony ground out between clenched teeth. Scarlet clearly failed to amuse him.

Were they lovers at odds? Amber caught herself wondering. There was certainly some kind of *tension* shimmering between them. She took another long drink. "What about you?"

Tony looked like she'd caught him in headlights. "What about me?"

"Your, er... animal?"

"Tiger!" he said, as if relieved. "Siberian tiger, to be exact." And as an afterthought, "You?"

"Cat," Amber said cautiously, and the heady drink made her continue when otherwise she might not have. "An Andean mountain cat, actually."

Tony's eyebrows raised. "I've never even heard of that."

Everyone said that.

"It's like a snow leopard," Amber explained. "But smaller, the size of a big housecat."

"It sounds pretty." The way he said it, gazing straight at her, made Amber warm to her toes and her cat purred in her ears.

She took another sip of her drink and, between the slight buzz of alcohol and the delight in Tony's attentive company, felt deliciously not herself at all.

The moment was doused by an unwelcome intrusion. "Are you finding your way around all right, Amber?"

Jimmy sidled up to her far side, and Amber felt obliged to turn politely, after casting a desperate look at Tony. "Ah, yes. Everything is quite well marked."

Her neutral tone was meant to be discouraging, but Jimmy sat on the stool beside her in chummy oblivion.

"You be sure to let me know if you need anything, then. I could arrange a fishing trip in the boat, if you're interested. Or a tour of the arboretum at Mr. Big's estate..."

Amber knew immediately that she hadn't hidden her transparent interest in the last quickly enough, and took another desperate slurp at the bottom of her drink with a non-committal noise before she could ask any encouraging questions about what kind of plants Mr. Big grew.

"We were just leaving," Tony said unexpectedly from her other side.

Amber looked at him in surprise and not a little delight. He sounded... jealous. Protective. It helped that when he stood up, he towered over them, and Jimmy actually shrunk back a little in instinctive alarm.

She gladly played along, pushing back her empty glass, then impulsively grabbing the drink umbrella as she stood up. "Thanks," she said, officially at Jimmy, but more meaningfully at Tony.

If Tony rushed her towards to the back door a little with his long legs, she scampered nothing less than eagerly with him.

CHAPTER 6

The air outside the bar felt cooler and fresher, and it was abruptly quiet as the door closed behind them. The colorful lights of the bar gave way to a thickly-scented, dark path, barely made navigable by a series of lights.

Tony felt the angry prickle that Jimmy had inspired immediately soothe as they paused to let their eyes adjust.

"I'm sorry," he said at once, looking down at the top of Amber's head. Her hair was sleek and touchable, and it was everything he could do not to stroke her in a too-familiar way. "I shouldn't have presumed to tell Jimmy that we were leaving. If you wanted another drink, or to stay at the bar..."

Amber tilted her head to look up at him, her eyes bright in the darkness. "You were my white knight," she said, with no hint of sarcasm. "That man will not take a hint. Seriously, maybe his animal is a *leech*."

"I'd put money on a rodent," Tony said, smiling.

For an oddly long moment, they stood and just stared at each other. Tony suspected that neither of them was thinking about Jimmy.

His *mate*. He couldn't believe how gorgeous and curvy she was, or how comfortable he felt, just being near her. He wanted her more than he had ever wanted anything in his memory.

When he bent to kiss her, unable to resist, she didn't even hesitate, but flung eager arms around his neck and kissed him back, standing on tiptoe to reach him. She tasted like alcohol and fruit, and her mouth managed to be both pliable and firm.

"My cottage," he offered, between kisses. He barely had the self-control not to wrestle her willingly into the fragrant tropical bushes.

"Mmm, yes!" she said, but she didn't stop kissing him, or raking fingers through his hair.

Even with her agreement, Tony found that he couldn't stop touching her or move his feet. Finally, he picked her up, and she gave a squeal of delighted laughter and wrapped her legs around his waist.

He could move then, though he recognized that he was staggering and weaving in his path. She didn't hamper him with weight, but the way she squirmed against him with her mostly bare legs drove him absolutely mad and her kisses left him dizzy. He had never realized how much having someone touch his shoulders could turn him on.

"Wait, wait!" Amber laughed against his lips, just as they turned on the path to his cottage.

"What? What is it?" His voice sounded like begging to his own ears.

"I lost my sandal!"

He put her down, carefully, sliding her down over the erection that was bulging his shorts, hands lingering at her waist.

She gave a gratifying moan of desire as her feet touched the ground, and she stood there leaning into him for a moment longer than was necessary.

"Your sandal?" Tony prompted.

"Screw the sandal," Amber said fiercely, and then they were tangled in kisses again as Tony tried to remember where he'd put his cottage key.

Between digging it out and trying to claim Amber's mouth for his own, Tony managed to maneuver them into the entrance of the house and finesse the door open—which is how it stayed as they began the erotic struggle of removing each article of clothing and finding the bedroom.

"Crap," he said suddenly, when he'd gotten her shirt off and she had thrown his across the room.

"It's not that complicated a bra," Amber promised, big golden eyes laughing. "I can help you."

"No, it's... condoms. I didn't bring condoms."

That gave her pause, but it was a grateful pause, and the smile that bloomed across her face was more reward than he had expected. "You really are a white knight," she said warmly. "I'm on the pill, if it makes you feel better."

The pause changed the timbre of the urgency, but not the magnitude. Tony wanted her more badly than ever, and gathered her into his arms for a deep kiss. He cradled both sides of her face, her silky hair spilling over his hands, and let his tongue explore the depths of her mouth.

She slid her arms around his neck and kissed back, licking and twining his tongue until they were both panting for breath.

He laid her down on the big bed and kissed down her neck, loving the way her body arched to his fingers. He stroked her bare arms, and over her bra, down her sides, and she closed her eyes and purred at him in delight. He put fingers along the waistband of her shorts, but when she raised her hips in invitation to remove them, only stroked her side again, and kissed between her breasts while she squirmed.

It was his first time with his mate, and he wanted to savor it as long as he could.

Amber had other plans, and gave a little frustrated growl when he ignored her signals. She pushed him off with more strength than he expected from her short frame, and he rolled over onto his back on the bed willingly while she straddled him. Her loose hair brushed his chest as she put an arm on either side of him and leaned down to kiss and nibble at his chest. Then she sat up again, and deftly unfastened her own bra, letting it spill off of her and release the breasts he had been vainly trying not to stare at all evening.

They were perfect orbs of firm flesh, with big nipples that were hard with desire, and he could no more keep his hands from them than deny that this woman was his one perfect, fated companion.

She moaned as he cupped them, threw back her head in ecstasy, and ground herself against the thick erection that was only a few light layers of clothing away. Tony wasn't sure what he would have done without those layers; he was at such a fever pitch that he would have embarrassed himself like a first-time teenager without the cloth to dull the sensation a little.

He used his thumbs to make lazy circles around her areolas, then dragged them across the erect nipples, and she gave a little cry of pleasure that made him feel proud and powerful. He did it again, with a little squeeze of his hands of the beautiful, soft flesh of her breasts. She cried out again in appreciation, scratching him reflexively, then tipped her head down to look at him and beg, "I want you..."

The shorts were no longer welcome in the bed, and there was an acrobatic flurry as they both tried frantically to shed them, without withdrawing from each other more than absolutely necessarily. The moment they were fully naked, he had to hold her against him, just enjoying the silky length of her warm body beside his, and then he was slipping into her wet, soft folds without a hint of resistance.

He gave her a slow, careful thrust, burying himself into her in one smooth, careful motion, fighting himself for control. To his shock, she arched in his arms, crying out in intense pleasure and shuddering in unexpected orgasm. He had to bite his lip to keep from taking her with abandon then, but gave a second slow, contained thrust, trying to keep her at that plateau of pleasure.

Her next cry was less, but still powerful, and she opened astonished eyes to meet his gaze as he rolled her onto her back without unlocking from her. His third thrust was less controlled, and she lifted her hips to eagerly meet him as her fingers raked across his shoulders.

It was like swimming in a hot pool of pleasure, thrusting into her. She was a heady mix of pliable and resistant, and the bite of her fingernails on his arms as she held him and moaned was an intoxicating aphrodisiac. Tony realized he was growling with need and kissed her, nibbling at her ear as gently as he could manage.

He had to stop doing that, his entire world narrowing to concentrating on putting off his own mounting release until he realized that Amber was crying out in orgasmic pleasure again; the sound of her delight was too much for him to resist and he was filling her with his hot seed.

His frantic thrusts slowed at last, and he was gradually aware again of the room around them, the chirps of insects and frogs outside, and the door of the cottage, still wide open.

CHAPTER 7

Amber came back to herself slowly as Tony's thrusts tapered off into a finishing rhythm. They continued to couple in the afterglow of the pleasure, as long as possible, and finally lay next to each other in gleeful exhaustion as their panting breath returned to normal.

When she had decided to treat the vacation as an excuse to cut loose, she had not expected it to feel anywhere near this... natural. She felt more comfortable with this complete stranger than she had ever been with anyone she had ever known, and he had taken her to heights she'd never dreamed existed. She hadn't even known it was possible to orgasm at a first thrust; this man was clearly no stranger to giving a woman pleasure.

His hand, still making lazy circles on her belly and breasts, promised more, if she was brave enough to accept it.

It's just a vacation fling, she reminded herself, and she thrust away the pang of regret that came with the practicality. Nothing about their encounter suggested he was any more interested in a relationship that extended past the boundaries of the resort than she was, and she ought to be grateful for that.

Her plan had always been to go home to Minnesota after a week of freedom, pick the least objectionable of the shy farmboys who made eyes at her at the garden supply store and start a perfectly respectable family. She couldn't let a magnetic tiger shifter tempt her away from that practical path, no matter how intensely her inner mountain cat was trying to convince her that this was something *more*, something *better*.

This week, she would take each day as it came and fixedly *not* think about what would come afterwards.

It was hard, though, to watch Tony get up and bring them towels to clean up with, and not think about how he made every one of those farmboys look spindly, pale, and utterly unappealing in comparison.

"I, ah... that was... thank you! Wow!" Amber said, not sure what else to say but aware that something was in order.

Tony smiled at her, a beautiful, confident smile that warmed Amber to her toes, and leaned over to kiss her possessively. "I was just thinking the exact same thing."

"I should get my sandal," she giggled against his lips after a lengthy kiss. "And close the front door..."

His cottage came with bathrobes, and she gratefully slipped into one and padded outside with a flashlight as Tony picked up their clothing and tidied the bed.

She leaned against the doorframe with her rescued sandal on one finger, watching as he deftly shook the comforter back into shape. It was refreshing, watching such a big, manly-looking male make a bed. His long arms served him well; he was able to fluff it with one smooth motion, where Amber would have been running from corner to corner.

He shot her a sideways smile that indicated that he knew she was watching him. "Seven sisters," he said. "Every one of them was a tomboy and I got all the housekeeping chores they could stick me with."

"That's adorable," Amber said wistfully. She shut the door behind her as she came into the room.

"You're an only child?" Tony guessed, and it was close to the heart.

"I... don't know," Amber admitted guardedly. "I was left on the front porch of a church, and I don't know if I actually had *any* siblings."

She expected pity. That was the usual reaction when she confessed the details of her childhood, and she already regretted bringing it up.

This was supposed to be a no-strings holiday fling, with no place for intimate discussions. They should be talking about fishing, or the weather, or the next time he was planning to tumble her into bed. Which was not nearly soon enough, as far as Amber was concerned. She had never felt such an odd combination of sated and needy.

"There's a shower," Tony suggested, gesturing towards the bathroom door. He winked and added, "It's big enough for two."

Amber let the bathrobe slide to the floor behind her as she sauntered in the direction he had indicated. "That's good," she purred. "Because I may not leave you any hot water, otherwise..."

Tony scrambled to follow her.

The bathroom was tiled in blue, with windows out over dark foliage outside. Amber had to stand on tiptoe to see out of them, but Tony would have no trouble enjoying the view... if he had eyes for anything but Amber. She loved the way he watched her, and left the glass door open while she slipped in and turned on the water.

His cottage was fancier than her own, and where she had only a narrow, simple shower, his was, as promised, plenty big enough for two, with a tiled bench along one side that she was already making plans for. His bathroom also had a Jacuzzi tub, opposite the shower, and Tony sat down on the edge of it with a wide grin, watching.

Once the water was warm, Amber soaped herself to a tantalizing lather, keenly aware of his gaze, and playfully dressed herself in bubbles. A glance showed that he was enjoying the show; his generous member was already beginning to swell again. She rinsed off the bubbles and soaped herself more earnestly, bending away from him to rub her legs and give a view of her wet ass, and then turning to pay exaggerated attention to each breast under the warm stream of water.

Tony had to adjust his seat on the edge of the tub, but remained an audience, rather than a participant. Amber felt like this was an unspoken challenge, and let her hands trail down her sides and belly, to lay one hand, fingers flat, against the mound of her entrance. She'd been uncertain about the Brazilian wax that she'd gotten before her vacation, but now it felt daring, and deliciously exposed. She let her fingers trail over each nearby thigh, and reveled in the smooth, velvety texture.

She peeked up to see if Tony was still attending to her and was pleased to see that he was at *full* attention. He had one leg stretched up on the ledge of the tub and his gorgeous member was erect again, as if it were reaching for her. Tony had both hands behind him, as if it was all he could do to keep his hands from himself, and Amber suddenly wanted to see him touch it.

She wriggled her hips a little, and let a single finger dip into the folds of her entrance, hoping he would take the hint.

Though she had done it for Tony's watching pleasure, she couldn't keep back the gasp of pleasure it gave her; she was still swollen and sensitive from their earlier activity, and the touch of her own finger brought her back to a fever pitch of desire and need. She gave another tentative stroke, and another, and looked up to find that Tony's look had intensified, and the lines of his hard body were rippled with clenched muscle.

He still hadn't touched the rigid hard-on that was all Amber could focus on.

She put a second finger in, enjoying the sensation, but so aware that it was nothing compared to the thick, solid member that was so close and yet so far away. She gave one slow stroke, and then another, unable to keep from squirming at her own touch. The water pouring over her shoulders added another dimension of sensation, and she closed her eyes to tip her head back and let it pour over her face.

A groan made her open her eyes, and she found that Tony was touching himself at last, not stroking, but holding his member tightly with a closed fist, as if he could keep his pleasure from mounting too fast by sheer will.

She didn't want to stop touching herself, but she was dizzy with desire for more; she wanted to be filled by his cock, not just admire it, and the memory of his movement inside of her was an ache. "Tony..." she moaned, and speaking out loud unlocked the moment.

Amber wasn't even sure how he crossed the room, but suddenly Tony was against her, lifting her onto the bench and kissing her neck as he pressed himself against her hungry folds.

She welcomed him eagerly, taking the length of him into her in a single, deep thrust that seemed to split her, fill her, and complete her, all at once. She didn't come at his first entrance this time, but did again after only a few of his strong penetrations, cresting into pleasure with a helpless cry.

He slowed, carefully, and then picked her up again and turned so that the water was spilling down over her back and she was straddling him as he sat back against the bench. She rode him, letting her fingernails trail over his shoulders and arms, reveling in the devoted attention he gave her breasts and the small of her back. He held her close, like she was a precious thing, while he met each of her bounces with a wild thrust of his own, and his embrace became a desperate clutch as he lost himself inside her once more.

CHAPTER 8

The practical side of Tony was dimly grateful that they were already in a shower and it was easy to clean up, but the rest of him knew he would never be able to take another shower without picturing Amber, her own fingers caressing herself, her gorgeous hair flowing wet over her bare shoulders, lips parted in concentration and desire.

He soaped Amber gently, and let her do the same with him. They explored each other's bodies curiously, fingers stroking over flesh like they were taking silent notes. She lingered over the angry scars on his back, but didn't ask. He stroked the faint scars on her wrist, but didn't ask.

It still felt unreal, finding her. He'd known his mate was out there, somewhere, but it was a distant certainty, playing no role in his real life. To find her, to so completely trust and love her so quickly, gave the whole world a new cast, as if the sun had suddenly changed color.

And the sex!

Tony grinned, looking down at her hair as she finger-combed the conditioner through it. What a wildcat!

They toweled each other off with the same gentle silence, and without conferring, each took a side of the big king bed and snuggled in together.

In the darkness, cuddled together, Tony felt like he could ask, "Was it hard, growing up without siblings? There were days I'd wish for it, when privacy was impossible to get in our little house..."

Amber was quiet for a moment, and Tony wondered if he'd pushed too far, too fast.

Then she said, "It was a small town, and they really did their best for me. The staff at the church where I was found, Saint Mary's, they still call me their little foundling and send me birthday cards every year on the anniversary of when I was found. And foster care was... it really wasn't horrible or abusive, like you read about in the news sometimes. But I was a difficult child even before I started turning into a cat when I got mad. I went through a few families before I aged out."

Tony held her tighter, nuzzling her neck in wordless comfort.

After a few breaths, she continued. "I finally found someone like me in high school—a bear shifter named Alice who told me there were others like us. We stayed in touch, even after she moved away, and we ended up sharing an apartment back in Lakefield after college. She's the one who convinced me to come here. I was... I was hoping I'd find another Andean mountain cat, like me. Maybe figure out where I came from, why I was abandoned."

The hopelessness in her voice would have cut Tony to the bone even if he hadn't already loved her. "You don't have to be alone anymore," he said fiercely. "You can make your own family."

Amber went rigid in his arms and Tony had a stab of doubt. Was it possible that she didn't consider him her mate, or that she didn't want him for family despite their connection? The idea that she might not feel their bond as deeply as he did made him suddenly, deeply uneasy.

They lay stiffly together, a chorus of frogs and insects loud compared to their silence, until Amber gradually relaxed in his arms. It took Tony a long while to realize that she had fallen asleep, and it took him even longer to fall asleep himself.

~

He woke up tangled in Amber, arms and legs entwined with hers. He'd never slept over with a girlfriend, always preferring to seek his own space, and he was amazed by how familiar it felt to come awake next to another person. It was fascinating to feel her breathing change against his chest, to feel her stir along the whole length of him, and come awake in parts; her toes wiggled adorably before the rest of her woke.

"Good morning," he said in her ear.

There was enough late morning light streaming in through the window to see her clearly. She looked confused at first, then wary, then smiled slowly.

"Good morning," she replied, almost shyly.

He bent over to kiss her, and she responded hungrily, wrapping her arms around his neck and holding him close to her. Any doubts that Tony had been left with from the night before were washed away in the wave of passion and the complete rightness that came from being so close to her. She could have no doubts about *his* interest; his member was rigid between them, and she was rubbing herself against it wantonly.

"We'll miss breakfast," she teased, drawing away from his kisses.

"I know what I want for breakfast," he growled back at her.

He slid fingers down into her and found that she was as ready for him as he was for her, wet and slick and warm. He touched her for a long moment, loving the way her breath caught and her body tensed.

"Oh, please, please," she finally begged, when Tony had teased her to a fine sweat.

He rolled over to straddle and take her, slipping, unresisted, into her folds as she moaned and gave a sweet cry of delight.

If waking to his mate in his arms had felt like delicious rightness, waking to take his mate so intimately seemed like heavenly choruses and perfection. He groaned in need and pleasure, keeping his strokes careful and tender.

She squirmed in blissful torture as he rode her, and cried out in abandon as he brought her to the crests of pleasure, not once, but twice, before he could no longer keep his own release in check, thrusting in increasing need and wildness until he was spent.

"I'm *sore*," Amber said, but it was with undeniable satisfaction. She held him tight against her until their breathing had returned to normal.

Tony couldn't help but feel pleased by the statement, and he nibbled her ear in wordless delight.

CHAPTER 9

Amber couldn't remember ever feeling so complete.

When she was with Tony, she forgot every insecurity she'd ever felt. He seemed like *family*, and it was easy to ignore the fact that she'd only just met him. Too easy.

She propped herself up on an elbow when he rolled out of the bed, and watched him go, mesmerized by the gorgeous curve of his ass as he went.

When he was gone, it was easier to remember that this was only a resort fling, that she was only a beach diversion, and he was only a last wild ride before she settled into somcthing... less.

Things this perfect don't last, she reminded herself. Too many foster families as a child had taught her to mistrust things that seemed so good.

She would enjoy this—to the bottom of her soul, she would enjoy this—and then she would go home and get on with her life, however she could.

Her determination to enjoy the day carried them through a swift shower—more utilitarian than the one the night before—to the dining hall for breakfast, where they found that service in the restaurant was already over. There was still an extensive buffet, with a range of breakfast and lunch choices (just being put out), fresh fruit, crusty bread, and an array of salty snacks and vegetables.

They piled plates high, and went out to a set of seats overlooking the pool.

"Are you eating raw broccoli? Ew!" Tony had taken a plate heavy on meat and bread, while Amber had been enraptured by the fresh options of vegetables and exotic fruits. They both had been unable to resist the rolls that had been brought fresh from the oven while they were serving themselves.

"You don't like broccoli?" Amber dipped a piece into a puddle of creamy dressing and ate it with relish.

"Not raw," Tony said, shaking his head emphatically. "And not unless it's smothered in cheese."

"I didn't like fresh vegetables until I started growing them myself," Amber confessed. "There's something about the taste of things you've put your own sweat and tears into." She had to admit that the selection here was better than anything she could grow, and she wondered if the resort had its own garden or greenhouse.

They compared favorite foods—agreeing on cheeses and breads, but disagreeing about meats.

"I like a meat you have to fight with," Tony said with a sparkling grin.

"I prefer mine fully cooked and not recognizable," Amber countered. "Give me a casserole or a sausage any day."

"You're from the Midwest," Tony said sagely.

They made short work of their plates and went back for a second round of fresh-ground coffee—Amber could not resist snagging a sweet roll on her way back to their table, and Tony took a second plate of food nearly as large as the first.

Amber enjoyed the warmth of the sun on her skin as she lingered over the combination of flavors in her mouth. She also enjoyed watching Tony eat, more than she'd ever thought she would take pleasure in such a mundane task. His fingers were so sure, and his jaw as he chewed was so obviously strong. He was wearing a short-sleeved, collared shirt that shrouded most of his shoulders, but the strength of them was still obvious, and his arms were thick and tanned. It was like watching a work of art, or a dance performance.

"What are your plans for the day?" Amber asked, when she realized she was staring at him again.

Tony looked reflexively at his wrist, though there was no watch there, or even a tan-line indicating he'd even worn one since he'd arrived. He scowled at the spot as if it reminded him of something.

"I hadn't made any plans." Then he grinned. "I wouldn't mind any day that ended like yesterday did."

Amber blushed, and was glad all over again that her skin wouldn't show it easily. She loved the way he looked at her, like she was delicious and desirable and perfect.

"I was thinking about swimming," she said with a nod to the pool to cover her confusion. "It's a lovely pool, and it might be too hot to enjoy in the afternoon."

Already, the temperature was baking hot, the sun beating down on the tile. Summer at Lakefield could get muggy and hot, but there was an intensity to the sun here that she wasn't used to.

She looked at Tony. There were a lot of intensities here she wasn't used to. "And then I was looking at maybe getting a massage or a pedicure, or something ridiculously girly like that."

Tony did his best to look innocent as he asked, "Are you planning to take advantage of the resort's skinny-dipping-encouraged policy?"

Amber flushed again. "I'm not that brave," she said with a laugh. "I brought a bikini that I barely have the guts to wear."

"I can't wait to see it," Tony said sincerely. He had the grace to not look disappointed that Amber wasn't going to be lounging nude on the pool deck and actually seemed eager to see the promised garment. "May I join you?"

"Of course," Amber said with a slow smile.

To her surprise, Tony took her invitation to mean the entire day. He scheduled his own tandem massage and pedicure with the manager of the spa when Amber did, before she retreated for her own cottage to procure the promised bikini.

"I don't plan on getting any toe polish," he said with a

wink. "But I do need a nail trim, and who doesn't like a little pampering?"

The idea of a big, manly man like Tony putting up with pampering gave Amber a skip to her step as she returned to the pool, too wrapped up in her thoughts of him to feel self-conscious in her admittedly skimpy swimwear. It helped that she passed a nude couple that gave friendly nods without the slightest trace of embarrassment.

With his closer cottage, he got back to the pool before she did, and she paused to observe him for a long moment in the shadowed entrance.

There were other guests enjoying the pool—one older man was swimming diligent laps, and a few individuals were sunning in the chairs at the other end of the pool—but Amber could only stare at Tony. He was wearing loose swim trunks, and lounging in one of the bar chairs with elegant ease and strength. His uncovered shoulders rippled with muscles that were pale in the golden sunlight. He had put on sunglasses, and looked like someone out of a movie, perfectly posed on a pearly white chair.

A spy movie, or an action-adventure, with that physique, Amber thought. *And he's* ***mine***.

Her mountain cat was in avid agreement. *Ours,* she purred. *Forever*.

The thought caught her by surprise and she delayed in the shadows another moment.

He wasn't hers, not really. And this was temporary, even more temporary than most of the people who moved through her life. As badly as she longed for *family* and *permanent*, she was not going to find that in a wild, tropical holiday affair. She didn't even know who he *really* was.

CHAPTER 10

Tony caught sight of Amber hanging back under the roof of the bar, just out of the sun. Her brilliant blue bikini wasn't nearly as skimpy as he'd been led to believe, and she looked like a goddess. He couldn't help but stare. The curve of her hip, the sexy slope of her shoulders, the sleek ponytail that curled around and was long enough to tickle the mound of her breast... it was a package that he wasn't sure he'd have been able to resist even if she wasn't his mate.

She took a deep breath and started walking towards him, padding as gracefully as a cat. Tony was mesmerized by the way she moved.

When she stopped at his chair, he had to catch his breath and keep himself from reaching up and pulling her onto his lap for a kiss with no care for the other guests on the pool deck. He was going to need a dip in the unheated pool, for sure.

Amber smiled at him, a slow, tentative smile that crinkled the corners of her eyes. "Ready for a swim?"

"You have no idea," Tony replied, glad that his swimsuit had a generous cut.

The pool was long and deep enough for laps in both directions. The far end, overlooking the beach, ended in a broad set of steps that went out of the water to a wide lower deck with umbrellas and chairs. Palm trees were spaced along both long sides, and the near end had narrower steps between twin waterfalls that fell from the deck nearest the bar and the buffet. A tinny radio was playing American rock, with commercials in Spanish. They walked down these steps holding hands, and Amber gave a little gasp at the chill of the water.

"Ooooo, I'm not sure this was a good idea," Amber exclaimed, shivering closer to him and laughing.

"It'll feel good once you're in," Tony promised, but he gave his own involuntary noise of alarm as his own package hit the cold water.

Amber balked as the water hit her belly. "A chair in the sun is looking really nice right now," she said reluctantly, but she was still giggling.

Tony took a chance. "You just have to get in all at once," he said. "Get the shock over with."

Amber looked up at him with big, alarmed eyes as he reached down and scooped her up. She squealed in playful dismay as he tossed her easily into the water before them before ducking himself in after her.

He was right, of course—once they were in the water, it felt no more than cool and refreshing.

Amber splashed him back, and they romped into the deeper water and then swam in leisurely fashion to the far end by the lower deck. Tony was aware of the indulgent looks a few of the guests gave them, but most of his attention was caught by his mate.

She swam easily, like a beautiful, curvy little mermaid, and when she ducked her head under the water and came out of the water beside him, he felt a rush of amazement and adoration.

They lounged at the edge of the pool, drinking in the sparkling sunlight, and Tony gathered her close to him, pausing at every step to give her a chance to protest the intimacy. He was grateful when she snuggled close to him.

"Costa Rica is as gorgeous as all the brochures promised,"

Amber sighed, her bare skin against his, cradled in the water of the pool. "*Pura vida* indeed."

"More gorgeous," Tony said, smiling at her.

"You aren't looking at Costa Rica," she said, smiling back.

"I know," Tony said, and he leaned in and kissed her, as he'd been longing to do since he'd first seen her at the edge of the pool. "But there's a beautiful banana tree behind you," he teased, once he finally released her mouth.

She twisted to look behind her. "That's not a banana tree," she told him. "That's just a palm tree."

"You sure it's not a coconut tree?"

"Quite sure," Amber said confidently. "See the way the leaves hang, and the shape of the trunk?"

"Mm-hm," Tony said.

"You're not looking at the tree," Amber scolded with a smile.

"Nope," Tony agreed.

This time Amber leaned up to kiss him first, and he drew her close against him, warm compared to the cool water around them. Her buoyancy gave the embrace an extra element of movement and excitement.

"We have an hour until our massage," she suggested in his ear, once he had released her lips at last.

The hint was all he needed. They scrambled from the pool, giggling like adolescents, and they barely took the time to towel off before slipping into their sandals and retreating for Tony's cottage.

This time, they managed to get the door closed behind them.

CHAPTER 11

The masseuses laughed off their tardy appearance to their appointment with knowing winks. "We are on tropical time here," said the woman with a thick Mexican accent. "I'm Lydia, please follow Andre."

The other masseuse, a lanky blond man with big, strong hands and an Australian accent, led them to a pair of tables in a private courtyard surrounded by beautifully flowering bushes.

Amber was amused to notice that the spa was set up for grooming animals as well as people, with a wide variety of currycombs and brushes hanging along the wall.

She nearly fell asleep during her massage, lulled by the conversation that Tony carried on with the two masseuses, all in lilting Spanish that she understood no more than a word or two of.

Afterwards, as they were getting dressed, she asked him, "You speak Spanish?"

He nodded before she could regret how foolish a question it was; clearly he spoke it very well.

"I took a little in high school," she said, feeling shy about it. "And a semester of French. Do you speak any other languages?"

"Russian," Tony said cheerfully. "Also French, Swedish, and enough Japanese and Mandarin to get by."

Amber stared, then laughed, pulling her t-shirt over her head. "Oh, just enough to get by. In construction management, you know..."

Tony startled and managed to look guilty and angry at the same time.

"Oh, look!" Amber was glad to distract him by pointing out a toucan making a lazy loop above them, but she knew that Tony was living some lie with her, and it reminded her too keenly that this fantasy had no place in either of their real lives.

A phone rang then and they looked around in surprise. Tony finally said, "Wait, that's me," and dug into his pants pocket. "I'm not used to having a signal," he said sheepishly. "Sorry, have to take this while I can!"

He left the spa hastily, already answering, and Amber was alone in the pretty little courtyard as she finished dressing.

Lydia returned with a smile. "Your young man left in quite a hurry," she observed.

"He's not my young man," Amber said swiftly.

That earned her a long, thoughtful look. "He certainly *appears* to be," Lydia said gently.

"Oh, no," Amber laughed desperately. "We just met, it's just… a vacation thing." She must sound terrifically shallow, she thought miserably. "I mean, I like him, it's just not a… he's got a… a..." a life he wouldn't tell her about. She thought about the phone call he'd had to take.

"Is he married?" Lydia asked softly.

Amber stared in horror. "No!" she said. Then, miserably, "I have no idea." She laughed, nearly hysterically. "I never even *thought* of that."

Lydia shook her head. "I do not think I would believe it," she said firmly. "Not the way that he looks at you, like he has never seen anyone *before* you."

Amber wondered if it was only because she wanted to believe Lydia so much that the idea of Tony being married really did seem impossible. It didn't feel like he was hiding a wife, it felt like he was hiding a *purpose*. Like he wasn't really here for a vacation.

He is ours, her cat agreed. *No one else's, ever.*

"These things work out the way they are supposed to," the masseuse said confidently, looking into her eyes. "Let yourself enjoy this. Seize it."

"*Carpe diem*," Amber agreed.

Lydia didn't press the issue. "You have been enjoying your stay, I hope?" she asked instead as she started to strip the massage tables.

"Very much," Amber said, grateful for the change of topic. "It's so beautiful here, and the food is amazing, and there's so much to do."

"Will you be joining us tomorrow evening at the dance?" Lydia asked.

Amber immediately imagined dancing with Tony and her breath caught. "I don't really dance," she said uncomfortably.

"I teach a class right before the dance," Lydia said coaxingly. "I can show you all of the steps you need to know."

Amber glanced over at her.

Lydia smiled innocently back.

Amber smiled back. "I'll come," she agreed.

CHAPTER 12

Tony could have kicked himself.

"Oh yes, I speak Spanish and Russian and Chinese," he mocked himself in a mutter. "Because *that* matches my cover story."

He hated that he had to continue to keep Amber in the dark about who he was, and kept ridiculously forgetting that he had told her the story he was using with the resort. It felt like he had known her forever, that she must know every one of his secrets.

Which is why he was getting Rochelle to send him the paperwork that would give him clearance to tell Amber what he was really doing there… if the WiFi would ever start working.

That was another conflict he'd had with Scarlet since his arrival. "We encourage our guests to disconnect," she had told him scathingly. "And we're on a private island off a foreign country generating all our own power; Internet reliability is not a priority. This is made clear in your rental agreement."

Tony wondered if there was more to it than that. It certainly was down at perfectly inconvenient times.

"It'll be in your inbox," Rochelle assured him. "And I promise not to breathe a word to Rick."

When he spotted Amber later, sitting on the bar deck overlooking the pool, it was like coming home. *Soon*, he thought. *Soon I'll be able to honestly talk about a* future *with her.*

She smiled and waved at him. "Want to get some food?" she asked, standing to greet him with a shy kiss.

"It's still a while before dinner is served," Tony said, automatically checking the spot on his wrist where his watch used to be. "But I could use some food now, too."

Amber slipped her hand into his as they walked, and he gratefully kept it; there was something satisfying about having even that tiny amount of contact between them.

The buffet had been replenished and freshened since they'd last been there. Both of them took heaping tacos that bore only a passing resemblance to their American fast food cousins, and ate them with relish and mess, licking their fingers and plates with laughter.

Amber took a glass of wine with her second plate. "I'm on vacation," she said defiantly.

"Don't have to defend yourself to me!" Tony chuckled. He took a beer, and they lingered over their drinks until the waitstaff began to set the tables for dinner and the sun began its journey to setting over the water.

"I haven't been to the beach yet," Amber said as they left the dining hall and paused at an intersection of the paths. Something in her voice suggested to Tony that she wasn't really interested in a walk.

"You aren't missing much," Tony said off-handedly. "Lots of sand, some crabs, maybe a dead fish."

Amber's eyes sparkled back at him. "I'm sure you have a much better idea?"

"There's a fine view of the sunset from my cottage porch," he purred at her.

~

Tony woke with Amber snuggled so naturally in his arms that he wondered how he'd ever slept without her.

"Did my stomach wake you up?" she asked with a giggle as it gave another hungry rumble.

They had skipped dinner in favor of talking about nothing and making slow love late into the night. His deck had a better view than Amber's did, and they sat on the loveseat watching the stars creep across the sky, fingers entwined, her sweet, strong body curled up close beside him.

Tony's stomach gave an answering growl. "I think it was my own stomach that woke me," he admitted.

The sun was rising over the resort and the sky was already light; they hadn't closed the curtains the night before, or the sliding doors. The surf was loud against the shore and there were birds crying in the jungle.

"We're in time to catch breakfast," Amber suggested, and it became a laughing race for clothes, hindered by tickling and kissing.

Their bellies were still giving a chorus of need when they arrived at the restaurant, and a grinning waiter who introduced himself as Breck seated them overlooking the bar deck and pool below. He brought them coffee with a flirtatious wink at Tony.

"What are your plans for the day?" Amber asked, sipping the froth from the top of her coffee drink.

Tony frowned, thinking about the dead-end he'd run into on his mission. He ought to be taking it more seriously, putting more pressure on the infuriating Scarlet, or pursuing more staff interviews. It was easy to forget he was at the resort on business; Amber seemed to drive all other thoughts from his mind.

"I was thinking about taking a yoga class later this morning," Amber suggested when Tony was silent. "Would you like to join me?"

"I have some... er... work from the office I should do today," Tony said awkwardly. He hated every word of the lie.

Amber smiled at him indulgently. "That's okay," she said understandingly, possibly thinking that he felt yoga was too unmanly for him.

"There's a dance tonight," Tony remembered. "At the event hall. Some kind of formal affair with a live salsa band."

"Oh, I saw that," Amber said, and Tony thought she looked a little wistful. "Lydia told me there's a dance class right before it to teach the basic steps."

"Would you care to attend with me, my lady?" Tony asked chivalrously. "I packed a suit for the occasion."

Amber's eyes glowed. "I would very much like that," she said shyly. "But I will definitely need to take the dance class beforehand."

"I will join you for that," Tony promised. "Leave space in your dance card for me."

Amber smiled and blushed in delight. "I will endeavor to do so," she teased.

Then Breck brought them plates of fluffy, cheese-smothered omelets with perfect toast and fresh fruit bowls and spread napkins in their laps. Conversation was forgotten in the need to fill their empty stomachs.

After a breakfast that had them both groaning and happily holding their sides, Tony gave Amber a swift kiss and she went to find the yoga class, protesting that she would be incapable of bending into the poses.

From the deck above, Tony discovered that Scarlet was at the bar; she appeared to be having a heated discussion with Jimmy, the lifeguard, and one of the handymen. Tony's eyes narrowed, wondering how long that would keep her, then swiftly turned and left by the back restaurant exit, taking the turn uphill towards her office.

He stopped at the Y in the path that split off to the spa and took a small device from his pocket. It separated into two pieces, and he tucked one into his ear, placing the other carefully beside the path to resort entrance. He walked past it twice to test the range and was satisfied that it would only alarm for someone choosing the path towards the courtyard.

He moved quietly, swiftly, and was relieved to find that the structure at the top of the resort was quiet and empty. They were far enough from the ocean that the sound of the plants rustling in the wind was louder here than the surf.

He prowled around first the outside, then the inside perimeter of the building. It was basically a large, square donut, with storage and utility rooms along three sides, Scarlet's office and what appeared to be a large bedroom suite on the downhill side looking out over the resort. There was a small, private lawn that opened off of it, and a patio with a table and a single chair.

Her office door was open to the inner courtyard, which Tony found odd. As private as the woman was, she seemed like the door-shut sort of person. His interview with her had been frustrating and useless; she asked him as many questions as he'd managed to ask her.

He went in carefully, scanning for alarm systems or electronics, and found nothing. A laptop sitting open on the desk was the most modern device in the room, everything else was clearly from the 80s when the resort was first built. Locking filing cabinets surrounded the window behind her desk, and potted plants filled most of the windowsill. The room had tall bookshelves on two sides, and one wall held a map of the resort half-shrouded in the trailing vines that looped all around the room. Tony left the laptop alone; he didn't have a warrant—yet—and everything that he could do legally should be done first.

He went to the closest bookshelf and scanned titles.

Like the décor, there was nothing more recent than the 80s, and every book looked well-read. He took out his phone and started taking photos of the spines. Rochelle might be able to come up with some kind of pattern in the titles, but he could not. There were foreign language books, several books on management and accounting, a range of classical literature, the complete Encyclopedia Britannica, books on botany and gardening, on mythical creatures, on maintaining small engines… and an entire row of Georgette Heyer. Not all of them were in English.

Tony took a book out at random, a book of Swedish to English, and found that it had tidy notations and cross-references in the edges.

He was just putting it back when the hairs at the back of his neck rose.

"Can I *help* you?"

Scarlet's voice—with him, at least—was always rather chilly, but Tony felt like the temperature in the room had just fallen ten degrees.

"The door was open," he growled, turning to face her.

She didn't look amused. "Most people are *polite* enough not to snoop through what is clearly a private office."

Tony scowled at her, feeling like he'd just been scolded by a teacher. A very severe teacher. "I was waiting for you," he lied. "My agency assures me that they've sent everything you asked for."

"Our service provider on the mainland has been having technical difficulties," Scarlet said tightly. "They assure me that our data should resume at full strength within the next day or two. I'm sure whatever has been sent will be here shortly."

"Awfully convenient," Tony muttered.

Scarlet's eyes flashed, but she didn't protest the accusation. "If there's anything else I can help you with?" she asked tightly.

There wasn't.

"Thank you for your time," Tony ground out.

"You're very *welcome,*" Scarlet said with exactly the same measure of sincerity.

She stepped aside, arms folded over her chest, and Tony left with his chin high and his temper higher.

The blare of the alarm in his ear surprised him, and he crouched into a fighting stance before he realized that he'd set off his own proximity alert. He went back two paces and picked the device out of the brush he'd put it in, staring at it curiously. How had she managed to get past without triggering it? The only other ways up into the courtyard involved hiking through the jungle or hopping over the wall that edged the top of the resort… and Tony couldn't imagine the terribly proper Scarlet doing either of these things.

He returned to his cottage and found that the bed had been made and the room straightened. He sat down with his laptop to jot down notes from the unproductive interview and download the photos, glancing at his phone and frowning to find that the WiFi was still down.

CHAPTER 13

Amber arrived at the event hall self-consciously smoothing down her sundress. It was not all that fancy, but it felt flirty. She hoped it wouldn't be too out of place.

Lydia greeted her cheerfully, dressed in a splashy red dress. The flirtatious waiter from the restaurant, Breck, was there as well, already walking slowly through the steps with a white-haired woman who was blushing and smiling at his attention.

Only a handful of people showed up for the class, Tony last and most importantly of all. Amber mistrusted the way her heart sped up and her belly clenched at the sight of him. She had hoped that the day apart would remind her that this was just a vacation fling, just a temporary, whirlwind affair that would be over with the week that was galloping by too quickly.

But his smile when he caught sight of her left her breathless, before he even stooped to give her a quick, possessive kiss.

It wasn't the kiss of a casual fling, it was a confident, warm kiss, with layers of expectation and promises of more.

But that was impossible, wasn't it? They were only living their short, false fantasies for a short time.

Tony, unlike Amber, had no need of the class and was clearly already comfortable with the step-step-step-pause rhythm of salsa. Lydia pulled him to the front of the class and used him to demonstrate the steps. Amber, terribly distracted by how incredible Tony looked in a suit, trod on Breck's toes a dozen time.

He grinned at her. "You found yourself a beautiful mate at our resort," he observed near her ear. "Step back."

Amber stepped forward and clashed her knee against his. "Oh, oops," she said, blushing. Mate seemed like an odd word to choose; Breck didn't sound English or Australian.

"The other back," Breck teased. "Step forward this time!"

She concentrated on her feet and the dance pattern with determination and made a successful circle around the room with the waiter before he led her to where Tony was dutifully practicing with the white-haired woman and switched partners with a knowing wink.

"You're really good at this," Amber told Tony breathlessly.

"You're beautiful," he told her, and Amber found herself drowning in his eyes.

There was a short break after the class while the band set up. They walked out to watch twilight falling over the cliffs and the ocean swirling beyond.

"After this week…" Tony started to say.

But there was no 'after this week' that Amber wanted to think about and she swiftly changed the topic. "Can you believe the view? Pictures don't even do it justice. I wish there was a way to hold onto the whole thing… the smell, and the sounds, and the heat, all of it." *You*, she didn't add.

Tony didn't press the issue, only agreed with her, and they talked inancly about the perfect weather and the beauties of the jungle, standing close together, fingers entwined.

The band began to play and they walked back through the gathering dark to the event hall, which had been transformed; it had seemed dim compared to the fierce daylight, and now it was brilliant in the surrounding darkness, filled with happy music and a gathering of satisfied guests and attentive staff.

Amber had been to dances in high school; they had been unmitigated hell. She'd been filled with longing for a connection, any connection, and had been rebuffed, sometimes even teased. She was an orphan, in a small town where everyone had family, and had been unfriendly and cold in an attempt to protect her sensitive heart. It didn't surprise her that no one wanted to dance with her, or be her friend, it only reinforced her suspicion that she was unlovable and undesirable.

But this night, this was everything her teenage self had ever dreamed of.

Tony danced every dance with her, and she was distantly aware that they were the focus of many amused and envious glances. He was tall and utterly dreamy, and Amber found it difficult to believe that *she* was the one in his arms.

They didn't talk, to Amber's gratitude, though they laughed often; she wanted to live this beautiful fantasy as long as she could. He made her feel light and graceful and complete as the music swelled around them, and it wasn't until much much later that Amber realized that her legs were aching and her feet were complaining.

"Can I get you a drink?" he offered.

She already felt drunk, Amber thought. Like she was drifting through the night in a seductive haze. "Just water," she said, out of breath.

They walked to the little bar set up at the side of the dance floor.

She felt Tony stiffen at her side and realized that Scarlet was behind the bar. The woman's serene smile felt chilly compared to the warmth of her staff. "Can I get you something?" she offered politely.

"Water," Tony said briefly and Amber shot him a look. The lazy, fairy tale bubble that they had been dancing in was gone and he looked unexpectedly cold and unapproachable.

"Very well," Scarlet said just a briefly, and she poured them two glasses from a frosty pitcher, handing them over the counter without expression.

Amber's feet were hurting in earnest now, and she was grateful when Tony led them to a chair at the side of the floor.

"It's so unfair," she said, trying to lighten the mood again as she bent to take her shoes off and rub her feet. "The cutest things are always the most uncomfortable."

Tony smiled at her, and it brought back every bit of the magical moment. "Not all of the cutest things," he said, and when he leaned forward to kiss her, it wasn't anything but completely natural to kiss him back. Amber gladly forgot about the severe red-headed resort owner, and all the secrets Tony was keeping from her.

CHAPTER 14

Tony was technically proficient at dancing, but he'd never particularly enjoyed it… until now.

Dancing with Amber wasn't a duty, or an expectation, it was joy. She was laughing and blushing in his arms, protesting her lack of skills but gamely enjoying herself.

She was his mate, Tony thought with satisfaction, and he could imagine nothing more perfect than this dance and this entire beautiful week since she had arrived and turned his life upside down.

But every dance had to end sometime and he finally walked with her to the edge of the floor, stared Scarlet down over glasses of water, and found free seats together at the quieter end of the hall.

As much as he wanted to continue kissing her—and do other things that he was sure Scarlet would descend on like a nun with a ruler—he pulled back. "After this..." he started, not sure how to go on. "Once I'm done..."

"After this, I'm expecting you to take me back to your cottage," Amber said, neatly deflecting the conversation about the future again.

Tony didn't have permission to tell her anything yet anyway. "Another turn around the floor first?"

"Not in these cute shoes," Amber said, her golden eyes laughing.

They rose to their feet and wandered out into the velvet night, Amber barefoot.

"Do you want me to carry you?" Tony offered, when they got to a place where the smooth white concrete turned to gravel.

"That's ridiculous," she said, giggling, but she didn't protest when he scooped her up and carried her the final steps into his cottage.

He put her down on the bed, kicking the door closed behind him, and kissed her passionately as she tossed her shoes across the room.

But it wasn't the same way that they had kissed before, and it wasn't the same ardor that had driven their previous lovemaking. She held his face as she kissed him, in no hurry to undress him, lingering over removing every layer.

Tony took his cues from her and they slowed, spending extra moments with lazy caresses and gentle, brushing kisses.

He knew her, so completely, in so short a time. He *knew* the touches that would make her breath hitch, and the places that made her eyes close in pleasure.

Everything felt different. It felt… like she was trying to memorize him, like she was trying to stretch each precious moment as long as possible.

Like she wasn't ready to say goodbye…

"Amber," Tony said quietly, when they lay together afterwards, a single sheet over them to keep the evening chill off.

Her breathing was slow and even.

"I… love you."

But she was already asleep.

~

A sharp rap on the door woke him.

Disoriented, Tony sat upright in bed, grasping at empty covers in the space where Amber had been. Sunlight spilled around the corners of the curtains, and he could see in the light that her clothing was gone; there was no trace of her anywhere. He rolled out of bed and staggered out of the bedroom as the knocking was repeated, more impatiently than before.

"I'm coming," he roared, and he nearly paused for the bathrobe before deciding that it served whoever it was right to meet them naked at the door.

Scarlet, dressed in a perfectly crisp linen skirt suit, looked entirely unfazed by his nudity.

Of course, Tony realized with chagrin. She did run a clothing-optional resort, after all. He, on the other hand, would have appreciated having a layer of clothing to give him some shreds of dignity. He settled for a dark scowl, crossing his big arms at her. "What do you want?"

"It's not what I want," Scarlet said, all business. "It's what you've been hounding me for all week." She thrust a file folder at him, all but forcing it into his hands. "I've cleared your background," she said, no hint of apology in her voice for her earlier obstruction.

"About time," Tony said gruffly, recognizing his own lack of graciousness. He opened the file folder to flip briefly through a stack of xeroxed forms, one for each of the missing shifters. He suspiciously wondered if Scarlet had purposefully delayed long enough to falsify the information she was giving him; there was something secretive about the woman that challenged his trust.

"You're *welcome*," Scarlet said coldly, and she turned on her heel and stalked away with a click of heels on concrete.

Tony shut the door behind her a little harder than he meant to, and crossed the room to the desk. He tapped a finger on the file folder, then looked through the open door to the bedroom with a furrow in his brow.

It bothered him that Amber was gone. It was deeply unsettling that she had been able to leave without waking him, and it gave him a pang of worry that she had *wanted* to.

Maybe she had just gotten hungry, and hadn't wished to wake him? It was mid-morning, maybe she was generally an early riser. Tony tried to find some peace in the idea, and failed to.

As much as he wanted to immediately go find her, he decided instead to get dressed, and get back to the job at hand.

He had work to do.

CHAPTER 15

The sunrise, peeking in through the gaps in the curtains, had pried Amber's eyes open, and she crept out of Tony's cottage using all the cat-silent skills she'd honed as a teenager. Tony barely stirred as she dressed herself, and she carefully latched the front door behind her, smiling to remember how it had gaped open while they made enthusiastic love their first night.

She had certainly taken her intention to have fun seriously. Her smile felt brittle, as she remembered that her time here would end altogether too soon, and she'd be saying goodbye to the big, charming man who had captured her heart.

The walk to her cottage felt impossibly steep and lonely, and she showered swiftly.

She put on a clean pair of shorts and a plain babydoll t-shirt that flattered her curves but wasn't as revealing as the shirt of the previous night and finished the look with a pair of low wedge sandals. She paused to look at her reflection, and grimaced at herself. Her long dark hair and slightly dusky skin could have been anything—Hispanic, perhaps, or Middle Eastern. Someone had once told her she looked Native American, and another had suggested east Indian. Her brown eyes were strangely light and golden, and her cheekbones not quite right for any specific nationality. Her diminutive height suggested Asian, but the shape of her eyes did not.

Maybe South American, like her animal form? Amber pushed the idea away. She certainly wasn't going to figure out her origins here, as she had half-hoped she might. She didn't look like any of the Costa Ricans she had met, and no one had ever heard of an Andean mountain cat shifter.

Her stomach reminded her that dinner had been very early the previous night, before a great deal of activity.

A sign at the dining hall door reminded visitors that clothing was required for establishments serving hot food, and there was a rack of bathrobes, in case someone was caught by surprise.

"Chef has something special on deck for breakfast this morning," Breck promised suggestively, winking at Amber as he pulled out the chair for her, and then spread a napkin in her lap.

"Chef," it turned out, was a distinguished older man who cared enough about his clientele to come out and check with her halfway through the exquisite meal.

"I've never had souffle before," Amber confessed to him. "And until today, I would have not guessed that I liked artichokes."

Chef looked ridiculously pleased. "The secret is fresh eggs and good cream," he said proudly. "The bacon crumbles don't hurt anything," he added conspiratorially.

Amber indulged in a second plate, with a side of fresh fruit pieces and another cup of strong, dark coffee.

Her table gave her a wonderful view of the dining area, and she people-watched shamelessly, enjoying the way that Breck doted on his customers, and how friendly and cheerful the other guests were.

One woman in particular Amber had to keep herself from staring at—she had clearly been there some time and knew all of the staff by name. She held herself like a queen, confident and assured as she directed her breakfast. She was gorgeous, with loose, waist-long, auburn hair and flawless makeup, and she was also the largest woman that Amber had ever seen. She honestly wasn't sure how the woman's chair held her up, and half-expected it to crumple beneath her at one dramatic gesture of her hand.

"That's Magnolia," Breck told her, refilling her coffee. "Isn't she just a dish? She's one of our long-term residents and we all just adore her."

Embarrassed to be caught staring, Amber quickly finished off her plate and drank the last of her coffee.

She had a moment of hesitation as she left the dining hall—an odd expectation that she ought to be somewhere, doing something, and she wasn't sure what that was.

"You're on vacation," she reminded herself. Most of her wanted to scamper straight back to Tony's cottage. But she didn't want to appear too desperate or clingy. *Just a vacation fling,* she told herself firmly. She turned her sandaled feet past the pool and down to the beach.

The winding stone paths led her to one edge of a long crescent beach, bright sand edged with emerald green shrubbery on one side and sapphire blue ocean on the other. She passed a cottage being renovated by two shirtless men who lent support to her theory about Scarlet's employment requirements including modeling. She smirked to compare them in her mind to Tony's gorgeous physique, then scolded herself for thinking about him again.

The beach had a collection of comfortable chairs, and a small open structure that held a tiny bar (with no bartender in sight), piles of fluffy beach towels, and an array of sunscreen bottles. There were even a few pairs of sunglasses and hats in various sizes. There were sturdy umbrellas, spaced along the beach. At the far end of the beach was a dock, where a sailboat was moored across from a larger boat with a Shifting Sands logo on the side.

But what made Amber stop and stare, gape-mouthed, was the lifeguard. Curled around the guard tower was a dragon, as big and real as life, gleaming green and gold in the early sun. She might have guessed it was some crazy jeweled sculpture, but it swiveled a long mobile face towards her, and blinked curiously at her twice before returning its gaze to the ocean, where a few people were splashing on body boards.

A dragon!

She had heard rumors of mythical shifters, but hadn't expected to ever meet one, and now that she was faced with one, she couldn't do more than stare in shock. She felt foolish for thinking she was special for being a rare cat shifter.

After a long moment, she gathered up a towel and chair, and found a spot near the end of the beach, where the sand curved around towards the head rocks so she could surreptitiously watch the dragon while still facing the water.

She closed her eyes, drinking in the feeling of sunlight on her skin, and tried to relax to the mesmerizing sound of the waves and the wind in the jungle leaves.

She was not surprised to open her eyes and find Tony, wearing only shorts, walking over the sand towards her, his own chair and towel tucked under his arm. The leap that her heart gave in her chest was both thrilling and unwelcome.

How many times was she going to have to remind herself that this was not a real relationship? The thrill of desire that went through her body at the sight of his muscled arms and strong legs was to be expected, but she needed to keep her emotions in check, and she was doing an utterly miserable job at that.

Ours, her cat purred rapturously.

You aren't helping, Amber replied.

"You left," Tony said accusingly, when he was standing right next to her. Clearly, she had violated some expectation of courtesy, in his mind.

Amber attempted to play it cool.

"I needed breakfast," she said offhandedly. "I was starving! And you know, no predation, so I figured I'd better head to the restaurant."

Tony set up the chair close enough to her that their armrests touched, and when he sat down, he took her hand and twined his fingers into hers.

"Was breakfast good?" Tony asked, tipping his head back so he could smile across at her.

Amber licked her lips in memory. "Exquisite!" she said enthusiastically. "You missed a treat."

"Alas," Tony said, with mock tragedy.

"Chef should be in a restaurant in New York City that you can't get reservations at for a week," Amber said, pretending she knew anything about high-end restaurants. "Scarlet has done an impressive job staffing this place."

She felt Tony's hand stiffen under her fingers.

"You don't like her, do you," she guessed, before she could stop herself. *None of your business, stupid,* she told herself.

"I don't trust her," Tony said. "She's been... obstructionist."

Amber tipped down her sunglasses and looked at him. "You're not really here for vacation," she said finally.

Tony squirmed.

"I'm sorry," Amber said swiftly, loosening her fingers so he could pull free if he wanted. "You don't have to tell me. It can be just a vacation if you want."

But Tony squeezed her back. "I'm part of a top secret government agency, Shifter Affairs, and I'm here as part of an investigation."

Amber blinked at him, but somehow wasn't as surprised as she thought she ought to be. And most of her was relieved that at least he wasn't *married*. "What are you investigating?" she asked.

Tony seemed to relax a little, the beach chair groaning a little as he settled. "Shifters have been going missing from this resort in particular for the past several years—sometimes they vanish on their way here, sometimes after they've checked out. One was mysteriously lost at sea during their stay, no body found. It's all been going on almost as long as Scarlet has been here. There's some thought that another government entity was poaching potential agents, but I think something more sinister is happening; the missing people don't all fit the profile."

"And you think Scarlet might have something to do with it?" The idea was chilling. More chilling: "And there's a government agency that knows about shifters? As in, the American government?"

"It's more like a... an... international x-file agency," Tony floundered. "That happens to know about shifters. We deal with all sorts of weird cases, but they aren't all shifters."

Amber glanced down the beach at the dragon who was still attentively watching the swimmers. "Is there a... registry?" She was sitting up in her chair now, all attention and no part relaxation. "Are they worried about... I don't know, an uprising, or a shifter revolution? Should we worry about being on a *list*?" Bad movie plots flitted through her head.

"Nothing like that." Tony shook his head with confidence. "Most shifters are peaceful and perfectly legal. We only deal with the criminal elements, and our records aren't public."

"Ooo," Amber couldn't help saying. "Criminal elements! You're like a James Bond superspy, aren't you!"

"But with a lot more paperwork and a lot less flying burning helicopters and disarming bombs," Tony laughed.

Amber laughed, then sobered and bit her lip. "You said you have *records*," she said, not sure how to proceed.

Tony was not oblivious to her train of thought, following her line of questioning to its logical conclusion. "You want to know if there are more Andean mountain cats, like you. Maybe your parents."

"I'm sure it's not as important as shifters disappearing today," Amber said, heart in her mouth. She gave a dry laugh. "And I have to *hope* they aren't on the wrong side of the law." But if they were, would that explain why they gave her up?

The combination of the idea, and Tony's intoxicating closeness, made her feel dizzy and unsettled. *Just a vacation fling*, she wanted to scream at herself.

"I can check," Tony said, making circles on the back of her hand with his thumb. "I will. If we've got any information, I'll find it for you."

Amber let the air out of her lungs all at once, not realizing that she had been holding her breath. "I'd appreciate that," she confessed in a small voice.

"It doesn't matter to me," he told her gruffly. "Where you're from, who your parents are. I don't give a damn." He looked at her so intensely, his brown eyes warm and direct. "I know who *you* are."

Amber blinked at him, overwhelmed. She could no more doubt him than doubt the air she was breathing, but it made no sense. Tony's eyes were full of promises, not empty flattery—promises of love and life together. She tried to remind herself again that this wasn't *real*, but could only see the warmth in his eyes and remember the way they had kissed and made love, and wonder if it could possibly be something more.

I don't get happy endings, she reminded herself fiercely. Too many times she had longed for stability, for family, only to have it ripped away.

James Bond never stayed with any of the Bond girls, she reminded herself. He had beautiful, casual beach flings and went away afterwards and was a spy again.

Just like Tony would.

Because that was all this was.

Right?

Amber couldn't make sense of the emotion swirling in her chest. "I have to go!" she said loudly, in terror and confusion, and she scrambled backwards out of her chair, tipping it over. She fled over the sand, stumbling and staggering over the uneven surface ungracefully.

"Amber, wait!" Tony said behind her and Amber ran faster.

The dragon lifeguard turned in alarm, hearing their commotion, but didn't uncurl itself from the lifeguard chair.

She made it back to the dining hall faster than she expected, winded by the uphill sprint, and she leaned against the stone wall panting.

"Amber!" It wasn't Tony, but Amber's alarm was no less. Jimmy was putting a cellphone in his pocket. "Your timing is perfect," he said with a big smile. "I was just organizing a tour of Mr Big's estate gardens for a few of the guests. Wouldn't you like to join us?"

His whole vibe was of a greasy salesman, but the idea was so appealing to Amber that she instantly agreed. "Yes. That is perfect. When are you leaving?"

“The van is already gassed up and ready to go,” Jimmy said brightly. “Be at the resort entrance in ten minutes!”

Something about his eagerness left Amber feeling dirty, but she was too grateful for an excuse to escape to examine the feeling.

She didn't want to think about any feelings, too sure that she had made a terrible mistake in losing her heart altogether.

“Is his name really Mr. Big?” she had to ask.

Jimmy laughed. “Not *Big*,” he clarified. “*Beehag*. It's an old English name.”

“Ah!” Amber tried to laugh with him, but it came out very dry and humorless. She suspected the mysterious man was going to remain Mr. Big in her head for a long time.

CHAPTER 16

Tony watched Amber flee with confusion and dismay, not even comforted by the exciting sight of her gorgeous little ass as she ran across the sand. What had he done wrong?

Had she heard his declaration of love the night before? Was she trying to tell him that she didn't feel the same? He felt the pull of his mate at an undeniable level, but every time he got close emotionally or tried to talk about the future, she seemed to get skittish, and this time he'd managed to scare her right off.

He scrubbed a hand across his face.

He'd also managed to tell her more about his agency than he was authorized to, and knew *that* was going to be some paperwork. There were a few shifters in his chain of command who might be tolerant about the slip due to the fact that Amber was his mate, but there were others who would definitely not.

And it was going to be a tough fact to prove, given that Amber was hell-bent on running away from him.

After giving a hefty sigh, he hauled himself up out of the beach chair. A glance down the beach at the watchful dragon lifeguard convinced him to fold up both his chair and Amber's abandoned one, and haul them back to the beach shed.

Back at the cottage, he booted up his laptop and picked up the cellphone, flipping open the folder that Scarlet had given him.

The signal was spotty. If it was cloudy, he'd be out of luck, but today he had solid bars. The WiFi, on the other hand, was *still* down.

He dialed the cellphone and waited, hoping the signal held. While he waited for the connection to be made, he flipped through the paperwork for a second time, hoping to find something new in the information.

"Rick," the voice at the other end finally said with disinterest.

"Richie!" Tony said.

There was a slight satellite delay, and Richard asked, "How's Costa Rica, Tony? Is it grrrrrrreeeeeeeat?"

"Har, har," Tony said, but he expected the familiar jibe. "Hey, listen up. I don't know how long my cellphone signal will last."

"Wow, Tony, you mean you've actually gotten some work done and have information? You're not just lying on the sand in the sun flirting with pretty girls at the *clothing-optional* resort on the agency dime?"

"I got the paperwork from Scarlet, finally," Tony said, without taking the bait. "And believe me, I had to work for it."

"Did you flex your muscles for her?" Rick teased. "Make promises? *Rise* to the occasion?"

Tony bit back his desire to tell Rick about Amber. He wasn't even sure what to tell Rick—was Amber going to continue to bolt away from him like he'd offended her in some way? Was it just taking her a little time to get used to the idea of a mate? Tony shook his head and brought himself back to the conversation. The satellite delay covered his confusion.

"There's nothing very helpful here," Tony said dryly. "Notes about food allergies and preferences, what activities they attended, what shifter type they were. Nothing seems to tie them together at all—they are all different kinds of animals, from different places. Some of them attended morning yoga, some of them didn't. One was allergic to peanuts."

"We can put it in a database and feed it to Rochelle," Rick suggested. "She can pick patterns out of nothing."

Tony was squinting at the pages. "Yeah," he said, distracted by a sudden thought. "I'll scan these and set them to email as soon as I've got WiFi or data again."

"Send me photos, too," Rick laughed. "Selfies that happen to have good beach babes in the background would be preferred. Clothing *optional.*"

Tony licked his lips. "Look, I have a favor to ask."

"One worth a great selfie from the beach? Maybe one that doesn't happen to have you in it?"

"I'll send you a dozen," Tony promised, smiling to think of getting the dragon in the shot, or the English boar couple who liked to bask in the sand in animal form.

"What's the favor?"

"I'm looking for a person, maybe a couple, on the run. One of them might have been an Andean mountain cat. They would have passed through Lakefield, about twenty-six years ago."

Tony heard Rick typing. The sound was strangely tinny over the poor connection.

"Lakefield Ontario, or Lakefield Minnesota?" Rick asked.

"Minnesota, I'd guess." She had a Midwestern accent and loved casserole, Tony thought. It was outrageous that he could know someone as intensely as he knew Amber and not even know if she was American or Canadian. "Look for a church called Saint Mary's. A baby was dropped there."

"Who happened to be an Andean mountain cat shifter," Rick guessed. "I've never even heard of an Andean mountain cat. Pretty, aren't they!" He must have looked it up on the Internet while they were talking.

Tony thought about Amber's petite, lush form, and her incredible golden-brown eyes. "You have no idea," he said. His thoughts were starting to form into a pattern.

"Pretty and... rare." He picked up the paperwork in front of him again, sifting through the pages with a fresh outlook. "One of these missing shifters was a white tiger," Tony said thoughtfully. "And one was a sand cat."

"You don't see many of those," Rick agreed.

"Another was a Borneo bay cat, and here's a Northern quoll." Tony said, unease rising in his throat as he skimmed faster, flipping through the pages, now with a specific field in mind.

"A what?"

Tony wasn't sure if Rick didn't know what a quoll was, or if he hadn't heard over the static on the line. "A quoll," he repeated. "It's an Australian marsupial." He wouldn't have known that himself, if it hadn't been noted on the form.

"I'm starting to see a pattern," Rick said.

"*Rare*. All of the missing shifters are *rare*."

"Like someone's... collecting them?"

"*Amber*," Tony said, ice in his throat. He dropped the phone, not even sure if he'd hung it up first, and bolted for the door. The files spilled off the desk behind him, but he didn't stop.

CHAPTER 17

"A few of the guests" proved to be just three other people—the English boar couple who turned up their noses at Amber's sandy sandals and simple tank top, and a flinty-eyed man who spoke Spanish with Jimmy without acknowledging Amber's presence.

Nothing less than grateful for his company to spare her Jimmy's attention, Amber went for an empty seat in the far back of the van, even knowing that the bumps would be the worst there. She had a bottle of water, her phone in her pocket, and a straw hat—courtesy of the resort—to keep the worst of the sun from her face.

Most of the drive was through thick jungle, over a rain-pitted road that wandered seemingly randomly through gullies and along ridges, further than Amber would have guessed possible on an island of finite size. She had drained half her bottle by the time the road finally resolved into a driveway and passed through a set of heavy iron gates. To her surprise, there were guards at the gate, each carrying a formidable-looking rifle.

Maybe Mr. Big—Mr. *Beehag*—just really liked his privacy.

The van drove past the very large house to a second structure, much more modest, and Amber was happy to escape from the deafening metal box and stretch her legs again. She was glad for her hat here; the jungle had been cleared a good distance around the estate —which looked more like a compound to her eyes—and the sun was beating down. They were higher than she thought they would be, and she could see far out over the jungle, to the distant ocean beyond and below.

Mr Beehag proved to be younger than Amber had expected of an island-owning eccentric billionaire, with a quick smile that showed perfect white teeth. The teeth seemed odd paired with the sophisticated English accent. Amber couldn't help but compare him unfavorably with Tony and then wanted to kick herself for thinking about him again.

Surprisingly, he all but ignored the English couple, who introduced themselves as the Bellinghams, and took Amber's hand.

"Welcome to my arboretum," he said smoothly. To her befuddlement, he kissed it. "You would be Amber, and you must call me Alistair." It wasn't so much a suggestion as a command.

"Alright," Amber said, raising eyebrows at him. "Alistair, then. Thank you for having us here."

She tried to include the others in her statement, but found that Jimmy and the Spanish-speaking man had both vanished.

The English boar couple looked unimpressed, but made vague polite noises.

"I assure you, the pleasure is mine!" Alistair's smile was distractingly white, and anything but vague.

Something about the way he looked at her made the tiny hairs at the back of Amber's neck rise, and she was glad when he led them all to the doors of the arboretum and unlocked them at a very modern-looking keypad.

The arboretum, at least, was everything that Jimmy had promised, and Amber was just as happy that he didn't reappear while Alistair showed them around.

The eccentric billionaire was an educated host, and he knew all of the plants in his collection. He had entertaining stories about most of them, and was clearly proud of some of the very exotic and rare flowers he had convinced to blossom.

Amber quickly forgot how oddly attentive he was, and found herself in easy conversation about fertilizer choices and the use of blooming chemicals. Costa Rica had a reputation for ecotourism and going organic, and Amber couldn't help but approve of the fact that Alistair was following that trend.

They were standing at the base of what Alistair insisted was one of the rarest palm varieties in the world when Amber realized that she hadn't noticed the other couple in an unusually long time—and also, she was starving! The sun was just beginning to descend towards the ocean.

"Did we lose the Bellinghams?" she asked. "And goodness, I should be getting back to the resort for dinner..." Her water was long since gone; she had been using the empty bottle to keep her hands from fidgeting for some time.

"I am a shameful host," Alistair said, with a glint in his eyes that made Amber suspect nothing was an accident. "We bored the Bellinghams back to the resort some hours ago; Jimmy took them. You must stay to supper with me while he returns, and I will show you the rest of my collection."

Amber's curiosity was piqued; they had passed several sets of electronically locked doors that she had wondered about, and the walls were all much higher than privacy on a private island really required.

"I..." she thought about Tony; was he wondering where she was?

I don't owe him anything, she told herself fiercely. *It isn't a real relationship.*

He hadn't even been honest about his profession, at first. But she couldn't help but remember his face as he told her she was beautiful, and the way his thumb made circles on her hand.

"I'd love to have dinner," she said firmly.

CHAPTER 18

Tony sprinted for Amber's cottage, and when he found a locked door, knocked ferociously.

"Amber!" he called. "Amber, answer me!"

When she didn't, he circled the place, and easily climbed onto the porch without resorting to shifting. His tiger roared for release, but he was a little afraid of the intensity of the fear mounting in his chest. The curtains on the big glass doors were pulled back, and the rooms inside were dark and empty. Unless Amber was cowering in the bathroom...

She is not, his tiger snarled at him.

He stalked back along the path, first trying the dining hall, then the pool. He didn't want to believe the tiger inside, who was insisting that Amber wasn't here, that she wasn't anywhere nearby. He stood at the upper entrance of the dining hall, breathing in the delicious scent of whatever Chef had invented for dinner and hating his helplessness.

Scarlet.

Scarlet would know where his mate was. Tony wasn't sure if Scarlet was behind the disappearances or not, but he knew to the bottom of his soul that she had secrets, and that she knew whatever was going on within the borders of her resort.

The path to Scarlet's office was half steps and half steep path, and he nearly collided with a curvy woman in jeans and cowboy boots who made Amber look diminutive but still barely came to Tony's shoulder. She was carrying her own luggage and she was on a cellphone.

"Jenna," the blonde was saying with vinegar. "Their mother, Jenna Bruin. Don't make me fly from Costa Rica to set you straight. Those are my kids, and if I have to, that *is* what I will do. You will not enjoy it if I end up leaving my vacation because of your incompetence, and your school will not be happy with the lawsuit I slap you with, so I suggest that you get it fixed immediately."

She was clearly enraged, and Tony's already activated tiger recognized the riled-up bear barely contained behind her fair skin. They glared at each other a long heartbeat on the path while whoever was at the other end of the phone sputtered and folded like a wet paper towel, and Tony, with gritted teeth, took himself carefully around her on the narrow walkway.

Even he wasn't going to mess with an enraged momma bear.

Scarlet was sitting behind her desk, frowning at paperwork with a familiar expression, and she didn't paste on a customer service smile when Tony burst into her close office without knocking.

"Can I help you?" she asked acidly.

"Where's Amber?"

Scarlet didn't even blink in surprise, only narrowed her eyes a small amount and gave Tony an appraising look. "She left with a group of visitors for a tour of the arboretum at the Beehag estate."

"How long ago?" Tony glanced at his wrist, and realized he still wasn't wearing a watch. Scarlet didn't have any clocks up in her office.

"About five hours ago," Scarlet said without having to check. "They should be back right about now." She was all business, green eyes narrow and thoughtful.

Tony wanted to break something, destroy Scarlet's office or

smash something valuable. It would serve the woman right if he unleashed his furious tiger right now.

It took all of his restraint to instead grind out, "Where?!" and let Scarlet, moving infuriatingly slowly, lead him out to the front gates of the resort.

The van was pulling up just as they got there, and Tony didn't even have to watch the British couple climb out. He knew Amber wasn't there as surely as he knew that the sky was above him. Jimmy, on the other hand, was there, getting out of the driver's seat as if nothing at all in the world was amiss when everything in the world clearly was.

It was only a few steps around the ugly van, and Tony could pull Jimmy the rest of the way out of the driver's seat by the lapels.

"Where. Is. Amber?" he demanded through bared teeth.

Keeping his tiger inside was like trying to keep a hurricane in a bottle.

Jimmy, all big eyes and clearly rising panic, stammered, "She was invited to dinner with Mr. Beehag. I was just told to drive these nice folks back to the resort."

The boar couple was clinging to each other, staring at the conflict with big, alarmed eyes. The gardener had materialized from nowhere and was watching them with a dark look, and a handyman who had been working on the stonework stopped his work to observe in interest and alarm.

"I will kill you if she is even the tiniest bit hurt." Tony said the words through bared teeth, very close to Jimmy's face, aware that he was holding most of the man's weight in his clenched fists.

"I swear," Jimmy wept. "I was just told to drive these people back, that's all I know!"

Lies! Tony's tiger insisted.

Jimmy changed underneath his fist into a squirming, snarling weasel, all clashing, razor-sharp teeth as his clothing fell away in Tony's hands.

Just as fast, Tony was changing, his clothing ripping from the striped fur and Jimmy's clothing shredded before his claws. The weasel was ripping at his front legs, all teeth and claws and crazed frenzy, and Tony swiped at him with a paw and missed as it swarmed at his face, snapping teeth across his sensitive nose.

Before he could react, Scarlet was moving forward with more speed than she ought to have in human form and she had the weasel by the scruff of the neck. Then she was suddenly holding a very naked, terrified-looking Jimmy with one hand at his neck as if he was no more than a misbehaving schoolboy.

"You!" she said ferociously. "I will deal with you myself!"

She met Tony's eyes and Tony could not figure out what animal he was seeing there, beyond sheer power. "You will go faster through the jungle than the road. Follow the ridge east. The estate is on the opposite side of the island."

Without pausing, Tony was off, every muscle of his huge tiger body tensing with one purpose: to rescue his mate. Behind him, he heard Jimmy whimper in fear.

CHAPTER 19

Amber felt under-dressed before she even walked in the ornate double doors to Alistair's house. The armed guards flanking the doors made her feel even more uncertain. It seemed sort of odd that there were so many of them.

The foyer was as big as her entire cottage and decorated with things that Amber immediately recognized as valuable and couldn't deny were tasteful. It was like a museum; clearly tailored to Alistair's personal taste for the rare and unique. Antique masks lined the walls, as well as colonial-era paintings that Amber felt like she ought to recognize. The furniture was all rich, solid wood, beautifully carved and subtly stained; Amber guessed that Alistair had never even seen the inside of an Ikea store.

She paused. A stairway led off to her right, curving up to a second floor. The dining room was open to the left, a decadent-smelling meal already laid out on a table long enough to run footraces.

"I'm not sure I should..." she stumbled, gesturing to her dirty sandals and worn shorts.

"My *dear*," said Alistair, and his hand at her elbow felt a little tight. "I insist. You are my... *guest*."

Amber went, because she didn't know how to deny what she tried to tell herself was a request. Although she could sense Alistair's interest in her, she didn't want to encourage it... and she wasn't sure how to discourage it politely. He wasn't like Jimmy, leering and making her feel dirty, but there was an uneasiness in Amber's stomach that she wasn't sure he deserved. Maybe it was just because she kept comparing him to Tony, and no one could measure up.

"Alright," she said, and she let the billionaire lead her to the table and pull out her chair. He even put her napkin in her lap. Maybe it was a Costa Rican custom, she wondered, thinking back to her breakfast service.

Breakfast had been very, very long ago, and when the servant put a plate of artfully arranged lampchops and tender vegetables before her, she fell into it eagerly.

"Your arboretum is amazing," she said, as her eating politely allowed. "I have never seen such an extensive collection of rare plants."

"It is charming to have someone who is enthused about it," Alistair said with an artful laugh, clearly enjoying his own food. "You are a botanist, then?"

Amber laughed. "I studied botany in college," she explained. "But mostly I just work in a garden shop. A very *rural* garden shop, where most people are concerned with strains of corn and pest control by the barrel. The most excitement I get is building hanging baskets of flowers in the spring. When it comes to exotics, all I get are aloe and jade plants. I love to read about things that grow in this climate, but I am a rank amateur when it comes to this stuff!"

"You undersell yourself," Alistair said, with a strange smile. "I find you very knowledgeable, and a delightful conversationalist."

Amber blinked at him and mumbled some shy thanks. Had she conversed all that much?

A servant took her plate, and she was startled into looking up at him. He seemed an awfully... military looking person to be waiting on a table with a towel over his arm, with short cropped hair and a thick, muscled neck.

"Dessert?" Alistair offered. "I believe the chef has prepared a *crème brule.*"

But the meal felt odd in Amber's stomach. She felt like her cat was on her metaphorical shoulders, every strand of fur on end, shrieking warnings in her ears.

"No, thank you! I'm... uh, on a diet. We really should call Jimmy to come collect me. I've imposed on you so much already."

"Let me show you the study and the private collection before you leave. It will take Jimmy some time to get back with the van," Alistair said, so mildly and logically that Amber couldn't figure out how to protest it.

She took his offered hand, and wasn't sure it was only politeness that prompted her to try to act enthused about it.

The study was a shock that took all of her acting ability to hide.

Taxidermied animals and pelts filled the cavernous room. A tiger's skin sprawled across a portion of the floor, and Amber thought immediately of Tony. There was a thick-maned lion hide in front of the fireplace.

"My grandfather's collection," Alistair said, unsettlingly close to her ear. "Of course that was colonial times, when the hunt wasn't illegal, and many of these weren't even endangered. People would even say it was immoral, but times were very different then."

"Of course," Amber said weakly.

"Come, this is not what I really wanted you to see."

He led her through the dim room, and Amber tried not to startle at the soul-less gaze of a stuffed gazelle, or the bear caught mid-roar beside it.

Alistair unlocked a sturdy wooden door with another keypad, and led her out into the warm night air. The dining room had not had windows, so Amber was surprised to realize that it was quite late. Crickets and frogs made a now-familiar drone, and a silvery moon hung in a field of glittering stars. Far away, a seabird cried hauntingly and went still.

They walked into a garden, edged with very tall fencing that after a moment, Amber recognized as cages. She was alarmed, but not as surprised as she should have been, when two guards from the door fell in step behind her.

"Much of my collection is nocturnal," Alistair said, and Amber could hear the excited pride in his voice. This was something he very much wanted to share with her, and it filled her with dread.

The first enclosure, a landscaped habitat with artful trees and a little hill with lounging rocks, proved to hide a small, agile ocelot, who jumped down from a branch to stare at them from behind the metal mesh. Amber, looking back at it, felt an odd connection. Maybe it was because she felt like she was being trapped as surely as it was.

"My father was the one who started this collection," Alistair said, leading her further down the path. "He recognized the limitations of taking the skins of these... animals, and began trapping them instead."

"You've continued his legacy, then," Amber said, trying to keep conversation casual. The next animal was a pacing tiger, white and black stripes rippling over agitated muscle. It roared as they walked past; Alistair gave no time to pause and observe. They passed a spotted deer that Amber didn't recognize, and a glass enclosure of little, thick-furred mammals. Each enclosure was carefully crafted for its residents. Amber was reminded of the best zoos.

"I've improved upon it," Alistair said proudly. "I've found some of the rarest and most precious animals, most of them just in the last few years. We've got a Borneo Bay cat," he said, his British accent pronounced. "Have you ever seen one?"

"I haven't," Amber admitted reluctantly. She was aware that her steps were slowing, and that her surreptitious glances for an exit or escape were becoming less subtle than she could wish.

"They aren't the rarest cat," Alistair said leadingly, and Amber couldn't hide her terror any longer. She came to a stop, and turned to find that only one of the guards behind her had his gun at ready. The other had a long-handled dog-catcher.

"Oh?" she said, incapable of anything more clever.

"I've been looking for an Andean mountain cat for a very long time," he said seductively. "And I think you'll be very happy in the enclosure I've made for you."

"Those skins in the study," Amber said with a sudden sick feeling in the pit of her stomach. "Were those all shifters?"

"Of course!" Alistair said in that accent that Amber couldn't hear as anything but terrifying now. "What sport is there in normal animals?"

She was spared having to answer that by a sudden, blaring alarm, just as the cellphone in Alistair's pocket came to life. He gestured to the guards behind them, and Amber couldn't get her frozen feet to move before the dog-catcher was dropped loosely around her neck.

"Show our guest to her new quarters," Alistair said lightly, as if there weren't a gun trained at her and a noose laying on her shoulders. "My dear, I hope you will forgive my lack of hospitality in showing you myself, but I have to deal with a slight problem at the perimeter."

He disappeared down a side path, and Amber was left with the guards, who prodded her into a staggering walk towards her doom.

CHAPTER 20

Tony ran.

As a tiger, he was an efficient machine of muscle and energy, and the jungle, unexpectedly, felt like home.

The jungle floor was springy, and surprisingly free of underbrush. Above him, tangled branches hid the night sky. Even with keen cat night vision, it was dark, and the drone of insects and frogs was like an ambient soundtrack to keep his pace.

His race at first was sheer adrenaline, but settled quickly into a punishing pace that ate the ground beneath him.

It was easy to follow the ridge as Scarlet had suggested, keeping to the high areas. It was steep here, and the land fell away from him on either side.

The forest thickened and the ridge began to tip downhill again.

He was just beginning to wonder exactly how long the island was when he burst out of the jungle onto a groomed lawn that made a perimeter around a tall stone wall. To one side, a lit driveway led to gates, and he immediately smelled the guards who lurked in shadows on either side.

He turned back to the edge of the jungle, fighting the tiger self who knew that Amber was behind that gate, and that she was in trouble. But training kept him in control; it didn't make sense to charge in without reconnaissance.

It took a long careful time to pace fully around the estate and return to the driveway; the compound was the size of a small town, and fully walled. There was only the one gate, the walls had broken glass and barbed wire at the top, and Tony noticed mounted cameras at several intervals. He suspected it was only darkness and luck that had kept him from being spotted when he had bolted out of the jungle, and was grateful for the natural camouflage of his tiger shape.

Tony even climbed into a tree, which groaned at his weight, to peer over the walls. The grassy perimeter meant he couldn't get close—jumping from the tree would have been impossible—but it gave him a view of the layout beyond the wall. A house was nearest the front gate, and what looked like an orchard lay to one side. Copious solar panels on most roofs suggested the source of their power. What puzzled him was the section behind the house, which was a sprawling labyrinth of squares with half-mesh roofs. It took Tony a moment to recognize that it looked like a zoo, and then everything clicked into place.

Relief flooded him; the collector was *keeping* the shifters he was capturing, not killing them, which meant Amber was *safe.*

Anger followed close on the heels of relief, because alive or not, they were keeping his mate from him, locking her in a *cage*, and Tony realized he was growling out loud.

He gave it some thought and decided, from his vantage, that the best place to scale the walls was back by the orchard. There was a natural rise in the grass at that point, making the wall a little shorter, and if he was careful, he might be able to take out the camera on his way over. There was a building just beyond that he thought he could hit with a good jump. They couldn't be expecting him, he thought. And what were the chances that someone was actually watching the monitors at that exact moment?

His tiger demanded action, and for once, Tony was in complete agreement.

He ran across the open lawn like a streak of justice, leaping for the wall. Walls meant to keep most animals out—or in—weren't going to stop a determined tiger, but it was still a stretch, and the barbed wire at the top drew blood across the pads of Tony's paws.

Tony wasn't as lucky as he'd hoped. He missed the camera, and landed with a heavy THUMP on the roof of the building beyond. Alarms immediately began to blare.

He leaped down from the building, and ran, full out, in the direction he remembered the enclosures being. If subtlety wasn't going to work, perhaps sheer force would.

Voices shouted behind him. He spun to find three black-uniformed guards. Two of them held guns, and the third had a staff that Tony recognized as a shock stick. He didn't care about them and turned in the direction that he knew Amber was, only to feel the sting of a needle in one shoulder. They were tranquilizer guns, he realized, and he was halfway across the orchard before he felt another one hit him.

The door separating the orchard from the zoo was wide open, and for a moment, Tony thought he was going to make it through—they couldn't possibly have planned their shots for a tiger's weight—when the effects of the drug hit him and his run turned into a stagger.

To his astonishment, his tiger legs were suddenly a man's, and he was crawling, naked and drunken, across the manicured grass. He didn't even realize he was lying down until a pair of stylish shoes made their way into his field of vision.

"A shame we already have a Siberian tiger," a crisp British voice said. "We don't have any use for this one."

"Could get a good price for him from the warlock," a Spanish-accented voice suggested.

"You... have... my... mate..." Tony managed to say. It didn't have the dramatic affect he intended, coming from a mouth half-stuffed with grass, and then blackness engulfed him.

CHAPTER 21

Amber walked meekly with the guards, trying not to be too obvious about looking around. The dog-catcher was lying unexpectedly loose at her shoulders, and when she glanced at the man holding the pole, he glared back and fingered a button on the handle. The other guard, walking behind her with the gun trained on her, cleared his throat, and Amber put her head down and continued to shamble with them. She was short, so it was easy to walk slowly and look like she was using a normal pace.

The looseness of the noose around her neck got her brain spinning.

They were expecting a mountain cat—an American mountain cat. A *big* mountain cat. If she shifted, the dog-catcher would be tight around the neck of a big cat. But around her small cat shape...

As quickly as the idea occurred to her, Amber put it in motion, shifting as she pretended to stumble.

Her clothing fell away from her cat form even as she jumped—straight through the noose—and scrambled for the wall of the mesh enclosure they were walking past. She heard the crackle of the dog-catcher rather than feeling it through her thick fur, and realized belatedly that it must be electrified. She wasn't sure if she would have made this attempt if she'd known that, but it was far too late now, and her coat, meant for cold mountain winters, had protected her from the worst of it.

She climbed in a panic, the agility of her cat form driving her, and as the guard behind her fired and missed, and missed again as she switched directions up the enclosure and reached the roof.

She heard the zoo erupt into roars and animal cries of encouragement. A human voice even cried out, "Go, kitty cat!"

"Shit!" the guards said in unison.

More wild shots followed her. Needles hissed by as Amber made it up to the roof of the enclosure. She ran and leaped to the next. She was already two cages away while the guards were still peering up onto the first. Then she switched directions entirely and leaped across the path to a new row of cages.

Her night sight let her see better than she had as a human, and her height gave her a clear view. Lights all along the wall had come on, showing her that she had no real chance of getting over them—though she could probably squeeze between the barbed wire with little damage thanks to her coat, she was too small to make it to the top of the wall to try; nothing was built up close to it. She noticed the cameras, too, now swiveling back into the enclosure to try to find her, and had a glimpse of a helicopter on one of the low roofs towards the back.

"Goddamn it, do you see it?" one guard called to the other.

"Beehag said it was a mountain cat, not a goddamn *little* cat!" the other complained.

Their voices were clear to Amber's excellent hearing.

Instead of immediate escape, Amber looked for hiding spaces, and found one in a pile of construction materials towards the end of the zoo. While the cameras were still re-positioning to try to follow her, she dashed out of sight down the side of one of the enclosures and flattened herself to fit in a tiny space on top of a pile of rocks, under dimension lumber and roof tiles. From here, she could see a dozen more hiding places that she'd be able to make it to in short order, and she had a good vantage for seeing oncoming intruders.

She could actually see that the entire zoo was actually much more suited for containing big animals. She'd be able to get out, she felt, with her first taste of confidence as the adrenaline began to release its hold on her. She just had to lie low, and she'd be able to sneak out of the front gates when the timing was right.

"Call it in!" one of the guards was saying.

"Fuck no, you call it in," the other protested.

Eventually, they worked out who was making the call, and the little two-way radio crackled in return as they explained their mistake.

"Escaped?" Even over the poor quality radio from a distance, Amber recognized Alistair's voice, and it made the hackles on her neck rise.

The guards fell over each other to justify their actions, and Amber gave a little cat smile to hear them describe her as basically supernatural.

There was a moment of silence in response, and then Alistair's crisp accent. "She won't get far. We've got her *mate* here."

Mate?

Amber knew without a doubt that they meant Tony, and it was everything she could do not to bolt from her hiding hole right then to find and defend him. But what did they mean by 'mate?' She could all but hear the emphasis that Alistair was putting on it.

The waiter at the resort had used the same word.

Whatever they meant by it, she knew that Alistair was right—knowing that they had Tony—that they might *hurt* Tony to get her, meant that Alistair had Amber as surely as if that noose *had* been tight around her neck.

CHAPTER 22

Tony came to through a haze of confusion and misery. Sunlight was just beginning to peer over the high walls, and he realized he was lying in a thin pile of straw over a concrete slab with fine chicken wire over it, and it was dreadfully uncomfortable in his human form.

There were thick bars all around him, and he could see more bars overhead. A small lean-to in one corner provided some protection in case of rain. There was a shallow tub of water.

He was aware of desperate thirst, and his tongue felt oddly thick. His hands and feet had fading scratches, and he remembered the barbed wire that had scraped them on his way over the wall.

Tony...

The voice in his head was not, he felt, exactly directed at him. It was an internal lament, a cry of pain and longing and confusion.

"Amber!" He said it out loud as well as through animal speech, reaching out for her with his mind.

Her surprise and relief did not exactly have words, but felt like a tackle hug. *How are we doing this?* she asked.

Some shifters just can, Tony explained. *Where are you? Are you alright? Are you... free?*

He got an impression of crouching in a small dark place with her answer. *I'm nearby, just to the east,* she said. *I can see you, but I don't want to show myself. They haven't caught me yet.*

Get out of here, Tony told her fiercely.

I'm not leaving you, Amber insisted.

They'll use me to try to capture you, Tony told her flatly. *Better that you aren't here at all. You have to get out.*

I'm not leaving you, Amber repeated stubbornly.

Use logic! You know you can't fight them all. You can get help, at the resort.

She didn't answer for a moment, then asked, *What's a mate?*

Tony sat up gingerly. The drugs had left his limbs feeling odd and as if all the joints were too big. *You're my mate,* he told her gently, mindful of how frightened she had gotten when he called her beautiful. *You're the one other person who completes me, the one true match for my soul and body.* He couldn't help but remember her body, all curves and velvet skin against him.

Amber was quiet in his mind, contemplating. *And you know your mate at once when you meet?*

Tony nodded. *With every inch of your spirit.* At least, he had. Had she?

Her laughter was a rich caress of his mind. *I thought I was going a little crazy when we met,* she confessed.

I had never seen anything in the world as gorgeous as you, Tony told her, deeply relieved. *And I will never forgive myself if you get captured because of me.*

You got captured because of me, Amber pointed out.

Tony had no answer for that, but wordlessly pleaded that she see reason and leave while she could.

Reluctantly, she finally answered. *I'll go,* she agreed. *But only to get help. I'm coming back for you.*

Tony had a sense of her, ghosting out of her hiding place and darting from shadow to shadow, her attention entirely on staying quiet and out of sight.

He wanted to implore her to be careful, but didn't want to distract her from her stealth. Instead, he stood, cursing his wobbly legs, and shifted into a tiger to explore the cage with the extra senses that came with it. The water smelled good, so he indulged in a deep, refreshing drink.

He smelled Beehag before he saw him: Indian spices, fine wool, and just a touch of whiskey.

"Ah," the odious man said, stopping before Tony's cage. "I like it when my guests stay in animal form. Some of them have to be... convinced to do so."

Mostly to spite him, Tony shifted back into a human, and stood up to scowl through the bars, arms crossed. He was actually glad for the week at Shifting Sands; being nude felt comfortable and powerful, when a week prior to that, it might have felt like a weakness.

Beehag frowned, but didn't look surprised. "Your cooperation isn't necessary, anyway," he said with an arrogant shrug. "You aren't really my goal here." His eyes glinted as his face slid into a smug smile. "She's a pretty little thing, isn't she? And surprisingly clever."

Tony wanted to reach through the bars and take the man by the throat, but knew it would be futile. There were two men with guns flanking the billionaire, and Tony suspected that they weren't *both* loaded with tranquilizer darts by the way the second guard was holding his.

Beehag had a black plastic box in his hand, and he lifted it. "She won't get far," he promised. "She wouldn't leave her mate. Not when he was in such agony."

Tony gritted his teeth, waiting for one of them to take a shot. But Beehag simply pressed a button on his box, and electricity jolted through him.

It was impossible to stand still, and there was nowhere to escape—the energy was coursing through the floor and the bars and not even the straw was enough to keep it from burning up his feet. The shock was not strong enough to kill him, but it was bitterly, burningly painful, and Tony couldn't keep back the yell of agony or keep his muscles from convulsing. It stopped just when he felt like he couldn't take another moment, and he stared through the bars at Beehag in impotent fury, panting and clenching his fists.

The smell of singed straw filled the cage.

"Do you know what a shifter's weakness is?" Beehag asked in his silky voice. When Tony didn't reply, he went on anyway. "A shifter can't help but shift if they are in enough pain..." He lifted the box again, and although Tony was braced for it this time, he was still not ready for the piercing pain.

True to Beehag's observation, Tony shifted without meaning to. He even tried to fight it, briefly, and was disappointed to find that the pain was no less in cat form. His tiger, however, was more capable of dealing with the pain, and his human self could only whimper at the torment while his tiger roared and flung himself uselessly at the cage.

Beehag stopped the electricity at last, and Tony paced the cage in tiger form, still staggered from the experience. He was not sure he would have been able to shift back if he had wanted to, he was so shaken by the torture.

"That ought to bring her," Beehag said, deeply satisfied. Somewhere down the pens, a single wolf raised its voice in a howl of sympathy. The rest of the zoo was eerily quiet.

CHAPTER 23

Amber darted from shadow to shadow, skittering through open drainage channels, under equipment, and across roofs, where she dared.

There was too much open space between the gates and house; she wasn't sure how to get from one to the other, or how to get through the gates once she got there. She tried to keep a map in her head, adding more to it as she noted landscapes and oddities, like the helicopter on a warehouse roof towards the back.

She nearly fell off the rain gutter when the pain began.

"Tony!" she cried, but he was too lost in agony to hear her or answer.

Beehag.

If he had been in her reach, she would have gleefully clawed his eyes out at that moment.

She nearly turned back, but she knew that the British asshole was just waiting for her. She wasn't sure what she was going to do, but it didn't involve falling into his trap like a stupid fool. It might have broken her heart to realize he was hurting Tony, but it didn't take more than a moment of rational thought to realize that he was doing it deliberately to draw her back.

It only steeled her purpose. She was going to return to the resort. She would ransack Tony's cottage—he must have secret government super-spy contacts she could reach. They probably had helicopters, or maybe squadrons of dragons. She'd tell them everything, and make them promise to send help, then come back and turn herself in to make them stop hurting him. She'd promise cooperation, if they let him be, and generally delay everything long enough for rescue to come.

When Tony's agony let up, she didn't try to contact him. She knew her will would waiver if she let herself touch his mind again.

Instead, she crept along to the front of the house, keeping to the valleys of the roof and watching for the cameras. She could hear a crash and commotion, and suspected that they were mobilizing—did they guess that she would try to escape? She expected them to be ready for her near Tony's cage; she had hoped that they would be distracted from the gates for that time.

To her surprise, the gates were open, and the beat-up van from Shifting Sands was wedged between them. Four guards with weapons—Amber had no idea if they were real ones or only tranquilizers, but wasn't willing to risk finding out the hard way—were surrounding it. They clearly looked flustered.

Jimmy was loudly protesting from the driver's seat that they were scheduled, that Mr Beehag had arranged a tour. "Just radio Mr. Beehag! I swear, he's expecting us!"

Amber's ears flattened against her head in confusion. The van was completely full of resort guests. As she watched, Magnolia made her ponderous way out of the side door, calling over one of the guards to take her imperious hand as the van tipped under her weight.

"Here, darling, stop waving that around and come help a lady down!" she commanded, and the guard actually did so, putting his hand out reluctantly to steady her.

The other resort guests weren't guests at all. Amber recognized a flash of Scarlet's distinctive hair in the passenger seat, and the person out after Magnolia was the surly gardener, who didn't so much as pretend to be friendly before punching the guard who had his hand captured in Magnolia's.

"So uncivilized," Magnolia said with a sniff as they began to brawl in earnest, but she didn't let go of the guard, demonstrating unexpected strength as he twisted and tried to break free. The gardener made short work of him, given his handicap, and Magnolia gently lowered the unconscious man to the ground after only a short flurry of blows.

Chef, out next, immediately asked if she was alright, not even giving the remaining three guards a glance.

"He didn't hurt you, did he?"

"I'm fine, sugar," Magnolia insisted, straightening her hat. "You're a dear to ask!"

Scarlet dismounted from the passenger seat like a queen, with her staff fanning out behind her as they scrambled out of the van like some kind of shifter clown car.

The remaining three guards fidgeted in place, swinging their guns from one target to another nervously. The youngest of them finally picked up their radio. "Um, sir? We've got trouble at the gate. Guests. Er... the resort lady. And... some staff, I guess. A guard is down."

"Tell Mr. Beehag that Scarlet Stanson is here to discuss some of the terms of our contract," Scarlet suggested sweetly, folding her arms and giving the guard a steely stare.

Several other guards ran up then, taking positions with partial cover and training their weapons on the motley crew. The first three took more confident stances and the young man with the radio looked back at Scarlet defiantly.

Then the last person disembarked from the van wearing a brilliant yellow lifeguard shirt, and shifted immediately into a dragon four times the size of the van. To a man, the guards all stepped back and re-positioned their hands on their guns.

The youngest guard picked up his radio again and said with a wavering voice. "Miss Scarlet is here... uh... to talk about a contract. They brought a *dragon*, sir..."

CHAPTER 24

Alistair Beehag stood in front of Tony's cage, looking almost bored. "You know," he said, condescendingly, "It isn't really worth all this fuss. I give my guests everything they could possibly need. I assure you that Miss Allen would be quite safe here. She would even stop trying to escape, eventually; they all do."

Tony shifted back into human form, because he could again, and because as a tiger it was getting difficult to keep himself from throwing himself at the cage walls in sheer fury.

He cursed at Beehag using every expletive that Rick had ever taught him.

It wasn't as satisfying as he had hoped and Beehag only laughed.

He went on conversationally, "Some of these shifters have been here for decades," he explained. "My father collected them when he was a young man, and passed his collection to me. Did you know that shifters live as long as humans even in their animal forms exclusively? It would be a wonder to the scientific community if they got their hands on some of my guests. Amber is quite young—I imagine she will live out a very long life here."

Tony might have flung himself at the cage even in human form if the bastard had kept going on, but fortunately one of the guards' radios crackled to life.

"Um, sir? We've got trouble at the gate. Guests. Er... the resort lady. And... some staff, I guess. A guard is down."

Beehag sighed, as if it was just a little inconvenience, but there was a glint to his eyes that Tony didn't like.

With an imperious gesture, Beehag sent half of the guards scurrying to the front of the estate like ants.

The remaining guards barked orders into phones, and didn't seem the slightest bit fazed when a panicked message came over the radio: "Miss Scarlet is here... uh... to talk about a contract. She brought a *dragon*, sir..."

Far from being alarmed, Beehag actually clapped his hands. "Oh, this is a good day," he said gleefully. "I have been unsuccessful in tempting that one away from the resort since it first arrived, but I've had a cage prepared for it all this time. And I've made all the precautions for capturing it." A gesture to the remaining guards sent them scurrying.

"I hope you will forgive me for bringing our conversation to such an abrupt end," Beehag said dismissively. "I am not yet sure if I will have further need of you, but I will keep you alive until I have the mountain cat safely in hand. Until then!"

Tony did fling himself at the cage then, roaring in anger and shifting as he leaped.

Beehag only laughed as he walked away, and flipped the switch on his control one last time to deliver blistering jolts of pain into the snarling tiger.

CHAPTER 25

Amber writhed in counterpoint to Tony, snapping at the air as she kept herself from bolting by instinct back to the terrible zoo.

When it stopped, she lay panting for a long moment, anger clouding her vision as much as the echo of Tony's pain.

More guards were spilling out of the house, taking cover behind a waist-high wall that had appeared merely decorative, but now seemed very cleverly defensible. Several had moved out along the walls, looking poised to close in on the gate if the interlopers moved out onto thc lawn.

Scarlet and her staff hung back, not entirely willing to leave the partial cover that the van provided or abandon their escape route. The staff, most of them unarmed, looked nervous, but Scarlet appeared unruffled, in her tidy business skirt and heels. The dragon roared, flaming into the air and snapping its big wings, but Amber thought it didn't look as intimidating once the shock of it had passed.

These new guards did not appear to be of the same easily-cowed stripe as the first ones, and Amber could hear them talking among themselves as weapons were passed out.

"These will turn 'em human, even the dragon," one assured another. "Aim for the bits between the big scales. Beehag wants them all tranqed because he's not sure what they are, especially the red-haired bitch."

Amber had a sinking feeling in her heart; the resort staff, plucky as they appeared, was no match for the uniformed, armored task force that faced them. There was little she could do, even behind the lines of the enemy. She was astonished by how many guards had boiled out of the estate—there must be two or three dozen men. Knowing that the guns they held were tranquilizers didn't make it any easier to take them out.

It was too bad she couldn't free the inhabitants of the zoo to fight with them.

As soon as the idea occurred to Amber, she was in motion, scrambling quietly back over the roof to the back of the house. If everyone was here, distracted by Scarlet's invasion, then there couldn't be more than a token guard back at the security room—where the locks to the cages must all be controlled.

She leaped easily down to the ground using a plumeria tree by the back door. To her frustration, it was locked. In human form, uncomfortably naked, she paced, trying to come up with some new plan, any shred of an idea.

She flitted back into cat form at the sound of officious footsteps and hid in the shadow of a big planter by the door.

Beehag.

He was smiling confidently and tapping a black box in his hands. With a lazy swipe, he used his keycard to open the door with a whir and a click.

Why wouldn't he be confident, Amber thought despairingly. He knew he had all the advantages.

Still, she wasn't going to give up yet. She held her breath, and darted in at his heels, as quiet as a whisper, pretending she was nothing more than a shadow behind him. She followed him down the corridor until they came to a closed door. Alistair swiped his card, and then put his thumb on a small screen by the security panel. The door whirred and opened with a little pop.

Amber followed him, barely getting her tail swished in behind her before the door closed with a hiss and a click. She knew she couldn't have made it in undetected if Beehag hadn't been so distracted.

One wall was a panel of screens, showing all the parts of the compound. Animals paced in dozens of cages, looking clearly agitated; they must know that something momentous was happening. Amber's eyes went immediately to search for Tony, and found several cages of tigers, one pure white and black, and two the more common orange and white and black. More screens showed the front lawn, and it was to these screens that Alistair immediately went.

Behind him, Amber's attention swung to the opposite wall, where a rack of weapons hung. She couldn't tell if they were real guns or tranquilizers, but it didn't matter to her now.

Quietly as she could, she shifted to human, standing up slowly and reaching for one of the rifles.

"Fools!" Beehag said mockingly, making her freeze in place.

But he was only talking to the guard who sat there, and the figures on the screen. A quick glance showed that Scarlet had moved away from the van and was speaking to guards, her hands up in a position of surrender. There was no sound from the screen, but Amber thought that her posture had more defiance than yield to it. She released the safety on the gun before taking it down, and a fortunate shift of a chair covered the sound.

As she suspected, actually releasing the gun was noisier, and both the guard and Alistair turned in alarm to face her as she swung it down, turned and aimed at them.

Their moment of shock gave her a chance to release a dart directly into the guard's neck, and she was gratified to see him crumple almost at once.

Alistair had an odd look of alarm and amusement, and Amber half-wished she had picked a gun with real bullets so she could wipe that smug expression off his face forever.

He put his hands up slowly. "What a clever little kitty you are," he said with an odd twist of his lips. "How did you get the resort staff mobilized? I was hoping to milk them as a source for my collection for much longer, but I knew they'd become a problem eventually. Your friend Tony just hastened that end, nosing around like he was. What I couldn't have hoped for was a chance to capture them all—I had thought they would all have to go down in the terribly *unfortunate* fire that I've already arranged."

Finger twitching on the trigger, Amber paused. "Fire?" she said.

As slowly as they'd gone up, Alistair's hands went down. "The resort is rigged," he said confidently. "Everything is in place to go up at sunset tonight. It's a shame no one will survive. But you know how unpredictable natural gas fuel can be, and construction regulations in a country like this can be a little *lax*. Besides, they're only shifters."

"You're a monster," Amber spat, thinking of all the innocent resort guests who would be killed in the tragedy.

"You're the ones who turn into *animals*," Alistair said in disgust, raking her naked body with his glance. "You have to keep me alive," he insisted. "If you want any chance of disarming..."

Amber pulled the trigger, racked the slide and fired again, sending a second dart straight into his chest beside the first.

Alistair's face twisted in anger and then went slack as he collapsed over the chair and fell to the ground as it rolled away. Amber resisted the urge to shift just so she could claw him in the face and dropped the gun to pounce at the control panel.

CHAPTER 26

Tony's roars subsided to growls as the pain from the shock faded. His anger was not the slightest bit banked, and he gnashed his teeth.

The inhabitants of other cages were agitated, many of them up and pacing at the front of their enclosures. None of them shifted into human, or tried to communicate.

He wondered how long Alistair had spent with his box of pain, training them to stay to animal shape, and how far gone they were, trapped within their non-human forms.

He longed to reach for Amber with his mind, but feared drawing her back in to Alistair's trap. With luck, she was far, far away by now, not even aware of the commotion that had drawn Beehag away from his zoo.

When the lock at his cage did an unexpected whir-click, Tony thought he must be imagining it. He heard other clicks, all up and down the row of cages.

Then a mind brushed his own. *Tony? I think I unlocked the cages?*

You beautiful, sexy genius, he answered, shifting so he could reach through and unlatch the door. *But didn't I tell you to get out of here?*

My social worker always told me I was unreasonably defiant when I was a kid, Amber said smugly. *Guess I never grew out of it.*

Don't ever, Tony said with a mental caress. *I love you just the way you are.* He gratefully left the cage and went to the one next door.

A maned red wolf stared back at him.

"You're free," Tony said, voice pitched to carry. "You're all free!" He unlatched the wolf's door, and it circled once before tentatively stepping out onto the pavement, still in wolf form.

Down the path, a few doors unlatched, and several naked people stepped tentatively out, blinking and flexing fingers curiously. More of the animals whined and refused to shift, waiting for someone to come open their cages; Tony had to wonder if they had forgotten how to be human, or if they were still just afraid. Several of them hid in the backs of their cages and didn't come out even when the doors were opened for them. A gazelle simply fled, hooves clattering on the pavement as it bolted in a zig-zag path towards the back wall.

The red wolf changed at last, into a crouched man with blazing red hair. He stood up unsteadily, then walked with more confidence to Tony. "You have a way to get us out of here?" he growled, as if his vocal chords hadn't been used in years.

On cue, Amber appeared, rushing from the house, burdened with an armload of guns. "They're tranquilizers," she panted. "And I heard one of the goons say they turned shifters human, too. We have to go help Scarlet and her staff at the front gate if we want to get out of here."

The red wolf shifter took one, checking the chamber expertly, and several other human figures ghosted forward to take their own. A white tiger, staying in animal form, shook his head and snarled, lifting one paw and unsheathing his claws suggestively. An ocelot and a red panda circled Amber curiously, but didn't shift. The other people and animals hung back, listening.

Tony took Amber's last gun, and swept her into a bone-crunching hug. "You were supposed to get out," he repeated.

"I saw an opportunity to do more good here," Amber said with the breath she had left from his crushing embrace. It was terrifically distracting having her up against him with both of them naked, but there were more important things happening.

Because just then, shots rang out from the front of the house.

The red-haired wolf shifter pointed to the east of the house, pointed at Tony, and pointed west. Without a word, he selected a handful of the fittest humans and the white tiger, then led them around the corner of the house at an easy lope.

Tony gripped the rifle in one hand and Amber's hand in the other and they broke into a run, a ragged sea of animals and people surging with them. It was a motley crew at best, broken-spirited animals and staggering humans—almost all of them naked. Counting the red wolf's crew, there were still only eight guns, between them all, and although some of the animals were predators, many of them were not. The only thing they had on their side was the element of surprise, and Tony prayed it would be enough.

"Oh, Tony, there's more," Amber said breathlessly, as they ran. "Beehag has rigged the resort to explode! At sunset! All the poor guests!"

Tony looked at the sky—midafternoon, and it was a several hour drive from the estate to the resort. "We'd never make it in time to disarm an explosive!"

"I saw a helicopter on the roof of one of the buildings in back," Amber panted. "Can you fly one?"

Tony had to laugh, because the whole situation was beyond crazy. "Of course I can," he said with mock arrogance. "I'm a super spy, right?"

CHAPTER 27

The scene that greeted them was even more chaotic than the one Amber had left. The dragon lifeguard had returned to human form and lay in a twitching heap in a patch of burnt lawn, riddled with feathered needles.

A giant polar bear was roaring over the waist-high wall. Its motions were a little drunken, and several darts hung in its brilliant fur, but guards were still scattering before its enormous paws. Scarlet was still in human form, crouched behind most of a wooden plank thick with needles as more of them hissed into her make-shift shield. Half a dozen unconscious humans lay naked across the lawn.

It was into this bedlam that Tony charged, firing quickly at the most competent-looking guards. The sea of animals and humans that were running with him spilled out into the guards, and though their enemies' shots were true, sheer numbers sent the ragged team forward. The polar bear made it over the little wall, but collapsed onto the guards with a whine and lay still, pinning several of them as it turned into Magnolia.

Amber shifted into her cat form, figuring she would be harder to hit if she were smaller, and felt a dart ruffle her fur as she hit the ground running.

She leaped onto the nearest guard, scratching at his face and hissing.

He staggered back and shot wildly into the air before falling backwards with a dart in his shoulder.

Tony fired the last dart from his gun and Amber caught a glimpse of him shifting into tiger form before she was dodging the swung muzzle of a gun from a guard who was out of darts. She hissed, and as she crouched to leap on him, he staggered backwards with a needle in his throat.

The red wolf shifter's team had flanked the guards from the other side of the house, and the red-haired man was taking down everyone in uniform with grim, sharp-shooting precision, taking a gun from one of the others in his team when he ran out of darts.

In a matter of moments, the battlefield had stilled to growls and hisses. A grizzly bear, shaking a dart from the ruff of its neck, staggered to where the polar bear had collapsed, and changed into Chef, gingerly pulling Magnolia's head into his lap as he sank wearily down beside her.

Scarlet put down her shield and stood up, as gracefully and self-possessed as if she weren't surrounded by the knocked-out bodies of most of her staff.

The animals from the zoo milled about uncertainly, and everyone who was ambulatory gradually found themselves in a loose semicircle around the resort owner. Amber put her hand in Tony's and squeezed wearily. Most of them shifted to human, but not all. The maned red wolf drew himself forward as their spokesman. "We're obliged for your assistance," he said gruffly.

At that moment, the gazelle charged from behind the house, skittered to the side when it encountered the mass of people and animals, and then fled wildly through the gate, leaping over anything in its path and finally charging over the van with a clatter of panicked hooves.

An elderly woman buried her face in her hand and wept. "I

don't know what I'll do now," she sobbed. "It's been twenty years since I saw my family."

"Some of these people have been here decades," Tony said, remembering. "Some of them may not remember how to be human."

"You have a home at the resort," Scarlet said, unexpectedly. "We can find beds and food for everyone, and the resort is as welcoming to shifters in animal form as in human." She lifted her voice to include them all. "Everyone who needs a place may stay there, until you can contact family, or as long as you need."

Amber clenched Tony's hand in her own, and as one, they said, "The resort!"

Scarlet's eyes drilled into them. "What *about* the resort?"

"Beehag," Amber said, then she explained as quickly as she could. "He says he rigged the resort to explode tonight at sundown. Tried to use it as leverage so I wouldn't shoot him."

"I hope that you did anyway?" Scarlet's voice was dry and hard.

"Twice," Amber said with remembered satisfaction, and she was rewarded by a grim nod from Scarlet.

"That's my mate," Tony said proudly.

"He said something about the natural gas," Amber remembered.

"*Jimmy*," Scarlet spat. "I caught him fooling with the hot water heaters earlier this week. He had some excuse about the settings being too high." She looked around suddenly. "Where *did* Jimmy go?"

A swift search revealed no sign of Jimmy among the unconscious on the lawn.

Tony hissed, "Beehag."

The three of them dashed for the security room at the back of the house.

The red wolf shifter remained behind to coordinate the dazed animals and secure the guards.

No one noticed the ocelot who followed them.

CHAPTER 28

Beehag was gone.

Tony roared, and curled his hands in fists by his side, barely keeping himself from smashing out at the computers.

Scarlet crouched at the floor, and picked up something small. A hypodermic needle, it appeared. "A stimulant, as an anecdote to the tranquilizer?" she theorized.

"The helicopter," Amber said urgently, tugging at Tony's arm as he muttered every curse word he knew.

Scarlet looked up sharply. "There's a helicopter?"

"We could get back and you could disarm the resort," Amber said, full of hope.

Tony both loved the way her trust in him made him feel, and shuddered to think he might not be able to do as much as she thought he could.

"You can fly a helicopter?" There was that dubious tone in Scarlet's voice again—as if she doubted he could drive a car, or possibly even operate a bicycle.

"Yes," he said defensively. As long as it was one he'd flown before, so he didn't have the humiliation of having to check the manual for the location of the fuel pump controls.

Amber immediately led them out of the room and towards the back of the compound, scampering as gracefully in human form as she did as a cat. Scarlet somehow managed to walk briskly enough to keep up without sacrificing her dignity and breaking into a run. Tony loped along beside her, and they all scrambled up the rickety steps outside the warehouse to the rooftop landing pad.

It was a relief to find that it was that it was a helicopter Tony had flown before, a common Bell 206, all sleek and glossy black.

It was less of a relief that the blades were already spooling up.

Jimmy was sitting on the far side, controls in hand, and Beehag was buckled in beside him, looking murderous and groggy. In his hand, pointed at them from the open cockpit, was a pistol. Tony strongly doubted that it was a tranquilizer.

If it had really been a spy movie, the words that Beehag was saying would have been something dramatic and threatening, but they were whipped away by the sound of the propellers coming to speed.

"We can't let him get away!" Amber shouted near his ear.

Tony cast about for something to stop him with, discarding the idea of throwing something into the propellers as too risky just as he realized that Beehag wasn't aiming at him, but at Amber, and that Amber was already sprinting for the helicopter as if she were going to wrestle him down with her sheer force of will.

Tony couldn't let her do that; no part of him was ready to lose Amber so soon after finding her again, and he went after her in a springing tackle, desperate to get her out of Beehag's sights. He caught her in two strides, wrapping his arms around her and rolling as he heard a heart-pounding pistol shot over the thump of the helicopter blades.

For a terrible moment that lasted far too long, he was sure he had moved too late, that she had been shot in his arms and the despair that washed over him was soul-deep and searing. Then she caught her breath, and squawked in protest. He remained atop her, knowing that Beehag would shoot again, and was surprised by a streak of motion.

Scarlet, he thought at first, but a second glance showed that

Scarlet was at its tail, a steel handrail she had wrenched from the stairs in her hands as she dashed across the rooftop.

The first shape was the ocelot from the zoo, already swarming into the cockpit and launching itself, snarling, at Beehag's face. Wild shots drew Tony protectively down over Amber, who was sensibly curled beneath him this time.

When he looked up again, Scarlet was pulling an unconscious Beehag out of his straps. Jimmy, face bleeding, was weeping and holding his hands up in surrender. Shots had spider-webbed the windshield of the helicopter, but Scarlet appeared untouched. The ocelot was staggering out of the cockpit, blood dark on one spotted flank. It walked several steps and then sat to begin grooming itself stiffly.

Tony rose, shaking his head, as Scarlet gestured at Jimmy to get out of the cockpit.

"I'll need him," he shouted at Scarlet. "He knows where the detonators are, and being with me at the resort with me, he'll have plenty of motivation to make sure they all get disarmed." The pistol was lying on the floor of the helicopter and he checked it. "One shot left," he said. Jimmy winced and cowered.

"I'll take that," Amber said over the thump of the rotors, at his elbow. "You'll have to fly us and I can handle a gun."

"You have to stay here, where it's safer," Tony said at once.

"You saw how well that worked last time," Amber said with a cheeky smile.

Tony couldn't help himself, but had to lean down and kiss her before striding around for the pilot's seat while she scrambled into the back seat with a not-so-accidental clip to the side of Jimmy's head.

Scarlet had gathered up the panting ocelot, and ducked back to a safe distance as Tony took the helicopter up, quickly getting used to the controls and handling. A quick glance showed that Amber had the gun to Jimmy's head, looking a little blood-thirsty in her satisfaction.

Tony had to grin as they went aloft. She was in every way his perfect mate.

CHAPTER 29

The island below them was an emerald jewel in an azure ocean, edged in black rock and golden-white crescents of sand. If it hadn't been for the spider-cracked windshield and the weight of the pistol in her hand, Amber might have believed that she was on the kind of tourist heli-tour she had imagined taking when she had first envisioned her tropical trip; they even got a gorgeous eyeful of a tall waterfall that cascaded into the ocean below.

She just hadn't imagined taking the tour nude, and the helicopter straps were not particularly comfortable without the additional padding of clothing.

Tony certainly looked comfortable enough, his muscles gleaming in the sunlight as he handled the controls with movie-style ease. Amber grinned. As much as he had protested being a super spy, he certainly played the role well.

Even the resort looked idyllic and perfect as they circled it. It was hard to remember that they were still in danger, everything seemed so peaceful. There were a few guests sunbathing in the late afternoon sun by the pool and on the beach, and if anyone had noticed that the staff was conspicuously missing, it hadn't raised any alarm. A few people glanced up at the helicopter, but more seemed not to notice it.

Tony came to a gentle landing at the front entrance. Amber noticed that he did not turn off the engine as he poked Jimmy out of the cockpit and followed him, taking the gun from Amber. If they failed to disarm the bombs, the two of them could escape, but Amber couldn't help but think of the guests—there weren't more than a few dozen of them, but they couldn't possibly all fit in the helicopter.

"Where are they?" Tony grilled Jimmy as they scurried, bent over, away from the noisy machine.

Jimmy, limp with defeat and clearly aware of the gun that Tony was holding, pointed. "They're at five of the tanks. They aren't large enough to destroy the entire resort, but the resulting fire probably would have done the job."

He showed them to the first, and Amber cheerfully took the gun back and stayed outside the mechanical room while Tony cautiously inspected the first device near Scarlet's office, comparing what he knew to Jimmy's cowed explanation.

Amber was not all surprised that Tony was able to disarm the thing; she was beginning to think there was nothing he could not do.

"It's a very straightforward model," Tony said with a shrug, when she commented to that effect. "Bombs are not usually as complicated—or as dangerous—as they make them out to be in the movies."

Jimmy made a noise of disgust, quickly muffled when he caught Tony's dirty sideways look. And despite what he said about the danger, Amber noticed that Tony moved very carefully with the components he removed, and was not eager to have Amber close while he did his work.

The next three were just the same, Tony having Amber stay back with Jimmy discreetly at gunpoint while he went in to do whatever arcane things with wires and explosives that he was doing. The sun was just beginning to sink towards the horizon, and Amber had to wonder how close to sunset the timers had actually been set; sunset itself was shockingly short this far into the tropics.

At the pool, they nodded to other guests who were packing up in preparation of a dinner that wasn't going to be ready. They were careful to keep the gun hidden, and Jimmy was behaving very meekly. Their odd company, and Jimmy's roughed-up face, got a few curious looks, but no one moved to stop them.

"It's not like *I* was hurting anyone," Jimmy whined, as Tony ducked into the last mechanical room, leaving Amber with a quick kiss and transferring the pistol to her.

"You *knew* what Beehag was doing," Amber reminded him. "And you were bringing him shifters that you knew he would be interested in."

"I didn't have a choice," Jimmy protested. "I had debts with the mob, and Beehag made me work for him to cover them..." He must have realized that Amber lacked any sympathy for his so-called plight, and subsided to sulky silence.

"That's the last of them," Tony said with relief, coming out of the mechanical room with the device in his hands. "If they make a movie out of this someday, I hope they use really jazzy music and up the countdown to something exciting, because this lacked drama."

Amber's attention was on Tony, not on Jimmy, nor the pistol she was holding, and she was caught utterly by surprise when the weasel shifter sprang at her, wrenched the gun from her hand, and turned it on her.

CHAPTER 30

Tony didn't want to admit to Amber exactly how dangerous what they were doing was. He downplayed the risk, but was keenly aware that the mechanical room door would not keep his mate from injury if he failed to perform his job. Fortunately, he wasn't lying about the simplicity of the task; these were very basic bombs, with a chunk of explosive, embedded detonators, and a timer. There were no deadman switches or boobytraps, and the wires could simply be clipped so the detonators could be safely removed.

Elementary.

He just had to think fixedly about the fact that he couldn't fumble the explosive, or cause too much of a static shock, and he grounded himself conscientiously, both mentally and electrically.

The last one was closer to the end of the countdown than he wanted to admit, and he breathed a sigh of relief as the wires clipped and he carefully wiggled the detonators out of the explosive material.

"That's the last of them," he said as casually as he could, coming out of the mechanical room. They were in a little alcove away from the pool, but he could hear people chatting distantly out there, as if he didn't have enough C4 in his hands to send parts of the wall and chunks of tile raining down on them. "If they make a movie out of this someday, I hope they use really jazzy music and up the countdown to something exciting, because this lacked drama."

He was just wondering if he was acting too casual, remembering Amber mocking his acting ability when they first met, when Jimmy turned on Amber and pulled the gun from her hand, using Tony as distraction.

Tony had witnessed many acts of desperate stupidity over his years as an agent, but none ranked with watching Jimmy take the pistol from Amber and try to take her hostage.

He was moving before Jimmy had even positioned the gun to her head. It took all the common sense left in him not to fling the only thing he had on hand at the scene, but considering that it would have been a chunk of C4, Tony was glad that he retained enough control to instead place it gently on the ground before he sprang for Jimmy and smashed him across the face with a fist, grabbing the gun and wrenching it away.

Jimmy crumbled before his onslaught, and Amber spun away from the action sensibly.

"How did you know I wouldn't shoot her?" Jimmy whined, putting up hands in surrender.

"There weren't any shots left in the gun," Tony told him. "I lied and banked on the fact that you wouldn't have been smart enough to count them when they were fired."

Jimmy cursed, colorfully, and Tony clipped him across the temple with the butt of the gun, knocking him out with a blow that he actually restrained.

Amber swallowed. "I guess you're a better actor than I gave you credit for," she said with a hiccup. "I believed you."

"That was what sold the deception," Tony assured her. He hadn't liked leaving her with such false protection, but he knew that as long as both of them had believed it, it would work.

Amber nudged Jimmy with a toe, drawing in a breath. The unconscious man didn't move, but Tony wasn't going to take a chance. He found a roll of duct tape on a shelf in the mechanical room, and bound his arms and ankles with more roughness than was strictly needed.

Amber helped tear off pieces of the tape, then stood back when they were finished. "You really are my white knight," she said, lifting her face to smile shakily at Tony.

Tony couldn't speak, too overwhelmed by the emotion rising in the wake of adrenaline and fear. He was suddenly, keenly aware that they were both still naked. What had become almost pedestrian was sharply important again, and he could not resist the silky velvet of her skin.

His first gentle touch raised goosebumps on her arm. His second made the breath catch in her throat, and he could see the fragile pulse at her throat quicken.

"The mechanical room has a lock," he suggested, voice husky with need. He wasn't sure how he was going to get politely back across the pool deck with the hard-on that was rising.

Amber didn't answer, only followed him into the dim room and scratched his arms lightly with her nails. Her eyes told him that she was feeling as much need and desire as he was, and he was not surprised to find that she was wet and pliable when he sent questing fingers to her folds.

"Yes," she breathed as he stroked her.

He cast about the room for a comfortable place to take her, but she was gripping him with more urgency now, and drawing him down to the floor, too consumed with her rising lust to care for comfort.

He willingly followed.

CHAPTER 31

Amber felt like she was on a roller coaster. She had spent the day afraid for her life, for Tony's life, and for their freedom. She had never realized how important another person could be to her, and now that the danger was past, she wanted nothing more than to be close to Tony, to feel his skin against hers, to feel him inside her, to have his big shoulders under her hands.

When he touched her, it felt like her nerves were on fire. Rational thought was gone, and when he stroked her lower lips, she thought she might explode.

But it wasn't enough, she wanted him closer, more a part of her, so she reached out and cupped his big, hard erection, drawing him towards her waiting entrance.

He gasped at her fingers, and shivered in need. Amber arched up to meet him, and he responded with the same urgency and animal desire that she was feeling.

He entered her with admirable restraint—Amber could feel him holding himself back, trying to stay gentle and controlled, and she was desperate for more. She was elemental, wild, and filled with need and want.

She moaned, drawing him faster, and clawed at his muscled

back, begging him wordlessly to hurry, to take her faster, harder, and when it worked more slowly than she needed, she bit him, drawing an excited yelp from him.

They rolled together on the utility room floor, colliding into a shelf with nearly disastrous results, and ended with Amber on top, straddling him. He thrust up at her hungrily, and she met his need with her own, riding him and clawing frantically. She wanted him deeper, closer, harder, and drew him into herself as if she could devour him.

He groaned, and drew her down for a kiss that completed her.

And then they were one, thrusting together in perfect sensual symmetry.

There was no thought for the hard floor or the hum of machinery, or for the trauma and stress of the frantic past day, it was only two of them, perfect mates fitted perfectly together like pieces of a puzzle. They moved together in beautiful, musical harmony, and crested into a peak of pleasure that sweated out the last of their fear and anxiety.

Afterwards, they lay together for a long moment side-by-side, panting, until the discomfort of the cold floor finally penetrated their afterglow.

Amber sat up, and felt an unexpected amount of satisfaction and soreness. "If this were a spy movie, they'd run the credits now," she said, rubbing at a spot on her shoulder that had gotten bruised.

"If this were a movie, they would have faded to black over the credits some time ago," Tony laughed with a rumble.

"Depends on the rating," Amber laughed back at him, then sobered. "What really happens now?" she asked.

Tony's eyes met hers intensely. "You're my mate," he said. "I belong with you, wherever that ends up being."

"You'd leave DC to be with me?"

Tony looked martyred. "Yes, I would even live in the Midwest with you." His voice suggested what a sacrifice he would consider this.

Amber pondered. "I've never been to the East Coast."

Tony looked hopeful. "Let me show it to you," he said. "If you hate it, we can live anywhere else."

"I hear the cherry trees in spring are quite the sight," Amber said thoughtfully. "And if I could have a garden..."

"I'll buy you a house in Maryland with an acre of land," Tony promised expansively. "You can grow anything you want."

"Talk dirty to me," Amber said, and she leaned over and kissed him, deeply. Like him, she wasn't sure it mattered where they went—as long as they were together.

CHAPTER 32

The laundry room was part of the mechanical room, and Tony found clean bathrobes in a laundry basket for them to put on. It felt distinctly odd to be covered again, after spending so much time nude by necessity.

They came out of the mechanical room to find that the guests were gathered in the bar, quite sure by now that something was up. The new bartender, a tall, muscular sandy blond with a thick Texan accent, had taken charge and was handing out drinks and snacks to the best of his ability, and he had ransacked the kitchen to provide a makeshift meal of grilled meat.

He immediately asked Tony if he knew what was happening.

"I'll... let Scarlet explain when she gets back," Tony said vaguely, not wanting to try to guess what story the owner was going to have for the events of the day.

The bartender seemed satisfied with the idea that she *would* be coming back, and went back to expertly flipping burgers and handing them out to the mystified guests.

It was hours before Scarlet finally returned, with Breck driving an overloaded Jeep at the head of a ragtag caravan of vehicles full of people and animals.

Scarlet did her best to give Tony the idea that he had handled everything completely wrong, and sent her people running for bathrobes and food.

"I could have been bartending in Las Vegas," the Texan muttered, bringing a pile of cold hamburgers from the walk-in fridge that the inhabitants of the zoo fell on as if it was ambrosia. No one offered him answers as to why Scarlet was one of the only ones still wearing clothing, or where the very confused and jumpy collection of odd shifters had come from.

"Thank you for saving the resort," Scarlet said grudgingly to Tony at last.

Tony had the grace to allow that the resort wouldn't have been at risk if he hadn't been investigating.

Scarlet raised an eyebrow at him but didn't comment further.

"What did you do with Beehag?" Tony asked.

Scarlet's face was inscrutable in the predawn light, but Tony suspected that full daylight wouldn't have revealed much more. "He didn't make it."

Amber gasped. "Did you...?"

Scarlet's look was the sort you gave hysterical people and over-enthusiastic children. "The stimulant Jimmy gave him to counteract the tranquilizers was too much for his system. He never regained consciousness. The lifeguard, Bastian, is a registered EMT, and we've already called it in to the mainland. I trust you have Jimmy? He'll be answering for that crime, among others."

Tony confirmed Jimmy's location and state of restraint.

"You didn't think he might shift out of duct tape?" Scarlet asked scathingly. She sent one of her handymen to make sure he hadn't, and to keep an eye on him.

"What about all the guards?" Amber asked. None of them were among the milling refugees.

"The cages will be serving their purpose until the authorities get there." Amber suspected it was satisfaction she was hearing in Scarlet's voice.

Scarlet turned away to answer a question about housing and was drawn back into the crowd.

"Amber? Scarlet says your name is Amber?"

Amber turned and furrowed her eyebrows at the stranger who hailed her. She was a short woman with straight brown hair that clearly hadn't been cut in years. Her brown eyes were light, almost gold in the poor light of the deck.

Amber sucked in her breath. "Yes, I'm Amber," she said.

"You're... you're a mountain cat, I saw you. An *Andean* mountain cat." Her voice was rusty, as if she hadn't spoken in years, and she winced when she walked closer to Amber, clutching at her side; blood had already stained through the white robe. She completely ignored Tony.

Amber realized, "You're the ocelot who helped us get the helicopter."

"Did you... know your father?" the woman blurted.

Amber swallowed hard. "I didn't know either of my parents," she said in a small voice.

Tears were spilling out of the woman's eyes, but she smiled radiantly. "Yes, I'm the ocelot," she confirmed hoarsely. "Your *father* was an Andean mountain cat. I never knew for sure if he got you out or not, but I told him I wasn't going to let you grow up in a cage. He didn't want to go, and I'm sure he didn't want to leave you anymore than he wanted to leave me. He must have been in danger, to leave you, and not return to me. I'm... sorry you never knew him. He was very brave."

Tony was holding her hand, keeping her up with the touch, and when Amber couldn't speak, he offered gently, "I think Amber gets that from both sides. You tipped the balance in our battle, and probably saved our lives and the resort."

Amber could finally speak. "You're my... mother?"

The woman opened her arms, and Amber fell gently into them.

"My sweet baby girl," the woman murmured, stroking her hair. "You grew up so beautiful."

Amber wept, and hugged her back too hard, making the woman gasp in pain. She garbled an apology, letting go and then squeezing the woman's shoulders more gently. She shook and laughed with the overwhelming emotion. “My mother!” She turned to grin in disbelief at Tony.

Tony drew himself up straight, suddenly the object of the woman's full attention.

“So, you're my daughter's mate,” she said critically. She sniffed, looked him up and down, and then said, “You'll do. Releasing us from Beehag's prison was a good first step towards earning my favor.”

“Your daughter did a lot of the hard work there,” Tony suggested, earning himself a warm smile.

“Yes, you'll do,” Amber’s mother repeated, more confidently.

They saw her to the room that Scarlet had assigned her, and Tony completely won her heart by making her bed—the staff had not had time to set up all the rooms.

“It's lovely to be human again,” she said thoughtfully, stretching her fingers. “A little odd, but I like the idea of clean sheets and a bed.”

Amber left her with a long, tearful hug and went with Tony to his house—anyone who could double up had, and she had already volunteered her house for a few of the refuges. Despite the fact that the sun was already rising, and Tony was exhausted in every pore of his aching body, he was not quite ready to climb between their sheets and find sleep, and he could sense that Amber felt the same way. They made their way to the deck and sat together on the wicker loveseat.

“Is being a super spy always like this?” Amber asked, snuggling against him.

“I promise it isn't,” Tony said sincerely. “Something like this means way too much paperwork. We're usually much more about donuts and meetings and Powerpoint presentations.”

Amber giggled, then asked seriously, “What would I do in DC?”

“Whatever you wanted,” Tony promised. “There are garden stores there, if you wanted to work. Or you could be a housewife, if you didn't.”

She froze beside him. “A... housewife? That would mean I was...”

Tony groaned. "I'm doing this all backwards again," he apologized, and he leaned over and kissed her head before getting off the loveseat to kneel at her feet. "I don't have a ring, I'm sorry."

Amber stared at him, golden eyes bright in the sunrise.

Tony gathered her unresisting hand into his own. "Marry me?"

The tears that appeared in Amber's eyes made Tony fear he'd done something terribly wrong until an amazed smile bloomed on her face.

"Yes," she whispered. "Oh, yes."

Tony surged up to take her into his arms, and kissed her passionately, fingers twining into her loose hair. She kissed him back, twining her tongue with his and wrapping her strong arms around his shoulders.

"I love you," Tony said, when he could breathe again. "I will love you forever."

"I love you," she replied. "Forever."

They kissed again, slower, and deeper, and Tony knew that forever wasn't just an empty word between them, but a promise, like the sun rising over the jungle.

"I'm going to miss this place," Amber told Tony, leaning into his side with her arm wrapped around him.

"Huh," Tony said with surprise. "I am, too." He had a feeling that Shifting Sands was going to stay under his skin for longer than there was sand in his shoes... and that was probably going to be a very long time indeed.

"*Pura vida*," he said. Pure life.

OTHER DUTIES AS ASSIGNED

This is a short story I wanted to write since I first introduced Tex near the end of Tropical Tiger Spy! He didn't even have a name in that book, but I already had big plans for him, and his first day of work was a little wild…

Tex and Scarlet ended their tour of the magnificent resort at the bar, and Tex felt like he'd just been handed the keys to the city.

His new domain for drinking was well laid out, with some tables out in the sun, and others in the shade of the restaurant deck above. The shelves were fully stocked; though he might have preferences for different brands of some items, none of them were substandard. Nothing about the place was substandard; even the napkins were linen.

The ice-maker had a quiet, pleasant hum, and everything was organized efficiently. Laminated menus were stacked at one end of a long bar with stools under a coconut, and there was a noticeable lack of a cash register. All-inclusive meant free drinks, and while Tex knew that there wouldn't be tips, he thought that the lush living conditions more than made up for it. He'd already been treated to a meal at the restaurant, and he'd been thoroughly impressed.

"If you have any questions or need any additional stock, please let me know," Scarlet said. She had been unfailingly polite throughout their tour, but lacked even a hint of warmth.

"Yes, ma'am," Tex told her, touching his fingers to his hat. "I'm sure it will go smoothly."

He settled his guitar into a corner of the bar. Scarlet gave it a long, skeptical look, but didn't comment. She had warned him that they were still somewhat under-booked, and that there might be downtime to fill. She'd also made it clear that she didn't expect him to be idling if there was any work that needed to be done, even if it was slightly outside of his expected realm of expertise.

"Other duties as assigned," Tex agreed. "Yes, ma'am."

"You may call me Scarlet," she said, thawing perhaps a degree. "I believe you have customers."

Tex gave the two women at the bar his most winning smile. "What can I get for you ladies?"

They gave him dazzled smiles in return and settled onto barstools. "A mojito," the taller of the two requested shyly. The other said nothing, blushing and pointing to one of the offerings on the menu she was holding.

"Extra mint in that mojito, ma'am?" Tex asked courteously, only hoping belatedly that they actually *had* fresh mint.

He needn't have worried; when the customer nodded, Scarlet showed him where there was a container of mint just off the back entrance of the bar.

"Now that's fresh," Tex said with approval.

"Don't waste any," Scarlet said severely. "If you have any urgent requests, please have them to me by this afternoon, as I will be placing an order tonight for pickup on the mainland tomorrow."

"Yes, ma'am," Tex said, tipping his hat to her politely.

He turned to make the requested drinks, more and more happy with the setup of the bar as he explored it. The blender was top quality, powerful but not obnoxiously loud. The glasses were all sparkling clean and free from cracks or chips. The ice-maker was an ancient beast, but was probably top of the line in the eighties, and well-maintained. It made pleasantly flawless ice cubes, and he served aesthetically pleasing drinks, topping them off with cubes of fresh fruit he found in one of the mini fridges and a jaunty umbrella.

The two women whispered together in delight while he found his way around the bar and put their drinks together. He couldn't resist giving the bottle of white rum a flip into the air, turning to deftly catch it, and they giggled and clapped.

Scarlet, also watching, did not appear as amused, but Tex thought she did look a little reassured, and she left shortly after, the sound of her heels clicking away over the tiles like a dismissal.

For a short time, Tex was busy; it was the height of the afternoon and several guests had been milling around waiting for a bartender. They didn't ask for anything he couldn't make, and he didn't once crack the bartender's bible under the counter. When an enormous woman with waves of auburn hair asked for a margarita, he tipped his hat and made her one of such strength and flavor that she laughed and extravagantly declared him her new favorite person in the world.

Then, there was a lull in activity, and he did a circuit of the bar deck, wiping down tables and arranging chairs. When no one else needed anything, he did the same for the pool deck, collecting a few lost bottles of water and dirty towels.

Finally, he returned to the bar and pulled out his guitar.

A red-headed woman, not as brilliantly-locked as Scarlet, came to the counter as he was tuning it, but when he started to put it aside, quickly insisted, "Oh, no, you can play. What kind of music do you like?"

Tex had to smile slowly at her, because his cowboy hat and belt buckle ought to give him away amply, and started the chords to a classic Hank William's song.

By the time he had finished that song, there were more drinks to make, so he reluctantly set aside the guitar and went to serve the guests.

He had long interesting discussions in broken English with a Russian visitor, and flirted kindly with an old woman from Brazil who smiled at him with a face wrinkled like a walnut, her tiny dark eyes full of wisdom.

"Have you seen the cook? Or the head waiter?" One of the waitresses from the restaurant deck asked him nervously, handing over a lengthy drink order.

"Not that I know of," Tex said apologetically, swiftly gathering ingredients.

The waitress wrung her hands in her apron. "The restaurant was supposed to open thirty minutes ago. I don't even know what the menu is supposed to be. Chef's not there, Breck isn't there. I went to see Scarlet, and her office was empty, too. No one knows what to do!"

"Don't you worry, darling," Tex said, as reassuringly as he could. "You serve these, I'll see if the lifeguard knows what's up."

But the lifeguard was also missing. The dragon hadn't even bothered putting up the 'no lifeguard on duty' signs—he'd simply vanished from the beach.

Tex returned to his bar, serving up a few more drinks and refilling the rapidly emptying bowls of nuts. The waitress scampered back in from the rear entrance. "There's still no one there," she told Tex, in a panic.

"It'll be okay, darling," Tex said comfortingly. "What's your name, sugar?"

"Angie," the waitress said, clearly fighting down her panic. "I'm new."

"That makes two of us," Tex said kindly. "Let's see if we can't get to the bottom of this little mystery."

He went back upstairs with Angie, to find a cold kitchen with a few baffled-looking staff. "I don't know how to cook," one of them said in a panic. "Chef always tells us exactly what to do!"

No one knew what was supposed to be on the menu, or what to do with the increasingly agitated guests. Tex pulled open one of the fridges and peered inside, half-hoping for a note of instruction, or possibly, the chef himself. He coaxed names from the cook staff: an agitated blond man named Angus and a frustrated-looking Hispanic man named Mateo.

"There's another fridge back there," Angie pointed out. That was a walk-in variety, and it offered no more clues than the first one had.

"They're getting hungry," Mateo said unhappily, running fingers through his dark hair in agitation. "They've already cleared out most of the buffet."

"Well," Tex said slowly, "we don't want them getting upset. Let's do the best with what we've got here and see about getting them fed." He looked around. "Is there a grill?"

Angus showed him where it was and lit it.

"There's plenty of chuck," Tex said. "And I'd have to give up my cowboy hat if I didn't know how to grill an edible burger." A hasty toss of the pantry turned up a five-gallon bucket of BBQ sauce in a back corner, and several sealed containers of rolls that looked on the fancy side for burgers. There were fresh tomatoes on the counter, in a crate like someone had simply dropped them off and left, and there were several heads of lettuce in the crisper. There was cheese, and jalapeños, and avocados, and a variety of condiments.

Angie left to announce the ransacked menu and collect careful notes from the guests about toppings and Tex got Mateo and Angus to chopping and peeling and setting out plates as he shaped hefty burgers and slapped them onto the grill.

Drinks were easier than they could have been, because nothing went so well with burgers as beer, so Angie popped the tops off bottles and hastily delivered them while Tex flipped meat and toasted rolls. Angus assembled the buns with toppings and threw on decorative garnish, adding artistic flare with swirls of BBQ sauce. There were bags of chips in back, clearly earmarked for the buffet, and each plate was topped off with a spicy pickle from a jar the size of a small keg.

Tex trusted Mateo to flip the burgers while he dashed back

downstairs and frantically filled drink orders, moving fast and sure-fingered, but not bothering with his usual bottle-flipping flair. When he returned to the grill, he saw that the properly-done burgers were put on each waiting bun according to Angie's careful orders.

"We've got a vegetarian!" she announced, coming in with orders from the last stragglers.

They all stared around each other for a moment, and Tex asked with dread, "That no-dairy kind?"

"Vegan," Angus supplied.

"Just said vegetarian," Angie said, eyes wide.

"Offer 'em a cheese, tomato, and avocado burger," Tex said desperately. "With...ah..."

"Cilantro?" Mateo suggested. "People seem to think that cilantro's fancy."

Tex shrugged. "Sure?"

Angie scampered out, while Tex went back to the bar to keep those customers happy as well.

He kept a keen eye out for any of the staff that Scarlet had introduced him to, but they were all weirdly absent. He spotted a tall, dark-haired man with a diminutive woman, both of them looking entirely disheveled and dressed in resort bathrobes. The man had been talking with Scarlet earlier, he remembered.

"Do you know where Scarlet, or the Chef, or the head waiter, or half the staff have gone off to?"

"I'll...let Scarlet explain herself when she gets back," the man said, an arm protectively around the woman. They both looked like they'd just come from a battlefield.

"I guess this is what she meant by other duties as assigned," Tex said, mystified but reassured that at least she *would* be coming back. Eventually. He returned to the kitchen, flipped more burgers, dashed down the stairs to mix more drinks, and when he came back, he found that there were finally no more dinner orders, and the several dozen burgers he'd already started were finished and then stacked on plates and carried back to the walk-in fridge.

The sky was pitch dark by the time Scarlet returned, and it was not a return to normal. With her came several loads of naked, nervy shifters in both human and animal form who stared around in wonder and fell upon the cold burgers that Tex hesitantly offered like they hadn't eaten in weeks.

"I, ah, sort of took some liberties, ma'am," he told Scarlet sheepishly. "The guests were getting hungry and restless. Was starting to fear a real stampede."

Scarlet gave him a scathing look that softened unexpectedly. "You did just fine," she said approvingly. "Thank you for your quick thinking, or for stepping up."

"My kitchen!" came a hearty roar from behind them. Tex had done no dishes, and he winced to think of the mess that had been left behind.

"I suggest you return to the bar and see if anyone needs a last call," Scarlet said wisely.

"Ma'am," Tex said, tipping his hat. "Do *you* need a drink?"

Whatever had happened that necessitated abandoning her resort and returning with truckloads of traumatized shifters, Scarlet looked remarkably composed, not a single red hair out of place.

She gave him an amused look. "I thank you for the offer," she dismissed him. "I think you'll fit in well here."

"It was an interesting first day," Tex said, leaving her at the railing of the restaurant with a polite tip of his hat as there was another wail of outrage from the kitchen.

The bar was almost deserted; the walnut woman from Brazil was the only one interested in a nightcap. She wanted to hear Tex play again, so he pulled out his guitar and checked the trueness of the tune before he launched into his favorite Willy Nelson song. "Crazy" seemed apt for the situation.

He tidied up the bar before he shut off the lights and wandered back to the hotel building where the staff was put up, pausing outside the door to look around at the midnight jungle and the star-sparkled sky in wonder.

As first days went, it was inauspicious, and if this was any indication, he was in for a weird and wild ride at this job, but Tex wasn't sure he'd ever been anywhere in the world that called to him so completely.

He had a bar that met his every desire, in a gorgeous place where shifters were free to be shifters, and if parts of the resort were odd and mysterious and unexpected…it would probably be boring, otherwise.

LOCKED

I wrote this story when I started compiling this omnibus edition and realized that I had never explained the origin of Neal's lock, which seemed like a shocking oversight in retrospect.

Neal parked the borrowed Jeep at the front of the complex. There was yellow tape strung across the broken gates.

No pasar, the tape said. Over and over again: *Policia - No pasar.*

Neal ripped the tape down and went in anyway, the crowbar that he had liberated from the resort on the other side of the island over one shoulder.

It was quiet, but aside from the police tape, it didn't look deserted. The lawn was still neatly mowed, and there was no sign that a savage battle had taken place; most of the firearms had been loaded with darts, not bullets, and they had all either been taken as evidence by the police, or cleaned up by the shifters before they left the scene.

Beehag had been experimenting with shifters and drugs, and no one wanted the authorities to start snooping around asking questions about the chemical cocktails. Shifters were secret here and wanted to stay that way.

Beehag.

Neal realized that his mouth was lifting into a snarl and his maned wolf was starting to rise inside him. He stuffed the animal back violently.

He'd been a wolf for ten years and he was done with it.

Ten miserable, angry years, forced to live in a cage as a power play for an asshole with a complex against shifters.

He'd tried staying human at first—most of them did. But Beehag had been adamant about keeping his collection in their animal form. Neal thought that some of the things he'd been shot up with were experiments designed to do just that, but they'd had the opposite effect, forcing a shifter to stay in their human form. He wasn't sure about some of the other things that had been tried on them. He still sometimes had nightmares of lights and operating tables.

The front door was locked. Neal broke the handle off and smashed in the door. It wasn't nearly as satisfying as he'd hoped, and there was no sound in response, only the endless tropical breeze rustling the nearby trees.

The complex was empty.

The rooms were still furnished and the clocks still showed the right time. If the authorities had taken anything, it didn't show. It was as if Beehag was merely out for the day.

The exception was his study; there were wide empty spaces and pale shapes on the floor and walls where the taxidermy shifter animals had been, frozen in forms of terror. The lion skin that had been before the fireplace was gone, and all of the stuffed heads.

Had the national guard taken them all as evidence of Beehag's crimes? Most of them had been endangered, some of them outright extinct. The official story that was being shared was that Beehag had trapped humans in his cages; they probably had no idea what the relationship was between the animals and the "human" victims that the resort staff had liberated.

Neal wandered through the house, out to the zoo behind it.

The zoo was empty, the doors propped open. It still smelled like the zoo, the rich floral scent of jungle not quite enough to cover the animals scents.

Neal blocked out his wolf as he paced down the aisles, trying not to flinch at the memories that crowded back. When he found his cage, he took the nearest bar in his free hand, half-expecting the jolt of electricity that was designed to cause crippling pain. Any shifter in enough agony retreated to their non-human form.

How many times had he tested it before he gave up for good? A year? Two years? Was he still trying after five?

Time didn't pass for his wolf the same way that it did for him.

Neal peeled his fingers off the inert bars and took the crowbar off of his shoulder.

It wasn't that he'd expected to find someone here to take his frustrations out on, but somehow he'd hoped. Beehag had the ill grace to die before Neal could get his revenge, and it left a hollow, burning place in his chest.

The cruel guards were all gone—fled or arrested, Neal didn't know or care.

The blow he landed on the bars of the cage was enough to dent them, and to make a shrill ringing sound through the deserted zoo. He followed it with a second hit, and a third, the rebound through the crowbar rattling back up through his shoulders.

It didn't do much damage to the cage, denting it, but not breaking through. Hitting the door only made it bounce, and everything Neal could do to it was cosmetic.

He scowled at the lock, the heavy box that he'd tried picking a hundred times, always driven back to his wolf form by the electrical shock protections.

It wasn't protected now, and Neal set upon it with the crowbar, straining and sweating for an undetermined time until he had pried it from the door and ripped the wires from inside the bars.

It was a heavy, unwieldy weight in his hands, ugly and dented. He considered throwing it into the ocean, or burying it, or finding a crucible he could melt it in. Then he curled his fingers around it. He would keep it forever, to remind himself that nothing could ever trap him again.

~

Scarlet was waiting at the entrance of the resort when he returned, but she didn't say a word about the fact that he'd borrowed her Jeep and hot-wired it without permission, then returned hours later looking like he'd gone rounds in a ring with a metal cage.

"Travis needs some assistance at cottage six," was all she had to say.

Neal shrugged and nodded. "Had some business to attend to."

"I'm sure that you did," Scarlet agreed without warmth.

There was a gazelle standing at the edge of the jungle, watching them both with big, dark eyes. Neal remembered seeing her fleeing the crowd of refugees from the zoo. He hadn't seen her shift since then and wondered if she even could. She'd been there even longer than he had.

He left the Jeep and took his prize from the zoo back to the hotel room he was sharing with several of Beehag's other victims. He thrust it under the far corner of his mattress, as if it was some kind of treasure that anyone else would ever want, then went to find Travis at cottage six.

Deep within him, his wolf whined, but Neal fixedly ignored him and locked him away in his head.

He would never be caged again, not by bars, and not by fur.

TROPICAL WOUNDED WOLF

CHAPTER 1

"I cannot vacation at a *nude* resort," Mary North said in horror. "I even have to change into my swimsuit in a toilet stall at the health club."

Her co-worker Alice, a bear shifter, rolled her eyes. "It's not nude, it's *clothing-optional*. There's a big difference and if you're shy, you can spend the whole time in animal form."

"Oh, I don't know," Mary sighed. "The pictures are lovely, but I'm not sure I like the idea of a shifters-only resort. It's in a foreign country and they have poisonous snakes there, probably. Plus, two women traveling alone? We might get robbed, or kidnapped!" She shuddered dramatically, and sniffed the coffee pot cautiously. Like the deer she could shift into, Mary was wary of everything. She suspected that the pot had been sitting out for hours on the burner.

"I'm sure they don't have poisonous snakes at a fancy all-inclusive place like Shifting Sands Resort," Alice scoffed. "And it's not like Costa Rica is some third world nation. Did you see the photo of the pool?"

"I did," Mary admitted wistfully. She loved swimming and the brochure made the pool look amazing: huge and crystal-blue in the sparkling sunshine, with pseudo-Greek columns, waterfalls, and palm trees around it.

"And the snorkeling!"

"I couldn't swim in the *ocean*," Mary said swiftly, deciding to dump the coffee out and wait for a new pot. She had just enough time before the next block of classes to brew one.

Alice snagged a cup before she could pour all of the coffee out, but Alice lived dangerously like that.

"Have you ever been in the ocean?" Alice asked, taking a sip of the molten sludge.

"They have sharks in the ocean! And stinging jellyfish and *eels* and things. Besides, this resort sounds expensive." Mary measured the coffee grounds carefully, shaking each scoop perfectly level.

"It's not so bad, once you realize that you don't have to pay for any food. It even includes massages and kayak rentals and guided hikes..."

"A tippy little kayak out on the ocean? You have to be kidding me!"

"... And I know you aren't spending your whole salary, living like you do. You haven't taken a vacation in years."

Mary smiled down at her second hand outfit. Alice wasn't wrong about her spending habits, and she did have a nice little nest egg put aside specifically for a vacation someday.

Still…

"I'm not sure. It's so far away!"

"That's a great deal of its charm," Alice said dryly. "And I'll be with you, so it's not like you'd be going alone! I speak Spanish like a native, and I can protect you from eels and poisonous snakes and strange men."

"But..."

Alice shook her coffee cup threateningly at Mary. "If you don't come with me, I will undoubtedly do something reckless and regrettable, and you will have to live with the guilt of not being with me to keep me from being foolish forever."

"I can't even keep you from drinking terrible coffee," Mary said plaintively, pouring her own fresh cup as the ancient coffee pot beeped its tired announcement of completion.

Alice grinned, probably sensing her victory. “But at least you won't have the guilt of not trying hanging over your head.” She drained the last of her bitter cup defiantly, just as the class warning bell rang.

Mary blew at her superior java as she gathered her teaching plan and purse. “I'll probably catch some terrible tropical disease and end up spending the entire vacation desperately ill,” she predicted direly.

CHAPTER 2

Neal Byrne turned the bottle of water in his hands. Even this early, the heat and humidity left a cloud of condensation on the cold surface. He traced a pattern in it until he recognized the tattoo he was drawing and wiped it entirely out with his thumb.

That wasn't his life anymore.

He lifted his gaze and looked out over the green lawn and tropical foliage. His life now seemed equally absurd: a gazelle cropped at the grass nearby, ignoring him.

"Aren't we a pair," Neal told her.

Neal made a point of searching her out every morning, offering an anchor of humanity and familiarity from which to start her path back to civilization.

The gazelle had been imprisoned in Beehag's horrific shifter collection for longer than Neal had been there, and he had spent ten wretched years in that place. Freedom and speech still felt strange to him and clearly the gazelle had not yet acclimated either, never shifting to her human form, barely tolerating bipedal presence at all.

Neal, by contrast, now refused his own animal form. Beehag had forced him to be a red-maned wolf in his zoo, for his entertainment. Neal rejected everything that reminded him of that captivity, burying his wolf so deeply now that he couldn't even hear its voice.

Mostly, he was ignored by the gazelle, his rusty conversation entirely one-sided, but he noticed that she came to this part of the grounds every morning, despite having the run of the island, so he continued to return, too.

"Breakfast is out," a cheerful voice announced. The gazelle moved swiftly to the far end of the lawn, ears twitching in alarm, then put her head down to graze again.

Breck, head waiter of the resort and a leopard shifter, came over to the bench where Neal sat, holding a heaped plate of food from the gourmet buffet, followed by Graham, the groundskeeper. Although the staff was allowed free rein of the resort food, they were not permitted to eat it in the guest dining room. The picnic table where Neal met the gazelle every morning had become a gathering place for a few of the staff, and somehow, despite his attempts to remain aloof, Neal had found a new place to belong in their motley ranks. He did whatever odd tasks were assigned to him and used his free time to work at getting the remaining survivors of Beehag's prison back to their lost families.

Strangely, he could face helping them, but not the idea of returning to his own life.

Graham, a lion shifter, sat down opposite him, grunting wordlessly in what Neal now recognized was a greeting.

Breck filled any conversational space left by the surly landscaper and the quiet refugee with practiced ease. "Today would be a great day to avoid Scarlet," he advised needlessly.

Scarlet, the owner of the resort, had a short temper and a ferocious will. Neal knew that he and the other rescued shifters were there by her generosity and was grateful for it, but kept out of her way as much as possible. He didn't want a reminder that he and the others were costing her money to keep, and he couldn't tell her when he was going to be ready to leave the insulated island.

Breck continued despite the stony silence. "I guess there are some legal inheritance issues with the island property now that our friend Beehag is out of the picture, and there may be some uncertainty for the long-term lease of Shifting Sands," he said conversationally, eating a slice of quiche with a fork. "We're over capacity in free guests, and under in paid." He paused, giving an eloquent shrug and nod at Neal. "No one blames you, but you might want to keep out of her way, just the same."

Neal shrugged back and Graham put an entire slice of the quiche in his mouth.

"What needs done today?" Neal asked, snagging an extra slice of the egg pie from Breck's plate over his feigned protest.

Neal hated any reminder of Scarlet's charity and avoided the dining hall whenever possible. It hadn't escaped his notice that Breck's breakfast plate had doubled in size since they first started meeting at this table, but none of them actually mentioned it out loud. Neal pretended he was stealing Breck's food, Breck pretended he was bothered by it, and Graham studiously ignored it all.

"There aren't enough guests to need any extra waitstaff," Breck answered him.

Neal was glad. While he could feign good manners and keep from swearing, he didn't fit in at the restaurant any better than the waitstaff uniforms fit him.

"Always weeds," Graham growled. "And the pool needs to be scraped."

"I'll do the pool," Neal volunteered. The last time he had tried to help Graham with the gardening, he'd pulled up a domesticated vine, and he actually thought for several moments that the lion shifter was going to deck him over the mistake. He could probably hold his own against the groundskeeper, but he didn't want to find out.

After eating half of Breck's plate of food and listening the resort gossip, Neal stood up.

"I want to get the pool done before it gets too hot," he said.

"Catch you this afternoon," Breck said cheerfully.

Graham grunted.

The gazelle gave him a long soulful look from across the lawn, then wandered away through the brush.

Neal shed his resort shirt at the supply shed and exchanged it for the long-handed algae scraper and net he would need for the pool job. It wasn't glamorous labor, but it was physically intense and the sun on the pool deck would be brutal later in the day. It was good work, requiring attention, and Neal tackled it with all of the frustration and bitterness that boiled in his blood.

He was about halfway down the first side of the enormous pool, sweating profusely and enjoying the burn in his muscles, when he felt his red maned wolf stir suddenly, deep inside.

"*No,*" he said ferociously out loud, and he scraped at the tile more vigorously, the thin velvet of algae dissolving before his assault.

To his surprise, his wolf growled back, the urgency of his message too keen to back down.

Without wanting to, Neal looked up and found his head swiveling to the deck by the bar.

A figure stood looking out over the bar deck, and Neal was grateful that she hadn't noticed him yet, because he had to stare for a long moment.

She was the kind of pale that only very new visitors to the resort could be, with mousy blonde hair and big, terrified eyes under a wide-brimmed hat. She had a bag clutched to her chest and one sandal-clad foot was tucked behind the other, rubbing nervously at the opposite heel.

She had the timid, diffident body posture that usually made Neal want to roll his eyes and avoid a person, but there was something about her—something more than the incredibly sexy curves that she seemed be trying to hide. Something that inflamed his senses and made him acutely aware of every pore of her perfect skin.

She's ours, his wolf told him firmly, and the conviction was so deep and determined that Neal had to turn away to fight it back down.

The worst part was, Neal knew he was right. That woman—that gorgeous, petrified woman—was his mate. He unexpectedly knew the iron core of her soul and could taste the gentle sweetness of her mouth. He wanted to kiss her, more than any urge he'd ever had, and was already fantasizing the feel of her pale skin under his calloused fingers.

He drew himself up short.

There was no way in hell he was going to subject her to himself. He was too broken from his years of captivity, his control of himself was too tenuous. It would be best for everyone just to keep his distance.

He shouldered the pool tools and headed the long way around the water to the service entrance where he would be able to avoid looking back at her. *Don't meet her eyes*, he told himself. *Don't let her see you.*

No matter how much he longed to.

CHAPTER 3

Mary had never felt so alone.

The owner of the resort, Scarlet Stanson, had been outwardly welcoming, but Mary couldn't help but feel like a grubby child in her tidy office. A grubby child who didn't quite measure up to the incredibly high standards of Shifting Sands Resort.

She had never been somewhere so polished and gorgeous. Even the walkways and steps were beautifully tiled, every plant groomed into the perfect shape. The buildings were all meticulous, even the ones clearly under renovation were well-contained and neater than a construction site had any business being.

Alice would have loved it here, Mary kept thinking, and she longed for her friend's boisterous company. Alice would never have felt intimidated by Scarlet's flawless hair.

But Alice had gotten chicken pox, of all the ridiculous things, and been forced to stay home. After everything she'd done to convince Mary that this would be the holiday she needed, Alice hadn't even been able to go. Getting on the plane by herself had been the bravest thing that Mary had ever done. At first, she'd considered refusing, but Alice had been adamant. *At least one of us is getting some enjoyment out of the cottage I booked, so you'd better go, or I'll come back as a ghost and haunt you for the rest of your days!*

Even pointing out that chicken pox was rarely fatal hadn't put a dent in Alice's fervor, and in the end Mary had reluctantly decided she didn't have a choice.

Clutching her map and her bag, already regretting her decision to come alone, Mary decided to go to the pool first, to familiarize herself with the layout and see if it was really as impressive as the photographs had made it out to be. The closest access was through the bar, but when she stepped out onto the deck, the ocean view arrested her before she even noticed the pool.

Even as far away as it was, she could feel the magnetic power of water and hear the waves crashing on the reef that protected the bay. There was a scent and a quality to the air that she'd never experienced before, salty and metallic and *alive*.

She couldn't even imagine swimming in such a thing. It was full of power and secrets and strength. Her shifter-self felt strangely stronger here, more alive than it had ever been in the sleepy little town of Lakefield.

She turned her gaze to the pool, but before she saw the pool itself, she saw *him*.

He was looking away, in that swift way people do when they've just caught themselves staring, but Mary was sure it couldn't have been *her* that he was staring at.

He had a shock of short red hair, mussed from exertion, and a stubborn tan you rarely found on redheads. That tan spread over muscles unlike any Mary had ever seen before outside of sports magazines. He had wide shoulders knotted with strength and arms like small trees. His narrow hips were clad in utilitarian shorts and his feet were bare. As Mary tried not to stare and failed, he gathered up his pool cleaning equipment and stalked away, never turning his face to her.

His exit left Mary feeling lonelier and full of longing than ever. Within her, something awoke and uncoiled. Part of her wanted to drop her bag and run down the stairs after the gorgeous man, even as the practical part said that was ridiculous and she was just reacting to a stunning male specimen after a dry spell in her life. It wasn't like she *really* believed any of that nonsense about fated mates or destined love.

Mary sighed and finally looked at the pool.

It was long enough for laps in either direction, with two waterfalls cascading from small pools at the bar deck she stood on down to the water level of the pool. Palm trees lined both sides, leaning over massive boulders on the left and spaced along a wide walkway to the right. At the far end, the poolside deck was peppered with chairs and umbrellas and guests lying out in the sun. Beyond that lay the terrifying ocean. Elevation hid the beach from her, but Mary guessed it lay below the pool deck; the island was quite steep.

No one was currently swimming in the pool and the last agitation from the gorgeous pool cleaner's efforts had already died down. Only the ripples from the water features disturbed the surface. Mary could see the deep bottom, the curved steps at the far end, and the globes of the lights that would illuminate the water at night. Would it be too scary to swim at night? It didn't look like there were very many lights around the pool.

As hot as the day was, the water looked deliciously cool. It was supposed to be unheated, something that Mary had been hesitant about until she stepped off the plane into the tropical Costa Rican heat.

A swim would have to wait, though, because she wasn't planning to change into her swimsuit here on the pool deck, no matter what kind of lax clothing rules there were at this strange place.

Mary took the exit that her map indicated was closest to her cottage and followed a pristine white gravel path to a charming little house with a beautiful private deck. It looked like something straight out of a tropical-themed issue of Good Housekeeping. Mary had another pang of loneliness and nervousness glancing at the bed in the empty second bedroom. If Alice were with her, she probably would have chased down the hunky man by the pool and insisted that he give them a tour of the resort and meet them for drinks afterwards.

For some reason, she could not get the picture of him out of her mind. Not just his juicy shoulders and ripped body, but the planes of the cheek that she'd gotten a glimpse of, the ruffle of his hair, and… something about the way he held himself. Like he hurt. Maybe not physically, but…

Mary ached for him, then shook her head and changed into her swimsuit. She didn't even *know* him!

CHAPTER 4

"Aren't there any jobs that aren't at the center of the resort?" Neal asked, trying not to sound whiny or ungrateful, though he honestly felt both. "Isn't there an urgent need to clear vines off the waterfall hiking trail or wrestle sharks on the other side of the island or something?"

It had been getting harder and harder to dodge the blonde with the big hat over the last few days. He always knew where she was, and he was beginning to suspect that she was actively looking for him. Already he had feigned illness to avoid being assigned to the waitstaff as she was heading for the restaurant and had shirked pool deck cleanup twice when he realized that she was there swimming laps. He knew he was in danger of being perceived as a slacker and avoiding Scarlet as well was turning navigation of the resort into a complicated challenge.

Travis, looking over the duty roster, made a noise of sympathy. "Unless you're secretly a certified electrician…?"

Neal had to shrug a negative.

"There's nothing left to do at the cottages I'm renovating until the wiring is in, and I won't be able to start in on that until tomorrow." Travis, a lynx shifter from Alaska, was apparently certified in every kind of construction and also drove the boat that ferried guests from the mainland when they didn't come by small plane to the airport on the other side of the island.

Neal was certified in plenty of things, but he wasn't sure how being able to set explosives and shoot the wings off a fly from a mile away would make him useful at the resort. He'd earned EMT certification, but that didn't distinguish him from the lifeguard, and any certification he had would be expired after ten years of captivity anyway.

"You could take the day off," Tex suggested with the drawl that explained his nickname.

Neal stared at the bear shifter bartender as if he'd grown horns.

"If you don't want to, *I* could use the day off," Bastian said with unexpectedly wistfulness. Neal was a little surprised—he knew Bastian liked to do his lifeguard duties in dragon-form, but Neal realized he had no idea what else he liked to do, or why he might need a day off to do it. As far as Neal knew, he spent all day, every day, on the beach, with one jeweled eye on the pool.

"I'm not qualified as a lifeguard," Neal said regretfully. The woman who was haunting him seemed to avoid the beach, staying to the pool and well-groomed grounds around the guest center. The beach might actually be a safe place to spend the day.

"Want to be?" the dragon offered cheerfully. "Costa Rican requirements aren't all that difficult, and I'm authorized to approve you if you can pass the swimming test and listen to me drone a bit in a crash course about waterfront safety."

Neal accepted gratefully; his swimming skills were strong, so passing didn't concern him.

Much later, gasping for breath, lungs burning and eyes watering from the saltwater, Neal decided that he should have been concerned.

"Nice work," Bastian said without irony after the final lap. "I'll have Scarlet print you up a temporary certificate in her office, and you can take over lifeguard duties for the afternoon."

Neal clung to the edge of the dock for a moment before heaving himself up. "I passed?"

"Oh," Bastian said, slightly sheepish. "A while ago, yes. I just wanted to see how much you could do."

"I'm going to kill you when I can move my arms again," Neal said, cheerfully exhausted. On the upside, he hadn't thought about his mate once since the test had started.

He would have gone straight for the buffet, starving from the exertion, but his unerring compass for the woman's location told him that she was already there, so Neal limped himself to the staff quarters instead, and collapsed on the picnic table in the sun.

Just as he was considering sneaking into the kitchen and braving Chef's wrath to steal food directly, Breck appeared with a plate of food and a bottle of water. He didn't even feign bringing it for himself but put it right in front of Neal.

"Well done on Bastian's brutal test!" he said admiringly, fanning himself.

"Saw that, did you?" Neal figured Breck was just teasing him. The head waiter flirted with everyone, men and women alike, but no one seemed to take it very seriously.

"The two of you, swimming around at the dock in those little shorts? Wouldn't have missed it for the world!" Breck winked and Neal was too tired to glare back.

"Congratulations on your certificate," a gentle voice interrupted them.

Neal sat up respectfully in his seat and stopped shoveling food into his face. "You heard about that, too, Mrs. Atheson?" he asked sheepishly, looking at the petite older woman who was smiling at him.

"It was a perfectly *lovely* show," the ocelot shifter said with a saucy wink. "A number of us were watching from the pool deck."

Neal blushed.

Then he realized that she was holding a small piece of luggage.

"You're leaving," he said in surprise.

Like the gazelle, she had spent longer in Beehag's zoo than Neal had, and she had very few belongings.

"Amber and Tony have bought a house in Maryland that has a mother-in-law apartment attached, and they're anxious to have me move back to the States. Tony has gotten the visa all sorted through his agency." She settled beside him on the picnic bench. "There are no more leads here to help me find my husband, and let's be honest, if he's even alive at all, it's unlikely he will come back to this island. If he does, Scarlet assures me she will send him my way."

"She will." Neal could say that with conviction. However temperamental Scarlet was, she was deeply honorable.

"More than that, I'm finally ready to be back out in the world," Mrs. Atheson said softly.

I'm not, Neal couldn't say out loud.

He only leaned over and let Mrs. Atheson enfold him in a motherly hug.

"Thank you for all of your help," she said. Near his ear, she whispered, "You'll be ready sooner than you think, too."

Neal gave her an extra squeeze and insisted on carrying her light bag up the last steps and out the resort entrance to where a Jeep was waiting to take her to the airstrip on the other side of the island.

Neal struggled with her departure, keeping a brave face over the stumbling uncertainty that he felt. Breck made no bones about crying as he hugged her goodbye, but Neal kept a stony face, not wanting to admit the empty hole that remained as the Jeep sped away. It was a gap made more keen by the impossible nearness and imposed distance he was keeping from his mate.

She was so close, he sensed, and part of him wanted to find solace in her touch. The rest of him wanted to save her from his poisoned brokenness.

CHAPTER 5

The pool alone was worth the grueling journey, Mary decided again. She had come to that conclusion her very first day at Shifting Sands, and every morning discovered it all over again.

The frightening foreign airport, the tiny cramped airplane ride, and the terrifying winding drive from the airstrip were all small payment for the delicious cool laps she could do in the stunning pool. Very rarely did she have to share the water with others, who seemed to prefer the beach or lying in the sun on the deck as humans or animals. There were never any raucous children running around to spoil the peace. The space was long enough that she could lose herself in the stroke and kick, and feel graceful and athletic, as she never did out of the water.

The palm trees made dappled shade that she could rest in at the edges, or she could choose a sunny spot to tip her face up to.

She got a massage the first day, and a pedicure and a haircut the second. The Spanish-accented woman who ran the spa, Lydia, offered to groom her in animal form, but Mary demurred; that felt a little intimate.

The staff as a whole was welcoming and friendly. The few times she'd seen Scarlet, the woman had gravely asked if she was enjoying herself, which Mary could always answer with enthusiastic affirmative. The handsome head waiter, Breck, flirted with her unexpectedly, skirting the very edge of too much attention to keep it easygoing rather than outrageous. Her housekeeper even apologized for the unseasonable amount of rain they were having, as if it were something they could control.

If it hadn't been for the mysterious pool cleaner who haunted her thoughts, Mary would have believed it was an absolutely perfect vacation.

After the first glimpse of him, she hadn't been able to erase him from her mind.

She couldn't quite stop herself from imagining climbing out of the pool and into the arms of the mysterious man she'd seen cleaning the pool. As she did her lazy laps, she lost herself in the idea of those strong arms wrapped around her, her mouth finding his as they slipped under the salty ripples of the water.

She continued to spot him nearly every day, always hurrying away from her with a loping stride that she wouldn't have been able to catch if she'd tried. She was beginning to think that he was avoiding her. She suspected that he felt the same pull she did, but sensed it made him uncomfortable, rather than intrigued. She still couldn't quite bring herself to believe it, but more than once she'd caught herself wondering, *Could mates be a real thing after all?*

It grieved her to think she was causing him discomfort, and she wanted to catch him, to say that she would never make him sad or unhappy, and that she was sorry she seemed to be causing him distress. She wondered if there was something she could do to help him—she could still feel the pain that crackled off of him.

She felt like one of her own students, enslaved to her own crazy adolescent hormones, and she could not stop fantasizing about him: about what it would feel like to kiss him, to slide her hands over his shoulders, to feel the weight of him on her when she lay in her wide bed.

Finally, three days into her vacation, she spotted him across the pool deck.

"Oh!" she said out loud, stopping in her tracks.

There he was, close as life, bending over a bucket of supplies by one of the lounge chairs; Mary would know his silhouette and the burst of his red hair anywhere, and she had a moment of near-terror.

She knew that he would find an excuse to leave at any moment, and it would have been easy to let him go. At any other time in her life, she would simply have lingered in the doorway a little longer and watched him escape from her again.

But she was here, being brave and courageous, in a foreign country by herself. She wasn't sure if it was the hot weather or the glamour of Shifting Sands itself, but she even felt like a more powerful shifter here; all of her senses were sharper than they'd ever been, and they were all focused entirely on *him*.

She gathered all of her resolve and walked decisively across the tiled deck, weaving around the chairs and tables on the deck without removing her eyes from him.

"I'm sorry," she said automatically, when she was finally at his side and, abruptly, the bravery that had carried her across the deck vanished. She was left feeling like a stammering fool, awkward and unappealing in her plain blue swimsuit and cheap flip-flops. She was keenly aware of the few other guests enjoying the late afternoon sunshine on the deck, including a sleek, manicured woman wearing almost nothing and the bartender who was strumming a guitar at the bar behind her.

"I'm sorry," she repeated. "I don't mean to interrupt you, it's just that... I... ah..."

He was looking at her with hazel eyes like saucers, as unable to look away as Mary was. He was more gorgeous up close than he was fleeing from her across a pool deck or down a path, built like an athlete, with wide shoulders under his resort uniform shirt and narrow hips in khaki shorts. Agile hands were clenched, white-knuckled, around the bucket handle.

All of the hurt she had sensed from him was there, intense and bone-deep.

"Oh!" she said in wonder. "You feel it too!"

Because, laid over the hurt was something else—the heat and lust and a depth of connection that Mary had never even dared to hope for.

This is our mate, her deer told her with no hesitation, pleased and excited.

Mary had always wondered if a destined mate could be real and hadn't dared to hope that her odd attraction to this stranger could be such a thing.

Meeting his eyes dissolved any doubt she might have had. She could feel a resonance between them that defied description. Magic seemed to crackle around them, and she reached out an automatic hand to touch him in wonder.

He flinched away, and the spell shattered.

His face shuttered, settling into an off-putting scowl, and he stood, towering over her. "I don't know what you're talking about," he snarled at her.

Then he turned on his heel and walked away, leaving Mary feeling utterly lost.

CHAPTER 6

Rejecting her was the hardest thing that Neal had ever done—watching her heart break into little pieces while he denied the pull of their mating bond was like being shot. He was worthless, terrible, the worst kind of jerk... and the biggest coward that had ever had the misfortune to walk the face of the earth on two legs and on four.

He sank down onto a picnic table seat, steepling his hands on the back of his head. He wanted to tear something into pieces, or burn something to the ground. His mate was hurting, and he couldn't do anything to protect her, because *he* was the one who had caused it.

What had *happened* to him?

At one point, he'd been part of one of the most elite teams in the military, a sharpshooter and explosives expert with a reputation for being fearless and unstoppable. He'd been confident with women and complicated missions alike.

Now he was reduced to doing odd jobs at a fancy tropical resort and failing even at that: fearful, prickly and unfit for any friendship, let alone the company of his own destined mate.

Why did she have to come here, of all places? Couldn't they just have been another unlucky couple who never had the grace to meet?

Something tickled at the side of his neck, a whuffle of air and short whiskers, and Neal snapped around to find that the gazelle had come closer to him than he had ever seen her, big eyes and mobile ears all focused on him. Familiar tension ran in every muscle along her neck. He saw that same tension in the mirror every day.

"There was a time you wouldn't have been able to get within a hundred yards without me noticing you," he told her dryly, letting his fists fall open with effort.

The gazelle only blinked in reply. There was a time she wouldn't have come within a hundred yards at all.

"I'm pretty awful at being a human being anymore," he continued conversationally. "Maybe I should have stayed in Beehag's zoo."

The gazelle snorted and Neal swore she actually rolled her eyes.

Even suggesting it sarcastically gave Neal chills and sweats. He could still remember the cold feeling of the bars as he pressed against them and the hot electric shocks that had been applied when he had tried to stubbornly remain in human form. He groaned and rolled his shoulders back.

"She's better off without me," he said firmly. "She doesn't need the mess that is me in her life."

Ears twitching, the gazelle dropped her nose to the hand that Neal had made into a fist again and touched it tentatively.

As far as Neal was aware, it was the first touch that she had tolerated since her release, and the honor of that penetrated his shell of self-pity.

He held his breath, not wanting to startle her away again.

"Neal."

The moment was broken by a completely unwelcome voice, and the gazelle was bounding away before he could even move to reassure her.

He was all prickles and anger and fury as he turned to face Scarlet.

The resort owner was dressed in a pressed khaki suit with a skirt to her knees and her hair, redder even than his own, was pulled in a tidy bun at the back of her head.

"You missed another staff meeting," she said, not sitting.

He stood up, not comfortable being shorter than her, but towering over her by half a foot did not seem to intimidate her in the least. She only gave him a flinty emerald gaze, her chin uplifted as she waited for his explanation.

"I'm sorry," he ground out, knowing he sounded anything but.

Unexpectedly, her face softened to pity and she gestured him to sit as she did the same, with all the confidence of a queen. Neal stubbornly remained standing, not wanting her pity.

"Neal," Scarlet said more gently. "You came to us under unusual circumstances, and you've worked hard to make yourself a place here."

Until this last week, Neal would have agreed with her. He didn't give her the satisfaction of a response.

"You've also been invaluable with the other refugees from Beehag's estate," Scarlet observed, which wasn't something that Neal had realized she knew about.

He continued to offer only the stoniest of faces.

"Most of them have been reunited with family and returned home now," Scarlet went on, unfazed by his lack of response. "And I'm not blind to the fact that you've played a large role in preparing them for that transition." She gestured across the lawn, and Neal noticed that the gazelle had not fled far. She was still standing in earshot, head upright.

"There's a limit, though." Scarlet's voice took on an edge. "To my patience, and to yours."

Neal braced himself.

"Shifting Sands is not your home," she said, like ice.

Neal almost had to sit. She was... firing him? Kicking him out? His first reaction was anger, followed by a drifting uncertainty and mournful feeling that she was right to. He buried it all behind an unwavering scowl, as deeply as he was burying his own wolf.

"You cannot make yourself whole here," she said, with all the haughtiness of a queen. "And I don't have the resources to pander to your cowardice forever."

Cowardice? No one had ever accused him of that—no one had ever dared, and Neal was not sure how to take it from the manicured woman who sat before him with her hands folded easily in her lap.

"I'm happy to remove myself," he said with automatic defensiveness, but even as he said it, he wasn't sure how he would do so. He had no money, no identity—he had undoubtedly been given up for dead by now, by his team and by his family.

A piece of paper seemed to materialize in Scarlet's hand as she outstretched it to him.

He took it, but didn't look at it, not wanting to show weakness by breaking their eye contact first.

"Those are the current contact numbers of the members of your unit," Scarlet said.

Neal had to look at the paper in shock then, nearly dropping it. How did she even know about them? He had been vague about his life before Beehag's zoo and discouraged discussion about it vehemently.

"There's also the number for your niece," Scarlet went on, as if she hadn't noticed his utter and complete shock. "I thought that might be easier than contacting your sister directly."

She stood and brushed off her skirt, looking as cool as could be in the muggy afternoon heat.

"I don't need your charity," Neal lied to her, crumpling the paper into his pocket as if he didn't care.

"Of course not," Scarlet replied. "I haven't given you any. But as a temporary member of my staff, please be reminded that I will not tolerate rudeness to my guests."

It made Neal feel prickly and angry and ashamed to think that she knew about *that*, too.

She left before he could find an appropriate rebuttal.

He was diving into his pocket before she was even out of sight, smoothing out the page and staring at the numbers as if they were ciphers to the locks in his head.

There was a landline in the staff building, but he wasn't sure he was ready to make any of the calls.

But there *was* one call he was ready to make.

CHAPTER 7

Mary stared at the magazine article until the words stopped making sense.

She couldn't even have said what it was about; every effort to read seemed to drift off into daydreaming about the red-haired pool cleaner. She couldn't stop thinking about the way his bare muscles gleaned in the tropical sun, and she kept remembering the frightful snarl as he pushed away from her.

She looked down at her skin, still pale against her utilitarian blue one-piece, and frowned at the curve of her hips and legs, resisting the impulse to pull a towel over herself. Maybe he was disappointed by her. Maybe he didn't want her for a mate. Maybe he wanted one of the taller, richer, tanned guests, in their tiny two-pieces and sparkly high heels.

Mary shook her head and put the magazine down. As familiar as the idea was, she couldn't bring herself to entirely believe it. Not after seeing into his eyes. He had wanted her as badly as she wanted him.

"You need a drink, honey?"

Settling into the deck chair beside her was a woman so enormous that Mary half-expected the chair to collapse, rolls of golden flesh barely contained by a fluttery, bright orange bikini.

"I'm sorry?"

"A drink," the woman suggested, lowering her sunglasses to peer at Mary with brilliant violet eyes. "Tex makes a margarita to die for."

"Oh, I couldn't," Mary said, flustered by the woman's intense gaze. "I don't really... I wouldn't..."

That earned her a tolerant smile. "Well, *I'm* ordering one," the woman chuckled, and she waved an imperious arm in the air towards the bar deck above them that made her chair creak in protest.

She must have caught someone's eyes, and her order must have been expected, because very shortly, Mary heard the distant whine of a blender over the waves crashing on the beach below them.

"I'm Magnolia, darling." The woman's offered hand was perfectly manicured, and her handshake was firm but gentle. Several jeweled rings decked her thick fingers.

"Mary," she answered, bemused, wondering what Magnolia took from her own handshake.

"You're in a knot about something," Magnolia suggested casually, leaning back into her chair and dropping her sunglasses back into place.

Mary had braced herself for casual conversation and was prepared to reveal the unstimulating truth that she was a math teacher from the Midwest and then talk about the lovely weather.

Magnolia's observation caught her by surprise and tears pricked at her eyes. She ducked her head and hoped that her hat's wide brim would keep her face from Magnolia's view as she muttered, "It's nothing..."

She was not so lucky. When Magnolia's chair groaned like a dying hyena, Mary looked up in alarm to find that the other woman had swung her legs around and was sitting up with both hands offered this time.

Mary mirrored her, letting Magnolia enfold her pale fingers in her larger ones. “Do you believe in destined mates?” she asked hesitantly, not daring to look up.

“Yes,” Magnolia said without any hesitation of her own. There was a richness to the single word, a depth of understanding that Mary hadn't realized she was hoping for.

“What if he... doesn't want me?”

Magnolia's laughter made Mary lift her head.

“It doesn't work like that, sweetie.” Magnolia said it very gently, as if to a small child. “You know that, don't you?”

“I don't understand, then,” Mary said, with all the frustration that had been building in her. “Why does he keep running away?”

“Finding your mate doesn’t always mean your fairy tale happy ending is at hand. Sometimes you need a little patience.”

Mary thought there was a note of sadness in her voice, and maybe a hint of dry amusement.

“His name is Neal,” Magnolia told her, and it took Mary's breath away to hear it.

It was such an odd sensation, almost like she recognized the name, but not quite.

A server appeared beside them, and Mary looked up to find that she was holding a tray with two margaritas.

“Oh goodness,” Magnolia said, releasing Mary's hand and taking one of the glasses. “I can't drink two of these.”

Mary suspected that Magnolia would have been able to down a dozen of them without effect, but she took the other anyway, unexpectedly eager for it.

“Tell me more,” she begged, once the server was gone again.

“Only Neal can tell you the whole story," Magnolia said, settling back into her chair again. “But I'll tell you what I know.”

CHAPTER 8

Neal pulled at the collar of the shirt.

It was a far cry from the well-tailored dress uniform he had attended military functions in, but it was more appropriate than the resort polo shirt and khaki shorts he usually wore. Travis, the resort handyman, had done an admirable job of fitting one of the waitstaff uniforms to him, as long as you didn't look too closely at the mismatched fabric under the arms.

"Don't pluck at it," Travis scolded, swatting at Neal's hands and adjusting the collar of the coat himself.

"Are you sure you aren't going to need backup, to see that you don't chicken out?" Breck added.

Neal bit back the automatic offense at the insult. Breck meant well and was only trying to be helpful. It wasn't like Neal didn't deserve a little ribbing for being a coward.

Tex strummed some dire chords on his guitar, sprawled across Neal's bed. "Do you want some musical backup?" he offered. "Women love to be serenaded."

Breck scoffed. "Sure, put her in the mood with a ditty about getting hit by a pickup and shooting a dog."

"I know some love songs," Tex chuckled, but the tune he played was anything but.

"Sad love songs don't count," Bastian said, shaking his head.

"You kidding?" Travis mocked. "Have you ever watched a chick flick? Girls love to cry."

Neal was not sure when this whole thing had turned into such a public affair, but his room in the staff housing was stuffed with supposedly helpful staff. Bastian was draped across his desk chair, and Travis was grinning at him from the footlocker.

"She's a deer, remember, so avoid predator jokes," Bastian suggested helpfully. Breck had risked his job and his skin by snooping into Scarlet's office for Mary's information and cottage number, to Neal's chagrin and gratitude when he found out.

"You should probably avoid *any* jokes," Tex added dryly. "You're not very good at them."

A determined knock at the door stilled the merriment of the room, and Breck opened it.

"Why, Graham," he said in mischievous delight. "I've been waiting for this day since I laid eyes on your gorgeous face!"

Graham scowled back and shoved past him to put the armload of flowers he was holding into Neal's hands.

The staff voiced their appreciation of the gesture with whistles of awe and murmurs of surprise; Graham was notoriously stingy about cutting his precious blooms. The staff liked to tell a story about him nearly coming to blows with Chef over using cut flowers in the dining hall without his blessing.

Neal took the bouquet with the same gravity that Graham had offered it. "Thanks, man," he said gruffly. He said it generally to the room and didn't wait to see their reactions, but simply marched out the door decisively, because he knew that if he lingered much longer, he would do exactly as Breck had suggested and completely chicken out.

The march across the resort grounds was as difficult as any mission behind enemy lines that Neal had undertaken, and he was sweating by the time he reached Mary's cottage, despite the cool evening drizzle and the downhill path. He was grateful for the shroud of darkness, but he paused when he reached her door, suddenly not sure if he should knock. Possibly it was too late for his visit. Maybe this was something better saved for daylight and safer times.

For a long moment, he hesitated. But then, gritting his teeth, he realized that this was something he *had* to do.

Making his hand land on the door was harder than any shot he'd ever taken and sounded just as loud to his ears.

A second knock was not going to happen, but fortunately, the door sprang open as if he had been expected, and he was frozen as Mary looked up at him, standing in a pale nightgown in the doorway, every curve a promise of forever.

"You came," she breathed, and Neal dropped the bouquet to catch her as she hurled herself into his arms.

CHAPTER 9

Mary's sense of where Neal was had never been terribly specific—she often found herself at a staff gate with the general idea that he was 'that way,' but she couldn't break the sanctity of a staff-only sign, too aware of how precious the privacy of her own teacher's lounge was.

So when she had a sudden awareness of his proximity, lying on her bed with a magazine, waiting for elusive sleep, it was a shock.

I should be wearing something sexier, she thought with chagrin. Her nightgown was old-fashioned and modest, something more appropriate for sleepovers with a girlfriend than a midnight tryst with her reluctant mate.

She was off her bed and halfway to the dresser to inspect her boring lingerie for anything less prudish than 'strictly utilitarian' when the knock came, and she couldn't keep herself from bounding across the room to fling open the door.

She ought to use a subtle touch, she reminded herself. If she was too forward, he might flee again; she needed to be the perfect combination of reserved and gentle.

But when she saw him, with that shock of short hair bleached of its red in the pale porch light, that handsome face a mix of longing and regret, all she could say do was squeak, "You came!" and throw herself at him.

Not your most restrained moment, she told herself.

He had no choice but to catch her, but instead of setting her sensibly on her feet, as Mary was expecting, he wrapped his arms around her tightly and pressed his mouth to hers.

Mary had never been kissed like Neal kissed her. She hadn't known a kiss like that was possible. It was deep and involved the entire mouth, and she was keenly aware of being pulled against him. The pressure of his body against hers was irresistible, sending her into a tailspin of desire and lust.

She had her arms around his neck, pulling herself deeper into the kiss, craving the closeness of his body and the honeyed salt of his mouth. She'd read of kisses described as electric, but she'd always thought it was a foolish expression—until now, with Neal sending shocks of pleasure to her toes and her fingertips. Her entire body was more alive than she had ever imagined it could be.

Her earlier fears were laughable now, her doubts that he may not desire her swept away in the way that he held her, cradling her at the small of her back and the base of her neck; the way he kissed her; and the most undeniable expression of lust that was pressing against her through his pants.

She was dizzy and lightheaded when he finally released her lips, and she gave a sigh of loss even as she gasped for breath.

"Can you forgive me?" he asked her, voice gruff and low.

Mary blinked at him. The kiss left her feeling confused and filled with head-spinning need. Did he want forgiveness for stopping the kiss? "Forgive you for what?"

His laugh was hesitant, like he didn't do it often. "I've been avoiding you. I told you I didn't know what you meant when you finally talked to me. I was a jerk. I was..."

Mary stopped him with a finger on his mouth. It was strange to feel his lips with her fingers. "I forgive you," she said simply.

"I should explain," he said reluctantly, and Mary could have drowned in the sorrow in those eyes.

"You don't have to," she said gently.

Neal stared back. Mary could feel the hesitation in his hands and the muscles of his body.

"I want to help you," she explained. "I want to know what happened to you. But you don't have to tell me until you're really ready. I know who *you* are. I know what you are to *me*."

He gave a great sigh of his own. His gaze softened, and Mary could feel some of his tension ease.

Not the important tension, though, and when he bent to kiss her again, she pressed herself against him like a cat in heat, unable to resist the demands of her own body.

He kissed her again, as her lips had been longing for, no less urgently than the first time, and she fumbled at his jacket buttons, desperate to put her hands against his skin.

They had to break the kiss to shimmy out of clothing, and Mary regretted her simple nightgown not because it wasn't sexy enough—slipping it off was a whisper of sensuality that she'd never expected—but because there weren't enough layers to it. She hadn't anticipated how much fun it would be to undress another person, or how exciting it was to peel through clothing to find the skin beneath.

Once her nightdress was off, Mary paused, and Neal stared for a long, mesmerized moment, holding the thin cotton garment in his big hands. The night air chilled goosebumps onto her flesh despite feeling flushed and hot. Neal gave a groan before tossing the gown to the floor and crushing her back to him for another of their long, deep kisses.

"It's not fair!" she laughed at him when her mouth was free. "I have so much clothing still to get through."

Neal was as impatient with it as she was, and the task was hastened: tie, shirt, and undershirt thrown aside with zeal. His scuffed shoes were wrenched off without untying and the pants were shimmied off to the floor until they both stood in only underwear.

Mary could not keep herself from staring. His briefs did nothing to hide his impressive desire for her, and she wondered if her inescapable dampness showed on her simple cotton underthings.

They were at the door of her bedroom now, and the sounds of

the room were the unending insects of the tropical night, the tapping of rain on the roof, and their own breath, ragged and eager.

"Do come in," Mary said at last, feeling suddenly shy.

CHAPTER 10

Neal felt as if he'd won some kind of lottery, and he mistrusted his luck, even while Mary's earthy, curvy beauty stunned him into silence.

The roundness of her hips, the softness of her shoulders—it wasn't just his maned wolf that Neal had to wrestle down. Everything about her brought out animal lust and desire in him. He had to struggle to keep his urgency in check, fearful of hurting her, of losing control and not treating her with the care and reverence she deserved.

When she invited him into the sanctity of her bedroom, he went willingly and instead of wrestling her down onto the bed the way he wanted to, he sat, and drew her into his lap.

There was no hiding his lust for her, no tempering the physical part of his need, but Neal forced his hands to be slow, and his kisses to her neck were whispers, not the bites he was so tempted to make. He teased around her breasts, lifting them, stroking them, defining their shape and softness, then finally brushing a finger across her nipples and delighting in the deep groan of need she gave.

She squirmed in his lap, driving him mad with the touch against his cock, and he feared he would embarrass himself before they even got out of their underwear.

He didn't realize that he'd frozen, trying to fight down the need that was rising to a fever pitch, until Mary pushed him back on the bed and slipped out of her underwear.

He stayed still while she wrestled him out of his own, lifting his hips to help her.

They both gave a gasp when his erection sprang free, Neal from the sensation of it, Mary in delight, as far as Neal could tell.

Then she was straddling him, drawing down on him, and Neal had to worship her swinging breasts and sweet flesh. She was slick with moisture, and beautifully, impossibly tight around him, each cautious stroke she made bringing him deeper into her eager folds.

Neal let her ride him, drowning in the incredible sensation of her skin and the honeyed smell of her, until he could bear it no longer. He reached up and rolled her over, never decoupling.

Sprawled beneath him, Mary's eyes were soft and glowing in the dim light of her bedside lamp. Her blonde hair tangled over the crisp white pillow like waves, and Neal had to reach out with one hand and trace the shape of her face, already so unexpectedly dear to him.

"I never thought I'd find you," she said softly, and even her voice was intoxicating.

"I never… " Neal couldn't find the words, too overwhelmed by smell and sight and sensation.

He wasn't sure if he had ever stopped moving, but now he was thrusting again, slowly, deliberately. Every movement was carefully controlled. He was painfully afraid of losing control, of losing *her*, and he wasn't prepared for her writhing moan of pleasure as she crested toward orgasm.

"Don't stop," she begged, and Neal could not have if he tried.

Her blissful sound of climax drove Neal out of his mind, and he only became aware again of himself as someone separate from Mary when the urgency merged into release and faded at last into gasping, grasping satisfaction.

His first thought, when he could think again, was for Mary. Had he hurt her?

Her brilliant smile suggested otherwise, and her laughing hands stroked his shoulders in a fashion that Neal wouldn't have expected to be so soothing.

"That was amazing…"

"I'm sorry… I didn't hurt you?" Neal had to know for sure.

"Hurt me?" Mary sounded amazed by the idea. "Are you kidding? Oh, Neal!"

She reached eager arms to wrap around him and kissed him soundly.

The way she said his name was all the reassurance Neal needed, and the way she kissed him made him wonder if she would be interested in a repeat performance. His basic need for her had been slaked, but the touch of her lips on his made him realize that he would be happy for another round.

He let her draw him down for an embrace and buried his face at her neck, breathing in the scent of her hair and her velvety skin.

I'm sorry, he wanted to say. *I'm sorry I'm not the mate you deserve, or the man I ought to be.*

But he could only hold her, and be grateful for her arms around him, and live in the moment for now.

CHAPTER 11

Mary was not particularly surprised to wake alone.

The bed was rumpled and the room smelled like sex and surrender.

Mary sighed and sat up.

Morning light was streaming through the big glass doors. Mary could see down to the hypnotic ocean over the tile roofs of the cottages in front of her and hear the rumbling call of it over the morning birds and the ceaseless chirping insects. She slid one of the doors open and was rewarded by a rush of humid air.

It had rained overnight, and the world was covered in jewels of water. It was already warming up, and Mary knew from the past few days that the sun would quickly burn off the lingering fog and evaporate the moisture. By mid-morning, it would be sweltering and blue again, and mid-afternoon there might be more warm showers.

There was a tiny lizard on the railing of the deck, and Mary eyed it skeptically. The first day at the resort, a lizard so close would have sent her scurrying back inside, but she was too wrapped up in thinking of Neal to mind it.

Mary continued to think, vacillating between frustration and warm, lustful memories, as she dressed and showered. She walked in a daze out of her cottage, only to turn in the wrong direction on the path and walk directly into a glittering spiderweb.

The sticky brush of it on her skin, the tickling of it in her hair and on her bare arms was bad enough, but out of the corner of her eye, Mary could see the giant orb of the viciously striped creature, bobbing on its tangled home. Bobbing *towards* her, hairy legs waving aggressively.

Mary screamed, skin crawling and adrenaline spiking, flailing her arms. The web was stickier and stronger than she expected, and the spider moved so quickly that she panicked, screaming again and leaping away.

A figure blocked her path, so looming and terrifying in its silence and menace that Mary barely recognized it as the landscaper before she was shifting out of instinct.

"Mary!"

It was Neal's voice, and it was the only thing that kept her from flinging herself in deer form in a panic through the brush—where there were undoubtedly more spiderwebs waiting to ensnare her.

She stopped in her tracks, quivering.

The landscaper growled at her and then went past. He went from frightful to horrifying as he scooped up the spider from its ruined web, right into his bare hands. "She wouldn't hurt you," he said accusingly, clearly more concerned with the spider than the deer.

Then Neal was there, sprinting over and snarling ferociously, hands balled into fists as he tried to figure out what was threatening Mary.

The surly gardener was the obvious choice and Neal did not hesitate to come roaring to Mary's rescue.

Wait! she tried to call to him through their bond, but he either didn't hear or was too deep in protective rage to notice, lunging for the man holding the spider.

Given his animal growl, Mary expected Neal to shift and was surprised when he didn't.

The gardener dodged with more speed than either she or Neal

anticipated and continued to cup the spider protectively in one hand while deflecting Neal's attack with the other.

Neal cornered with the kind of strength and reflexes that could only come from intense training and shifter advantages, snarling and striking at the other man while Mary wailed *Stop!* and Neal didn't seem to hear her.

The landscaper fought only defensively and was hampered by carefully holding his arachnid friend, but still managed to block most of Neal's rain of blows, absorbing the rest with an impressive show of imperviousness. Mary had never seen such combat outside of movies and was stunned by the ferocity and might of Neal's attack.

Finally, she managed to get enough of a hold on herself to shift back to her human form, and she ran forward, knowing she had to try to stop this. "Neal, no! He didn't do anything, it's okay! It wasn't him!"

The look he leveled at her was feral and full of panic but faded abruptly at her words, and he pulled the blow he was landing, letting the momentum of it pull him forwards into a slumping crouch. Mary went to him at once, putting her hands on his shoulders without hesitation. He flinched, then looked up in chagrin. "I'm sorry, Graham."

The gardener wiped away a trail of blood from his mouth and shrugged, looking genuinely unconcerned as he turned to deposit the spider gently onto a branch.

"It was just a spider," Mary explained soothingly. "I walked into a spiderweb and it scared me. That's all that happened. I guess… it was a shifter spider?" She looked at Graham for some confirmation, but he only scowled at her and then walked past them, not offering an explanation before he vanished down the path.

Neal's shoulder shook beneath her hand and Mary realized after a moment that it was a weak laugh. "No," Neal said wryly. "I'm sure it was just a regular spider."

CHAPTER 12

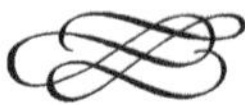

Neal knew he was a fool.

Graham may not hold the attack against him, but he'd humiliated himself in front of Mary and proved his unworthiness beyond a shadow of a doubt. He hadn't stopped to think when he saw the deer with Mary's clothing loose on its form. The flash of her fear had been driving his steps and, between his wolf snarling for freedom inside of him and the rush of adrenaline at the thought of his mate in danger, he'd made a snap attack, not pausing or assessing. It was the worst kind of behavior in a soldier—a terrible slip of control.

No one who was whole, who was thinking clearly, would have reacted so poorly. Surely Mary must know how broken he was now.

"I'm sorry."

Mary's hands on his shoulders felt like weights of guilt, like judgment, and Neal was surprised when she knelt in the damp grass beside him, one arm still draped around him.

The press of her body at his side was distracting. The buttons of her blouse had popped off when she shifted and it hung loosely now, open in the front to show glimpses of her luscious breasts as she moved.

"You seem to apologize to me a lot," she observed without judgment.

"I'm broken," he said. The simple words came out without effort, and he was astonished by how much better he felt for having said them.

Mary didn't try to deny his words, and Neal was grateful for that. "Broken things are worth fixing," she said gently. "*You're* worth fixing. You don't have to be sorry, you just… have to let me in."

Neal lifted his eyes from the mesmerizing curves under her open blouse and looked into her face.

She looked back without wavering, which was something Neal couldn't do with his own reflection, and the compassion and emotion in her eyes undid something old and rusty in his chest.

"I don't know how to do that," he confessed. He could be nothing but truthful with her.

"Just trust me," Mary told him simply, as if trusting her was just that easy.

And unexpectedly, it was.

Morning flowed into noon as he told her everything—everything that had happened to him, and its consequences. It streamed from him in a rush of words that he couldn't stop and didn't try.

He told her everything backwards, from the escape of Beehag's prison to the terrible ten years of his stay there. The dart at his throat, and the journey to the Costa Rican island where he was caged and tormented into remaining in wolf form. He recounted the day he was in Columbia, on the first day of their mission to stop the turncoat Marine who was using school children to shelter his drug business. He even told her about Afghanistan, from years earlier, and the nightmares he had suffered ever since, and they laughed together about playing kick the can in the cul-de-sac, growing up in different small towns.

Mary added her own observations occasionally, but mostly she listened. Not once did she act shocked or judgmental about his revelations to her. She just absorbed everything he told her with solemn attention.

Neal's voice was raw and hoarse by the time he came to what he felt was the end of his narration, or the beginning. The sun, dappled through the plumeria tree above him, had burned off the clouds and dried the lawn. Downhill from them, the gazelle was grazing. She was in earshot, he thought, with those big dish-like ears, but strangely, the idea didn't bother him.

He sat with Mary in silence for a long moment. It felt comfortable and natural, as nothing had felt in a very long time. He'd gotten used to feeling tightly coiled and filled with anger, and he felt strangely empty now. Empty—and yet filled at the same time, because of the woman who sat beside him.

"You helped all the other shifters go home, after you were freed from the prison?" she finally asked.

"Almost all of them," Neal agreed, looking out over the green carpet to where the gazelle was pretending to ignore them.

"But not yourself."

Neal was silent, familiar tension rising in his throat.

"Does your old unit know what happened to you?'

"No."

Mary squeezed his arm. "They must think you went AWOL?"

"By now, they'd think I was dead," Neal guessed.

"You must be pretty angry about that."

Neal opened his mouth to deny it, then snapped it shut. He'd spent so much time trying not to think about it that he hadn't recognized how furious it all made him, or how much that frustration was leaking into all the other parts of his life.

Mary, with a thoughtful look that suggested she saw his revelation, went on. "I imagine you're pretty pissed that you never got revenge."

"Beehag died," Neal said shortly.

"His heart gave out over the antidote to a sedative. I don't imagine there was any satisfaction in that."

Neal realized his hands were balled in fists. He sighed and uncoiled them.

"Are you a therapist?" he asked, not entirely teasing. Some of the staff had tentatively suggested he talk to one, but they had stopped dropping hints after he reacted poorly.

"I'm a math teacher," Mary said with amusement. "At a middle school."

Neal saluted. "I should have known you worked in a combat zone."

"Because of the way I screamed about a spiderweb in my hair?" Mary's sideways look was rich with humor and self-deprecation.

Neal might have let her brush it off with humor, but their talk had left him raw and observant. She was genuinely embarrassed about her fear and felt bad for her reaction.

"I was the only deer shifter in a family of big cats, a throwback to a great-grandmother who was a deer," she explained shyly. "I guess I got used to being protected, and everyone … just expected me to be afraid of things. I think it's just a habit, now."

"It's okay to be afraid," he said roughly and, unexpectedly, it was true for more than just her.

Into the silence that fell after that, Mary's stomach rumbled audibly and she giggled. Neal let out a rusty guffaw with her, startling himself, and said, "It must be after lunch. Damn, I was supposed to help Travis with some cement work…"

They unwound themselves from each other and stood.

"You have to take care of yourself first," Mary said.

"Why do I get the feeling that's advice you don't always take?" Neal asked suspiciously.

He knew he was right by Mary's blush.

"I'll meet you later?" she deflected.

"I'll be working until late," Neal said apologetically.

"Then I'll meet you late."

"By the pool? I'll be closing the bar."

Mary nodded. "I'll be there."

An awkward moment of silence followed. Neal felt as if all the words had been dredged out of him and he had none left to offer.

"Later, then," Mary said shyly, and she moved to leave.

Neal couldn't let her leave like that and caught her after only a few steps for a passionate kiss. The blouse that had been barely staying together slipped off one shoulder at last. Her mouth was hungry under his, salty and tantalizing. Neal kissed her mouth and down her neck to that deliciously tempting bare shoulder, then went back to her lips for one final kiss before setting her back from him firmly.

"Later, then," he agreed, and he walked away with a rare smile at his mouth.

That was a proper goodbye.

CHAPTER 13

Mary got to the bar just before last call.

There were only a few guests left—a determinedly drunk elderly man with a thick Russian accent, and a cold blonde in high heels and little else. They both took Neal's last call as gospel and grumbled back to their cottages after downing unusual choices (he had something with an umbrella, and she had a vodka, straight). Spanish music played quietly from a tinny stereo behind the bar.

Mary took a shy seat at the counter.

"I just have to wash up a few glasses and wipe down the tables," Neal said.

"It's no problem," Mary said. It occurred to her that for the first time, his explanation had sounded more like a statement than an apology. She smiled, and the memory of his goodbye kiss made her squirm on her stool.

It was certainly no hardship watching him clear up. He scrubbed the tables with more vigor than skill, and the resort issue khaki shorts and polo shirt did nothing to hide the incredible physique beneath. Mary caught herself staring at his ass as he bent over to scrub a stubborn spot and had to look away before he turned back, blushing like a schoolgirl.

He toweled off the last clean glasses and put them away before he turned off the radio and flipped off the bar lights, plunging them into relative darkness.

Mary gave a little squeak of fear. "It's dark," she said, as he came around the bar to her. In the darkness, he was a little frightening, big and looming and featureless.

"I'll protect you," he offered, and his voice reassured her.

"I'd like that," Mary breathed.

Then he was gathering her into his arms for a kiss in greeting, and it was every bit as breathtaking as his goodbye kiss had been.

"It's starting to rain," she said, when she could again. Her eyes were starting to adjust to the darkness.

"Are you made of sugar?" Neal teased her.

Mary laughed. "No, but I am a little cold!"

"The pool is warm," Neal suggested.

"I didn't wear my swimsuit!" Mary protested.

"The resort *is* clothing optional," Neal pointed out. "Besides, I'm sure your underwear is less revealing than most of the bikinis I've seen here."

Mary sputtered. "Oh, I couldn't… it's… I could never…"

"Never say never," Neal persuaded.

Mary found herself drawn to the steps into the pool, flanked by the waterfalls. Running water and insects were the only sound outside of her own heartbeat that she could hear; the resort was otherwise quiet and anyone sensible was tucked into their beds, safe from the drizzling rain.

She let Neal pull off her shirt, enjoying the sharp intake he gave at the sight of her lacy bra, holding her breasts snugly. She shimmied out of her own shorts while Neal shed his own clothing down to briefs that did nothing to hide the impressive bulge of his cock.

"Sure you want me to stop?" he asked, putting a finger into his waistband teasingly.

Mary was quite sure she didn't, but she wasn't ready to admit that. "This is a terrible idea," she said, giggling like a misbehaving child. They crept down the grand steps to the water, and Neal pulled her down into the pool before she could balk.

Compared to the chilly night air and cool rain, the pool was warm and welcoming, and it glowed with blue orbs of lights underneath the surface. The effect as a whole was eerie and alien, and Mary felt deliciously not herself. Neal's hand was firm in her own and, when he tugged her closer, she glided to him willingly.

Her legs tangled around him and she pulled him close to kiss, unwittingly nearly dragging them under as they forgot about treading water in the passion of the moment.

They swam together for the edge of the pool near the waterfall where it grew shallower. Neal hooked an elbow on the ledge there and drew her close. They were protected from the view of anyone who might chance by on the bar deck, as slim a possibility as that was at this hour.

The sensation of the water all around her, her legs entwined with his, and the delicious pressure of his member against her nether areas was intoxicating. When Neal added his mouth, Mary found herself writhing in need.

"Don't stop," she begged him, when he pulled away, but then he touched her thighs with his hand, stroking at the edge of her lace panties and she could only whimper in pleasure.

She clung to his shoulders, panting and clawing at him as he used his talented hand to explore her through the wet fabric. When he finally slipped a questing finger under the elastic and into her folds, she gasped and cried out in release.

"If we weren't in the pool, you'd be able to tell how wet I am for you," she said near his ear when she could breathe again.

"Can you tell how hard I am for you?" he answered, and Mary found his proof with her own hand. He wasn't bulging now as much as he was straining against the soaked undergarment, his erect cock pulling the elastic away from his legs. There was little resistance from the underwear when Mary pushed it aside, the better to touch the firm, velvety flesh.

Floating in water was significantly different than tussling on the bed, and it meant a great deal more accidental touching as they struggled to keep their heads out of the water and their bodies in contact. Every touch was electric and new, caressed by the flow of water around them.

When Neal pulled aside her underwear and slipped into her, it was like being lit on fire. Even the friction of his member inside of her was new for being underwater, and the grip his hands felt fluid and different.

With touches and thrusts, he brought her to the crest of pleasure, not once, but twice, then pulled away, gasping, "Too hard…"

"Just hard enough," Mary laughed back at him, but she followed willingly to the far edge of the pool, and they tumbled out of the water onto the edge of the pool, where they kissed and touched and slipped on the wet tile. The rain had faded to nearly nothing.

Neal tugged her up onto one of the padded lounge chairs, and Mary shimmied out of her underwear to welcome him, not sure where his briefs had disappeared to in the darkness, but glad they were gone. He slid fingers under her wet bra strap, and she gleefully unclipped it to let her breasts swing freely.

He worshipped them with his hands, cupping them and running thumbs over the erect nipples, and Mary felt her yearning reach another fever pitch.

He entered her in a rush, and Mary rose to greet him, moaning softly in satisfaction. Having him close, having him inside her, seemed to fulfill her in a way she'd never known she was missing.

Clever fingers and the perfect rhythm of thrusts brought her to peaks of pleasure again, and this time, Neal joined her at that crest of orgasm, and finally sank down to embrace her tenderly as their breath returned to normal.

CHAPTER 14

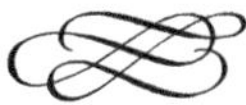

When the chill in the night air finally drove them off the damp lounge, Neal discovered that his briefs had been left behind in the pool and were floating just beyond the reach of the pool net.

After grumbling, Neal finally slipped back into the water and swam to retrieve them. Mary greeted him with a thick towel at the edge of the pool.

They walked the steps back up to the bar deck where they had shed their clothing and pulled them on. Neal couldn't help but stare while Mary dressed; all of her curves in the dim light were enchanting and mesmerizing while she struggled to get tight clothing over damp limbs.

He walked her to her cottage, hand-in-hand, running the last few steps as the rain started up again.

"Stay with me?" she asked softly as they stood in the doorway, almost begging.

Neal almost broke at the gentleness of her voice, feeling his heart aching inside him. He took her face in his hands for a gentle goodbye kiss.

"I… don't sleep restfully," he said regretfully.

"So I'll sleep in after you leave in the morning," Mary cajoled. "It's a big bed…"

Neal cut her off with a second kiss and a shake of his head. "Soon," he suggested, and he didn't want to think about how true that had to be given the little time they had left.

She didn't try again to persuade him, only gave him a curvy embrace and reluctantly let him go.

He left her sighing in the open door, lit from behind as he went back out into the dark, back to his own bunk to catch a few hours of sleep before waking to do the morning chores.

As promised, it was not restful sleep. He lay awake for far too long, thinking about how short his remaining time with Mary at the resort was. Her stay was only a few days more, and he…

While he couldn't imagine staying after she left, he also couldn't imagine fitting into her life. She was a math teacher. He was a broken soldier. She suited a quiet, domestic life. He wasn't fit for anything.

Close to dawn, he finally dozed off, and the afternoon's confessions dredged up terrible memories to work into nightmares of horror and guilt. He woke in a sweaty tangle of blankets, his pillow already ejected to the other side of the room.

He took a utilitarian shower in the tiny hotel bathroom, and when he went to pull on his clothing, he found the paper that Scarlet had given him in his pocket.

It was already worn; he must have taken it out and refolded it a dozen times over the past several days. Some of the pencil had rubbed off, but Neal had already committed the numbers to memory.

He could hear some of the other staff rising and heading off to work as he made his way to the empty common room. He could smell the breakfast that Chef must have been working on for several hours already.

The rain had let up, but it was still cool, and a thick mist lay over the resort. Neal tried to absorb some of the peacefulness from it as he lifted the receiver. While it rang through the international lines, Neal stared at the black TV screen across the room. Travis and Bastian had tried playing a shooter game with him a few weeks back, but his hands had shaken too much to aim at the animated bad guys. It was a far cry from his steady-handed sniper days.

When his unit commander, Judy Washburn, answered, her voice was a jarring reminder of his long-ago life.

For a moment, he could only consider that she probably wasn't still a major, and it seemed terribly important that he didn't know what rank she had now. He stabbed the button to hang up without speaking and buried his face in his hands.

He wasn't ready for this yet.

Mary would tell him he didn't have to be, he thought, and just the idea of her brought him back into balance. He could almost hear her voice in his ear, reminding him to take whatever time he needed. He didn't have to heal in a day.

He almost dialed again, but was interrupted by Travis, who walked briskly into the room and said, "Oh, good timing. I'll be needing your help at Cottage twelve this morning to get the new interior walls raised."

Travis said nothing about the phone that Neal still held in his hands, and Neal didn't volunteer anything.

"I'll be right there," Neal said, hanging up the receiver and standing.

"Neal."

They both turned to find Scarlet in the doorway. She looked out of place in the shabby room, with the pearls at her throat and her starched linen skirt.

Neal stood at attention out of instinct and caught Travis doing the same out of a corner of his eye, though he didn't think that Travis had any military background.

"I'll need you out of the resort this afternoon." While Neal was still trying to process the speed of his ejection, Scarlet continued, "Go with Bastian on a mainland boat trip, or head out to clear the waterfall trail, I don't care, but don't come back until late tonight or even tomorrow."

Neal furrowed his eyebrows. If he wasn't being thrown out…

"I've got an investor coming here with Beehag's heir, Benedict, and I don't want any… *incidents.*"

"I don't know what you think I would…"

Scarlet raised a silencing hand. "This is not a topic that is open for discussion."

Neal remembered Mary's quiet assessment that he'd never gotten revenge and surprised them all with a grim smile. "Yes, Ma'am."

Scarlet nodded and swept out as abruptly as she'd come.

"We'd better get to work while we can then," Travis said, looking bemused.

"Right you are," Neal said cheerfully.

CHAPTER 15

Mary couldn't swim her laps without blushing and remembering the night before in vivid detail, so it wasn't long before she was crawling out of the water and toweling off more vigorously than usual. Neal had been nowhere to be found since breakfast, but the head waiter had winked at her and said, "He'll find you for lunch."

Scarlet-cheeked, Mary slipped her sundress on over her damp suit and went to the bar for a cold water.

Tex was behind the bar, strumming melancholy chords on his guitar along with the radio, but he put it down as she approached.

"What can I get you, darlin'?" he drawled.

"Just ice water, please," Mary said, putting the towel carefully over the barstool before she sat.

"Coming right up." Tex reached up to get the glass and filled it with a swift scoop of glittering ice from the ice bin.

Mary wondered how much he knew, or if anyone had caught sight—or sound—of their pool activities the night before.

"We're all happy to see Neal smiling again," Tex said warmly as he put the sweating glass down in front of her.

Mary's cheeks felt even hotter. "I, uh. Yes, me too. I mean, it's a great smile."

"I wouldn't flirt with that bartender." Neal's voice surprised her from behind, and Mary swiveled on her stool to find him standing at the back entrance, shirtless and dirty and sweaty.

It was a heady combination, and Mary wondered exactly how red her face could become.

She gulped down some of her cold water as Tex protested, "Come on, now. Why shouldn't she flirt with me?"

"You're unlucky in love," Neal reminded him.

"It's a tragic truth," Tex agreed mournfully. "You're better off with this one," he said to Mary.

"I think so, too," Mary squeaked.

Neal's shirtless proximity was terribly distracting.

"I thought we might take the boat out snorkeling this afternoon," Neal told her, accepting his own glass of water from Tex and downing it in a few determined gulps.

Mary felt the color finally drain from her face. "Oh no," she protested. "I don't… not in the *ocean*. I couldn't."

Neal shrugged. "We could head over to the mainland with Travis, then. Do some shopping, or take the horseback shore tour."

"Horseback?" Mary shivered. "I can't ride. They're so big, and no. No. I can't. I don't need to go shopping. No. Boats, no. Can't."

Tex and Neal blinked at her.

"I'm afraid of boats," she confessed sheepishly, feeling their surprised scrutiny.

Tex found some glasses to wipe, politely looking away.

"It's perfectly safe," Neal suggested, looking baffled at her terror, but her look must have expressed her distrust adequately. He counter-offered, "How about a hike, then? There's an easy loop that goes up by a really gorgeous waterfall. It's about five miles, no boats. We'll take a picnic lunch."

Mary wanted to balk. There were bugs, and snakes, and scorpions out there in the wild jungle, and she'd already had closer relations with a spider than she ever wanted to again. But she didn't want Neal to think she was a complete ninny, either.

"That sounds nice," she said weakly.

"I'll grab a shower and get us a bagged lunch," Neal said briskly.

"I'll change clothes and pack a few things," Mary offered with a brave smile. How bad could it be?

'A few things' proved to be her entire purse stuffed full, and Mary was glad she had opted for the kind that swung over a shoulder; bottles of water were heavy and she wasn't planning to go out without sunscreen and bug spray, or the pocket first aid kit. Spare socks and her raincoat made the bag bulky and awkward. When Neal caught sight of her, his expression said more than he needed to.

He was carrying a single water bottle in one of the cargo pockets of his shorts and, aside from the wicked-looking machete that hung from his belt and the promised lunch, appeared to have nothing else extra on him.

Mary had changed into long, lightweight travel pants and sneakers. She wished she'd brought heavier shoes, especially once they had hiked out the first mile.

Neal's idea of an easy walk was clearly not her own, even though they stopped several times for Neal to hack back the encroaching jungle vines.

Mary was sweating and itchy and hating the smell of the bug spray she had saturated herself with by the time they stopped for lunch. She picked a rock to sit on that at least gave her a view of any insects that might try to sneak up on her and could barely eat the lunch that Neal had packed for keeping an eye on the beetles and ants that were crawling around on the jungle floor. The dappled light through the jungle canopy made everything look as if it were always moving, and Mary spent the meal trying not to twitch at every rustle and skittering leaf.

"I'm sorry," Neal told her, as they were finally packing up the dirty wrappers. The crumbs were swarmed by ants in a terrifying show of swift insect utility.

"There you go apologizing again," Mary said with a weak attempt at a laugh.

"You're not having fun."

"I'm not an outdoors person," Mary confessed. "I'm sorry."

Neal looked conflicted. "We could go back, but I'm supposed to stay away from the resort until Beehag's heir is off the property tonight."

Mary forgot the bugs momentarily, staring at him in shock. She recalled their conversation from earlier, when she'd pointed out he'd never had his revenge for what Beehag had done to him. "Oh. I can see why Scarlet might not want you around for that."

Then it occurred to her. "We'll be out here until *tonight*? After *dark*?" She hadn't brought a flashlight and the idea of these big, looming trees after dark, and all the *things* that would be hiding among them, was enough to bring her to hysterics.

"I plan to be back right about sunset," Neal said soothingly.

"Oh," Mary hiccuped. "Okay."

She lifted her chin. "I can do that."

It didn't sound as bold as she would have liked it to, but Neal smiled at her in a way that melted her knees, and she felt able to sling her bag across her body and start hiking again.

CHAPTER 16

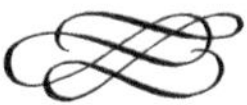

Neal watched Mary trudge courageously in front of him, distracted by the sway of her hips and the glimpses he got of the curve of her ass. He wished she had brought less with her, mostly because the bulky bag covered his view.

He wanted to praise her bravery, for continuing to hike out in a wilderness she was clearly terrified of, but he was fairly sure she wouldn't believe him, and he didn't want it to sound like empty flattery.

Shortly after their lunch, it began to rain. At first it was a light drizzle that they heard on the leaves above them more than they felt, but within fifteen minutes, it had turned into a deluge. Mary put on her raincoat.

"I'm glad I brought this after all," she said cheerfully, pulling the hood over her head. "I know you thought I brought too much."

Neal was wise enough not to agree with her.

It was still warm, so Neal didn't mind that he was shortly soaking wet, but it slowed their progress as the ground became slick and hazardous.

The trail itself was not wide, knobby roots were constant obstacles to clamber over, and the moss grew slippery as the rain continued.

Conversation proved difficult, between their concentration on walking and the noise of the rain; the jungle canopy acted like percussion under the raindrops, and the fall of the rain was all collected on leaves that would then dump on them unceremoniously when full of water.

Mary struggled on gamely and offered Neal an overly-bright smile whenever their glances crossed.

This was a terrible idea, he told himself. *Way to go, Romeo.*

He would have berated himself further, but then they rounded the corner of the trail and there was an opening in the trees. The view suddenly expanded, showing a tiny cove below, cradled by cliffs, and the waterfall he'd wanted to show her when he'd suggested the hike. Everything was shrouded in mist, so the ocean below was reduced to a single line of breakers before vanishing and the sky above melted into foggy trees above them.

The waterfall itself was a silver ribbon from the cliff to their right, crashing past them down to the sliver of beach below.

"Oh!" Mary said beside him. Her fingers found his as they stared. "It was worth it."

If he had not been standing right beside her, Neal would not have heard her over the fierce roar of the little fall and the pounding of the ocean.

He looked at her skeptically. "Are you sure?"

Her hair, once neatly braided, was wild and half-loose, plastered against her wet face. Neal wasn't sure what was sweat and what was rain. Even her raincoat was limp in the wet, and her pants clung to her curves. But her face, already red-cheeked, had lit up at the gorgeous view, and Neal thought that she looked utterly gorgeous in all her disarray.

"I'm sure," she said, giving Neal an impulsive hug, a little hindered by her soggy purse and wet raincoat.

He squeezed her tightly in return, and the curves of her body pressed against him made him forget the miserable trip and even the beautiful view. When she might have drawn away, he kissed her, and she wrapped her arms more tightly around his neck and kissed him in return.

Her mouth tasted like honey and promises, and her breasts beneath the crinkly raincoat were firm against his chest. Neal was tempted to peel her out of it right then and there and lay her down on the jungle floor to make love to her on the spot. He settled for caressing her through the unwieldy garment.

"It was definitely worth it," Mary declared with a smile, once he had released her.

"We do still have to walk back," Neal cautioned. The rain had reduced to a faint drizzle again, and he even thought it might be clearing in one area of the foggy sky above them.

Mary winced. "The same way?"

Neal shook his head, and showed Mary where the trail switched back behind them. "It's a little steep down here, and then we'll be walking back along the cliffs to the resort."

Mary looked dubious. "Along… the cliffs? Are they very high?"

Neal noticed that she was staying well away from the drop off by the waterfall. He wouldn't be surprised if she were afraid of heights, too. "Oh, no," he reassured her. "Twenty-five feet or so above the ocean?" They were twice that high here.

"That doesn't sound so bad," she squeaked, and she turned to lead the way down the steep switchback. One side of the trail was tight against the path they'd just followed and the other dropped away over the little cove. It was narrow, narrower than the last time Neal remembered walking here, and rainwater runoff was spilling down from the upper path. The earth was soft and spongy underfoot, beneath the slick surface.

It took Neal a moment to put all the warning signs together, and just as he opened his mouth to caution Mary, the trail beneath her crumbled away into nothing.

Moving as only a shifter could, Neal reached for her and pulled her back to solid ground—only to find that the ground he'd assumed solid was anything but, and then they were both falling, crashing and sliding down the side of the cliff to the jungle foliage below.

Neal, still holding onto Mary's arm, rolled to protect her. It was a far cry from his experiences of jumping from aircraft, hindered by Mary and her handbag and distinctly missing a parachute, but he was able to turn them so that she was protected in his arms, just as they crashed into the first of the trees.

Branches whipped them across every exposed surface and snapped beneath them, jarring impact after jarring impact that Neal could only grit his teeth and weather. One against his head had him seeing stars, then another smashed against an elbow, but all he could think was that he had to keep Mary safe, at any cost.

Air was impossible to draw into lungs. Every blow drove it out again. Then there was blazing pain and he lost his brief battle with consciousness.

CHAPTER 17

Mary left her eyes shut even after they'd at last been lying still for a long moment, catching her breath and trying to make sense of the last few crazy moments. Neal had only let her go at the very last moment, and they lay close enough together that she could hear his labored breathing.

When she finally opened her eyes, she was alarmed by how pale and still he looked as he lay in the sand and the awkward angle of his body. She moved to sit up, and cried out in surprised pain. The arm of her raincoat was ripped open and a broad gash beneath was oozing blood. Her shoulder felt wrenched and, when she tested the rest of her limbs, she suspected a sprained ankle—if it wasn't actually broken. Her sides ached and she guessed she would be peppered in bruises the following day.

She glanced up at the tree they had fallen through, littered with fresh broken branches, and the cliff beyond. Shrouded in fog, it looked very high above them indeed. The scar of the mudslide they had started was darker than the rest of the rock around it.

It was a miracle that they had survived.

Neal groaned, and Mary scooted to his side just as his eyes fluttered open.

"Are you okay?" she asked, feeling ridiculous the second the words were out of her mouth.

"Are *you*… okay?" he asked in response, voice rough and weak.

"I'm fine," she said, and she had to laugh a little in relief that he could speak. At no other time in her life would she have considered her current state 'fine.'

She winced to see that all of his exposed skin had been whipped raw by the tree. Several of them qualified as gashes, bleeding freely. He lay oddly, still looking dazed, and Mary struggled to remember her first aid training.

"I'm going to look you over," she said properly.

Neal started to try to sit up. Mary told him sharply, "No! Let me have a look first!"

He protested less than Mary thought he should, sinking back into the sand with a low sound of pain.

Starting at his head, she found the lump at the base of his neck that was probably the cause of his dazed state. He moaned when she touched his chest and offered, "Probably a broken rib."

She was gentle, working her fingers down his side, but he still sucked his breath in sharply and added, "Maybe two."

Moving his elbow made him give a hiss of pain as she examined his arms. Mary suspected a sprain. At any other time, she would have been delighted for the excuse to run her fingers over the magnificent muscles, but now, she was simply concerned for him. None of the abrasions seemed major, and she moved to his chest and stomach, not finding any problems. His legs lay in odd ways, but he was able to help her move them straight, which is when Mary found the worst of his problems.

"Oh," she said in quiet alarm.

"Hurts," Neal admitted shortly.

"You… landed on your machete," Mary said, moving the tool out of the way. Blood was flowing down into the sand below him. The wound was along the outside of his right hip. She didn't think he could have nicked the artery, but the amount of blood was alarming. "I don't know how bad it is, but Neal, you should shift."

"*Don't ever tell me to do that!*"

Mary rocked back on her ankles, not even minding the shooting pain as she did so. Neal was snarling, pulling away from her. "No, don't move!" she said, alarmed at how the bleeding ramped up as he struggled.

His eyes were feral and filled with pain, but Mary could not let him drive her away. "You lie still," she said, as firmly and gently as she could. "I'll do what I can."

Neal subsided, the wildness in his eyes fading to only agony, and Mary unclipped the machete from his belt to use it to cut away the rest of his shorts.

The injury was shallow, she was glad to find, but it was dirty and bleeding merrily, even as his other scrapes and wounds seemed to be slowing. She balanced the machete between her knees and was able to cut her shirt—the only passingly dry article of clothing between them—into a bandage, but it wouldn't be long enough to tie around his massive leg. She could tie the arms of her raincoat around him. It had stopped raining, at least.

She knew she ought to clean the wound first. "I'm going to get water," she said.

Neal only growled.

Her handbag had been thrown clear, and Mary limped over and dumped it unceremoniously onto the sand to find her water bottles. One was empty, but the other was nearly full. It would have to be enough—she didn't trust the water from the waterfall, and she knew that seawater wouldn't do. She scooped up the first aid kit, too, wishing she'd brought a larger one.

Neal made a guttural noise as she washed out the wound. She wasn't satisfied with the way the sparse water washed out the ugly flap of skin, but short of other choices, Mary didn't know what else to do. The little drizzle of water seemed to get out most of the grit, and Mary squeezed the two tiny packets of antibiotic onto the gash. It looked like pathetically little against the long slice.

She folded her shirt onto the wound and wrapped the raincoat around it, tying the arms as tight as they would go.

She stepped back. "Well, that's hideous," she said. "But hopefully it will do."

Neal gave an attempt at a laugh, but it turned into a dry cough and he lapsed into pained silence.

Mary completed her examination down his legs to his feet, but found nothing else of great concern.

She returned to his head, frowning. "Neal, I'm going to shift."

"Fine," he said shortly. "Just don't ever ask me to."

"You'll heal much…"

"*Don't*. Ever."

Mary knew a losing argument when she was in one, and backed away. She took off her soggy shoes and socks, wincing as her ankle protested the activity. Her own aches and pains were back with a vengeance and even the simple act of undressing was agony.

She looked up to catch Neal watching her with warm eyes.

"You're beautiful," he said in a whisper.

Mary blushed. "Oh, no. I know I'm not." She wanted to cover herself, but something about the reverence in Neal's eyes as he looked at her made her hesitate to do so, instead letting Neal watch as she unclipped her bra and tried to get out of her soaked pants and underwear without angering any of her worst injuries.

"How could you think that?" Neal asked her.

Mary was so surprised by the question that she answered it frankly. "Well, I'm fat." She had to sit down to pull the legs of her pants off, her ankle too fragile to support all her weight at such an awkward angle.

He laughed at her, and it was the most encouraging sound she'd heard from him since their fall. "You are not fat, you are glorious, and I adore every curve," he protested. "*Magnolia* is fat, and she is the second most beautiful woman at Shifting Sands, so your argument has no meaning at all."

Mary had no counter for that. She couldn't doubt his sincerity and it pleased her more than she thought it ought to please a modern, independent woman. "My hair is limp," she added, but it sounded as ridiculous to her ears as it did to Neal's—she knew it was plastered to her face with rain and sweat, and she could tell by the stinging of her face when she smiled that it was as whipped with branches as Neal's was. She gave a mock falsetto and continued merrily, "My makeup is simply ruined, and my dress! Oh, my stars, I could never go to the ball like this!"

Neal chuckled, as he was supposed to, and sobered as his ribs reminded him how much that hurt.

"Seriously though," Mary said, "I am going to shift now and wander around to see about how we're going to get out of here."

"You do," Neal said shortly, clearly in pain.

Mary hesitated. She had never shifted in front of anyone but family before and she felt terribly self-conscious.

Then she was thinking about grazing and leaping and sun on her flanks, and was walking forward as a deer.

CHAPTER 18

Mary as a deer was a beautiful as she was as a human. Her brown coat was smooth and glossy, and her big ears were expressive and mobile.

She came over and touched Neal with her whiskered muzzle, then pranced away, limping only slightly.

Neal was glad when she disappeared through the brush towards the base of the waterfall, because he knew he'd done a dismal job of holding himself together in front of her, and he didn't want to admit just how much agony he was in. The leg that had been cut was like a throbbing fire, but the pain in his chest worried him much more.

Every breath caused a stabbing pain, and there was a tightness to his chest and dizziness that Neal strongly suspected was a collapsed lung—if not fully, at least partially. They had no sort of catheter to release the pressure he was feeling, so he saw no reason to admit it to Mary. Let her keep believing it was just a few broken ribs and a concussion. He couldn't bear to see her worry, and there was no treatment here that could fix an injury like that.

You could shift, his brain betrayed him. Deep inside, Neal could feel his red maned wolf stir.

Neal snarled and refused to think of it any further. He drew himself slowly into a sitting position, verifying with each dry cough and agonizing breath that his diagnosis was correct.

There was an old piece of driftwood that had been flung up high on the beach, and it had a root piece that was exactly the angle of a reclined easy chair. Neal manage to drag himself over to it and prop himself into the crook, just as the deer returned and shifted seamlessly into Mary.

"You shouldn't be moving!" she said in alarm.

Neal grunted. "Got tired of the view there. This one is better."

The sun was fighting through the clouds and fog, and blue sky was beginning to show above the mist. Late afternoon sunlight made the little cove glow. In truth, Neal would have been hard pressed to pick a more lovely scene. Golden-white sand in a perfect semi-circle met gentle ocean, lapping at its edges. Emerald jungle plants fringed the bottom of dark cliffs on all sides, and the waterfall they had hiked to see made a silver ribbon that fell down the cliff and crawled to the ocean like a bit of discarded Christmas wrapping on the sand.

"I'm beginning to reconsider what I said about the view being worth the hike," Mary said. "But it does seem to be doing its best to be picturesque."

She frowned at him and felt his forehead, and then carefully untied the raincoat. She didn't pull off the shirt bandage, but seemed satisfied that it hadn't soaked through with blood and re-tied the raincoat.

"I guess we'll want a fire," she suggested, leaning back on her ankles without wincing. She moved more easily now and the raw vine whips on her face had faded significantly, even more than Neal would have expected from a shifter's ability to self-heal. "And some food? I have two granola bars left."

"Water," Neal suggested, concentrating on not coughing. His lungs were crying for more air that he couldn't get, and it was making him dizzy.

"I can fill the bottles at the waterfall," Mary said dubiously. "I had a good drink as a deer, but we ought to boil it for you."

She said it without being pointed, but Neal still winced and set his teeth, ready for a fight about shifting again.

Mary stood up and walked to where she'd left her clothing. She held up the soggy garments, clearly decided not to put them back on, and spread them on the driftwood to dry instead. The fog was burning off quickly, and the heat of the sun was drying a halo of gold from the hair that had escaped her braid.

Watching her gather up the contents of her bag and sort them neatly for inventory was a treat when she was nude, and she seemed to lack self-consciousness about it for the first time.

"The wood is too wet to use friction to start a fire," Neal said. He didn't think it mattered if he drank contaminated water given state of the rest of him, but building a fire would give Mary something to do. "Do you have any lenses?"

"I have sunglasses," Mary suggested.

"No good, they have to be clear." Neal looked at the odd selection of things. "You brought condoms?"

Mary blushed. "I thought this was going to be a romantic hike, not a death march through the rain capped by falling down a cliff," she said tartly.

Neal laughed and gritted his teeth at the pain of it. When the wave of dizziness had passed, he explained, "We can use that to start a fire."

Mary blinked at him. "A condom?"

"A condom full of water," Neal added.

"This is why I like math," Mary complained. "Math makes sense."

Neal smiled but didn't attempt another laugh. "I'll show you. We'll need dry tinder, and good kindling, and water."

Mary stood. "I can get those."

She scooped up the two empty bottles and the cavernous handbag. "There were some driftwood piles at the other end of the beach that might be dry in the middle. I'll try there first."

Neal lost his battle against the urge to cough and regretted it, able to do nothing but helplessly watch her walk away.

CHAPTER 19

Mary didn't like the Neal's pallor or the rattle of his dry cough, but she knew that was nothing she could treat.

The sand was getting warm beneath her bare feet, and wading through the cool stream was unexpectedly pleasant. Mary paused at the first pile of driftwood. There were probably things in the dark recesses of the wood—biting things and maybe even venomous things. She gritted her teeth, wished she was wearing her soaked clothes, and reached in to rattle a few branches loose, snatching her hand back quickly.

No swarms of snakes or spiders came pouring out at her and, after a moment, Mary tackled it again, pulling the wet wood off the top to reveal a dry inner cavern with an armload of good driftwood. She filled her bag, before adding some of the crunchy dry seaweed she found there, hopeful it would make good tinder. The second heap of driftwood was wet through, but there was an overhang at the end of the beach that had a pile of larger pieces. She heaped her arms full of them, and only as she was returning to the stream did she realize that she hadn't poked the pile or checked it for bugs before she picked it up.

Her skin crawled at the idea she might be carrying ants or spiders, and she dropped her armload unceremoniously by the stream. She filled both her water bottles and capped them, then gathered her wood back up more carefully, flicking a single tiny ant off with a leaf.

The fog had burned off by the time she returned to Neal with her treasures, and she was relieved to see that his driftwood prop was at least partially in the shade. He was dozing, though his face, even in sleep, was still twisted with pain.

Mary gathered up some rocks, only once biting back a shriek of terror when she disturbed the creature—she wasn't sure what it was—which was living beneath it.

Though she suspected it wasn't necessary, she built a fire ring with the rocks, and was pleased at how domestic and camp-like their little space looked with the addition.

Neal woke, and was appropriately pleased by her building efforts. He walked her through setting out the wood for the fire and pouring the condom partly full of water.

"You're essentially making a lens with it," he explained.

Mary made a tiny nest of the seaweed tinder and squeezed the pocket of water in the condom until she got two tiny points of light that she could focus together.

"Hold it just a few inches away," Neal advised. "Have you ever burnt ants with a magnifying glass?"

"No," Mary said with disgust. "I have definitely never done that."

Neal chuckled and then coughed, swearing under his breath. Mary resisted the urge to drop her make-shift firestarter and go comfort him.

When his coughing subsided, there was still nothing happening. "How long does this take?"

"It could take a while," Neal said hoarsely. "A long while, I'm afraid. It's a game of patience now, and the sun is past its strongest point."

Mary settled into a more comfortable position. "Alrighty then."

There was a moment of silence, and Mary listened to the pound of the ocean on the shore and the noise of the waterfall and concentrated on holding her points of light still on the seaweed.

"Tell me about one of your missions," she finally suggested, not wanting to watch Neal lapse back into sleep. "How about that last one you were on?"

For a moment, she thought he was going to refuse, but then he started speaking, slowly and carefully. "The short version of the story is that we were stopping a drug lord in South America."

"That sounds exciting."

"The longer version, which I will spare you, involves an AWOL Marine, Lewis, who had set himself up as a local kingpin, a school being used as a switchhouse, and a mysterious billionaire funder."

"That version sounds even more exciting!"

Even with his breath shallow and his words unnaturally slow, Neal had a wonderful storytelling voice.

"Lewis knew we were coming, somehow, and he knew that some of us were shifters. He used children as hostages and made us surrender ourselves before we could call in for support."

Mary whistled. "That doesn't sound good."

"It wasn't. Major Washburn—Judy—was fitted with some new tech that we didn't want them getting their hands on, so we staged her suicide."

Mary gasped.

"It was a ruse, don't worry. Ended up luring in one of the mercenaries and blowing up half the compound. We focused on getting the kids out and were able to call for backup once we were on high ground."

"Did you get Lewis? Did everyone get away?"

"I don't know," Neal admitted with frustration in his hoarse voice. "I was darted in the neck during our escape. Lewis is the type to throw every man, or child, he has at his own escape, so it wouldn't surprise me if he was still on the loose."

Mary had no answer for that, guessing that he felt guilty for not being able to protect his teammates. She lapsed into silence, staring at the point of light focused on the seaweed.

It was several moments before she realized that it was starting to squirm, and she squealed so loudly that Neal startled.

"It's smoking! It's smoking! What do I do?"

It was everything she could manage not to drop the condom in her excitement.

"You'll want to blow on it, very gently, to encourage a flame, and immediately feed it the smallest kindling," Neal explained.

Mary leaned over awkwardly, holding the condom water balloon in one hand and tiny tinder in the other, giving it a cautious puff of air. Her heart fell as the smoke danced and seemed to disappear, then gave a whoop of triumph when the tiniest flicker of flame appeared.

It vanished almost immediately back into smoke, but a second, more careful puff of air brought it back, and Mary fed it tiny dry twigs with trembling hands.

"It worked!" she crowed. In no time, she had a small, happily crackling fire, and Mary felt like she had just conquered a country or taken down her own drug lord.

CHAPTER 20

Watching Mary's little triumphs was the best thing that Neal had ever witnessed. He'd been in survival situations more dire than this, but it meant a hundred times more to her to do something basic like make a fire than it ever had to him. Each task was a tangible victory, and Neal loved watching her face scrunch in concentration and light up in celebration.

Once she'd gotten the fire going, she put an empty mint tin and her sunglasses case to work as vessels for boiling water, using a sock for a potholder. They boiled quickly, and she set them aside to cool before putting them into the plastic bottle. She hummed as she worked, clearly proud of her accomplishments and delighted with every little success she managed.

If she couldn't quite mask her concern for him, Neal didn't blame her. His chest felt like it was wrapped in steel bands that were being tightened by the minute. Every breath was painful and difficult. He knew that if he hadn't been a shifter, he would already have been dead, and the possibility still existed that he wouldn't weather an injury of this gravity. He wasn't even sure if shifting would help him now, and he continued to refuse to think of it as an option.

"I thought we could split one of the granola bars tonight and save the other for tomorrow morning," Mary offered, bringing the foil-wrapped treat to Neal with her hard-won half-bottle of boiled water.

Neal wondered how much of his dizziness was hunger. He certainly didn't feel like he had much of an appetite, but it had been a long time since their picnic lunch. He drank the still-warm water gratefully and held out a hand for the offered food. Mary broke it in halves and gave him the larger chunk.

Neal didn't have the energy to argue with her or try to insist she take the larger portion, and he suspected she'd completely refuse it anyway. He chewed the sugary bar obediently.

"Do you think they've noticed we're gone yet? They'll probably start looking for us first thing in the morning, don't you think?" Mary suggested, sitting beside him carefully.

The sun was just beginning to go down, casting long shadows along the beach towards them.

"Yes," Neal said soothingly. "At dawn, no doubt."

He didn't consider the worrisome idea that Travis had taken the boat to the mainland for an overnight, and that Scarlet probably thought they were on it and not due back until tomorrow afternoon. Only Tex knew that he'd changed his plans to take a hike instead. When would Tex notice that they were missing? It was hard to think past the pounding pain in his head and the vertigo that was swamping him.

"It'll be dark soon," Mary said. Neal could hear the quail in her voice before she steeled it to add, "I want to take another look at your leg, while there's still enough light."

Neal let her unwrap it and peel off the shirt.

"I think it looks better," she said uncertainly, poking gently. "A little, anyway." Blood still oozed along it, but it was sluggish compared to the original flow and the shirt wasn't completely soaked. It didn't look infected, at least. "Let's put the clean socks on for bandages now, and I'll wash this blouse out so we can use it tomorrow if we need it."

She stood, brushing sand off of her legs briskly. She put on her pants and bra, now that they were dry; the sun was losing its strength as it plunged for the horizon, and she put most of the remaining wood onto the fire. "I'll get another load of wood and water, too."

"Mary," Neal said, as she started to stride away. "I'm proud of you."

She was back at his side in a flash. "Don't talk like that," she said fiercely.

Neal was trying to fight back one of the wracking coughs that his battered lungs were insisting they needed. "Like what?"

"Like you don't expect to be here when I get back." There were tears in her blue eyes, gathered but unfallen. "I'm not blind. I know you're more hurt than you'll admit. I know I can't help you, and you won't help yourself, but damn it! Neal, you'd better hold on until someone else can get here and help you, because I'm not willing to lose you."

Neal felt like the band on his chest tightened three notches, and he envied Mary her easy sobs. "I'll fight to the last," he promised. "I'm too tough to die here."

"I'll hold you to that," she said fiercely, clinging to one hand and bending over him. "I didn't chase you across half the resort just to let you get away this easily."

Neal wheezed a laugh for her. "I've never been so happy to be caught."

Mary sniffed and drew in a deep breath before standing. "It's almost dark. I have to get wood while I can." Neal wasn't sure if the tremor in her voice was fear or some other emotion, but he marveled at the way she squared her shoulders and marched off into the growing gloom.

CHAPTER 21

The cheerful afternoon sun was gone, and the final direct rays had vanished by the time Mary made it to the stream. She refilled her water bottles and tucked them to the bottom of her voluminous bag. The stream was less friendly in the dark—no longer a Christmas trimming, but a stream of blood, reflecting the final light of the sunset. She rolled up her pants to wade across it cautiously.

The last light was gone by the time she made it across, and it took her eyes several moments to adjust. Every shadow seemed full of chirping insects and singing frogs, and every bush rustled with some sort of creature in it. Continuing to walk forward was one of the hardest things she had ever done. Behind her was Neal and the safe, cheerful glow of her fire, but before her was darkness and mystery and danger.

There was a bright moon overhead, so she wasn't walking entirely in blackness, but the shadows were thick. Mary wanted to walk further away from the treeline than she had in the daylight, and was alarmed to discover that the tide had come in: the beach was a much thinner sliver than it had been earlier, and the terrifying ocean was threatening to encroach on the places she wanted to walk.

A tiny crab skittered across her path, making Mary startle and bite back a shriek. The last thing she needed was to make Neal try to come after her.

The thought steadied her.

Neal needed her.

She had to be brave for Neal.

She marched forward again, and faced down the menacing driftwood piles with a determined scowl. "I don't like you, and you don't like me," she told them fiercely. "But I need wood, and I teach middle school, so nothing you can do can scare me off."

As declarations of bravery went, it lacked panache, but the ridiculousness of it buoyed her spirits and Mary was able to plunge her arms into the unknown depths and find more wood that was dry to the touch. The sun had even dried some of the driftwood she had rejected earlier.

She couldn't see each piece well enough to identify bugs, so she could only brush at each one and try not to image that each little tickle was something with too many legs and antenna.

She filled her bag to bursting and piled more into her arms before turning back towards their piece of the beach—and stopped in alarm.

The tide had come in even further as she worked, and where there had once been a clear path back to their fire, there was now ocean, lapping right up to the trees in places.

She could try to scramble back into dense jungle foliage, or she could wade through dark water—dark *ocean* water. Dark ocean water that was probably teeming with biting, stinging things.

Mary took a tighter grip on her armload of wood. Trying to climb through the jungle— which was undoubtedly full of scorpions and snakes—would be nearly impossible with her load of firewood.

She stopped to roll her pants up further, up above her knees, and as she was patting them smooth, recognized that she was just trying to delay the inevitable.

"I teach middle school," she reminded herself.

She gathered up all of her wood again and settled her bag firmly across her body.

Then she stepped into the lapping water and waded across to the other side of the crescent.

Walking in the ocean was not like wading in a stream. The stream knew where it wanted to go and went merrily there. But the ocean was a different matter altogether.

The ocean caressed her. It tickled at her, and swirled around her ankles, and tried to take the sand away from the bottoms of her toes. It surged up almost to her knees and tried to pull her out with it in a salty partners dance. It subsided and relented and teased her, making her shiver as it played against her bare skin. Mary closed her eyes, willing herself just to keep going—and then she was walking out of it, close to Neal's driftwood chair, and she could see the glow of her fire on the undersides of the trees again. Licking her lips, Mary wondered now why she had been so frightened. The ocean against her legs hadn't harmed her. In fact, it had felt… almost nice.

She actually stopped and turned around, dipping her toes into the lacy foam right at the edge. It was partly greeting and partly in thanks. She knew she would never have to fear the ocean again.

CHAPTER 22

True to his promise, Neal was still conscious when Mary returned with her heaped armload of driftwood, but it was more of a fight than he liked to admit.

She dropped her burden beside the fire, shimmying out from her laden bag strap in a manner that would have boiled Neal's blood if he were in better shape. She was lit by the cheerfully crackling fire in warm hues that accentuated every gorgeous curve, and there was moonlight giving her a cool halo from behind. Clad only in torn pants and a bra, she was all womanly perfection in shape and grace. Even half-dead, he wanted her to the very core of his being.

"How are you feeling?" she asked, kneeling beside him.

"I've been better," Neal said truthfully. "But I'm not worse."

If he kept his breaths painfully shallow, he could keep the chest-buckle feeling from reaching excruciating levels, and the worst of the coughs seem to have passed. Maybe he was just getting used to fighting them back.

Mary felt his forehead and Neal willed himself to think cooling thoughts. He could feel her frown through the darkness.

"Neal," she started.

"I'm not shifting," he growled at her. At this point, he wasn't even sure if he could; it had been so long since he'd had a hint of his inner wolf that he wasn't sure any of it was left. Could a shifter lose his animal self?

"I won't ask," Mary said. "But …"

Neal gave a growl, sure that the 'but' would involve shifting.

"Remember your promise," Mary said simply. "Just keep fighting. I love you, and I don't want to lose you."

Neal lost a precious breath at her words and had to cough again. Mary held his shoulders while he struggled back to his precarious balance of shallow breathing, dizzy to the bottom of his soul.

She loved him.

Neal knew he ought to say it back, that he ought to confess that the tangled up mess of his heart was all hers, whether she understood everything that entailed or not, but he couldn't.

She was everything to him already, but when he thought about telling her that, it felt like he was ensnaring her, trapping her in the miserable downward spiral of his life. He couldn't tell her. He could barely admit it to himself.

He closed his eyes when Mary went to put more wood on the fire, missing her presence beside him as soon as she was gone.

Nothing used to scare him. He took the most dangerous jobs without quailing, faced the most terrible enemies. Now here he was, facing mortality with the woman he was afraid to love, and he was more terrified of admitting to himself that he cared about her than he was of the cold reality of his death drawing near.

He felt Mary return, warm against his side. She shivered and then shifted, laying her gentle deer's head on his good thigh.

I love you, he thought he heard, like a distant echo, or a memory.

CHAPTER 23

Mary woke in darkness.

The moon was gone, and the sprinkle of stars in the bottomless sky did little but frost the edges of the shadows.

For a terrible moment, she thought that Neal's stillness beneath her head was complete, and she shifted to her human form as she sat up.

He was still breathing, but if his breaths had been shallow before, they were almost nothing now. His skin felt clammy and chilled under her fingers.

"Oh, Neal," she said, her own chest feeling tight and hopeless.

He stirred, but didn't wake.

Mary got up and went to the fire, which had died down to glowing coals.

Tears blurred her vision, and she nearly put the embers out in her haste to feed in small pieces of driftwood. Finally, though, it was crackling again, flames licking at the rock ring, and Mary had her sobs under some semblance of control.

She knelt by Neal and drew his head gently against her, burying her hands in his ruddy hair.

"You're safe," she murmured. "You're safe with me."

He stirred and muttered, but didn't wake from his restless sleep.

"Neal, listen to me. You have to shift, you have to. I can't heal you, I don't know how. But your wolf can, if you let him."

He didn't snap this time, far too deep in his fever to register her words or fight the idea—but too far, also, to understand the urgency.

Would he die this way, stubbornly resisting his animal form to the very end?

Mary's hands clenched reflexively. She couldn't let that happen.

Neal, she said firmly, without speaking. *Neal!*

There was no answer, just muffled silence behind her closed eyes.

Dammit, Neal, I love you, and I'm not going to let you go like this.

Deeper and deeper she fell into his mind, through fever-crazy dreams and prickling fears.

I won't leave you, she told him.

Then, abruptly, Mary was kneeling in a sunlit plain with no sky, her deer standing beside her. Neal's human form was limp in her arms, ghostly transparent and cool to the touch. She looked for his wolf form, expecting to find it lying nearby in the tall grass.

You have to find him, her deer told her urgently. *They need each other.*

Mary tilted her head back and shouted with all of her strength, "Neal!" It echoed back to her through the strange cavernous space, mockingly. *Neal! Neal!*

As the last echo faded, he came.

Mary had expected him to be injured, as the human self was, but the red maned wolf pranced through the grass on long springy legs, eyes feral and mocking and full—unexpectedly—of anger.

He needs you, she said, and she heard her deer say the same in chorus with her.

He doesn't want me, the wolf said slyly. *He rejects me.*

His look for Neal's ghostly form was full of contempt.

He is hurt, Mary told him. *He will die without you.*

He is weak, the wolf retorted.

You will die without him, Mary's deer said, and she paced in circles through the grass, tossing her delicate head.

I am not weak, the wolf scoffed, and he circled the deer hungrily.

You are angry, said Mary with sudden clarity. *He is not the one who hurt you, but you have no one else left to blame.*

The wolf paused, and the deer put her nose down to touch his in his moment of stillness, fearless and determined.

I can still run, he replied at last.

I can run faster, Mary's deer said gently.

The wolf pulled his lips back in a snarl, but the deer did not back down, keeping her velvety nose against his.

You can heal him, Mary begged, watching Neal's human form fade further and threaten to blow away altogether.

He can heal you, her deer added to the wolf.

The wolf flicked his big ears, staring back into the deer's eyes without words.

Then Neal stirred, and sighed, and said, *Come home.*

Mary woke with a start, her fingers buried in a coarse red mane, not Neal's short hair. She looked down in wonder at the creature lying beside her. He had done it. Neal had shifted. He had overcome years of trauma and fear and terror and found his way home again.

The red maned wolf still slept, but his breath was strong, and when Mary felt through his fur to his skin, his heartbeat was steady. She wept, exhausted, and buried her face in his fur.

CHAPTER 24

Neal woke from dreams of dark-skied sunlight and bones that cracked back into their proper places with blood-chilling sounds. Mary was curled at his side as a deer, head resting against his neck, and it felt comfortable and right, as very little had felt comfortable and right in the last decade.

Looking down at his body, he found that it was not strange or triggering to have paws again, and his wolf was not a painful thorn in his mental side, but a trusted companion once again.

Sunrise was beginning to color the ocean before them, and the tide was out again, revealing a golden-white semicircle of pristine sand.

He was breathing easily again, he realized, and took a particularly deep experimental inhalation.

It still hurt, and his chest still felt tight, but it was markedly better. His leg had only the barest of aches.

Neal was surprised. He knew how deadly even a partially collapsed lung could be, and while he knew that shifting could heal many ills, he had not expected this level of improvement.

Mary's breath changed and Neal put his nose to hers and gave a grateful, tender lick as she woke.

Her shift to human was seamless and smooth, and Neal wondered if he had ever shifted so gracefully. His own transformation was rockier—he could feel the injured places inside stretch and change as he returned to his human shape. As his body remade itself, it tried to make itself properly, healing the leaking places in his lungs.

"Oh, Neal." Mary was weeping, wrapping her arms around his neck as he rose to gather her up for a close embrace. "I thought I'd lost you."

"I love you," he told her, holding her tightly against him. He still felt weak and slightly dizzy, but the feeling of her skin against his made his strength return. "I love you," he repeated.

She snuggled closer, and Neal could feel her smile against his neck. "I know."

"I'm sorry I was so stubborn," he said sheepishly.

"There you go apologizing again," she teased, but she said it lightly.

I forgive you, his wolf said loftily, as if he'd been the recipient of the apology.

I missed you, he admitted to it, wondering what his response would be.

He got in return a lupine laugh, lolling tongue and all.

"Mmm, you are feeling better," Mary observed, and Neal realized that he had a terrific erection, pressing between them.

"I have lost time to make up for," he said, running a thumb along the slope her neck to her shoulder. "Here we are, lost in the romantic, tropical wilderness, and all I wanted to do was lie in the sand and let you make fire and save us. At the very least, there should have been more snuggling together for warmth."

He followed his thumb with his mouth, kissing to her collarbone, and she hissed in pleasure.

"Will you be very disappointed if I tell you I don't want to just snuggle right now?" she asked slyly.

"I'll take a raincheck," Neal suggested. He didn't stop at her collarbone, but fell to her bountiful breasts, kissing until he had to cough.

"You're still not fully healed," Mary said, drawing back in concern.

"A few more shifts to get everything back into proper shape," Neal guessed, battling his breath back. "But I'm well enough for this." His erection had not ebbed after his coughing fit, and his hands were hungry for Mary's soft skin.

"Maybe you should let me look you over," Mary suggested. When she put her hands on Neal's shoulders, pushed him back down onto the sand and straddled him, he let her.

"You need a proper inspection," she said with a laugh.

First, she kissed him on the mouth, firmly but gently, slowly and with breaks so that he never ran out of air, then started to work her way down his body. Every scratch got a feathery kiss, and spaces between got licks and caresses. She worked her way down his chest, pausing to tease his nipples, and Neal had to draw in a sharp breath as she teased down his abs on a sure course towards the member that was acting as a flagpole below.

"Mmm," she said. "Scratches, bruises. Nothing needs stitches, but this needs a little… attention." Her fingers made a loose loop around his cock, stroking him once from base to tip.

Neal groaned and couldn't quite keep himself from thrusting up at her.

"Uh, uh!" Mary scolded merrily. "Keep still for Nurse Mary, or I'll have to bring in an orderly to tie you down."

Obediently, Neal kept himself still as Mary continued to touch his throbbing member, stroking the skin gently, and scratching tenderly at his balls.

She teased him and tortured him exquisitely, until Neal knew that he was going to lose whatever precious control he had remaining.

"You have to… I'm going to… oh…!"

His pleasure rolled over the top, but Mary had slowed her finger strokes down just enough, to just the correct rate, and he had a moment of sheer bliss without actual release.

While Neal was still reeling from that treatment, marveling at the little miracle, Mary straddled him, bringing her hot, welcoming folds around him.

She was no less gentle riding him than she'd been with her hands, keeping her rhythm slow and deliberate, even as she moaned and clutched fingers through the sand beside them.

When she came, crying out in irresistible pleasure, Neal found a second crest of sensation and lost himself, thrusting back, his own cry of pleasure twining with hers.

CHAPTER 25

Mary stretched and laughed, feeling sated and satisfied to the furthest reaches of her toes.

Her stomach rumbled, a reminder her that one part of her, at least, was not in the slightest fulfilled.

"I have a granola bar left," she remembered, springing to find it.

The wrapper had come unsealed at some point, and Mary was dismayed to find a trail of teensy ants inside. At one point, not many days previous, she would have shrieked and thrown it away, but she was hungry, and there weren't that many ants. Mary peeled the granola bar and spent several moments carefully flicking each tiny ant off before she brought it to Neal, who was lying with his hands behind his head, looking up at the clouds skidding through the morning sky.

"I believe they call that a shit-eating grin," Mary said, handing him half of the bar.

Neal accepted half of the bar as he sat up, and Mary was relieved to see that although he winced, he moved easily, and his breaths were deep and steady.

"I cannot wait to get back to the resort and take a shower," she said, squirming. "I have sand in very uncomfortable places.

"We could go for a swim," Neal suggested—though immediately looked trepidatious, probably remembering Mary's near panic-attack from just a few days ago.

It seemed like a very long time ago that Mary had been so afraid of the idea of the ocean, and she found herself looking thoughtfully out at the lapping waves.

"I like the idea," she said, and she looked back at Neal's upraised eyebrows. "I know! I'm as surprised as you are, but after falling down a cliff and sharing a granola bar with ants, I'm up for all kinds of new adventures."

She did insist on putting on her underthings before wading out. "I don't want something swimming up in there," she insisted, at Neal's skeptical look.

He laughed, then teased, "Except me, right?"

Mary laughed back. "Swim on in any time, handsome."

They shared a deep kiss. Mary only pulled away because one of the waves came higher than the others, startling her with a splash of cool water.

Hand in hand, they waded out into the rolling water, and the sand beneath them fell away until they were swimming. Mary was astonished at the clarity of the water and the brilliant blue color of it. She dove down and found shells at the bottom, surfacing with a handful of aquatic treasure.

"Oh, look," she said, sharing the shells with Neal.

He duly admired them, but Mary thought he was really admiring her more; his glance was filled with a tenderness and joy that didn't seemed aimed at the shells she was sharing.

Then one of the shells sprouted legs, and she shrieked and threw them all away from her. "They have crabs in them still!" she exclaimed, and she was laughing even before they hit the water and began to sink back to the sandy bottom. Neal wrapped his arms around her in comfort, and she giggled weakly against his big shoulder as they half-floated in the water.

"I'm such a ninny," she said apologetically as the adrenaline began to ebb.

"You're not," Neal chided. "Look where you are, what you're

doing! You got us firewood in the dark, and ate a granola bar crawling with ants."

"It's easy to be brave for you," Mary said thoughtfully. "You needed me."

Neal's arms tightened around her.

"Besides, I was really hungry," she teased. "And ants are probably good protein."

"I am going to spend the entire afternoon at the buffet when we get back," Neal agreed.

Mary was silent for a moment. "What are we going to do when we get back?" she asked solemnly.

"Buffet," Neal repeated. "All of it, if Chef doesn't stop me."

Mary hit him gently in the arm. "I meant after that. I'm supposed to fly home tomorrow morning."

Neal stilled against her. The waves seemed very loud in his silence.

Mary turned in the circle of his arms so she could look into his face, squinting against the bright sunlight that dazzled off the water at them.

"I love you, Neal, and I think you are well on your way towards healing, but you've got a lot of unfinished business. Your military unit thinks that you're dead, and you have a family who doesn't know what happened to you. You want revenge that you'll probably never get, and even your wolf can't heal everything you've been through."

She watched his face flit through a dozen expressions as he took in her words.

Acceptance was the final look, and Neal drew her close again. "You're right, of course. I have a lot of things to work through, and I don't know how it will all shake out. But if you'll have me…"

"I will," Mary said emphatically.

"... I'll go wherever you are."

"I have a tiny apartment in a tiny town where I have the extra glamorous job of teaching math to middle school students in the throes of puberty. Would you be happy there?"

"I'd be happy anywhere I could be with you." Neal scooped her up and kissed her until they were both dizzy.

"When do you think they'll find us?" Mary asked when they had broken apart, smiling foolishly at each other.

That struck the smile from Neal's face. "Could be late today, or even tomorrow," he surmised. "Travis took the boat to the mainland overnight, so it might be afternoon before they get out on the water, unless they call in for help earlier."

"Could we swim back by ourselves?" Mary suggested nervously. It wasn't as terrifying as she had expected here in the water, and she knew she was a strong swimmer, but the ocean was more alive than any pool she had ever been, and she had no idea how far it would be along the coast to the resort.

Neal considered. "It's a fair way," he said reluctantly. "And there are a few places we'd have to swing out pretty far to avoid rocks. We'd be better off staying where we are and waiting for them to come for us."

Mary smiled slowly, actually pleased by the idea. The cove, now that Neal was no longer at death's door, was a pleasant little oasis. If they could both shift, they could drink the water from the waterfall, and Mary suspected she could forage for food as a deer, as Neal could as a wolf.

Now that it was sunny and perfect, it was almost better here than at the resort.

Mary's stomach grumbled.

Almost.

CHAPTER 26

They swam back to shore with easy strokes, pausing to embrace and kiss at lazy intervals, enjoying the sparkle on the water and the musical sound of waves on the shore. As if to apologize for the earlier rain, the day was crystal clear and gorgeous, with just enough of a cool breeze to keep the heat of the sun from being oppressive.

Halfway back, Neal took Mary's arm and pointed.

She squeaked in alarm and clung to him, but gradually relaxed as the turtle under the water swam closer to investigate them and then moved on. A jellyfish got the same reaction, and a school of fish earned only giggles as she swam backwards away from them.

Neal found himself wanting to show her everything. Her excitement and nervousness were adorable, and he loved the way she got past her immediate alarm every time and boldly went forward to new experiences and adventures. She may have considered herself a coward, but she was easily the bravest person Neal had ever known.

When Neal pointed out the whales on the horizon, surfacing and blowing a spray of water up into the air, Mary *ooh*-ed and *ahhh*-ed, and nearly pulled them under in the excitement of spotting one flip its tail above the surface.

He shifted when they gained the land, and he could feel his breath come even easier in wolf form, dark paws dancing the surf. Mary slipped out of her underthings and frolicked beside him in deer form. While she found beach grass to nibble on, he found the scent of some small rodent, which he tracked down to a pile of driftwood and devoured.

He returned to find her trying to coax new flame from her neglected fire, and he cheered her success by lifting her into the air and spinning her around, grateful for strength in his arms once more.

They made love in the sand as the sun moved across the sky into afternoon, and Neal felt like he was discovering her all over again with his own healing body.

The scrapes across her skin had faded to almost nothing, and even the gash along her arm was nothing more than a silver scar now against the deep tan she was developing.

She moved like the ocean under his fingers, rising to his kisses and scratching his shoulders in passion as he entered her.

She was tight and willing at the same time, welcoming and yet deliciously resistant, and Neal wanted to do nothing more than capture the moment forever.

He kept his strokes slow and deliberate, teasing and tantalizing, and bringing her to the brink of pleasure again and again until she was writhing and begging and clawing at him, breathing his name in a way that made his toes clench.

Finally, she came, and Neal couldn't stop his own pleasure at the same time, his release like a triumph.

They lay together, and Neal was deeply grateful for the way his breath went all the way to the bottom of his lungs.

His wolf, grinning in satisfaction within him, was no longer a hated reminder of his trials. He knew that whatever happened, they were partners again.

He rolled over up on one elbow and looked down at Mary, who smiled up at him contentedly.

"You are so amazing," he told her frankly.

She made a funny face. “I have sand in awkward places again,” she laughed.

He laughed back at her, and it was as much a delight as breathing again, to open his mouth and hear laughter.

“Do you hear that?” Mary suddenly said, freezing and clutching at his arm.

Over the now familiar roar of the waterfall and the endless lapping of the ocean on the shore, Neal heard a faint, mechanical hum.

“A boat,” they said together. Mary fell over herself reaching for her scattered clothing, totally forgetting about the sand she had just complained about.

Neal sprang to his feet without regard for his own nudity, and ran for the beach, desperate to catch the eye of whoever might be out there.

He needn’t have worried: if Travis’ eagle eyes had not spotted them from the little boat, Bastian suddenly swooping from overhead would not have missed them.

“Shirking your jobs again, are you?” the dragon teased, shifting into human form within a few steps of his neat landing. He was a clothing shifter, so he remained neatly attired in his lifeguard uniform with a first aid kit strapped to his waist.

Neal folded his arms and offered a smile in greeting as Mary came up to hand him what remained of his tattered clothing.

Travis looked alarmed at her blood-stained shirt, but Mary quickly waved him off. “I’m fine, really. Neal was the one who was hurt.”

That earned him a head-to-toe look from Travis.

“I’m fine now,” Neal said blithely.

“You should still be looked at,” Mary said firmly.

Bastian and Travis exchanged amused looks that would have had Neal gnashing his teeth in irritation just a few days earlier. Now he only shrugged, with a tolerant half-smile.

“Partially collapsed lung,” he said off-handedly. “It’s better now.”

Mary stared at him. “I thought it was just some broken ribs,” she said in outrage.

“I didn’t want you to worry,” Neal said seriously. “There was nothing either of us could do about it.”

Mary’s eyes were flinty. “I would have appreciated being in the loop anyway.”

Neal squirmed under her scrutiny. “How about I put on my clothes and we go back to the resort for a good meal before you read me the riot act.”

Travis and Bastian smothered snickers.

“I’ve got some energy bars,” Bastian offered peaceably.

“I’ve got spare pants,” Travis added.

Neal suspected that the boat ride back would have been more uncomfortable if Mary had not been immediately enraptured with the whole affair.

Mindful of her previous fear of boats, he offered her a seat in the middle, but she quickly gravitated towards the edge, looking over the edge at the rippling sea bed below them and squeaking and holding on to him every time that they bounced over a particularly large wave. The resort boat was not the most modern vessel, but it made short work of the journey back to Shifting Sands, and was too loud to allow easy conversation at its top speed.

CHAPTER 27

Mary climbed out of the boat onto the dock with a grin. "I want to do that again sometime," she told Neal, as he clambered out behind her and took her hand. She wasn't sure why she had ever been afraid of it. "But maybe a shower first?"

"Then you want to go straight back out on the boat?"

"Then the buffet," she laughed. "For a few hours."

"Yes," Neal agreed merrily.

"Maybe not," Travis cautioned as they walked up the dock to the beach.

Neal sobered with alarming speed, eyes narrow. "What's up?"

Travis glanced at Mary, who tried to look serious and trustworthy back at him. "Beehag's heir Benedict is still here. He brought an… investor."

"Investor?" Neal blinked.

"The investor isn't exactly the savory type, and he's interested in buying the island and ending the lease with the resort. Renegotiating, they're calling it."

Neal whistled. "Scarlet can't be happy about that."

"That's an understatement," Travis agreed. "And that would be tense enough…"

"Do they know about the shifters?" Neal guessed.

"No one is sure," Travis explained. "But these guys are bad news."

"Beehag's nephew didn't fall far from the asshole tree," Neal growled.

"There you go with the understatements again."

Travis paused at the bottom of the steps up from the beach. "It's not an easy time," he cautioned. "Everyone is on edge, and there are a lot of… bodyguards that came with the investors. Armed bodyguards. Creepy, well-armed bodyguards who are not exactly acting respectful of the guests." Travis nodded at Mary. "Especially the female guests," he added apologetically.

Mary felt Neal's hand tense in hers.

"Probably mercenaries," Neal guessed from the description. "Have there been any incidents?"

"Nothing worse than leering," Travis said, to Mary's relief. "But it could get awkward if they said the wrong thing to Magnolia and she took offense. On the upside, Virginia finally put on clothes and stopped draping herself over the furniture like meat."

"That's a sign of dire times," Neal observed dryly.

The walk up the numerous steps from the beach to the pool deck that had Mary blushing with memories took very little time, and they abruptly came to the top of the stairs to find a collection of people having a heated discussion.

Beehag's heir, Benedict, Mary guessed, was the greasy, scrawny youth—he looked barely old enough to be admitted to the resort, and he was scowling defensively.

Scarlet was looking at him like he was some kind of small worm, and lesser men than he would have squirmed the way he was.

"We have a contract," Scarlet was hissing, and Mary guessed by her fists that she was keeping herself tightly in control. "It has clauses for breach."

"My lawyer assures me that everything about this transaction is completely legal," Benedict whined. "There's a more than generous severance fee."

Scarlet was clearly unimpressed by the figure they were offering her, though Benedict seemed to think it ought to assuage her ire.

She turned her icy attention to the investor. "There are other resorts for sale. More accessible locations."

"There are no other resorts like *this* one," the investor replied with a chuckle. "Shifting Sands has several unique properties that appeal to me particularly."

The mercenaries, were, true to the warnings, looming figures, each of them easily the size of Neal and armed with wicked-looking guns. Mary glanced at Scarlet and back at them. She didn't think that Scarlet was actually afraid of any of them, but considered herself unpleasantly bound by the contract.

The investor was wearing a suit and standing with his back to the party coming up the stairs, and he turned to glance at them with an unconcerned, sleazy smile.

In an instant, everything shifted.

Neal's hand in Mary's became an anchor, wrapping around her fingers even more tightly than before, as he hissed, "Lewis…"

CHAPTER 28

Neal did an automatic assessment of the situation as they crested the stairs, taking stock of the bodyguards—six bruisers—and the other figures standing there. The bodyguards looked bored, but professional; Neal knew at once that he had been correct about guessing they were mercenaries by the way they were subtly assessing each other as well as the newcomers, fingers lazy on their weapons. He dismissed Benedict as a useless youth with too high an estimation of himself and no physical skills. He knew better than to discount Scarlet as an asset, though he had to lump her into a total unknown category.

The figure with his back to them was the most intriguing. The suit was clearly fine quality and perfectly tailored, and the body beneath was unexpectedly large and powerful. From the expense of his dress, Neal guessed he had to be one of the investors.

Then, he turned, and Neal saw his face.

Lewis recognized Neal in the same moment that Neal realized who was standing at the top of the stairs and, with a gesture, directed all of the mercenary attention on him. Weapons that had been held loosely were at ready. The men that had looked the laziest were suddenly sharp-eyed and alert.

"Mr. Byrne," the drug lord said in oily tones, turning all of his attention from Scarlet to Neal. "How… pleasant to see you again."

Neal forced a smile onto his face. "I wish I could say that that was mutual, Lewis."

Scarlet glanced from one to the other, frowning thoughtfully, but said nothing.

Mary's hand in his tightened, and Neal wished her anywhere else as Lewis' glance turned from him to her.

As polite as could be, Lewis offered his hand to Mary. "My dear," he said slickly. "How lovely to meet you. Mr. Byrne is an… old friend."

"I, uh, I'm Mary North," Mary said in a quavering voice. She had to reluctantly let go of Neal and very tentatively shook his hand. It didn't escape anyone's notice that he held onto it a little longer than she wanted him to.

"I wouldn't say friend," Neal ground out, holding his anger tightly in check.

Lewis gave a toothy smile. "No need to be pedantic. Business associates, if you'd prefer?"

"My mission was to kill you," Neal said flatly.

Mary's breath hissed in alarm, and Neal could feel the air around Scarlet chill. Behind him, at the top of the steps, Travis shuffled his feet and Bastian flexed his hands. Benedict sweated in the muggy air.

"Fun times," Lewis laughed. "But come now, you aren't even considered alive by your old unit. Surely we can put a failed mission behind us."

"Not when the failed mission was to take down a turncoat drug lord who hid behind school children." Neal's wolf growled from his throat.

"There's no reason to escalate this," Lewis said smoothly, turning away from Neal to address Scarlet. "We simply need to finalize the paperwork"

"What am I supposed to tell the guests?" Scarlet asked. Neal immediately found the calmness of her voice deeply suspicious.

"That they should have purchased travel insurance," Benedict suggested with a snigger.

Lewis shot Benedict a squelching look that silenced the laugh mid-breath. "The resort is simply changing ownership. The staff has their jobs, if they want them, and the guests are welcome to stay for the remainder of their reservation. I'm sure you'll understand why I will insist having *you* escorted off the island, Ms. Stanson."

"Of course," Scarlet said, ice in her voice.

Neal wondered what Lewis knew about Scarlet that the rest of them didn't.

CHAPTER 29

"And you, Ms. North," Lewis said, turning back to her.

Mary startled, and clung to Neal's hand.

"I'm sure you understand our desire to keep things from escalating."

Mary, keenly aware of everyone's attention, squeaked, "Yes. Of course."

Lewis smiled at her. "Than I'm sure you won't mind coming with us. As assurance of peaceful resolution."

Neal's hand threatened to cut off circulation in Mary's fingers and Mary's world went white with terror. Go with these frightful men and their gigantic guns?

Lewis continued, talking directly to Neal now. "I know that you are debating whether or not to shift, and trying to decide whether or not you could get to my throat before bullets could get to her." He glanced over their shoulders. "And you, you're trying to decide if being in dragon form would intimidate my men. I assure you, it would not. I've generously offered you your jobs. But unemployment doesn't need to be the worst of your problems."

Mary heard Bastian shift his weight on his feet behind them.

"We can draw up the necessary paperwork in my office," Scarlet said coldly. "And I'm sure you won't mind if I pack a few of my things."

Lewis nodded. "I appreciate keeping things… civilized." He put a hand imperiously out to Mary and snapped his fingers.

Mary felt Neal's growl rather than heard it.

No, Neal! Mary said wordlessly at him.

She wasn't sure if the speech would work in human form, but he stilled, and let her step away from him.

He won't hurt me if we all do as he says, she tried to reassure him, not entirely convinced herself.

A wordless wave of deep skepticism and reluctant acceptance was the only thing returned to her.

Trembling, Mary put her hand in Lewis' and he tucked it into his elbow as he turned away, pulling her forward.

She had time to give Neal one quick goodbye glance, hoping she looked brave rather than simply terrified, and then they were climbing the resort steps past the bar towards Scarlet's hilltop office.

Benedict looked between the mercenaries who dropped behind at Lewis' gesture and the party making the climb, then dashed to catch up with Lewis.

CHAPTER 30

Watching Mary walk away with Scarlet on one side and Lewis capturing her hand on the other was one of the hardest things Neal had ever done. His wolf snarled helplessly inside him and for once, they were in reluctant harmony.

"Well," Travis said, coming up on one side. "That answers the question of whether they know we're shifters or not.

Two of Lewis' hard-faced men had been left behind, assault rifles at hand. They clearly expected to be feared, and that gave Neal an idea.

"You don't mind if I sit, do you?" he asked casually, and he sank down into one of the lounge chairs without waiting for their answer.

He smiled, delighting in the way the mercenaries shifted on their feet and kept their faces carefully stony. It was never comfortable knowing that your enemy wasn't taking you seriously.

"Lewis always had one fatal flaw," he said cheerfully, leaning back into a deck chair, looking for all the world as if he had nothing better to do than lounge in the sun overlooking the pool while his mate was hauled off as a hostage.

Travis and Bastian exchanged brief, mystified looks, but played along willingly, pulling up their own chairs.

"What's that?" Travis asked, swinging his feet up on the lounge and settling his sunglasses over his eyes.

Bastian picked up a magazine, hamming it up even further.

"He always underestimated shifters," Neal said merrily. "Like, he didn't know about the other things we can do."

It was the mercenaries' turn to exchange looks, and Travis immediately caught Neal's intentions.

"He doesn't know we can turn invisible?"

"He doesn't know a thing about that," Neal agreed. "I bet he even thinks the silver bullet thing is a myth and thinks that those standard bullets would stop us." He nodded at the gun the nearest mercenary was holding in what were now white-knuckled hands.

The second mercenary made a skeptical noise, and when the shifters looked at him, broke his cold facade to scoff, "You wouldn't be saying those things with us listening if it were true."

Bastian laughed lightly. "We'll just use a forget-me field on you… if we let you leave at all."

"Because really," Travis added swiftly. "How do you think shifters have stayed a secret this long without those extra tricks?"

The first mercenary scowled at his partner. "Quit talking to them, Jake."

Out of the corner of Neal's eyes, a flash of movement caught his attention. The gazelle was browsing on the lawn by the deck—suspiciously close, for her.

Jake, defying the other's suggestion, mockingly said, "You wouldn't have let Lewis walk off with your girlfriend if you could have stopped him."

Touché, Neal thought, scrambling for a cool response through the flare of anger at the memory of Mary's last fearful glance.

"Didn't have to stop them," Travis said, before Neal could think of anything. "They're walking right into Scarlet's trap, after all. Mary's safe as houses with her."

How safe are *houses?* Neal had to wonder, and he would have shot Travis a grateful look if he hadn't been concentrating on appearing cool and in control of the situation.

Jake's partner hooked him by the elbow and pulled him out of easy earshot, toward the lawn where the gazelle was still pretending to graze so they could exchange whispers.

Neal kept a practiced eye on their weapons, judging how they were held.

Bastian nudged a shoulder towards them and raised his eyebrows, subtly asking Neal if they should try to take them by surprise. Neal concealed his head shake by raking fingers through his hair lazily. Whatever else these soldiers were, they were professionals, and their attention was complete enough that their weapons could be brought to bear before the shifters could take them down. They looked rattled, but not entirely distracted, glancing around often.

At a moment when they weren't watching him, Neal gave a wave to the gazelle, who was still grazing in earshot. He wasn't quite sure what she could do to help them, but another source of distraction would give them more options.

The gazelle lifted her head and with slow, cautious steps, walked to where the men stood with their guns.

At her first deliberate steps, the guards were at full attention, discussion over whether to call Lewis and warn him about the supposed trap at a standstill. Jake lifted the muzzle of his gun to point at her, while the other had his rifle down, but a finger at the trigger, swapping his attention between the gazelle and the shifters lounging on the pool deck.

She scented the air as she walked forward, one slow hoof after another. Jake lowered his gun, dismissing her as a threat; despite the long, spiraled horns, she was very small and delicate looking. Then she riveted all of their attention—and Neal's as well—as she rippled and shifted.

A woman knelt there, shrouded in waves of waist-length hair in mixed black and white. At first glance, she was an old woman, the white in her hair and the gauntness of her limbs giving an impression of age. But her face, though haunted, was free of wrinkles, and her eyes were wide and full of youthful innocence as she looked up through her hair at them.

"You are bad men," she said chidingly.

She had all of their attention, much more than she ought to, and it took Neal a moment to shake off her spell himself and realize that the soldiers' hands had gone slack on their guns.

He rose to his feet, waiting for either of the bodyguards' attention to snap back to him at the sound of the lounge chair creaking underneath him. He poked Travis, who blinked stupidly at him for a moment before turning to put an elbow in Bastian's side.

Bastian actually pinched himself to complete his release from the gazelle's hypnotic spell.

Neal rushed forward, realizing that this chance wouldn't last forever, and Bastian and Travis followed him into action.

Taking the weapons from the men was laughably easy; they didn't even startle until the shoulder straps were released and the gazelle was leaping away in her antelope form again. They blinked stupidly at Neal and Travis, but it didn't take a lot of time to convince them they were beaten. They gradually shook their heads and put their hands up, scowling.

CHAPTER 31

Mary looked from Lewis to Scarlet as they walked into the courtyard that opened onto Scarlet's office and personal quarters, glanced at Benedict and the men with the guns, and then turned her attention back to the most important two.

Scarlet's face was a perfect mask, utterly impenetrable, but Mary could feel the anger sparking off of her, and knew beyond a shadow of a doubt that the woman had no actual intention of turning her resort over to these men. Neal's revelation that Lewis was a criminal had changed the transaction for her, turning it from something inevitable that she would have to accept to a battle she was bracing herself to fight.

Lewis must have sensed the same thing Mary did.

"There's no reason to make any of this unpleasant," he said, voice silky, but threatening. "You know that you don't have a choice in the matter. It's all quite legal and above board, and no one needs to get hurt if we do it the easy way."

Mary bit back a squeak as one of the mercenaries pointed his rifle more obviously at her.

"Take only what you need, I will have my men pack the rest to ship to you on the mainland within a week's time. I assure you I pay them well enough that they won't be interested in your belongings."

"You aren't going to just let us leave," Scarlet said, her own voice chilly and skeptical.

Lewis chuckled. "*You* may, lady, and any of your staff that chooses to go. It's quite true that I can't leave Neal free to tell tales."

Mary startled, and sudden terror for Neal overwhelmed her own fears.

"But you owe him nothing," Lewis continued smoothly to Scarlet. "Our history is none of your concern, and you can preserve the remainder of your staff and take advantage of our very generous monetary offer simply by using a little good judgment."

Scarlet's face betrayed nothing as she turned to walk into her office, but Lewis stopped her anyway.

"No, I think you should not go into there yourself," Lewis suggested, and he looked to the closest and burliest of the mercenaries with a question on his brow.

He got a surprisingly toothy smile in return, and a nod. "This is one of the strong places, one of the places of power," the man said.

His words crystallized something that had been bothering at the back of Mary's mind. Scarlet's office had always left her feeling unsettled, but the mercenary's words made her recognize that it wasn't Scarlet herself, but something deeper and older, something asleep beneath the resort. She felt like a more powerful shifter here, and she suddenly wondered how much of a role that power had played in Neal's swift recovery.

"No surprises," Lewis warned, and all of the mercenaries felt so tightly wound that Mary expected them to snap.

"It's not a power that can be controlled," Scarlet said, her voice full of warning.

"You mean *you* can't control it," Lewis scoffed.

"I mean it doesn't like to be controlled," Scarlet said softly. "If you wake it, I don't think it will appreciate either you or your actions."

"That's a risk I'm willing to take."

Mary felt adrift, like a child listening to a conversation that adults were having, understanding their words, but not their meaning. Benedict looked nervous, and Mary caught him crossing his fingers superstitiously.

Scarlet went into her office with the bodyguard and carefully gathered a few things—a handful of files and a laptop were tucked into a rolling bag, and she picked up an unadorned wooden box, all under the scrutiny of the watchful bodyguard and Lewis, who stood with his arms crossed, watching through the door.

"Let's see you off in the Jeep then," Lewis said, almost merrily. He seemed to think that Scarlet's quiet was a sign of her defeat, but Mary strongly suspected otherwise. "Our plane is waiting at the airstrip to take you back to the mainland."

They walked through the courtyard, two mercenaries in the front, and two trailing. Lewis, still holding Mary's hand at his elbow walked behind Scarlet and Benedict.

Benedict was babbling something like an apology to Scarlet. "I'm sure you understand. The offer was just too good. I couldn't turn it down…"

No one paid him any mind.

CHAPTER 32

Neal left the mercenaries well-wrapped in duct tape, disarming them of an array of knives and small weapons first.

"We're outnumbered," Neal said as the shifters climbed the steps to the bar deck. "We've only got these two guns against five of them." He automatically discounted Benedict Beehag as a combatant, but he was not foolish enough to think that Lewis was not still in prime fighting form, whether he had traded his fatigues for suits or not.

"And a dragon," Bastian reminded him, flexing his shoulders but not shifting. "Two guns and a *dragon*. That counts for something."

"Beehag had a tranquilizer that changed shifters back to human," Neal cautioned. "We have to assume that Benedict has given that formula to Lewis."

Bastian scowled, but nodded.

"Hey Tex," Travis called into the bar. "Want to join a reckless, doomed rescue mission?"

"What are we rescuing?" Tex asked with a lazy drawl, not putting down the towel he was drying glasses with.

"His mate," Travis answered, jerking a thumb at Neal.

“Scarlet,” Bastian added.

“Shifting Sands,” Neal finished gravely.

“You had me at reckless and doomed,” Tex said, grinning. He put the glass away carefully and came out from behind the bar.

“Would Graham…?” Neal started.

As if summoned, the landscaper materialized from the back entrance to the bar, a wicked machete in one hand. He didn’t offer an explanation, but Neal had to guess that he had spotted the strange party headed for Scarlet’s office and recognized that something was afoot.

At his heels, was Breck, still in his waitstaff uniform, but looking uncharacteristically grim-faced.

“These are starting to feel like better odds,” Travis said confidently. “I can get Magnolia, she’s a polar bear who’s good to have in a fight, and where she goes, Chef goes.”

“I can keep them from being able to leave,” Breck offered. “It wouldn't take much to disable the Jeep.” At Neal's nod, he trotted away with the grace and speed of his leopard.

“They still have more ranged weapons,” Neal cautioned. “And hostages. We need a plan. And a backup plan.” He set his jaw. “I’ll need your phone, Tex.”

The list in his pocket had long since dissolved to unreadable, but Neal didn’t need it. He dialed Major Washburn's number as if he’d always known it.

“This had better be good,” Judy answered, her voice painfully familiar even after ten years.

Neal could hear the whine of engines in the background, and guessed she was at an airport.

“Judes,” he said roughly, and he walked across the bar for whatever privacy he could get.

There was a moment of silence at the other end of the line. “Who the hell *is* this? How did you get this number?”

Neal recognized the deep thrum that underlay the airplane engines. A carrier. The team was somewhere on the flight deck of a carrier. But what ocean? Were they close enough?

“Judes,” he said again. “Listen up, I need a support team at the coordinates of this phone. I've got Lewis, but don't have the resources to hold him myself. There are civilians at stake." *My mate*, he didn't say.

"Lewis? What the—Neal, is that *you*?"

"It's me," Neal assured her, and it was odd to realize that he meant it. He felt more like himself than he had in ten years. He was alive again, and on the hunt. His feet were on solid ground, his wolf was in alignment with him, and he had purpose.

"Where the hell have you been? It's been ten fucking years, you jack—"

"It's a long story," Neal cut her off. "A really long story. And I promise I'll split a bottle and tell you the whole damn thing, but not now. I need the team. Lewis has at least four bodyguards, moderately armed, and two hostages …"

Without waiting for her agreement, he detailed the basic lay of the resort and Lewis' resources.

"I don't know how fast we can get there," Judy said when he was finally done. "These things need approval from upstairs."

"Damn," Neal laughed. "It's been longer than I thought if you're waiting for approval these days. Aren't you a general yet?"

"When you hit colonel they start making you write your own fucking reports," Judy groused.

"You haven't changed a bit," Neal laughed. He sobered quickly. "Come as fast as you can. I have to go."

He knew that Lewis wouldn't wait docilely for the team to arrive, and his mate was at stake.

CHAPTER 33

They were standing by the Jeep, waiting as the driver poked under the hood, cursing and casting nervous glances at Lewis.

Scarlet was so tightly coiled that Mary didn't feel safe standing next to her, but a quick glance showed the red-headed woman looking utterly serene, her laptop case in one easy hand, the box tucked under the other arm. Every strand of her hair was in place.

Her crimson hair reminded Mary of Neal's and she shifted on her feet, worried sick. They hadn't heard any shots, and surely she would know if her mate had been unceremoniously dispatched.

As if in response to the idea, she heard Neal's voice in her head.

Mary…?

She looked down, letting the curtain of her dirty hair cover her face.

Neal? Are you all right? Lewis says he's going to… She stopped herself, trying to rein in the hysteria that came with even the idea.

We're free, he replied quickly, with a rush of comfort like a caress. *We're* fine. *Can you make a diversion?*

"Oh!" she said out loud, and that got her the attention of the two guards.

"Is there a problem?" Lewis asked sharply.

Mary squirmed, realizing that as diversions went, this wasn't well thought out. "I, ah, just realized that my flight is in just a few hours. I'm probably going to miss it, and I won't be able to re-book unless I call in advance."

Lewis looked disgusted.

Mary set her jaw. "Maybe an airline flight doesn't mean that much to you," she said with pepper. "But I'm a math teacher, and I saved up a seriously long time for those airline miles."

She had their attention, but not all of it.

"You may be some big-shot millionaire jungle gigolo, but some of us work for a living!" Exhaustion and adrenaline made her feel jittery and hollow, but Mary dredged down to try to recall the worst of her students' dramatic fits. "This isn't fair!" she wailed, and she stomped her foot and set her hands on her hips.

"I saved all my money for years to come to this place, and all I got was marooned in the wilderness and kidnapped! This was supposed to be a lush vacation, and it's been horrible and it's not fair!"

The effect must have been ridiculous, with her unwashed hair, crusty from saltwater, and her ripped, blood-stained clothing, but it had the desired result: she had the attention of all of the guards, and even Scarlet was staring at her as if she'd lost her mind.

"I need to make a phone call," she whined. "You have to let me call the airline, *right now*."

When they glanced at each other, clearly not sure what to do with her, Mary stomped her foot again. "It's not fair!" she shrieked, and burst into noisy tears.

"Oh, give her a phone," Lewis said in disgust, and after a moment, Benedict dug out a shiny modern smartphone, unlocked it with his thumbprint, and handed it to her.

Mary sniffed, and made a great show of wiping her tears away. "Can anyone get the phone number for Costa Rican Air?" she whined after a moment of fiddling with it, waving the phone around. "I can't seem to get data on this one."

One of the mercenaries pulled out his own smartphone. "I'm detecting wireless on this, but I need the passcode."

Scarlet, still inscrutable, shrugged. "I'd have to check my log—I change it every week."

Another guard pulled out his own smartphone. "I've got a bar of data, wait, no, I've lost it."

"You could just call information," a third suggested.

"I've let this fall asleep," Mary said sweetly, handing the phone back to Benedict. "You'll have to unlock it again."

The timer she had discretely set to a ringtone went off just as he took it, and he almost dropped it, then fumbled trying to figure out how to answer it. "What the hell?!"

"I don't know!" Mary said defensively, using her very best clueless student voice. "It's your phone!"

"For fuck's sake," Lewis snarled. "Is the goddamn Jeep fixed yet?"

They all looked towards the driver, to find him slumped on the ground. Tex stood beside the Jeep, a baseball bat in his hands. A leopard was crouched beside him.

"You know you shouldn't drive and use your phone at the same time," Neal chided from behind them.

Mary's heart lifted to see him, holding a gun in steady hands, training it on Lewis. Travis was to one side with another large gun, and Graham was flanking the guards on the other, a machete held grimly in one hand; one of the guards was lying at his feet. Behind him, a massive pair of bears, one a polar bear, one a giant grizzly, were growling.

The remaining bodyguards reacted quickly, re-pocketing their phones smoothly and regaining their grips on their weapons. But Lewis was faster than any of them, and before Mary could react, she was being held against him by her wrists, a handgun at her forehead. Beside her, one of the guards did the same with Scarlet.

"You didn't think this out well," Lewis sneered, and Mary wanted to agree.

A giant, dark shape passed overhead and landed with a deep

thump on their far side, green wings like vast sails folding into jeweled sides. *A dragon.* Mary could only see it in her peripheral vision, but she could see the reaction in the mercenaries: fear and uncertainty.

Well, she could relate.

CHAPTER 34

It was a standoff, at best. The two forces were evenly matched, in Neal's estimation, and Lewis had hostages. He was smart about it, too—holding Mary where Neal couldn't get a shot at him without risking her too. It did, however, mean that his back was to a dragon. Neal was sure that was worth something. He kept his sights trained on Lewis, and knew that he just needed to keep him talking until an opportunity presented itself, or backup arrived.

Patience, he reminded himself. He concentrated on keeping his breath steady, and his shot clean.

A week ago, he wouldn't have been able to hold the gun without shaking, he realized. He wouldn't have been centered enough to get this far. He'd probably have done something stupid and suicidal already, and risked Mary's life as well.

A week ago, he'd been a different man.

"You're getting sloppy, Lewis," he said gravely. If Lewis was talking, he wasn't shooting, and Neal had backup on the way. "Last time we tried this, you had a tranq dart waiting for me."

"I didn't think you'd survive in Beehag's cage," Lewis scoffed. "I'm surprised you're alive. Your team doesn't think you are. I'm sorry, that's your *ex*-team, of course. The funeral was lovely, according to my man on the inside."

Neal set his teeth. Lewis had someone on the team? Cold fire ran through his veins. Was it Judy? Was the backup he had planned in vain?

He couldn't let any of that show in his voice. "Might have known you had someone from the team in your pocket. Is it Remmy? Gobber?" He didn't add Judy to the list.

Lewis seemed confident that he had the upper hand. "It's amazing what power money has. Especially when family is involved. Especially family who's sick and needs the kind of care only money can buy."

Neal dredged into his memory. Remmy's sister had gone through cancer treatment, not long before their fateful last mission together. She hadn't had insurance that would cover it, and Remmy had been worried... and then strangely unconcerned not long after.

"So, it's Remmy." Neal shrugged. "That's not much of an infiltration."

"You've been out of the loop," Lewis reminded him. "Remmy's not just the comms guy now, he's second in command."

They'd given a traitor his position? Neal had to rein in his temper, and wondered suddenly if Lewis was playing him. Whatever else Lewis was, he *was* clever.

The idea steadied him. "You know much about your boss?" he asked, raising his voice to carry further to the bodyguards standing around them. "You're new hires, don't you wish you knew what kind of circus he was planning to drag you into? And did you ever wonder what happened to his last crew?"

Though he kept his gaze through the sight of his gun on Lewis, he could feel the barb hit home. A few of the younger mercenaries shifted their feet and Neal knew they were listening.

"Lewis offers a lot of money for loyalty," Neal continued derisively. "You're probably thinking that it's worth what he's paying for a little danger. But Lewis really hates to pay his bills, and since he's a traitor himself, he doesn't trust anyone else either. It's funny, what a mortality rate his mercenaries have. Usually *after* the danger has past."

They were all listening to him now, and Lewis was scowling. He shifted Mary in his grasp, effectively keeping her between Neal and himself.

Lewis' phone gave a sudden blurble, and he carefully reached down to check it. A toothy smile spread across his face. "Speaking of turncoats," he said cheerfully. "I guess your team is on its way now. Cleverly done, Byrne. Too bad that they won't get here in time."

Mary gave a squeak as Lewis tightened his grip on her.

Neal fought down his urge to act and reminded himself to be patient, to wait. "You don't need Plan B if Plan A is still going well," he bluffed cheerfully. He pitched his voice to the mercenaries. "We won't hurt anyone who surrenders. You have to ask yourself which party you think is going to end up treating you with more humanity—the resort staff of animal shifters, or the turncoat who relies on people betraying their friends and hides behind women and children when things get tough."

Mercenaries tended to have a code of honor, and it often excluded using civilians as hostages—especially children. The fact that Lewis was using two apparently defenseless women now played well into Neal's speech.

Behind Lewis, the dragon shifted his wings and growled, and Lewis turned to glance at him, finally offering the shot that Neal had been waiting for as his finger relaxed from the trigger of the gun at Mary's head.

As tempting as it was to put a bullet in Lewis' forehead, Neal took the harder, more humane shot, right through the arm holding the gun.

Lewis howled, dropping the gun as Mary spun out of his grasp and sensibly dropped to the ground with her hands over her head.

Neal heard his own shot in that crazy moment, and Bastian's dragon roar, and another several rounds being fired. He didn't see what happened to Scarlet, but heard a crunch of breaking bones and glanced to find the guard falling away from her, shrieking in pain and cradling his gun arm.

Then Neal was driving forward, leaping over Mary to tackle Lewis and bring him to the ground. He heard howls and grunts and more ear-splitting shots as the rest of the staff took on the remaining mercenaries who hadn't been swayed by his speech, but he focused on Lewis, who was reaching with his off hand for his dropped gun.

"I don't think so," Neal said firmly, and smashed him in the face with the butt of the assault rifle he was still holding, taking cathartic delight in watching Lewis' eyes roll up in his head.

The sounds of fighting died out quickly, and Neal looked around to find Tex relieving the last guard of his weapons. Graham's mercenary was on the ground, whimpering and holding his hands up for mercy. Bastian was human again, looking disappointed at not having anyone left to fight, and Benedict was cowering against the car with his hands over his ears being completely ignored. Magnolia was back in her human form, brushing her flowered dress back into shape as Chef picked up her wide white hat.

Graham had been grazed with one of the wild shots, and Bastian offered to clean it up. Graham looked down at the blood oozing down his shoulder and shrugged, wincing. "It'll heal," he said.

"You all right, Scarlet?" Travis asked.

"He missed," she answered calmly, smoothing her blouse and tucking a strand of artistically loose hair back.

Neal wasn't sure if he believed her or not.

"Oh, Neal," Mary said, uncovering her ears. "You saved us!"

Neal gathered her up into his arms, holding her tight. "I owed you one."

She wrapped her arms around him, and Neal could have sat there and held onto her forever.

Tex cleared his throat. "What do you want us to do with these guys?" he asked.

Neal reluctantly let go of Mary and helped her to her feet.

Scarlet was scowling at Benedict. "You've certainly laid a mess of trouble at our door," she said coldly. "I presume that the sale is off and you'll be cleaning this up?"

Benedict opened one eye and looked up at her. "Oh. Um, yes. I'll be calling my lawyer immediately and canceling the whole thing. I didn't know he was a… a… drug lord or whatever."

Neal snapped his fingers at Benedict. "I need to make a phonecall first."

Benedict obediently handed it over.

"Are you getting any bars of data?" Mary asked merrily.

Neal had to stop laughing before he could dial the phone to warn Judy about Remmy.

CHAPTER 35

While Neal stepped away to make his phone call, Mary felt like the weight of the past few days was suddenly upon her. She became intensely aware of how dirty and tired and hungry she felt, and how ragged and stained her clothing was.

Scarlet, by comparison, still looked like she'd just stepped out of a salon.

"You are welcome to stay longer at the resort," she offered. "If you can change your plane tickets, I will give you another week in the cottage at no charge. Your Shifting Sands experience should not be so heavy on surviving in the wilderness and being held hostage."

"I'd like that," Mary said with a weary laugh. "But right now I'd mostly like a shower and about four hours at the buffet."

Scarlet laughed with her, and Mary thought it was unexpectedly genuine sounding. There was relief in her face, and Mary realized that she hadn't just been angry about losing Shifting Sands and being shuffled off the island. She'd been afraid.

It was somehow comforting to know that there were things that someone like Scarlet was afraid of, too.

"We'll leave the staff to clean this up," Scarlet suggested. "And I'll need to add duct tape to my list of supplies to reorder."

Mary watched Scarlet go off, waiting for Neal to finish his phone call.

He came back with a familiar dark scowl on his face. It lightened when he caught sight of Mary again, and he bent to give her a lingering kiss.

"We've got this," Bastian said, waving them off. The mercenaries were being neatly trussed and completely disarmed, and marched off to… Mary didn't care where. She assumed that they would be kept until the Costa Rican authorities could get there, and was just as happy to look forward to the promised shower.

"I still have sand in awkward places," she told Neal. "My cottage?"

He took her hand and walked beside her down the steps. The sun was making its wild lunge into the ocean for sunset, and everything was cast in golden light. The few clouds near the horizon were fuchsia and orange, and the ocean made its siren song over the sounds of birds and insects.

The smells wafting from the dining hall almost made them turn in their tracks.

"A very fast shower," Mary said, despite the grumbling of her stomach.

"A very fast one," Neal agreed.

That vow lasted only as long as it took to stagger to Mary's cottage and strip each other out of their clothing.

She could not keep her hands from the planes of his muscles, and although she got the shower started and pulled him in after her, soaping herself seemed like a terrible use of her time when she could be kissing him, and letting him caress her and lift her up onto the bench with her legs eagerly spread.

He entered her, slick and shamelessly inviting, and Mary had to bite back cries of pleasure and peaking desire.

"Don't, don't stop," she begged in his ear, nibbling at his neck and clutching at those amazing broad shoulders.

"Don't let go," he told her back, lifting her effortlessly along the wall to get her into a position where he could thrust easily into her, over and over again until she was drowning in pleasure and her begging was incoherent.

Then he was coming too, thrusting with increasingly urgent strokes until he made an animal noise near Mary's ear and then coursed into her with his seed.

They stood slowly as they regained control of their breath and the waves of their pleasure ebbed away. Neal knocked a bottle of shampoo off the rack and caught it deftly, but not before it had spilled onto Mary's shoulder.

"Close," she said, scooping it up and redepositing it on her head.

After that, the shower was more utilitarian, but if Mary lingered a little longer than was strictly necessary in some spots while lathering Neal with soap then it was understandable, and he certainly didn't object.

CHAPTER 36

Neal felt like a new man. Showered, dressed in clothing that (mostly) fit, and sitting across from Mary in the open dining hall, it seemed like it had been more than just a few scant hours since they'd been rescued from their private cove. It seemed insane that they'd been taken as hostages and rescued themselves in that time, and Neal still found it hard to believe that Lewis—Lewis that he'd been sent to bring down ten years ago—was in custody.

"How does it feel?" Mary asked quietly.

Their plates were empty between them, though they'd been refilled several times.

Scarlet had insisted that the staff be served in the restaurant, and Breck, Bastian, Travis, and Tex were regaling a rapt audience with a version of the situation that Neal suspected had little resemblance to the actual events.

Neal shrugged, not sure what Mary was asking about.

"Lewis is why you went to Beehag's prison," she reminded him. "Does it feel like closure to finally capture him?"

Neal frowned, trying to pinpoint why he didn't feel vindicated. "Not exactly," he said thoughtfully.

"Did you really set Benedict's phone to ring when you handed it back?" Breck called across the dining room, interrupting them.

Mary laughed, looking up at him. "I just set a timer," she explained with a shy shrug. "Anything to be disruptive."

"Honey, you are a mastermind," Breck said with approval. "Let me bring you guys dessert."

Despite having polished off several plates of Chef's braised pork cutlets and tender vegetables with red potato wedges, Mary and Neal both accepted the tall, fluffy slices of angel food cake smothered in fresh berries and whipped cream.

Neal was chasing the last blueberry across his plate when he heard the distant sound of chopper blades, and his restlessness finally made sense.

It was several moments before Mary noticed it, and Neal spent those moments watching her face as she savored the last morsels of her cake.

"What is that?" she finally said, listening.

"That was Plan B," Neal said cryptically. At her quizzical look, he explained. "That's my old team. I called them as soon as we got free of the first group of guards. You're hearing a heavy helicopter, just a few minutes out."

Mary's eyes grew wide, but she took that as beautifully in stride as she had their entire adventure.

"How does *that* feel?"

It was a valid question, and one that Neal didn't have an answer for, even when they were standing together at the parking area at the top of the resort outside the gates—the only clear, level place at the resort with space for a landing.

Mary stood close beside him, clinging to his hand. Though he suspected that it was for her own comfort, he took an equal amount of strength from it. She shielded her eyes as the helicopter whirled to a landing, but Neal just squinted at it in the darkness. Judy would be using radar to make the landing, and she must know that he was already there, waiting at a safe range by the entrance.

Watching his team exit the lit helicopter was odd, the familiar shapes of their shoulders beneath the armor they were wearing; the way they each moved and held their weapons; and the other, more subtle differences that weren't apparent until they stepped into the light by the gate.

Judy had dyed her hair a deep nut brown and let it grow out a few inches more than Neal had ever expected she would, almost to her shoulders. Gobber still had no hair, and refused to wear a helmet except to battle, but he had more years of wrinkles in his face, and there was a new scar by his ear. Jessy was still tiny and fast, but had braids in her black hair now, and a stiff motion that suggested a healing shoulder injury.

Remmy—Neal's gut clenched. Remmy still had that too-young look, as red-headed as Neal was, but twice as freckled, with big innocent eyes in his round face. When Neal met his gaze, Remmy flinched so quickly Neal almost doubted that he'd seen it, but when he looked at Judy, he knew at once that she had seen it too, and that it was the last confirmation she'd been waiting for.

She gave a quick, professional gesture, and Thomas, who was giant and umber-skinned and hadn't aged a day, was swiftly behind Remmy, disarming him with practiced hands before Remmy could even blink. Jessy lowered her weapon in a not so subtle way, keeping it trained on Remmy.

"You got here fast," Neal said, not wanting to comment on the action, even as Remmy started to protest, "What's going on guys?!"

"Don't make it worse," Judy warned him. "I had my suspicions before I heard from Neal. You couldn't expect someone like Lewis not to rat you out, could you?" She added a few choice insults, then turned her back on Remmy and said blandly to Neal, "We didn't want the Costa Rican authorities to get here before we could. Jurisdiction often comes down to who gets there first, and I'm not letting that asshole slip through my fingers again."

Scarlet had appeared at Neal's side without his notice, a fact that would have alarmed him with anyone else. "Well, we certainly appreciate having this mess cleaned up as quickly as possible," she said, all business. "This way, please."

Not one of the soldiers had a problem accepting her authority and falling into step behind her, each of them giving Neal a grin and a not-so-gentle punch in the shoulder as they went past. All except Remmy, who only glared.

"I can't believe you'd take his word over mine," Remmy grumbled. "You don't even know where he's been for ten years."

Judy was the last to pass, and she alone stopped at Neal, and after a moment of staring at him, broke into a grin and enfolded him into a fierce hug. "You son of a bitch," she said fondly. "You could have called sooner, you know. They've got phones here, I hear."

She stepped back and inspected Mary with critical eyes.

Neal wanted instinctively to step between them, but paused.

Mary swallowed. "How do you do," she said formally. "I'm…"

"You're Neal's mate," Judy finished for her. "That's good enough for me."

Without further formality, she gave Mary a punch in the shoulder and turned to follow the rest of the team into the courtyard where Scarlet had Lewis and his men lined up in duct tape restraints.

Mary rubbed her shoulder and turned mystified eyes to Neal.

"Sorry," Neal said. "Judy takes a little getting used to."

"I like her," Mary said, with a surprisingly large smile.

CHAPTER 37

The courtyard was crowded with nearly a dozen restrained men, Neal's team, and Scarlet's staff. Tex, Travis, and Bastian seemed to feel that the handover required their direct supervision, and Benedict, who was not restrained, kept wringing his hands and muttering about his lawyer.

Judy gave Lewis a toothy smile, clearly enjoying his furious sulk. "I told you I'd be back for you, you bastard."

"I should be so flattered," Lewis snarled back. "You're only here because Neal went whining for his *girlfriend* to come and save him."

"And he did a fine job before we even got here," Judy answered, not in the slightest ruffled. "Because you're an incompetent jackass who surrounds himself with other incompetent jackasses and turncoats and then wonders why you can't inspire loyalty."

"How did you get free of your guards?" Tex asked in an undertone as Judy talked about the legal details of taking custody of Scarlet's prisoners.

"Gizelle," Neal said. "Er, the gazelle. I've been calling her Gizelle in my head. I have no idea what her name really is."

"What, did she skewer one of them?"

"Turned into a human and hypnotized them," Neal said with a sideways smile.

"Neat trick!" Tex said.

"Not as neat as a 'forget-me field'," Travis scoffed. "Seriously, Bastian, what was that? You didn't think that was just a little bit impossible?"

"We've already had this discussion," Bastian said with mock seriousness. "You just don't remember it."

"We want to get these guys back on American soil as soon as possible," Judy said, concluding her discussion with Scarlet. "So we'd best get going."

"You're welcome back any time," Scarlet said warmly.

"I thought the resort was for shifters only," Judy said with a searching look. "We're not all shifters."

"We can make exceptions," Scarlet said with a meaningful look in return. "Any of your team is welcome to stay here."

"Does that team include you, Neal?" Judy's voice was a challenge, and Mary felt Neal's hand tighten in hers.

But Neal shook his head. "Not any more," he said, and Mary could hear the mixture of regret and determination in his voice. "I've got a lot of healing left to do, and I'm ready to settle down and do what needs to be done. No more hiding."

Mary felt a little surge of relief. She would never have asked him to give up his team, but she knew that she'd have a hard time being away from him during his missions, missing and worrying for him.

"We'll miss you," Judy said frankly, clasping his arm. "We *have* missed you. But I'm not surprised. I'll be back for that drink and the story you owe me."

Neal let go of Mary's hand to embrace her. "I'll be waiting," he said hoarsely.

Judy turned to Mary. "Take good care of him," she said firmly.

Mary drew herself up. "I intend to," she said just as firmly.

CHAPTER 38

Neal woke with a start, disoriented, until he realized that he wasn't in his own bed. He was snuggled up close to Mary's warm, curvy form.

Part of the disorientation was that he hadn't woken from nightmares, but from sweet, restful sleep, for the first night that he could remember.

Sunlight spilled around the edges of the curtains covering the big glass doors at the foot of Mary's bed, and she stirred as Neal sat up.

"I am never taking clean sheets for granted again," Mary purred, as she stretched and opened her eyes.

Neal couldn't find words to answer her, just taking in the beautiful curves of her body under the silky sheet, and the splay of her hair on the pillow. She smiled up at him, and Neal could read the warmth and affection in her expression.

She felt like home. Like safety and wholeness and happiness. Like forever and happy endings and things that Neal had never guessed he could claim for himself.

He was still staring at her, he realized, as her expression became quizzical.

"I'm glad you could get your plane tickets changed," he said. It was the truth, if not the whole truth.

"I feel so terrible for the substitute. A whole week of those students, all wound up from spring break." Mary chuckled. "But not terrible enough to regret it."

"I should have my visa sorted in time to go back with you," Neal said, and he was glad of it. He wasn't sure he could stand watching Mary get on a plane without him.

"What do you want to do this week?" Mary asked.

"I… guess I figured I'd keep working," Neal said, blinking. He hadn't really considered himself a guest at the resort, though he supposed that Scarlet's invitation to stay on as a guest had included him. "And you'd enjoy the pool."

"I was thinking we might go parasailing," Mary suggested shyly. "And maybe snorkeling? It seems like a shame to come all the way to Costa Rica just to sit by a pool."

Neal grinned at her. "We could go hiking."

Mary hit him with a pillow, and Neal caught it easily, reaching to wrestle her down and tickle her.

"I have a better idea," they said in one breath to each other.

His mouth on hers was the perfect ending.

UNLOCKED

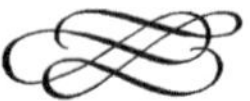

The second story I wrote specifically for this omnibus collection, and a matched pair with ***Locked****. Gizelle's point of view is always a delicious challenge to write.*

Her name was Gizelle.

Neal had given her the name and it was hers.

Gizelle.

It was as if having a name made her a person inside her gazelle.

She liked Neal. He felt safe, like she didn't have to always run, and he never tried to touch her or speak loudly. Her gazelle liked Neal, too, and they often grazed nearby, because it made him feel better to have her near.

He was sitting on the picnic table where they had shared many meals over the days and weeks, Gazelle browsing at the short, delicious grass.

But he didn't have food today, and he was dressed curiously. There was a backpack next to him, and he wasn't wearing shorts.

He felt different inside, too; his maned wolf was noisy in his head again, unlocked from the cage he had been in for so long.

"I know you can shift now," Neal said. "And so do you. You don't have to stay like this forever."

Gizelle continued to graze, letting a flicker of her ear be the only hint that she'd heard him.

Neal didn't offer to chase her across the lawn or cajole her into shifting.

"I brought you this," he said, and he set something heavy down at the end of the picnic table, as far away as he could reach.

"I can shift now, too," Neal said conversationally. "We're on good terms again, you know, me and my wolf."

Of course she knew that. But her careful observation of the people in this place suggested that most of them weren't paying much attention to all the things going on inside of others. It was like they couldn't hear anything but the loudest of mouth noises.

She grazed closer to the table, wild with curiosity, but pretended that she wasn't eyeing the object. It was metal, Gizelle thought, but she couldn't tell what it was.

Finally, she shifted, keeping the end of the table between them.

Neal watched her, trying not to look like he was. Gizelle put a trembling hand to the thing and picked it up. It was heavy and not very beautiful, but she supposed that she shouldn't judge it by her own aesthetic standards. Everything in this form was bright and full of garish colors that her gazelle couldn't see.

"What is it?" she asked with her voice because she could not ask with her human ears.

"That's the lock from my cage in Beehag's zoo," Neal said gently.

"It's... noisy," Gizelle observed. "Noisy with feelings. What do I do with it?"

Neal shrugged. "I only know that I don't need it anymore... and maybe you do?"

She cradled it in her arms as if it was a fragile child, not a heavy, dented chunk of metal and mechanics. "No one has ever given me anything," she said in awe. "I don't have anything to give you in return." And he'd already given her her name.

Before Neal could assure her that he didn't expect anything back, she shook her head. "I will," she promised. "I will. Or, I did."

Then she wilted. "You're going away."

"I'm going home with my mate," Neal said gently.

Gizelle was shaking in earnest now, distressed; her knuckles were white around the lock. "You're *leaving.*"

He was the thing here that she knew the best.

"You'll have the lock," he said coaxingly. "It can anchor you."

Gizelle had only the foggiest idea what an anchor was. Something heavy. Something to keep her from floating away in fear.

"You are safe here," Neal said. "Scarlet will protect you."

Gizelle nodded. She trusted Scarlet. Scarlet was kind and strong and everywhere on this side of the island. "I would like to help," she said softly. "This is a *nice* place."

"I bet that Tex would like your help at the bar," Neal suggested.

Gazelle nodded. "I could try that," she said. The weight of the lock kept her hands from trembling quite so much. Maybe that was what it was supposed to do. She looked down at herself, all her pale, fragile human hide. "I would probably have to wear clothes." She had been watching everyone for a long time. She saw how they dressed and walked, on two legs.

She longed to be like them but wondered if she ever would. And now Neal, the person she knew better than anyone else, was leaving.

"Gizelle," he said gently.

That was her name. He'd given it to her and she didn't have to give it back. She realized that she was clutching the lock to her chest and it was making uncomfortable marks in her skin. Should she carry it around with her always? Maybe she needed a hoard, like a dragon, a safe place to keep all of her things. This was her most precious thing so far.

Next to her name.

"You gave me a name," she said gratefully. "You unlocked me."

Neal smiled at her. "You're going to be okay," he said gladly.

Gizelle thought that maybe he hadn't been sure of that before he came to see her, that he was looking to her for reassurance, to make sure that it *was* okay. She didn't like the idea of him leaving, it made her want to run and run... but she thought that he'd be happiest going away with his mate Mary and she didn't want to be the one to hold him here.

"I'm going to be okay," she agreed.

Neal stood slowly and offered his hand to shake, but Gizelle knew it would be too much noise, too much color, and she backed away instead. "Goodbye," she said because she somehow knew that she'd regret not saying it if she didn't.

"Goodbye," Neal echoed her.

Then he turned and went away.

That night, Gizelle went back to the zoo on the quiet side of the island. She found a place where the wall had fallen down and dashed inside on two legs, because she could not carry the lock with her on four legs. She explored the empty aisles between the open cages, peering in each one like it might have the answers to all her many questions.

She didn't remember being in a cage, not like Neal did. She didn't remember anything before her escape, jolted suddenly to awareness in the midst of chaos and battle. She'd fled to the jungle, drawn to the peace in the trees, and spent several days wandering the forest until she was drawn to the resort on the far side of the island.

There were people there. People like her.

She found her human skin when she had to, and remembered ahead how to speak.

Neal was safe. But Neal had left. Was leaving. Would leave? Time was different for a gazelle than a person.

Gizelle used her gazelle's nose to find the place where she must have lived for so long, and she sat at the door in her human form until it was too cool and her trembling wasn't all fear and uncertainty. She stayed there a few days, mostly as an antelope, but she wouldn't eat the grass close to the cages.

She thought about all the things that she'd seen and felt and tried to make sense of them: good people and bad people and friends and *mates.* All the voices and people and animals.

Then she returned to Scarlet's side of the island, carrying the lock that Neal had given her, to find clothes and be useful.

She wasn't sure what okay looked like, but she thought she was a little closer to it now.

TROPICAL BARTENDER BEAR

PROLOGUE

FIVE YEARS AGO

Tex Williams met the eyes of the waiting customer and slid the beer glass expertly down the bar into his waiting hand. He tipped the brim of his hat and was unable to resist feeling like Tom Cruise in Cocktail when the customer gave him an enthusiastic thumbs up and the patrons between them applauded.

"Last call!" he hollered, in a voice that carried.

Then he turned to the gorgeous sepia-skinned woman who had just come in and staggered up to the bar. She was leaning heavily on it, wearing a tight, deeply-scooped magenta shirt and a short skirt. Knee-high, high-heeled boots completed the look.

"What can I get for you, ma'am?"

"Whiskey," she said boldly. "Neat. On the rocks."

Tex smiled indulgently at her. "Which one?"

She blinked back, confused. "Can't it be both?" she asked in a stage whisper, glancing at the next customer at the bar; she was packing up her purse and paying them no notice at all.

"Yes, ma'am," Tex replied in a matching whisper. Neat was a

straight shot, on the rocks was over ice, so there was no way to do both. He turned to pour her a seltzer on ice with a twist of lime. "On the house," he said, not trying to swindle her.

She took it with no suspicion at all, gulping it down and shuddering as if she had just downed the strongest stuff that Tex had.

"You need me to call you a cab, honey?" Tex asked. He had a few cabbies that he trusted with cases like this on speed-dial.

The woman stared at him, clearly trying to make sense of his words.

"You got a friend here?" he asked gently.

"A friend?" She furrowed her brow, adorably trying to figure him out. Alarm passed over her face and she put a manicured hand to her mouth. "There was someone…" Her eyes widened. "Do you think that he could have put something in my drink?"

Tex was immediately on alert. No one was going to be slipping drugs to ridiculously innocent young women at his bar on *his* watch. He peered into her dark brown eyes, which were glassy, but not dilated. "What have you had to drink?" he asked her intently. "Did you ever leave your glass, to go to the bathroom? Who were you talking with?" His bear senses were at full strength—she smelled like hand soap and laundry detergent and leather and richly of alcohol, but not like drugs.

"I had some iced teas," she said, gazing back into his eyes trustingly. "Three Manhattan iced teas. Or New Jersey iced teas. Or something…?" she furrowed her brows again in that childlike way.

Tex relaxed. "Long Island iced teas?" he suggested. That matched the smell on her breath.

She tried to snap. "That was it!"

"You don't drink a lot, do you." Tex didn't make it a question.

She giggled and shook her head. "No."

She was a full-bodied woman, all her curves in just the right quantities for Tex's tastes. But if she wasn't used to drinking—which clearly she was not—three Long Island iced teas would explain her inebriation quite completely.

She was still trying to snap her fingers.

"What's your name?" Tex asked her, trying not to let his amusement show.

He needn't have worried; she was oblivious to anything but her disobedient fingers. "Jenny," she answered distantly. "Jenny Smith."

"I'm Tex." If she had been more sober, Tex might have guessed she was picking a generic fake name.

She must have realized that, as she raised sparkling eyes to him and added. "Well, it's really Jennavivianna Rose Smith. My parents didn't want me to have a boring name, and were devastated when I told them I'd rather be Jenny."

"You sit right here, Jennavivianna Rose," Tex told her, indicating a stool. "I'll make sure you don't pass out or do anything stupid. I'm going to give you a glass of water and a cup of coffee, and you put down whatever you can, you hear me?"

She gave a sloppy salute with a face-splitting grin as she clambered carefully up onto the barstool. "I trust you," she said. "I don't know why, but I trust you."

Tex poured the last few drinks for the other customers at his bar, keeping a careful eye on Jenny while she sipped her water and played with the bar napkin. The other customers gradually filed out as they finished their drinks and Tex failed to provide further inebriants. Tex wiped down the bar, and gathered up all the dirty dishes for the cleaning crew. The waitress began putting chairs upside down on tables and gave an old man nursing his last drink by the door a good-natured scold.

"How you doing, kitten?" Tex asked Jenny, wiping the counter around her. "Feel like being sick?" He'd been a bartender long enough to know the usual progression of a drunk that thorough.

She was clearly flagging as the alcohol wore slowly out of her system, but she shook her head firmly. "I don't usually drink," she confided. "This is all very out of character for me." Her gesture included her outfit and she pulled the shirt up at the shoulder self-consciously.

"You want to tell me about it?" The offer was automatic on Tex's part, but he meant it whole-heartedly.

Jenny looked at him with a hazy smile. "Yeah, I do. I mean I wouldn't usually, but hey, while we're being out of character, why not?"

Tex was pleased to see that her speech was clarifying. He was certain now that nothing was ailing her more than a bit too much to drink and he was able to shake off the vaguely guilty feeling that had been dogging him at the idea that someone could have slipped her something on his watch.

'It's not your bar,' he reminded himself. 'And you can't save every hard-luck case that comes through the door.'

She didn't look like a hard-luck case, though. Her hair was neatly trimmed, and her makeup was perfect. Her hands had the soft, subtly manicured look of someone who had gone through life without doing labor more menial than loading a dishwasher.

Even her voice as she spoke sounded educated. "It was my sister's idea," she confessed in a whisper, though the waitress was across the room closing things up well out of earshot.

"She thought you needed a night out on the town?" Tex gave her an encouraging smile.

Jenny rolled her eyes. "She thinks I'm a stick in the mud," she scoffed, forgetting to be quiet—or forgetting *how* to be quiet.

Tex wisely did not agree, but only made a sympathetic noise.

"She always has all the fun," Jenny complained. "I'm the responsible one, studying hard, scholarship to the University of Texas. She's so smart, she just skates by without working at all. She could be anything! She's so stylish and has so much fun." Her voice was full of affection and envy. "These are her clothes," she added wistfully.

"They look great on you," Tex told her sincerely. They certainly fit her just right.

"They look great on her," Jenny corrected him. "I look like a fraud. I feel like a fraud. I'm graduating in three months with a degree in law and I feel like I'm ready to panic and run away and do something crazy and reckless and throw it all away because I'm not as good as my grades say and who would even *let* me practice law and there's the bar and maybe someday I'll be a judge but that's just absolutely nuts and it's all just really overwhelming."

"It's pretty normal to feel like that," Tex assured her. "I've probably seen a hundred students in the last few months of their degrees who say variations of that. And it's okay to take a little break and be out of character and go out to a bar for a good time."

Jenny's look of relief was almost comical. Tex wondered how long she had been waiting for someone to say that to her.

"'Course, I have to say that because I work in a bar," he teased her, and was glad when she picked up that it was a joke and laughed richly.

"Did you go to college?" she asked, then backpedaled, "Sorry, that was probably too personal."

"Nah," Tex drawled easily back at her. "I never had the smarts for that. Thought I might make it as a musician, never really got further than amateur night and karaoke."

"I bet you sing really well. You have a great voice."

Tex wasn't sure if the warmth in her own voice was still the alcohol, or if she was flirting. "Thanks, sugar," seemed a safe enough reply.

"I'm leaving!" the waitress hollered, making true on her statement with a bang of the back door.

"Dreams are important," Jenny said firmly. "You shouldn't give up on being a musician."

"Dreams change," Tex said with a shrug. "I still like playing, but it's not a career I'd choose."

"What would you choose? Bartending?" From some people, it may have sounded condescending, but Jenny was genuine and naive; her question was sincere.

"Honestly, yes," Tex admitted. "I'd love to have my own place—maybe somewhere tropical."

"You ever seen…"

"Cocktail," Tex finished. "Yeah, I may have watched that at an impressionable age. Practiced juggling liquor bottles for hours to get it right."

Jenny sat up. "Let's see!"

Tex chuckled and picked two bottles from the counter. "Pro tip… full bottles have different balance than empty ones, and half-empty ones are worse. That lesson cost me half a paycheck when I dropped a 16 year old single malt."

He set the bottles easily in motion, spinning them in his hands and dipping them behind his back, even tossing one of them and catching it with a flourish.

Jenny squealed and clapped her hands appreciatively. "Oh my gosh, you have reflexes like a shifter!"

Startled, Tex fumbled the bottle, and then miraculously caught it before it hit the edge of the counter. Jenny's eyes went wide and she clapped her hand over her mouth. She met Tex's eyes and he knew that he had betrayed his understanding of the term with both his reaction and his reflexes.

"I mean… ah…" Jenny bit her lip. "I suppose we've eliminated the possibility that I was drugged into stupidity, but can I blame the iced teas for that slip?"

Tex had to laugh at her earnestness. "I hate to break it to you, but you're almost past that excuse, too."

Jenny gave a mortified groan.

"You're a shifter?" Tex asked. Somehow, she didn't fit into his expectation.

Jenny shook her head. "No, but otters and wolves run in my family. And I'm usually much better about being discreet about them."

Tex chuckled, replacing the bottles on the shelf. "Long Island iced teas can do that," he said understandingly.

"What's your animal?" she asked wistfully. "If you don't mind me asking."

"Bear," Tex said. "Brown bear."

"I didn't know there were brown bears in Texas," Jenny observed thoughtfully.

Tex leaned in. "Want to know a secret?"

Jenny nodded, eyes dancing.

"I was born in Oklahoma. And I don't admit that to just anyone."

Jenny laughed, an unlady-like snort of pure humor. "I can understand why."

Tex straightened up again. "Now you know all my secrets!"

"I won't tell a soul," Jenny promised. She rubbed her temples ruefully. "I don't think I will ever drink again, so I promise that this secret will be better kept."

"Circumstances were stacked against you," Tex drawled understandingly. "And anyway, it was part of the whole escape out of character."

Jenny cast her eyes down, giving a little half-smile. "It would be out of character for me not to go home alone, too," she suggested with an unexpected invitation.

Tex actually considered it. She was sober enough now that he trusted the offer was made with sound mind, and she was utterly, completely gorgeous, with warm brown eyes and dark, thick, shoulder-length brown hair. Her skin was a rich mahogany, the magenta shirt did little to hide the swell of perfect, overflowing breasts, and the tiny skirt hugged the sexiest hips Tex could imagine. In every way, she was everything he'd envisioned in his perfect mate. But something was holding him back, some sense that she wasn't quite right for him, and the only feelings she activated were protective.

"You don't want me, honey," he told her gently. "I'm unlucky in love. And I wouldn't want to be mixed up in the hangover you're going to have."

She looked disappointed, but accepting, and when Tex refilled her water glass, she gratefully drank it.

"Can I call you a cab?" Tex suggested gently.

This time Jenny nodded. "My sister was supposed to meet me here, but I'm guessing something came up with her job. I'll read her the riot act tomorrow, let me tell you."

She slipped off of her barstool to use the ladies room while Tex made the call, and he was pleased to see that her steps were no longer more wobbly than strange, high-heeled boots would indicate.

He finished cleaning the bar while she was busy, and when she came out, the cab was already waiting at the curb.

Tex came around the bar to unlock the front door for her.

"Thanks," she said shyly, looking up at him with those beautiful brown eyes. "I feel like you came to my rescue tonight."

Tex tipped his hat at her. "Just doing my job, ma'am."

Jenny stretched up on her tiptoes and planted a chaste kiss on his stubbly cheek. "You're my hero," she told him.

Then she was slipping out the door for the cab, and Tex was locking the door behind her in bemusement. Somehow, he didn't think he'd seen the last of her.

CHAPTER 1

PRESENT DAY

Laurelangelina Smith woke in a hot panic, every one of her senses blazing, and she was out of bed and running into an unfamiliar wall before she remembered that she was not at her tiny condo, she was at Jenny's apartment, and... *Jenny*.

Laura reached for the odd psychic connection that she shared with her twin and found only emptiness.

Jenny was gone. There was no sense of her, anywhere that Laura could reach.

Still disoriented, Laura pulled one of Jenny's sensible bathrobes on and staggered out to the kitchen. Her head was pounding, but she knew that wasn't the reason that she'd woken up, or the reason that Jenny was so gone from her head.

You're an idiot, she railed at herself. *How could you have trusted those jerks? You knew better than to get mixed up in that scene.*

She expected a snarky response from her wolf, but only got wordless worry and grief in return.

Laura shuddered and opened the fridge. Nothing looked appetizing, and there was no Irish cream for her coffee. A drink, maybe a drink would calm the whirlwind in her head.

There was nothing more alcoholic in the cabinet than a rum fruitcake leftover from Christmas.

She nearly jumped out of the bathrobe when the phone on the table rang, and she was puzzled when her thumbprint didn't open it. Dammit. Jenny had grabbed the wrong phone on her way out, and left her own behind. The screen told her: Fred. Fred Kesser worked at the same firm that their father had worked at, where Jenny worked now. Trust Jenny's work to be calling at oh-god-hundred in the morning on a Monday.

Jenny…

Jenny was *gone*.

Laura buried her face in her hands and sank into a chair at the tiny table. She should *never* had sent Jenny to go shopping in her car. Had they blown it up? Sent a sniper? Shit. She never thought these things through.

Getting involved in the mob-like organization of the LA cartel had been so easy, so innocent. John had offered her good money at a tight time, and everything they asked for had been so simple and easy. In her small, gray wolf form, she could make discreet deliveries and pickups. She never saw what was in those little packages, never asked questions, never wanted to know.

But some part of her always knew, knew at least that it was bad news, and that she was being willful in her ignorance.

Then, finally she'd heard too much, seen too much, and she knew she couldn't continue.

Getting out was harder than getting in, of course.

She swallowed to remember Blacksmith's eyes, and his threat. "You tell anyone about this, and shifting won't save you."

And now Jenny, *Jenny* was *gone* and there was no *way* it wasn't related.

Laura hadn't smoked a cigarette in two years now, and she had never wanted one so badly.

Hours later, when the cops finally knocked on the door, she had still not found anything to drink.

"Ma'am, are you Jennavivianna Smith?"

Laura blinked. "Jenny," she said weakly. Jenny hated her full name.

"Ma'am, I'm afraid there's been an accident. Your sister's car was just pulled out of the water by Handle's Curve."

Laura gripped the door frame tighter. They'd probably cut the brake lines, or tampered with the steering or something. In the dark, in the spring rain… and Jenny wasn't as good at driving as Laura was—she commuted by bus or train and didn't even own a car.

"No body has been found, yet. The search is ongoing."

Then it hit her. They thought that *she* had gone off the road. They thought that Jenny was standing here, and that her hapless, screw-up sister Laura was the one who had died. Laura gave a little moan of pain.

The second cop reached out a hand to her and offered words of sympathy and support that Laura brushed off, not even hearing over the buzzing in her head.

"Yes, thank you. I'll be okay. I've got… friends, yes. I'll be okay. Yes, please keep me updated." She brushed them off as best as she could, going through the puppet-motions as she imagined Jenny might.

They didn't say a word that implied they might think it wasn't an accident and Laura said nothing to suggest it, either.

When she'd finally shut the door behind them, she leaned against it for a long moment. It had all been one long lie, from 'I'll be okay' to 'Thank you.' But it had been easier than she guessed to put herself in Jenny's shoes.

Jenny's phone showed a voicemail alert. Laura unlocked it with the code they'd used for bike locks when they were little and listened to it.

"Marty thinks you should go to Costa Rica to represent the firm," Fred said after a brief opening ramble about contracts and files. "You're the one who got the old contract annulled and the new one ready in time. And you're totally due a break. Give it some thought, and find your passport. The World Mr. Shifter finals are just next week, so we've got to make the airline reservations right away."

It was one of the few things that the sisters had in common—a weakness for ridiculous pageants. Mostly, it meant snarking together over pints of ice cream on the couch. A shifter pageant—was it just a gimmick, or was it actually a male beauty contest for shifters? And Costa Rica… she had always dreamed of going there.

It suddenly occurred to Laura that Costa Rica was more than just a tropical destination—it could be her escape. She wouldn't be able to maintain the facade of Jenny's life very long; she could fit what she knew about contract law in a pen cap with room leftover. But she could start a new life in a foreign country where no one knew either of them.

It didn't take Laura more than a few moments to find Jenny's passport—the whole apartment was ridiculously tidy and well-organized, and passports and important cards were thoughtfully filed at her desk. The same passcode that had opened her phone unlocked her laptop, but Laura couldn't bear to look through it.

With a deep breath, Laura called Fred back.

She didn't have to feign the tears that came as she explained why she wouldn't be in to work. "My sister… there was an accident." *It was my fault*, she didn't say. *And it wasn't an accident.*

Fred fell all over himself trying to comfort her as she choked out the parts of the story that she could.

"No, of course you don't need to come in. We'll give your cases to Julie, naturally. Don't feel bad, take whatever time you need."

Painfully glad that Fred had not pressed her with any details about those cases, Laura hesitantly said, "The… the Mr. Shifter contest—"

"You wouldn't have to go, of course," Fred said quickly, then seemed to stumble and reconsider. "But you could, if getting away sounds good. You know, a change of scenery. While you… ah… recover."

As if she could ever *recover* from this. The best Laura could hope for was *escape* from this. "A change of scenery sounds good," Laura saved him gratefully.

"I'll get Marty to put everything in order," Fred assured her. "We'll get you the tickets right away, send you the itinerary. Do whatever you need to do."

"Thanks Fred," Laura said sincerely. She tried not to think about how poorly she would be thanking him, abandoning Jenny's job and fleeing the country altogether.

"Anything you need," Fred repeated. "Anything you need, you let me know."

"I will," Laura lied. *I need my sister.*

She pulled out her wallet after she hung up and stared at the photo on her license.

The face—her face and Jenny's—was so familiar. The name wasn't hers anymore. Jenny's hefty kitchen shears split the photograph, and the shreds of the card were cast into the garbage disposal. Laura's credit card, already maxed out anyway, followed swiftly. Jenny's passport would get her out of here, and she had enough information and identification to access her accounts through her laptop.

Even dead, Jenny was saving her butt.

CHAPTER 2

The conference room behind the restaurant was stuffed to the seams. Tex wryly thought that if they were going to keep adding staff members, they would have to start meeting in the grand event hall where they held exercise classes and weekly formal dances.

Tex chivalrously stood when a strange woman in the Shifting Sands housekeeping uniform edged into the room and glanced around for a chair.

"Merci!" she said sweetly, with a grateful smile. She sank gracefully into the offered chair.

"Too bad we don't have new French maid uniforms to go with the new French maids," Breck, the headwaiter, hissed near his ear appreciatively as Tex backed up to the wall with folded arms.

"I think she's French Canadian," Tex whispered back. She smelled like too much perfume.

Not that Breck would care where she was from. Breck appreciated all women, and all men, for that matter.

When Scarlet entered, the chatter died to a murmur and then turned into an attentive silence at her frown.

"As you know, we've got a lot of new staff to welcome," she said briskly. "We aren't in preschool, so we aren't going to go around the room and introduce ourselves, but do take a moment to look around and see who's new and make a point of saying hello to those you don't know. On your own time." Her green eyes traveled apprais-ingly across the room and Tex met them briefly.

"The World Mr. Shifter finals will officially begin one week from today, but we'll be getting new guests every day between now and then, and they'll be doing a lot of the early interviews and photo-shoots starting in two days. Travis?"

Travis, a lynx shifter from Alaska who was in charge of repairs and maintenance, looked like he hadn't gotten sleep in several days. The impression was probably accurate; he had been pulling all-nighters since the resort had gotten the news about the event's last-minute change of venue, desperate to get enough of the housing into shape to house the influx.

"All of the primary cottages are ready for occupancy, and the hotel has been brought back up to code. The hot water in the west wing isn't working yet, but should be by tonight. The toilets..."

Tex let Travis' report flow over him as he assessed the new staff. There were at least half a dozen new housekeeping staff, two new kitchen assistants, two new waitstaff who would split time between the dining hall and Tex's pooltop bar, a green-looking carpenter to work with Travis, and a second lifeguard to relieve Bastian. Even Graham, the stand-off-ish lion shifter in charge of landscaping, had been assigned a new helper, though Graham had already made it clear the young man would be do nothing but the most basic tasks, like lawn-mowing and hauling clippings. Tex suspected that he found the whole idea of an assistant deeply offensive, and the gardens had gone from immaculate to some new state of perfection, even while the gardener cleared vast new swathes of jungle encroachment back from the cottages that were being put back into use and tamed it into hedges of flowers and thick leaves.

"You want us to move?" Bastian said unexpectedly, in response to something Travis said.

Tex turned his wandering attention back to Travis, who squirmed and looked guilty, glancing at Scarlet for support.

"It's not that we'd have to," he said defensively. "It's just that the houses on the south cliffs are set up as a large private family manors, never made for individual rentals. It would take a lot of work to convert them into private rooms, and they'd be a hard sell the way they're configured now, with shared bathrooms and living space. But they're in fine working condition, and if the staff moved to those three houses, we'd free up twenty more rooms in the hotel."

Scarlet was nodding, paying no mind to Bastian's disgruntled muttering about sharing a bathroom. "Let's make this happen. I understand that it's not ideal," the withering look she gave Bastian was as much sympathy as he could expect out of her, "but our waiting list has never been this long, and this is a chance we can't let escape us."

She glanced around the room. "Chef?"

"Travis has the new freezer working," the distinguished older man reported, "and it's fully stocked. Our supplier on the mainland says there should be no problem filling the orders we've put in for the next few weeks, and I've got everything that can be made ahead ready to go." He nodded at his new assistants. "I'm confident my team and I can get you meals that will do the resort proud."

He earned the tiniest hint of smile from Scarlet. "I'm glad to hear that. We'll need to coordinate an extra trip to the mainland mid-week, from the looks of the order forms, but that shouldn't be problematic. Tex?"

Tex sat up straighter. "We're well-stocked in everything hard, but the white wine shipment came in four cases short."

Scarlet frowned. "Four cases?"

"I counted twice," Tex assured her.

"I'll call and have words with the distributor," Scarlet said, and Tex was glad that he wouldn't be on the receiving end of that call. "We may need to pick some up on the mainland if they can't get the replacement here by next week."

"We'll have a better idea of how well stock is holding up pretty quickly," Tex agreed. "Maybe they'll all be red wine drinkers. Incidentals are in good order, plenty of napkins and tiny umbrellas, and the fruit shipment exceeded my expectations this week."

Scarlet continued through housekeeping, and then got a thumbs up from Lydia, the black swan shifter who managed the spa. Other than a few minor supply concerns, and Travis' warning about overtaxing the septic system, they seemed ready for the oncoming crowd. Scarlet seemed cautiously optimistic.

"I'm really pleased with how well you've all stepped up and gotten everything together," she told them candidly, and Tex was as surprised as he was proud; Scarlet was notoriously stingy with her praise.

"We've got a busy few weeks ahead of us and I know you'll be asked to do more than usually do. It's going to be crowded and we're all going to be under a lot of scrutiny. I trust you can handle it, and that we will make this a *pleasantly* memorable event. Go make it happen."

The meeting broke up with high energy and cheer. Breck immediately introduced himself to the new French-speaking housekeeper.

As Tex slipped out past Scarlet, she took him aside. "I haven't seen Gizelle in a while." It wasn't quite an accusation.

"She's still not good with crowds, ma'am," Tex said apologetically.

Scarlet nodded thoughtfully. "She's going to have a rough few weeks," she said pityingly.

"I think we all may," Tex said candidly, earning a dry laugh from Scarlet.

Except for the extra staff, Shifting Sands didn't look any different. It still had that peculiar poised energy that Tex thought was due to the way the sun glittered off the white tiled decks and retaining walls. Photographers were already on site, taking light readings and doing test shots of the dramatic pool steps.

Gizelle was sitting behind the bar polishing silverware that was already clean, her salt-and-pepper hair obscuring her face. She scrubbed at each fork with a corner of her sundress, then held it up to the light critically. "Not much of a hoard," she said critically, when Tex found her.

"I'm not a dragon," he reminded her gently. "I'm a bear. Bastian is the dragon."

"Bastian doesn't think he is a good dragon," Gizelle said airily.

"Scarlet noticed that she hasn't seen you around in a while," Tex told her, crouching down and taking the basket of forks that she handed him.

"Scarlet notices things," Gizelle agreed, unconcerned. "She notices the sky with no sun. But she can't see the whole island."

"There's going to be a lot of people coming here in the next few days," Tex warned her. They'd talked about the upcoming Mr. Shifter event several times, but he wasn't really sure how much of it made sense to her.

As far as anyone could tell, Gizelle had spent her entire childhood as a gazelle, a captive in the zoo of a sadistic shifter collector. She didn't know her own name, or have any memory of parents or human shape before coming to Shifting Sands. She could have been twenty-five, or fifty; the white streaking her dark hair made her look ancient, but her face was unlined and innocent. She had a tendency to flee at the slightest hint of conflict, shifting into her gazelle shape and leaping high into the air. There had been several times Tex wasn't sure how she avoided breaking one of her fragile-looking legs as she landed.

Gizelle looked up at him, big eyes behind her wild, loose hair. "I know," she said reluctantly. "Too many people are coming, so *loud*, and there will be photographers to avoid. But I'll still help. Graham lets me rake sometimes, and Chef lets me wash the dishes. I broke a glass, to see how it would sound, but he told me I could still do the silverware."

Tex ruffled her hair gently, a privilege she didn't allow everyone. "You'll be fine. You want to go help Graham with that raking?"

She nodded with a slow grin and stood up, padding silently away on dirty, bare feet.

As Tex was giving the basket of forks a quick sift for anything unexpected, she popped back into the bar and warned him, "Some of the people are going to be bad. Listen through your nose!"

Then she vanished again.

CHAPTER 3

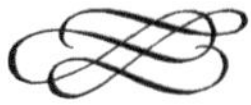

Shifting Sands was everything the brochure promised, Laura thought, looking down at it from the entrance.

Cottage roofs scattered through jungle greenery stepped down the hill before her, dipping down to a gorgeous crescent beach and a shimmering green ocean, waves lapping invitingly, even from this vantage. A few bigger buildings were artistically arranged to the south and an enormous pool gleamed from a white tiled deck.

The grounds were lush shades of green with riotous flowers everywhere providing spots of color and a distinct, dreamy scent.

"Excuse me," an impatient accented voice said behind her, and before she could move, she was being elbowed aside by a man carrying a suitcase whose bland white suit did nothing to hide the fact that he was clearly a bodyguard.

"Excuse *me*," Laura snapped, moving back inside the entrance. It was a little more crowded than the brochure had suggested. The courtyard was filled with people waiting to check in, and heaps of suitcases and travel bags lined the walls. They were clustered in groups—little flocks of attendants for each of the Mr. Shifter candidates, with their dark glasses and celebrity expectations.

"We'll need fresh linens every day, of course." The woman's American accent was strident and demanding.

"Of course! We'll do everything possible to make your stay pleasant and memorable." Laura recognized the clerk's silky, Spanish-accented tone at once. She'd worked in hospitality before; that was the 'your coffee will be spit into twice daily, but I'm going to smile' voice.

Beside the American woman, a man was leaning on the counter. He was definitely one of the Mr. Shifter contestants, his shirt unbuttoned halfway showed plenty of tanned pecs and he caught Laura's glance to give her an overly white-toothed, leering grin.

"We'll need breakfast delivered promptly at 9 each morning," his assistant continued.

"I'm sorry ma'am, food is only served at the restaurant. It is open 24 hours with a limited self-serve buffet, and has regular meals at..."

"There's no room service?" Her voice raised a scale. "What kind of fly-by-night resort is this?"

The clerk's voice remained steady. "I think you'll find the breakfasts our chef makes are worth the early trip," she said cheerfully.

"What are the bar hours?" the Mr. Shifter contestant asked in a lazy Californian accent. That clinched Laura's guess that this was the American representation and she was already embarrassed for her country.

"Wine and beer are available in coolers at all hours, the staffed bar is open until midnight each night." The woman pushed their keys over the counter with a pamphlet. "You're in cottage eight, here is a map that shows you the way; your cottage is circled in red. There's a schedule of events listed here."

"You don't have anything closer to the beach?" It was half whine, half kissing up, in a lightning fast swap of attitude as the assistant realized that she might need leverage with the clerk.

Laura was impressed by the clerk's sweet, even response. "I'm sorry, we're booked solid for the next week."

"Well, I suppose it will have to do, then."

From her tone, Laura could already imagine the Yelp review

that the American assistant was composing in her head. 'Resort was not able to accommodate my many and ridiculous demands. Terrible service. Spotted several insects. Staff in foreign country had actual accents.'

She was smirking over the idea in her head when Mr. America caught her eye again and he seemed to think her smile was about him. He winked, and Laura could feel the smile on her face freeze and turn brittle.

She was done with men. Pretty faces and nice muscles and her own destructive attraction to self-centered jerks had gotten Laura into this mess in the first place.

She wasn't going to make all those same mistakes again.

She scowled back and Mr. America looked surprised. She stalked back to her modest pile of luggage and waited while his assistant fussed about having their bags delivered and kvetched about how far it was to walk and how steep it looked. She admired the courtyard instead, with its lovely planters full of exotic things. Green vines draped down in veils from the center of the open yard, and the indirect light was gorgeous and otherworldly.

The Americans finally left, and two sets of Asian contingencies checked in. These, too, were clearly Mr. Shifter contestants with their assistants and a bodyguard apiece. The one that Laura guessed was Mr. China did his own registration, an assistant and an older man who may have been a trainer or a bodyguard waiting behind him. The other let his cheerfully forward assistant handle everything while he smiled and nodded a lot.

The last one before Laura in line was an eastern European man with incredibly green eyes and thick dark hair. A tropical white shirt did nothing to hide his incredible physique. He waited haughtily across the room with their luggage reading his phone while his secretary tripped across the room to complete their registration. She was uselessly giggly, had lost the confirmation number, and it took several extra moments while she fumbled for the correct credit card.

"I'm sorry it's taken so long," the woman behind the counter said with her lilting Spanish accent when Laura was finally able to approach. Her nametag said "Lydia."

"No worries," Laura said warmly, giving a wry smile of understanding. "You've had your hands full. Jenny Smith."

Lydia's professional smile became more real. "Do you have your confirmation number?"

Laura had used her copious waiting time to find her numbers and get Jenny's credit card, and she gave them both to Lydia.

"Perfect," Lydia said gratefully. "We've got you in the hotel, room 320 on the top floor." She said it neutrally, probably knowing how it sounded after the fancy cottage assignments she'd given to the Mr. Shifters before her.

"That sounds great," Laura said genuinely.

Her pamphlet had a map of the resort with the narrow hotel building circled. "You'll want to use the second door," Lydia said, indicating it on the map with a little blue dot. "And go ahead and use the staff elevator, it's directly on your left when you go in. Ignore the sign; there's no keycard required for it." She gave Laura a warm wink.

"Thanks," Laura said, and they shared a companionable smile.

"I've got a sunrise yoga class in the event hall if you're up." Lydia added shyly, pointing to the schedule on the back of the pamphlet.

Laura's smile slipped; sunrise and Laura didn't really get along, but she knew that Jenny was an early riser. And if she was going to maintain the charade… "I'll... try to wake up in time."

"Jetlag can be a drag," Lydia said kindly. "You'll be welcome if you can make it."

"Thanks," Laura said weakly. Jenny had been dedicated if not enthusiastic about her yoga classes, even if her efforts hadn't given her a shape any different than her lazier twin sister's.

Laura took her key and turned back to her bags. At first, she thought it was another Mr. Shifter contestant who was stalking up; he certainly had that Mr. Shifter physique. Then he started to take her bags, and Laura recognized that he was wearing a staff polo shirt with a nametag: Graham.

"I've got these," she said, before he could pick them up. "They stack, and have wheels, so I'm fine."

He grunted and shrugged, and went to fetch another pile of luggage without so much as a sideways glance. He picked up half the pile without a hint of effort and left as abruptly as he'd come in, festooned with bags.

Well, that one wouldn't have gotten far through the personality competition, Laura thought wryly. She slung her purse over her shoulder and just as she was about take her bags and find her hotel room, she heard, "Jenny! Jenny!"

It was a heartbeat before Laura remembered that she *was* Jenny, and she turned with a resigned sigh to smile and wave weakly at Fred as he came in with the next surge of guests in the single courtesy van from the tiny airport.

It had just become a dozen times more difficult to maintain her cover.

CHAPTER 4

A scream broke the hot afternoon lull. Tex dropped the drink he was making and vaulted over his counter without a second thought, bringing the baseball bat he kept there automatically. It was a short sprint out the back door and he spent those strides wondering what insane threat to expect this time.

For such a quiet little resort, Shifting Sands got some strange events. In the months that Tex had been working there, there had been a hostage situation with South American mercenaries, someone had wired the resort generators to blow up, and a crazy rare shifter collector had been kidnapping guests. Once, he'd had to break up a lion and bear fight. What would it be this time, the mob?

No, no, he told himself, this was Central America, probably it was the *cartel* here.

Graham materialized from a hedge with a machete just as Tex made the back entrance of the bar. There they found the new maid with the French accent standing on the sidewalk, clutching her armful of fresh folded towels and shrieking at the top of her lungs. A wide column of ants was making their merry way across her path and she was backing up from them in horror.

Graham lowered his machete, gave her a dirty look, and

vanished back into his beloved greenery. The few guests who had followed him to discover the source of the commotion decided there was nothing to see and returned to the bar, grousing about dramatics.

Feeling as sorry for Graham's disgusted look as he did for the ants, Tex leaned his baseball bat against the doorframe and crossed the ants with one extra long stride.

"Don't worry, ma'am. They occasionally get it in their little ant heads to march from some place to some other place, but they'll be done in no time at all. It's the jungle, after all, you've got to expect some insect encroachers. Graham does his best to keep them off most of the paths, but there's a limit to what even he can do."

The maid—her nametag said Marie, which was just perfect—threw herself into Tex's arms, towels and all.

"There's so *many* of them!" she sobbed. Her French accent was strangely gone.

Tex looked at the ants in some bewilderment. He'd gotten used to them, and suspected that Marie would not last long at Shifting Sands if she wasn't able to handle a simple ant migration. "You should see what happens to the cottages if people sneak food back to them," he said, patting her on the shoulder and hoping that the humor was reassuring.

She continued to sob on him.

"Now there, it's okay. You can just step right over them, they won't even notice you."

She made a noise of alarm and clung to him harder.

"Alright, then, ma'am, hold on."

She was barely an armful, even heaped with towels, and Tex was able to swing her up and carry her over the offending column of ants. He set her down on her feet, but she continued to hold on, clutching the towels between them.

"You're safe, ma'am," he said, slightly strangled. "You can let go now."

It took a more obvious effort to pry her off before she released him. "*Mon dieu*," she said, wiping at her eyes. "You are my hero."

Tex wondered if he'd imagined her French accent vanishing, it was certainly thick enough now. He tipped his hat at her. "It's the least I can do, ma'am."

Marie gave a little moan. "Oh, *mes serviettes*!" she said, shaking her head at her rumpled armful.

"Your… oh, your towels? They haven't suffered any," Tex reassured her. "I'll help you fold them and no one will know a thing about their brush with the army of *formicidae*."

She furrowed her brow at Tex adorably, and he smiled at her. "Ants," he explained. "Just ants."

Her face brightened in understanding, and Tex helped her shake the towels back into presentable shape and fold them neatly into squares again.

"My hero," she repeated, and the look she shot back over her shoulder as she trotted away down the clear trail to the cottages suggested that she was willing to reward Tex's chivalry.

Tex wasn't sure why the offer was so unappealing. She was a good-looking woman, with very definite charms. Dating within the housekeeping pool didn't offend Tex's good sense about not seeing coworkers; he would never had been even tempted by someone who worked the bar with him. But although he appreciated the view as she walked away with a little extra swing in her hips, he didn't find himself wanting to chase her down.

It wasn't just that he felt the weight of his bad luck in love, he felt like he was… waiting for something.

With a shrug, he collected his baseball bat and returned to the bar. Dropping the drink had not broken the glass, but there was a mess of spilled syrup to clean up, and an impatient crowd of guests had gathered while he was away.

"Sorry folks," he said, swiftly stepping up to give the mess a brief swab. "A lady screams, you've got to be ready to drop things and run to the rescue," he said smoothly. He added a wink for one of the older ladies at the counter, and was repaid by watching her grouchy expression turn to a delighted blush.

"What can I get for you?" he asked the first person at the bar. He got all their requests while he remade the interrupted drink.

They were all duly impressed when he could remember what

each of them had asked for without pausing to write anything down, serving even the most meticulously-ordered drink exactly as dictated. He spun a bottle on each hand as a finishing touch, and got a scattered round of applause from the ones who had remained at the counter to see the whole show.

"I'll take a Shifter's Mate," a familiar voice said from the end of the counter as the others dispersed. A sunhat and a wave of dark hair obscured her face as she bent over the laminated drink menu, shoulders slumped. She lacked the manic energy that the rest of the resort seemed to have right now.

"Coming up, ma'am," Tex said automatically, trying to place the voice and figure out why it was giving him such an unexpected electric thrill. He dropped the ingredients into the shaker with a few cubes of ice and shook it efficiently while he filled a glass with clean cubes in the other hand. An umbrella and a wedge of fruit at the rim finished his own invention.

"Pretty," the woman said, finally looking up.

"P-p-pretty," he echoed her, unable to come up with anything more. He remembered that face and those brown eyes, but that last time he had seen her had been nothing like this.

She is ours, his bear roared gleefully.

Jennavivianna had been gorgeous then, but now she was something infinitely more. Every curve of her body was an invitation, every wave of her dark hair was a promise. The planes of her lovely face were perfectly composed and the eyes—those limitless, bottomless, aching eyes! A man could drown in those places, if he let himself go.

And Tex was ready to jump.

CHAPTER 5

It would be a short and easy trip to become a drunk in the wake of her sister's murder, Laura thought, but she knew she needed her wits about her. She had hoped that Shifting Sands would be a safe escape from anyone who knew Jenny, the perfect place to springboard a new life in a foreign country. The resort had people from all over the globe and she planned to make use of her time to get to know some of them, maybe even get a lead for work that wasn't too careful about looking at visas. It didn't have to be in Costa Rica, she could get her return ticket changed to anywhere!

But she hadn't planned on Fred.

Fred had decided to join her at the last minute and, while he was fortunately not able to get all the same flights as Laura, he was staying at the hotel just a few doors down.

"I didn't like the idea of you off in some foreign place so soon after the loss of your sister," he said, so earnestly that it was impossible to hate him for fouling up her strategy so completely. "Isn't it lucky they were able to open up a few new rooms?"

It was only lucky if you counted *bad* luck.

Now, instead of planning her escape in two weeks, Laura was agonizing over everything she said and did—did she say that like

Jenny would have? Was she walking like Jenny did? She chose to wear the modest one-piece that Jenny would have, though she'd been surprised to find a sky blue bikini in her sister's closet. She even kept a sensible hat on, though her brown skin wouldn't burn. She had used jetlag and headaches as excuses for avoiding Fred at meals so far, but she knew that wouldn't last long. She was dreading the time when he'd finally try to talk work with her, and she'd have to stare at him blankly.

He was such a nice guy and he'd been such a good friend to Jenny and their parents over the years that Laura felt awful for brushing him off so coldly. She consoled herself by thinking that he would probably assume her chilly behavior was because she was grieving.

Her grief felt oddly far away. She couldn't really believe that Jenny was gone. They still hadn't found a body by the time she'd left Los Angeles, but there was no way she could have survived the crash or the ocean… was there? The police had given her no reason to hope. But it still wasn't *real* that she'd died. Despite the silence of their psychic bond, Laura couldn't help but expect her just to walk into the bar and scold her for slouching.

She felt restless, but she didn't think that's what grief ought to feel like.

She scanned the laminated drink menu, trying to decide which one Jenny would pick.

"I'll take a Shifter's Mate," she called to the bartender who'd been showing off at the other end of the counter without looking. It called itself a 'Shifting Sands original, a Mai Tai with a Costa Rican twist.' It would be like Jenny to take a fruity house specialty and it would undoubtedly be mostly cheap juice and a plastic sword.

She only watched the bartender's ridiculous drink-making out of the corner of one eye, not lifting her hat until he set the drink before her.

"Pretty," she had to admit, and then she made the mistake of looking him in the face.

He was as handsome as any of the Mr. Shifters, with a tan and build that Mr. California himself would envy. His easy smile was not as fakely white, and his hands were both strong and gentle on the glass he hadn't let go of. He was wearing a cowboy hat, of all the ridiculous things. Laura had no patience for the pretentiousness of cowboys and hated their music.

She wanted to dislike him at once but, instead, she was utterly drawn to him. His brown eyes had crinkles of kindness and humor around them and Laura had never wanted to touch a jaw as much as she wanted to touch his. The almost-scruffy stubble, the straight nose, and the stunned look—he was straight off a Western romance book cover.

"P-p-pretty," he echoed her.

Laura wondered if he was as stunned as she felt, or if he was just an idiot. Being an idiot would simplify things, at least.

He's not an idiot, he's ours, her wolf told her firmly, canine voice singing in delight.

He blinked and shook his head, which gave her just enough space to do the same.

"You're Jenny," he said, to Laura's shock. "Jennavivianna Rose."

Laura had no words. She'd come halfway around the world to escape her life, just to meet a bartender who knew her *sister*?

"We met in Austin, half a dozen years ago. Over spring break." He sounded baffled.

"Oh wait, yes!" Laura blurted. Jenny had told her about this, when she returned her borrowed boots. "You were very kind to her—to ME. You were really sweet. To me."

Ours, not hers, her wolf said jealously.

"Can I get you something?"

Laura barely avoided asking him to take his pants off and make love to her right there in the crowded bar. "You, ah, already took my order," she reminded him. "You're still holding onto it."

He gave a confused guffaw and let go of the glass. His fingers left bare spots in the gathering drops of condensation. Laura put her own fingers there and wondered if she imagined the little electric shock it gave her.

She knew what this was from the stories and from her inner wolf's animal glee. She'd never really believed she'd find her own mate, but she knew it was possible. Love at first sight, it was supposed to be. Like this, except not complicated by the fact that she was masquerading as someone else. Someone he'd already met.

She concentrated on his cowboy hat and worked at keeping her expression blank and casual. It was something she had a lot of practice with lately; act stupid, keep her head down, try not to put too much together.

"Can I get *you* something?" she asked, chilling her voice deliberately.

He actually blushed as he realized he was staring at her. It was one of the most adorable things she'd ever seen. He put his fingers to his hat in a gesture that could only be automatic. "I'm sorry, ma'am," he said humbly. "It's… ah… a surprise to see you again."

"It was a long time ago," Laura agreed with a careless shrug. It was tricky pretending disinterest when everything about him made her heart race and her breath catch. "Small world."

'He's a cowboy,' she reminded herself. 'You *hate* country music.'

She clung to that and took a sip of the drink.

He was still staring at her.

For the first time on the trip, she was actually glad to hear Fred's voice. "There you are, Jenny!"

She turned with a warm smile for the bartender's benefit and a little wave. "Hey Fred."

Fred plopped down beside her on a barstool, completely innocuous and out-classed in his flip-flops and sunburnt balding head.

The bartender's face, when she snuck a look, was a hilarious mixture of jealousy and confusion. Laura might have laughed out loud under different circumstances. "This is Fred," she introduced casually. "We work together." She wasn't actually that sure where in the hierarchy of the law office Fred fell, or for that matter, what Jenny's exact position was, which did nothing but complicate her acting efforts.

The bartender tipped his hat automatically to Fred. "Pleased to meet you," he drawled. "I'm Tex."

Of *course* he was. Laura had to keep her eyes from rolling.

"We met a few years back when I was in Austin for spring break," Laura offered.

Fred extended a sweaty hand for a handshake. "Did you go to college down there?"

Tex looked abashed. "No, sir. I'm not a college man. I've been a bartender since the law let me."

"Nothing wrong with that," Laura snapped in his defense before she could stop herself. She'd never managed more than a semester or two of college herself and Tex's embarrassed look hit her in several ways.

"Of course not," Fred said jovially. "It's not for everyone."

Laura gritted her teeth as his patronizing tone, but couldn't say anything. She was supposed to be Jenny, who'd done seven or eight years of higher education, so she shrugged and took a sip of her drink, nearly stabbing herself in the cheek with the stupid umbrella.

She let Fred and Tex fumble through a conversation without her, sipping at her drink like it would save her. A "Shifter's Mate," it was called, and just like the real thing, it was sweet, with a kick of intoxication and a twist of sour.

Her mate. She'd found her mate.

Our mate, her wolf corrected, practically purring in her ear. She, for some reason, did not seem to consider the cowboy hat a deal breaker. Nor did she mind that Tex was a bear, something that they both seemed to instinctively know.

These things don't matter, her wolf said dismissively.

How about the fact that we're masquerading as our twin sister and he's already met her. That might confuse the issue.

Aren't you humans used to confusion by now? You certainly seem to thrive on it.

Sometimes Laura felt like Jenny was the lucky one, not being a shifter.

She caught herself watching Tex out of the corner of her eye. He was telling Fred his choices of high end gin for a gin and tonic. Fred was trying to look knowledgeable about the selection.

Laura emptied her drink, wishing it had been four times as strong, and ate the fruit off the umbrella stick. "I have to use the ladies," she said, hopping down off her barstool. Fred would probably wait here for an hour or more before he figured out she wasn't coming back.

"Wait," Tex said too loudly. Other patrons of the bar turned to look curiously, and a pause in the tinny Spanish radio music gave the moment a surreal edge.

Laura turned back, and gave what she hoped was a cool stare back at him.

"I'm pretty sure I don't have to pay," she said dryly. "This place is supposed to be all-inclusive."

"No, of course, it's just…"

He was adorable, fumbling through his obvious confusion. Laura could not get over how expressive his mouth was, or how perfect the line of his jaw was. She'd been turned on by men before, but none of them had ever made her as literally weak in the knees as this. Between the tropical heat and the sanity-eating lust this man was igniting in her, she thought she actually understood why heroines in dirty novels sometimes swooned.

"Can I see you, later?" he finally stammered.

She wanted to say yes. She honestly didn't want to leave his presence; every move away from him felt like betrayal.

But he was a complication in a plan already made painfully complex by Fred. A mate wasn't a mandate and she was past the point in her life where she let her loins lead her around.

"I'm not interested," she lied. She was entirely too interested. "Sorry," she softened it, hating the lost look in his eyes.

Before she could change her mind, she turned on her heel and left.

CHAPTER 6

"Mr. France was disqualified because he was a dragon," Bastian said with a snarl. "Everyone knows it. Specism is a thing and mythical creatures get the short end of every stick."

"I don't know," Travis said thoughtfully. "They said it was drugs. Besides, Mr. Ireland is a pegasus."

"Maybe they just have something against dragons, then, and not sissy flying horses. And what drugs could possibly survive a dragon's bloodstream?"

"It was some designer thing, specific to dragons," Travis explained, reading from his tablet. They call it goldshot, and it has some kind of *enhancing* properties."

"Enhancing what?" Breck asked suggestively from across the room.

"Hey, there's Graham!"

The surly landscaper made a brief appearance in the background of the interview on the screen, scowling and vanishing as soon as he realized he was in the field of the camera's view.

In person, Graham grunted and took a drink from his beer.

The Mr. Shifter competition was on the staff television,

streaming through the Internet, rather than broadcast television. Shifters weren't acknowledged in all of the countries represented, which made the competition more complicated, and the contest was being hosted through a webpage. At least part of the contestant elimination was done through Internet voting, though there were also a half dozen celebrity judges wandering the resort acting important.

Tex sat at the other end of the couch from Graham, nursing a beer and paying the barest of attention to the screen he was staring through.

"Damn, this place looks great on camera," Travis said proudly. There were aerial shots of the pool, zooming in through the palm trees to the Greek columns and grand steps, flanked on each side by waterfalls. Mr. India was stepping out of the water, and the camera lingered on the water slipping off his dusky skin and the tight, shiny spandex of the very spare swimsuit he was wearing. It was a bit of a disconnect, seeing the sunlit resort when the darkness outside was so complete.

"Man, that French villa is wishing they hadn't screwed up their contract," Breck agreed. Every shot made the resort look good, with gleaming cottages and landscape that was dripping in riotous flowers. There had been multiple shots of the pristine beach, with its jeweled jungle backdrop and crystal blue water. It was the kind of advertising you couldn't buy with money.

"That probably had something to do with Mr. France's disqualification, too," Bastian muttered acidly.

"It could have just been that Mr. France couldn't fake his way through the part of the contest where he had to actually speak in complete sentences," Travis suggested.

"Not that he has to for the swimsuit portion," Breck countered merrily.

Bastian's face went dark and he rose up out his seat with a growl, but he only pivoted on his foot and left in a grouchy huff.

"What's his problem?" Tex asked, momentarily distracted from his own problems.

Breck shrugged.

Surprisingly, it was Graham who answered. "He had to move his hoard. It's a dragon thing."

"Oh," Breck, Tex, and Travis said in understanding unison.

Bastian had been in a vicious mood since they'd moved out of the hotel, though any of the other staff would have cheerfully said that the house by the cliffs was actually a step up. It wasn't as private, but the rooms were bigger, and the common areas were stunning. The only real problems were that the toilet clogged if you flushed anything larger than a grape, and that Breck refused to tie his bathrobe closed when he was wandering around early in the morning drinking coffee.

The pageant stream went to a sponsored commercial for energy drinks and Travis muted it.

"I have a question," Tex finally started, and stalled out. He had his guitar in his lap, but his fingers were uncharacteristically still on the strings.

"Out with it, Cowboy," Breck prodded him.

"Do you… believe in mates?"

"Hard to deny them," Travis said solemnly.

Graham just grunted, but Tex thought it sounded affirmative.

"I just hope it never happens to me," Breck said, clutching his neck in a choking motion.

"But if it does," Tex pursued. "If it does, it's supposed to be at first sight, right? You're supposed to know immediately."

Even Graham nodded at that.

Travis said, "My grandfather used to say that if you aren't sure, it's just lust."

"It's not just lust," Tex said before he could stop himself.

The others stared at him.

"Cheers!" said Breck. "Who's the lucky girl?"

"You lucky dog," Travis added. "The sex is supposed to be amazing."

Graham gave him a crooked smile and raised his beer can in a toast.

Tex groaned and put his face in his hand, tipping back his hat.

"I just—I don't understand. We met before and it was nothing like this. Not even a spark. And now, she acts like… like…" Tex flailed. "Like she doesn't feel what I do."

"You already met once?" Travis asked, puzzled.

"Years ago, in Austin. Had a little after-hours chat when I was closing a bar I worked at."

"Just a chat, eh?" Breck could make anything sound suggestive.

"Just a chat," Tex said firmly. "She needed a little help and, even though she was gorgeous and willing, nothing actually happened."

"And this time…?" Travis prompted.

Tex pulled his hat back down over his eyes. "Sweet daisies help me. I cannot get her out of my mind. I want to do unspeakable things to her, and I want to get down on my knee and propose on the spot, and she's looking at me like I'm a sun-touched fool."

"Is she a shifter?" Breck asked.

"No," Tex said, just as his bear inside him said, *Yes.*

"*What?*" Tex said in confusion.

"Well, if she's not a shifter, she might not know about mates. Probably, she isn't sure why she's all hot and bothered for *you* in a crowd full of Mr. Shifter contestants." Breck's explanation was plausible.

"Doesn't explain why he didn't get the lightning bolt the first time they met," Travis added thoughtfully.

"Not you," Tex said impatiently. "My bear says she's a shifter. But *she* said she wasn't."

That earned him curious looks.

"Bizarre," Travis said with a shrug.

Graham looked darkly suspicious.

"Have you always been able to tell who's a shifter?" Breck asked curiously.

"Sometimes I can smell it on them, but not always," Tex said, baffled. He poked at his bear curiously, but his companion was distracted, all attention focused on their distant mate. All he could get was— "A wolf. She's a wolf shifter."

"Can you tell what Scarlet is?" Travis asked avidly. Most of the staff had bets going on the topic.

Tex shook his head, shrugging.

Graham shushed them, pointing at the screen, and Travis turned the volume up as the program returned with the interview and videography of Mr. Austria, an eagle shifter with Alps for muscles and a thick Germanic accent.

He was just explaining his plan for implementing world peace when there was a timid tap on the door.

Breck rose to answer it.

"*Excusez-moi!*" came a familiar voice. "I wondered if Tex was free to, how do you say, walk with me? If he is still up, I know it is late."

"Is that her?" hissed Travis.

Graham gave a lopsided grin and raised an eyebrow at him.

Tex grimaced and shook his head, but rose to his feet and came to the door to see Marie, elbowing Breck out of the way.

"Ma'am," he said politely, touching the rim of his hat. When she stepped back away from the door, he felt obligated to come out into the tropical darkness with her—there was no way he was inviting a lady into the bachelor house to the attention of his house-mates. He closed the door behind him, knowing it wouldn't do much good because the house had no air conditioning and all the windows were open. "Let's step up to the staff garden."

She took his arm gladly and Tex tried not to sigh too loudly.

"You have been so kind to me," Marie said, laying her head against his arm. "I just wanted to find some way to thank you."

"Marie," he started, once he thought they were out of easy earshot. There was a bench under a flowering magnolia tree and he sat with her there while he tried to find a way to let her down easy. A single garden lamp barely lit the little garden.

Without warning, Marie launched herself at him, her mouth landing on his demandingly.

Tex didn't want to hurt her and awkwardly tried to pry her off without manhandling her, finally standing up to escape her ardent kisses and insistent hands.

"*Qu'est-ce qui ne va pas*?" she asked breathlessly. "What's wrong? Have I offended you? Am I… not attractive?"

She was wearing something frilly and very low cut; somehow it had slipped off one shoulder as Tex struggled to get away. As she spoke, her breasts heaved in a way that would have been very distracting indeed if Tex couldn't help but compare them to the shape that Jenny's must be.

Tex had to laugh a little. "Marie, ma'am, you are lovely, and any man would be lucky to win you."

Her eyes were dark and glittered with tears in the faint light. "But you do not find me worthy."

"It's not about worthy," Tex promised sincerely. "If things were different… but there's…"

"Someone else," Marie's voice had an iron edge. "There is another *amour*."

Tex thought about Jenny's haughty dismissal of him and sighed. "It's complicated," he said.

Marie drew her shirt up over her shoulder and sat back, offended dignity in every line of her posture. "If it were not for her?" she pouted.

Tex was already thinking about Jenny again, the flash of spirit in her brown eyes, the curve of her perfect mouth. "If it weren't for her," he agreed plaintively. If it weren't for her, he could sleep at night, could close his eyes without picturing her. He shifted on the bench, embarrassed to find that he was having a physical reaction to just imagining her.

He didn't want Marie to think he was reacting to her, so he focused on where he was again. "Marie, let me walk you back to your room. You're at the next staff house up, right?"

Marie graciously let him escort her, keeping her hand on his arm, but not leaning on him this time.

"Thank you," she said thickly, when they arrived at her door. Tex could hear the sound of the Mr. Shifter contest blaring from the screen in their house, female voices laughing and appraising the contenders. "You are a true gentleman."

Tex tipped his hat at her. "Just trying not to shame the mother who taught me manners," he promised with a little laugh to lighten the mood. "Have a good night, ma'am."

"Oh, I will," Marie answered. Tex couldn't identify the tone of her voice, but was happy that she went inside without further protest.

He walked back down the manicured path to his staff house, decided he was done watching the contest for now, and slipped quietly to his own room.

He shucked off his staff shirt and lay down, to slide at once into dreams about Jenny.

CHAPTER 7

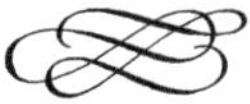

"I am very well-known in most of Europe," the photographer told Laura. "Practically a household name. Everyone knows who Juan Lopez is."

Laura made an uninterested noise that was taken as an interested noise by the gold Speedo-clad man wearing so much suntan lotion he looked as greasy as he sounded.

"I would love to photograph you," he said, slipping his sunglasses down to give her a look that was only barely not a leer. "You have this *joyous life* to you. I wish to capture it on film."

Laura knew a line when she heard it. She hooked a finger on her own sunglasses and looked at him over the top in a deliberate mirror of his own. "Nude, of course," she said dryly.

Her sarcasm was lost on him. "Of course. It is the only way to do you justice!"

Laura settled back into her sunchair, realizing that subtlety was not her friend here. "Nope."

"You won't get another opportunity like this! I am an artist..."

"Go find some other naive woman with low self-esteem to try this on," Laura suggested. "I'm not interested, I won't be interested, and I'm not above reporting you to the staff if you continue to harass me."

She tipped her head back and closed her eyes, every other sense alert. "Get lost." She curled her fingers around her water bottle and prepared to throw it at him if the matter escalated.

The photographer sputtered in surprised outrage, then muttered an insult and took himself somewhere else.

"Don't mind if I am," Laura muttered after him, then took a sip of her water. The old her would have fallen for his flattery. He wasn't bad looking, if perhaps a bit outclassed at a tropical resort filled with male pageant contestants and staffed with men who could have given them a run for their money.

But she knew better. He'd picked her because she was wearing a modest one-piece by the pool and wasn't model thin like so many of the beauty coaches and personal assistants. She was probably obvious about dodging Fred at this point, so she looked like easy pickings for the self-esteem pickup… he'd flatter her, she'd decide to do the pictures to make herself feel better about her looks, there would be drinks, a pass that she wouldn't feel good about saying no to. Men suck, she reminded herself. She was done with them.

Except that she couldn't get Tex's face out of her mind. That gorgeous, stunned smile, those clever-looking fingers. The perfect laugh crinkles around his big brown eyes.

No, she thought fiercely. *Done with men.*

Tex was behind the bar, handling the light traffic of the sweltering afternoon. Laura couldn't see him from the pool deck, but she knew he was there. It was hard to pretend that she wasn't irresistibly drawn to him, but he'd been impeccably professional when she had returned to the bar the evening before. He'd clearly been confused by her and Laura hated the longing hurt in his eyes, but chivalry seemed to be his first order of business. He'd filled her drink order without grilling her or pressing her further, keeping conversation to the business at hand.

That was how it was going to be, then. She would pretend there was nothing there, and he would respect the distance she was insisting on.

Laura was wryly aware that this plan would not have worked with anyone less than a perfect cowboy like Tex.

"Can I get you anything, Mademoiselle?"

Laura sat up to find that a young dark-haired woman in a crisp white housekeeping uniform had a tray full of bottled water, one of them open.

"Thank you, no," Laura said, settling back on the lounge. She indicated the half-full bottle she had contemplated throwing at the photographer.

To her surprise, the woman didn't move on right away. "You are enjoying your stay at Shifting Sands, I hope?" she asked leadingly.

Laura considered. If she hadn't been stressing so hard about maintaining her cover, this would have been a perfect vacation spot. The bar was well-stocked, the hotel was comfortable and well-appointed. She loved the aesthetic of the whole place, with its shining tile and riotous jungle gardens. The restaurant could get crowded between the Mr. Shifter events, but Laura recognized that this was a temporary state of affairs and had learned to schedule her visits to the services during times when most of the guests would be busy with the pageant games. If Jenny had been with her, she might have wanted to spend more time watching them like so many of the other visitors, but without her, if felt empty and disappointing.

That, and she kept comparing the contestants to Tex.

It was all too complicated to explain to the maid, so Laura simply said, "I'm having a great time." It wouldn't have been a lie if she hadn't been working so hard to hide her true identity.

"And you know Tex, I think?"

Laura was trying so hard to figure out what kind of accent the maid had—it didn't sound Spanish, she thought—that she wasn't expecting Tex's name, and she started. "I… er… we met once a few years ago. In Austin." It was mostly the truth.

"I see." The woman's icy tone surprised Laura, but as quickly as she recognized it, it was swept away in a bubbling laugh. "He is a great bartender! We love his juggling!"

Taken aback by the pendulum swing of the woman's demeanor, Laura laughed hesitantly along. "Yeah, he's great at it."

"He plays and sings so beautifully, as well, you have heard him?"

Laura shook her head.

"Always with the saddest songs. You are sure you do not want a fresh *eau*?"

"Ew?" Laura said, then her brain caught up with her ear. "Oh, *eau*, water, no, no thank you." A French accent, then.

"Another time," the housekeeper suggested firmly, and her shoes clicked across the tiles firmly. Laura thought it was odd that she didn't pause to offer one of the other sunbathers any water, but perhaps Laura simply hadn't heard her talking to them earlier.

The poolside sun brought her no comfort after that and after a few more moments trying to get comfortable in the chair, Laura abandoned her magazine and decided to return to her room.

Jenny's laptop was sitting on the desk, and Laura sighed and opened it, emotions in a jumble. She was desperate for some kind of closure, some closeness with her lost sister. She probably had some of their email exchanges, neatly filed. Maybe reading over them would make her feel better.

Jenny's wallpaper was a serene tropical scene with a white beach, which made Laura smile crookedly. If only she could see the view out Laura's own window now.

Before she could open the email program, Laura was stopped by a shortcut on the desktop labeled finances—will and life insurance. Of course Jenny would be so organized. When Jenny was halfway through law school, she'd insisted that Laura file a will. Laura had left everything to Jenny, and Jenny had done the same in return. Was there a life insurance policy that named her? But no, they thought it was Laura that was dead, and she'd never taken out a life insurance policy, and she didn't have any money to inherit.

Did Jenny have a policy that named *her*? Jenny was always looking out for her.

Laura wiped away a tear and clicked on the shortcut. It opened a folder with more links—Jenny's bank, copies of legal-looking documents...

A tap on the door startled her, and Laura had to take a deep breath and remind herself that it wasn't like she was *stealing* Jenny's money.

She ignored the person at the door, hoping they would go away, until there was a scratching at the lock that made her realize it was probably housekeeping.

"Oh, thank you, no," she said hastily, getting to her feet. "You can come back later. Or not at all. I can make my own bed, really."

She went to the door, not sure if they'd heard her, and pulled it open to find Fred putting something in his pocket.

"I was worried," he said. "You've been so distant, and have so much to deal with. I wanted to make sure you were alright." He stepped towards her and Laura instinctively moved back, inadvertently inviting him into the room.

Laura smothered a sigh. Would tears only encourage him to stay and try to comfort her? She settled for trying to feign a brave face.

"I'm okay," she promised. "It's hard, and sometimes I just need a break. There are so many people here, you know. It's sometimes a little overwhelming." She gave a trembling smile. "Laura would have loved this place." Too thick?

Fred patted her arm, a strictly paternal and comforting move that still felt awkward. Jenny may have been good friends with him, but Laura hadn't seen him since she moved out on her own nearly ten years ago.

He glanced around, as if he found the moment as awkward as she did, and his eyes fell on Jenny's open laptop. Laura suppressed her urge to leap for it and close the lid.

"There aren't too many people in the restaurant right now," Fred said coaxingly. "There's some kind of photo thing down at the beach, so we could go now and get a good seat for dinner and make an early night of it tonight."

As if sleep would make everything better.

Lacking a good excuse, Laura agreed, closing the laptop as unobtrusively as she could manage before reluctantly following him out.

"Are you enjoying the resort?" Fred asked carefully, as they were served a generous plate of baked fish slathered in a creamy sauce, topped with fresh herbs and served on a bed of fluffy rice.

The restaurant usually only had two gourmet meal selections, but what it lacked in choice, it made up in quality. If she wasn't in the mood for what was available, the buffet always had sandwich ingredients and a few staple dishes to choose from. But Laura had never been less than delighted with what she was served.

"It's lovely here," Laura said, though she knew her tone was lack-luster.

"You're not… sorry you came?" Fred pressed. "I know you haven't been enjoying the pageant events as much as you thought you would."

Laura put on a brave smile. "I'm not sorry I came," she promised.

Fred drew an exaggerated hand over his forehead. "Whew," he clowned. "I would hate to be responsible for convincing you to go on vacation and have it turn out terrible."

Laura felt for him. He was trying so hard to make sure she had a good time, and had been such a good friend of the family. She remembered how he'd been there when their parents had died, making bad jokes to try to cheer them up, and handling all the paperwork and finances that they'd floundered with.

"Have you thought about what you'll do next?" he asked unexpectedly.

Laura froze, and then reminded herself that he was undoubtedly not talking about her plan to disappear in a foreign country.

She toyed with the fog on her water glass and looked down at the suddenly unappetizing fish. "I haven't thought about it," she lied.

"You'll need to have a memorial," Fred told her gently. "I know neither of you would want a fancy funeral, but you should have something."

Laura took a sip of the ice water to try to loosen the sudden lump in her throat. Jenny deserved a fancy funeral. Probably her lawyer friends would come, all in business black. Her neighbors would turn out, with their neatly-dressed offspring.

Who would come to *her* memorial? Ex-boyfriends? Her grouchy landlady? The guy who delivered her favorite Chinese take-out?

The cartel?

Not for the first time, Laura was certain that the wrong person had been in that car.

"Yeah, you're right," she agreed faintly, knowing she looked sick.

Fred patted her hand. "You leave all the details to me, sweetie. I'll arrange a nice, quiet memorial and can take care of all the paperwork."

It was an echo from years ago, and Laura felt like she was seventeen again, lost and afraid and adrift.

The only difference was that Jenny wasn't here to cling to.

There was a sudden rise in the hum of conversation at the restaurant as guests began to arrive en mass, laughing loudly about the beach-side sunset photoshoot.

Laura choked down the last of her fish and told Fred she planned to head to bed early. "There's a marathon kick-off pretty early tomorrow that I'd like to catch," she said, mostly meaning it.

He gave her a fatherly hug that she couldn't politely dodge and stayed for dessert while she fled.

CHAPTER 8

"What's next on the Mr. Shifter schedule?" Travis asked, collapsing onto a stool at the end of the bar. "I got the generator for the laundry room back up again, but I have no idea how long it will keep working. Tell Breck that the second washer needs his special kick."

Tex poured him an orange juice. "I see a bed in *your* schedule," he suggested.

"One more stop," Travis protest, downing the orange juice. "Broken fan in cottage three."

"Hasn't that fan been broken twice this week already?" Bastian, just off lifeguard duty as the sun went down, slid onto a recently abandoned stool. Most of the post photo-shoot crowd had milled off for dinner at the restaurant and Tex could hear them on the deck above, laughing and carousing. He'd just sent a tray of fancy drinks up with one of the waitresses who was running her tail off.

"I'm beginning to think they're breaking it on purpose," Travis said darkly.

"Probably, they're just enjoying watching you climb up on that ladder," Bastian teased. "Everyone's in the Mr. Shifter mood for a little show."

Tex served Bastian a shot of cinnamon whiskey, neat, and consulted the resort schedule. "To answer your first question, Travis, it looks like early tomorrow morning is the Mr. Speed event, the marathon to the airport and back. And tomorrow evening is the Mr. Fur, Fins, or Feather animal event."

"How does that even work?" Bastian asked, tossing down his shot. "I mean, how would you judge between all the different animals? Cage match?"

Travis laughed, pushing his glass back over the counter. "I think they are evaluated against species ideals and assigned values by expert judges. I know Lydia's got her girls booked for the entire afternoon for grooming services. Guests are grumbling about how hard it is to get any spa services."

"I know we should be grateful that business is so good after a long dry spell, but I will be very glad to have things back to some kind of normal," Tex said wearily. He glanced longingly at his guitar, leaning in the corner of the bar. Most days, he had plenty of opportunity to sit behind the bar and play. This week, between the madhouse of guests and assisting Travis in getting the resort into top working order, he hadn't touched the strings. Every spare moment was spent restocking, or cleaning, or repairing.

"Speaking of normal," Bastian said, raising an eyebrow.

Tex looked at him blankly.

"What's up with your mate?" Travis finished for him.

Tex was glad that a guest sidled up and requested a drink, but when they wandered off to the pool deck with it, Travis and Bastian were still staring at him expectantly.

"Aren't you too busy for gossip?" he asked crossly. "I am."

Travis and Bastian exchanged knowing looks.

"She still denying it?" Travis asked pityingly.

"It doesn't make any sense," Tex said, knowing he sounded as whiny as he felt. "I mean I've always felt unlucky in love, but this is ridiculous. How can she not feel this?"

"Why do you always say that?" Travis asked. "That bit about being unlucky in love."

Tex shrugged. "It just always seemed that way. I'd get my

courage up to ask a girl out… right after she got asked out by the high school jock. Or that date where my truck broke down on my way to the restaurant and she ended up marrying the waiter."

"Brutal," Bastian agreed. "And now your own mate is pretending there's no bond between you."

Tex let out a breath he didn't know he was holding. "I can't stop thinking about her. I can't get her face—or her body—out of my mind. I don't sleep without dreaming about her."

"Sounds like those songs you love to sing," Travis teased kindly. "The sadder the better, right?"

Tex groaned and pinched the bridge of his nose. "I don't know what to do," he confessed.

"Another round of margaritas!" one of the tables called.

The harried looking waitress scrambled through the back door with a tray of empty glasses. "I need a sidecar, a ginger snap, two blended margaritas and one on the rocks, no salt. Two pilsners, one Guinness, and a Budweiser."

"Who the hell goes to a tropical luxury resort and orders a Budweiser?" Bastian asked, getting up from his stool to let Tex get back to work. "Come on, I'll hold your ladder, Travis, and make sure no one tells you about anything broken before you can get a decent night's sleep. Breck can kick the generator if the laundry room goes black again."

"That's what I'm afraid of," Travis said darkly. "He can handle the machines, but I don't like him doing the electrical stuff. I've seen what that man can do to a fusebox!"

They left Tex to mix drinks and think dark thoughts about things sadder than any country song he'd ever sung.

CHAPTER 9

Sunrise yoga in the recreation center hadn't even started when Laura joined the growing throng at the very top of the resort.

Laura yawned and wished she'd thought to swing by the restaurant for a latte before coming to the start of the marathon. Several smarter guests carried steaming to-go cups.

The view was arguably worth the early morning. To one side was the vista down over the terraced resort, with it's charming cottages and grand architecture. The pool from here was a huge blue jewel, and the ocean beach beyond was a sliver of white caressed by turquoise water. The early morning sun set silver light in the jungle treetops, casting dappled shadows everywhere.

The other side was a sea of beefcake. The finalists were all wearing the barest of running shorts, and only one of them had opted for a tanktop... and it was one so tight and scant it was barely worth the effort.

There was more gleaming manflesh, stretching and warming up in provocative positions, than Laura would expect to find in a magazine for lonely women.

She found her cheeks heating, just watching the spectacle, but she kept thinking about what the bartender, Tex, would look like. She hadn't gotten a glimpse of his ass, but she could imagine that it was much like Mr. Brazil's, given their similar body build. Mr. Brazil obligingly bent over to stretch his hamstrings and gave her an amazing view of his spandex-clung butt and the barely contained package beyond.

The girls next to Laura giggled and fanned themselves.

It suddenly occurred to Laura to wonder if Tex had a pair of assless chaps, to match his other over-the-top cowboy accessories, and then, of course, it occurred to her how much *fun* such a garment might be.

We could find out, Laura's wolf suggested.

We could not, Laura replied sternly.

One of the celebrity hostesses, a little bottle-blonde woman named Jessica Linn, looking more than a little hungover, banged on her clipboard. "Are you rolling?" she asked the cameraman.

"When you're ready," he said.

"I'm ready to get this over with," she snapped. "Why would they schedule this so early?"

"Gets too hot later," Mr. Canada guessed over his sunglasses. He looked as dragged out as Jessica did.

Mr. Ireland, by contrast, was bouncing in place, obviously eager to go.

"Alright," Jessica said. "Listen up, studs. We're going to go over the rules before we turn on the cameras and I don't want to have to say things more than twice." She pointed down the road behind them. "You'll be running down that road to the airport, and back up. It's about two miles each direction, lots of winding, lots of hills, mostly under jungle cover. We've got cameramen in several key spots, and the video camera will be in a Jeep behind you for part of the way. There's also a drone that will be following you. There is no shifting allowed, this is human legs only."

Laura wasn't surprised—it wouldn't be much of a race between a pegasus and a peacock, but Mr. India looked lean and fit; she thought he might give Mr. Ireland some competition.

"The winner will be awarded the Mr. Speed trophy in the final awards ceremony, and there's a ribbon or something for the second place. I don't know, who cares." Jessica fanned herself with her clipboard. "I'm bound by the insurance company to let you know that you are not covered for egregious injury due to special shifter riders, blah blah, don't be a dumbass and step in a gopher hole. We're not medi-vaccing you. Do they even have gophers here? Oh, let's just get this started. I need some cheers, ladies."

She fluffed her hair and pinched her cheeks, pasting on the most plastic smile that Laura had ever seen and gestured at the cameraman in the back of the poised Jeep.

"Welcome back to the World Mr. Shifter events!" she squealed. The girls gathered around Laura gave ear-splitting shrieks and applause, and the Mr. Shifter competitors stepped up their stretching and posing as the camera panned around.

Laura clapped half-heartedly.

"Oh, it's such a shame Mr. Ireland is married," one of the audience members near Laura lamented.

"I thought that being single was one of the criteria!" another protested.

"No, that's the *International* Mr. Shifter competition, this is the *World* Mr. Shifter. These guys don't even require that you have modeling experience. Mr. Ireland doesn't."

"What does he do?" The first woman was practically drooling.

"Firefighter, I heard."

"Oh, he can put out my fires any day."

"Show us your best cheeks, gentlemen!" Jessica was saying enthusiastically.

The Mr. Shifters lined up at the white chalk line that had been drawn on the road, pausing to flex and preen and dust invisible things off their shoulders.

This would have been a lot more fun with Jenny to snark with, Laura couldn't help thinking. Or if she could stop imagining Tex as a contestant. He looked like he could make a steep, four mile jog without getting winded.

Probably carrying a tray of drinks.

In assless chaps.

Laura shook her head firmly, and turned around to walk back down into the resort before they finished the introductions and the starting gun was fired. Maybe this way she could beat the rush on the restaurant and get a good seat and a peaceful latte.

CHAPTER 10

The restaurant was one level above the bar, with an expanse of open indoor seating and a spacious deck that looked down over the bar deck, the pool deck below, and the beach beyond that. Tex found that looking down over the uppermost deck gave an interesting perspective to the view that he usually enjoyed as he worked.

Tex closed the bar about midnight and wasn't often up this early, but when the sun rose at five and the birds came alive with the light, he gave up the pretense of trying to sleep and came to rustle breakfast from the kitchens. Chef, raising an eyebrow at him, didn't question his early appearance or the circles under his eyes. He just gave him a plate with a fresh bun stuffed with an arcane egg and sausage scramble.

Marie had been helping in the kitchen and gave him a long, plaintive look, but she didn't attempt to stop him when he left.

Scarlet allowed the staff to eat anything they wanted from the kitchens or the buffet, but discouraged them from mingling with the guests to eat their food. Tex had every intention of heading back to the conference room with his culinary prize, or even retreating to the closed bar to eat it there.

But then he felt her. *Jenny*, he thought and everything was wrong about the way her name sounded in his head.

He hadn't caught more than a glimpse of her the day before, desperately busy during the morning helping Travis piece together some questionable plumbing at one of the smaller cottages, and even busier at the bar after dinner until midnight. Celebrities, he found, came with more ridiculous demands for their drinks than any clientele he'd ever served. Never had so many olives been found unsatisfactory or mixing methods been called into question.

He'd been grateful not to have the time to think about Jenny, because she came with such a pang of pain and confusion.

Now, though, she was here, at the same level he was, being seated at a table that completely blocked a subtle escape. He either had to walk within arms reach behind her or walk out straight in front of her.

Frozen with indecision, Tex only watched her, doing what he suspected was a terrible job of camouflaging himself in the potted plants near the railing.

Even from here, she was so beautiful. Her dark hair was soft over her mahogany shoulders. Tex was mesmerized by the little motions she made with her hand as she ordered and the flicker of a smile over her mouth at some joke of Breck's.

He was shallowly glad when she responded coolly to the head waiter's obvious flirtation and irrationally angry when Breck was able to make her laugh with his pout.

Tex took another bite of Chef's breakfast concoction and finally made the decision to try to creep behind Jenny. It was possible she wouldn't notice him on that route, even if it would take more willpower to be that close to her and keep going.

Then he paused, trying to figure out what felt so wrong.

The sounds of the restaurant were all exactly right: the low murmur of conversation with the occasional laugh, and the clink of cutlery and the sounds of eating. More guests were arriving as the morning grew later, and there were the sounds of chairs scooting as they took their seats. It was busier than it usually was, but that had become the new normal with the booming event business.

Nothing looked out of the ordinary; servers bringing plates of food and specialty coffee drinks, clearing off tables and refilling coffee and water. The guests varied between bleary-eyed and clearly fighting hangovers, to energetic looking, probably fresh from Lydia's morning yoga. The early light shimmered over the open deck in ripples through the potted plant leaves.

There was nothing out of the ordinary about the little breeze that blew in over the open dining area, or the birds that sang.

It was the smell.

It wasn't just the food, and the breakfast drinks, and the tang of the jungle plants. He could also smell each person, under whatever cologne or deodorant they were wearing, and whatever they had brushed their teeth with. It was a tangled, many-faceted sense, and part of it was… wrong.

Bear was roaring in his head as Tex dropped his breakfast, shifting as he leaped across the room.

In one swift swipe of an enormous paw, the latte that was being served to Jenny went flying, to shatter against one of the support columns.

After an understandable flurry of gasps and shrieks, the chairs that Tex had knocked over stilled, and the dining room went silent. Tex was aware that he was the focus of absolutely everyone, forks frozen over plates, some of the guests even standing in alarm. Jenny's latte dripped slowly to the floor in a foamy mess.

He opened his mouth to explain, but it came out in a rumbling growl.

"What is the meaning of this?"

Tex heard the distinctive click of Scarlet's shoes before he saw her, pacing decisively towards them.

"I had to save her," Tex tried to say, but it was an ursine whine.

"Would you care to explain this, Mr. Williams? I suspect your human shape would be more useful to communication." Scarlet crossed her arms and waited.

Tex sheepishly shifted, realizing that he was completely naked and that his staff uniform had been completely destroyed in his rush. He was keenly aware of Jenny, plastered back in her chair in shock, and to some lesser degree, aware of Breck, who was still holding an empty hand out to her, frozen in place. He glanced behind him to realize that he'd broken one table leaping over it, and cracked several chairs. His hat was tottering on the edge of the railing, next to a broken planter littered with shreds of his polo shirt. Graham was going to have words with him about that.

He cleared his throat. "I apologize for the disruption, ma'am," he said to Scarlet, with a nod to Jenny. "I… ah, smelled something."

One of Scarlet's eyebrows inched towards her neat hairline. "You smelled something."

"Yes ma'am," Tex said firmly, drawing himself up to his full height despite his urge to grab a napkin from the table to cover himself with. "A bear's nose is more powerful than a bloodhound's, and I smelled something." He pointed at the coffee drink that had puddled on the floor. "That's poisoned."

The gasp from the audience was theatrically perfect.

Scarlet's second eyebrow joined the first. "Poisoned?"

There was the snap of a cellphone camera shutter, and Scarlet's head pivoted to glare at the photographer. The woman gave a quavering smile against her glower and put her phone sheepishly down on the table at once.

That released a titter of quiet conversation and speculation and Breck sat down heavily in the empty chair opposite Jenny.

"Damn, Tex. Give a little warning next time you're going to be a two-thousand pound brown bear and slap a mug out of my hand," the waiter said breathlessly.

"It's Jenny, right?" Scarlet said to the wide-eyed woman.

At her silent nod, Scarlet extended a hand. "I apologize for the disruption of your meal, but if I could ask you a few questions more privately?"

Jenny stood up, exchanging a brief, terrified look with Tex.

"Breck, please see that we have a record of everyone—staff and guests—that were in and out of here this morning." Scarlet's voice was deceptively calm. "Collect as much of the coffee as you can, and keep the pieces of the mug. Get the rest of this cleaned up and make sure that our guests enjoy their breakfast."

Breck came to his feet smartly, and immediately started getting his dazed staff in order as people slowly (and suspiciously) returned to their meals.

Tex trailed after Scarlet and Jenny protectively, shaken by the stark fear in her eyes. He didn't know what she was so desperately afraid of, but he knew that he had to protect her.

CHAPTER 11

The bear should have frightened her. A gigantic, snarling brown bear had loped across the deck at her, destroying tables and chairs, and smashed the coffee cup from her very fingertips. Laura knew that she should have been quaking in her shoes at the near-assault, and she wasn't sure why she hadn't feared for her life at any point in that blurry moment.

It was Tex's words that shot cold terror into her heart.

Poison.

Her latte had been *poisoned*.

That meant the cartel had found her. She'd been followed under her sister's name to this foreign resort and they were still trying to get to her.

There was no place in the world that was safe for her.

"What kind of poison was it?" Scarlet asked, once they were out of the restaurant and in a little office off the kitchens with the door closed. Laura sank into the only available chair without asking, sure that her shaking knees weren't going to hold her any longer.

Tex took an apron off a hook near the door and used it to do a poor job of covering his nakedness. Laura was grateful for that much coverage; a completely naked Tex was extremely distracting. She kept imagining what she would do to him, what his skin would feel like if she touched him.

"Rattlesnake venom," Tex said confidently.

Scarlet frowned at him. "We don't have any rattlesnake shifters registered among the staff or the guests. Are you sure?"

"I'm sure, ma'am," he said firmly. "We found a rattlesnake nest on the ranch when I was a kid, and I will never forget that scent."

Scarlet turned her sharp emerald eyes to Laura, and Laura shivered at the intensity in them. Surely this woman was looking right through her flimsy disguise.

"Do you know why someone would attempt to poison you?"

"No," Laura lied, hoping her squeak sounded sincere. She could think of at least two reasons—either the cartel she'd been reluctantly working for thought she'd snitched, or the rival cartel had figured out who she was. Either one of them would want her out of the picture, and had already tried to do that, taking her sister instead. She swallowed the grief that welled up in her throat.

"Would rattlesnake poison have killed you?" Scarlet's gaze was direct and unnerving.

It would have killed Jenny, Laura realized with a start. Her sister wasn't a shifter. Laura might have burned off the poison if she'd shifted, but Jenny definitely wouldn't have been able to. She felt safe giving an uncertain shrug, not really sure who she was answering for.

"You represented Mr. Stubbins, the producer of the Mr. Shifter event, when he broke contract with the previous resort, didn't you?" Scarlet suggested. "Could there be some hard feelings there?"

Laura had only the foggiest idea what Jenny had done with the contract, or how she had handled that case; most of what she knew about law was based on sensational cop shows. "I suppose there could be?" she said hesitantly, hoping it wouldn't raise questions about the details.

"Wouldn't that mean Mr. Stubbins was a target?" Tex suggested. Laura could have kissed him. Not that she didn't already want to kiss him, with his gorgeous, suntanned muscles not at all covered by the tiny apron he was wearing.

Scarlet pursed her lips thoughtfully and said decisively, "I'm going to have some trusted extra security assigned to him. Tell Graham to clean up and report to the office. Travis has got too much to do." She looked at Tex appraisingly. "You keep an eye on Ms. Smith." Tex thought there was a hint of a smile in the corner of her mouth. "I'll report this to the authorities, of course, but they're not likely to react quickly."

Authorities were the last thing that Jenny wanted to involve, but she couldn't very well say that. Everything was unraveling far too rapidly for her to follow.

"I'm very sorry that you've run into this trouble at our resort," Scarlet said sincerely. "We will do our very best to find the person responsible and keep you protected in the meantime."

Was Scarlet afraid of a lawsuit? Laura abruptly remembered that she was supposedly a lawyer and it was probably a valid concern. "I'm sure it's not your fault," she said faintly. Probably that wasn't very lawyer-y of her to say.

Scarlet gave her an unexpected smile. "I'm sure it's not," she agreed dryly. Then, to Laura's dismay, she added, "I would love to consult with you at some time regarding the Shifting Sands contract. I've been butting heads with the owner's lawyer about some of our lease details, and I would appreciate an experienced set of eyes on the wording."

It was everything Laura could do not to squirm and start crying. One wrong word out of her mouth would betray her masquerade now. She kept her gaze locked with Scarlet with effort, but she knew that her hands would be shaking if they weren't clenched tightly in her lap.

"I would pay for your time, of course," Scarlet added, guessing the cause of her discomfort incorrectly. "Now, I've got paperwork to file and samples to store. I'll be taking witness statements from the guest and staff most of the day. If you need anything, be sure to let me know."

Then she was sweeping out, pulling out her cellphone as she

went, and the silence in her wake was awkward and deep as Laura kept dragging her eyes away from Tex.

Who was still wearing nothing but an apron.

"I'm so sorry I frightened you," he said, in that thick southern drawl.

Laura gave a strangled sound that was meant to be a laugh. "Frighten me?" she chuckled. "You saved my life." She found that tears were gathering in her eyes against her will. All of her resolve seemed to have vanished in Scarlet's wake.

Tex looked horrified. "Oh, ma'am, no!" He knelt before her, taking her unresisting hands in his own big ones.

"Don't call me ma'am," Laura sniffed.

"Jenny..."

"I'm not Jenny." The words were out before she could stop them.

Tex blinked at her, but kept looking at her with those painfully trusting eyes. "I thought...?"

"Laura. I'm Jenny's twin sister, Laura. Laurelangelina Lily."

"You're... not... Jenny."

Were they back to 'he's an idiot?'

It was just a shame he was such a *gorgeous* idiot.

"Why would you do that for me?" she asked before she thought about it. "Save me, I mean."

"I love you," Tex replied.

Laura's breath caught in her throat. "What?!" It was absurd. Mating wasn't *love*. It wasn't *love* that was making her nethers heat up. It wasn't *love* that made her think about the way Tex's hands would feel on her skin.

But somehow, hearing him say the words was a knife-twist to the gut in a new and agonizing way.

It felt like hope.

Flustered, Tex twisted the apron in his big hands, which made it cover even less of him. Laura caught a tantalizing glimpse of his half-hard member before he shifted uncomfortably.

"I don't mean I *love* you, exactly. I hardly know you. And apparently I know you less than I thought, since the you I knew wasn't you. But I… I couldn't let you get poisoned. Not that I'd let anyone get poisoned, but you… you're *everything*."

It sounded like a line. In his ridiculous cowboy accent, it sounded like it had been written for the most awful movie in the world.

And Laura believed every syllable of it.

She believed that she was everything to him, that, however deluded he might be, he believed she hung the stars. No matter what happened, how stupid she was, he would come galloping for her over any obstacle. He was her knight in a cowboy hat. He was her… *everything.*

Without meaning to, Laura reached out to touch his face.

He was looking up at her adoringly, and when her fingertips brushed his jaw, he caught her hand in his own and kissed it.

Was there no end to his dramatic gallantry? His mouth on her knuckles was more potent than the liquor he'd served her, and Laura was grateful she was sitting; her knees were suddenly very shaky, and she was uncomfortably aware of all her intimate parts.

When she didn't make any motion to withdraw her hand, he turned it over and kissed the inside of her wrist, a place that Laura would never have guessed was so sensitive. Every nerve in her body was on fire, desperate for more of this man's gentle touches.

He wasn't half-hard any longer. The apron was a tent across his lap and Laura was mesmerized by the promise of it.

She swallowed hard. "I'm not in a good place right now," she said, her voice husky. "There's a reason I was pretending to be my own sister."

Tex looked up at her trustingly, not relinquishing her hand. "I'm sure it's a great reason," he said, and there was a catch to his breath that told Laura he was as affected by her presence as she was by his.

"Don't you care what it is?" Laura wondered if she should feel insulted by his lack of concern. But she'd had plenty of experience with jerks who only wanted sex and this didn't feel anything like that.

Tex kissed the inside of her forearm, the stubble of his jaw tickling her skin. Then he looked up at her and said sincerely, "I will protect you from anything. Whoever you fear, I will fight. Whenever you flee, I will find you. Whatever you choose to tell me, that will be enough."

Laura had no defense equal to those words, and fell forward to press her mouth to his.

CHAPTER 12

The apron had been flimsy protection, but when Laura flowed into his lap, the cloth was suddenly an imposition.

She was more intoxicating than the finest whiskey, her mouth was sweeter than chocolate. Tex, slid his hands up her shoulders to cup her jaw so he could kiss her more deeply.

His words had barely scraped the surface of his feelings. He craved her, wanted to be buried inside of her, but more than that, he wanted to protect her, to worship her. She felt like forever.

Then her hand reached beneath the apron, giving him just the barest touch, and he had to gasp for breath.

"You can't go back out there like this," Laura teased him, her voice quiet near his ear.

"The resort *is* clothing optional," Tex wheezed, trying to match her light-hearted tone and failing.

"Clothing is one thing," Laura said chidingly. "This would be just obscene."

"Not… sure… what… to-" Tex couldn't even come up with a coherent sentence, not with her nails sliding tantalizingly over him.

She leaned in and kissed him again, and this time, Tex had no doubt how she intended to make him presentable again. He stroked the silky skin of her neck, keeping his fingers from clawing her with effort, and tugged the straps of her tank top and bra down to expose a soft shoulder to kiss.

"Besides," she said, in a rich, husky voice as she pulled back, "I don't want to share this view with anyone."

Tex had to bite back a whimper—one of her hands was teasing his hard cock, and the other was pulling the apron off over his head.

"You have an advantage over me," he said as he kissed her. "Let me… oh…"

Her fingers circled his member distractingly and when she pulled her hand away, he groaned at the loss, only to be delighted when she used it to help shuck off her tank top and unclasp her bra in one smooth motion.

Tex froze, mesmerized by the swell of her breasts, and the beauty of her exposed belly. Her nipples hardened in the chill of the office and Tex reached to rub his thumbs over each of them.

Laura gave a noise of pleasure and Tex pulled her closer with a hand cupping each breast, to kiss her jaw, her earlobe, her neck, and then feast on a collarbone before letting himself kiss his way down to the luscious breasts.

He couldn't pause there long, too wound with need and it didn't take much to wrestle her shorts and lacy underwear from her curvy hips. He lay her down on the clear desk and kissed his way down her stomach to pause for a moment at the lightly furred mound above her treasure. A careful breath made Laura cry out wordlessly, and a soft kiss made her arch up to him in need.

"Fuck me," she said, when he might have paused or tried to take a softer path. "Just fuck me, Cowboy."

Tex was eager to oblige.

He slid her to the edge of the desk and lifted her willing leg. If he'd been any harder, he felt he could have burst on the spot and when he pressed himself at her waiting entrance, she was already slick with her own juices.

Entering her was like perfect music; a slow crescendo of pleasure from a plateau of anticipation and need that already felt like a new high. He had to bite his lip not to simply thrust at her like an animal in rut. She deserved a crafted love-making, a worship of luxurious intimacy. Bad enough that he was sneaking with her in Chef's office instead of laying her down on silk sheets in a shower of flower petals, he wasn't going to make a schoolboy's hash of their first coupling.

His bear had other thoughts.

She is ours, he growled inside Tex's head. *Ours to take and love and protect. Our mate. Our all.*

Tex had to find the melody of a slow song in his head to keep his rhythm from becoming frantic. At every sweet thrust, Laura rose to him with a moan of delight and desire. Her hands at his arms left scratches of need and when she writhed in the grip of an orgasm that drove a blissful cry from her perfect lips, Tex lost any sense of slowness and simply fell into his own frantic release.

CHAPTER 13

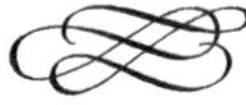

Laura was used to sex as an escape from her crappy life. She enjoyed the way problems dissolved for a short time in the hot wake of passion.

But it had never been like this. She didn't feel like she was using Tex for a few moments of ignoring reality and she didn't for an instant feel like he was using her.

He loved her, however he stumbled over the semantics of it.

His touch wasn't just about his pleasure, or even about her pleasure, or their pleasure. It was a bone-deep need, a connection at a level beyond skin. She felt like she'd been placed on an altar and worshiped, not taken in a tiny, barren office on a chilly metal desk as a matter of convenience.

Even after they were done, breath ragged and heartbeats loud in the little room, he didn't let go of her, pulling him up so they were both standing. His strong arms held her up, and he continued stroking her back and shoulders as the moment passed.

"I will never call myself unlucky in love again," he declared, to Laura's amusement.

"You might reconsider that when you realize what you've gotten into," she told him, finally drawing away.

She recovered her tank top and dressed. Tex gave the apron a wry smile and put it back on, then settled back to watch her getting dressed.

"Enjoying the show?" she needled him, shimmying back into her shorts. She gave him an extra, unnecessary jiggle.

"It's almost as much fun as watching you take them off," Tex promised.

Once they were basically presentable, Laura crossed her arms and regarded him thoughtfully.

Tex gazed back, unafraid, and Laura felt like it was a challenge.

"Let me tell you what's going on," she said, settling into the office chair and putting her feet up on the desk.

Tex rather belatedly locked the door and then took a seat opposite, mirroring her posture. He wiggled his bare toes at her.

Laura didn't let herself smile at them.

"I worked for the cartel in south Los Angeles."

Tex took his feet off the desk, but continued to gaze at her as she had hung the moon.

"I didn't mean to," she promised, suddenly not wanting to betray that naive trust. "I have—I've had—terrible taste in men. One of my old boyfriends got me a job, an easy job. They found out I was a shifter, and they had me pretend to be a pet, and I could make… deliveries. I swear, I didn't know who I was really working for, I didn't ask questions about what I was taking places. They paid well, and… I was tired of asking Jenny for money. I thought I was being responsible, finally taking care of myself."

Laura made herself shut her mouth around the continued excuses she wanted to give.

"And your sister?"

Tears unexpectedly welled up in Laura's eyes. Every time that she remembered Jenny, it was like the shock of her loss was all new again.

Tex was around the desk before she could stop him, gathering her into his strong arms. "It's okay, kitten. I'm here. You can tell me."

"She was the best sister," Laura sobbed into his bare shoulder.

"She was so smart and kind and *good.* As soon as I found out what I was doing, I tried to get out. I told them I quit, and I went to Jenny and told her everything. But they told me not to tell anyone, and they must have found out, because when she took my car out, it crashed, and she never came back, and they must have *done* something, because she's a good driver, and she wouldn't make a mistake like that."

Tex rocked her in his arms, holding her tight and smoothing her hair back from her face. "It wasn't your fault."

Laura pushed him away, viciously, tears still streaming down her face. "It was entirely my fault," she cried. "They sabotaged my car, and she got caught in the cross-fire. If I hadn't been tangled up in the wrong people, if I hadn't gone to her for help, if I hadn't let her go get things for me..."

Tex looked conflicted, but resolute. "It wasn't your fault," he repeated. "You don't know for sure it wasn't an accident."

Feeling almost hysterical, Laura insisted, "What else would it be? And now they've followed me here, and I'm not safe anywhere..."

Once again, Tex gathered her into his arms, slowly, gently, giving her every opportunity to push him away.

Laura didn't want to push him away. She wanted to snuggle up against those burly arms and beautiful shoulders and let Tex keep everything bad in the world away from her. She wanted to let him be her hero and save her from everything.

Even if she knew he couldn't.

Once she had cried herself out, Tex offered his apron to wipe her cheeks. "Could Fred have tipped them?"

Laura scoffed. "Fred? No. He thinks I'm Jenny, which let me tell you, is getting hard to pull off. I swear, he keeps talking legalese and finance at me and I have to nod and stuff food in my mouth instead of answering. I'm going to gain a hundred pounds if I keep this up."

"You both knew him?"

"He was a friend of our dad's, and worked at the same law business. They were up for partners in the firm at the same time. My dad got the spot, but he and my mom died in a car accident just a few weeks later. Fred was really great to us during that time, helped us get through everything after they died, and set up the loan that got Jenny through school. He even helped Jenny get a job with the firm, after college."

Just as Laura realized she was babbling, there was a knock at the door, and the two scrambled to their feet, looking guilty.

"Why is my door locked?" Chef demanded from the other side.

Laura straightened her tank top one last time and nodded to Tex when he went to open the door.

"Sorry, Chef," he said contritely. "We were just leaving."

Chef, a large, distinguished older man, stood with his arms crossed, glaring them down. "What have you done in here?" he demanded. Then he pinched the bridge of his nose. "No, I don't want to know. Just get out. And don't ever bring that apron back."

Glancing at each other like erring schoolchildren, barely able to keep the giggles from their lips, Laura and Tex fled, hand-in-hand.

"Don't worry about Chef," Tex told her, giving her a quick kiss at the back door to the restaurant. "He's just grouchy because Magnolia isn't here this week and we rented her cottage to someone else for the event. He doesn't even use this office most of the time."

He escorted her chivalrously to her hotel room, acting nonchalant about his apron-clad bare body, and Laura noticed with amusement that everyone they met took it perfectly in stride.

It was, after all, a clothing-optional shifter's resort, hosting a male beauty pageant.

Nothing seemed too odd for this place.

CHAPTER 14

One advantage to being a bartender was that Tex got a front-seat to all the best and worst of the guest-watching at Shifting Sands.

He got to watch the producer, Gregory Stubbins, have a shouting show-down with his cameraman, Bam Stagger (Tex guessed it was an assumed name, but never heard him referred to as anything else). Gregory didn't go anywhere without his new black-suited bodyguard since the attempt on Jenny's—Laura's—life, and Tex felt sorry for the stoically sweating rock of a man who shadowed the obnoxious jerk.

Jessica Linn, the tiny blonde celebrity host, got falling down drunk every afternoon at about 2, to sober up in time for whatever evening event she had to announce. She was at best unkind to the resort staff, and at worst, a raging harpy. She thought Tex was a dreamboat, though, so she was slobberingly pleasant to him.

Tex would have rathered she wasn't.

The photographer, Juan Lopez, was constantly taking candid photographs that Tex strongly suspected would be sold to tabloids later, or used for blackmail, when he wasn't hitting on woman after unsuspecting woman.

Tex's opinion of the Mr. Shifter competitors who frequented the bar ranged from sheer pity, through amusement, into active dislike. Mr. Canada completely failed to uphold his country's reputation for politeness. Mr. India was a class act. Mr. South Africa made Tex very, very wary and raised his bear's hackles. Mr. Brazil was a complete jerkface, flanked by a beauty coach who was at least as bad. Tex thought he might like Mr. United States, even if he was almost a caricature of laziness. Mr. Ireland never took off his glittery green pageant banner and never stopped talking (though his charming wife often stepped in and pointed him in the direction of distractions with a wry smile).

Tex sniffed, literally and figuratively, making even more conversation than he usually did. He got Mr. Ireland talking about his job, firefighting, and then despaired of ever getting him to stop. He got Mr. Austria talking nostalgically about growing up in the Alps, and Mr. India, after a few beers, talked about living in the slums of Delhi. Mr. Japan's beauty assistant was a shy woman that would only take lemon tea, but Tex got her to tell him about climbing Mt Fuji and laughed over her fear of bees.

"They are very large bees," she said, with an embarrassed smile.

Tex commiserated with a story about being chased by angry bees on his farm and convinced her to tell him about Mr. Japan and how she'd gotten involved in the contest.

None of them seemed to have any motive for hurting Jenny. Or Laura, as far as Tex could tell. Most of them only knew who she was because of the incident with the latte.

It was everything Tex could do not to blabber about Laura himself. He wanted to tell everyone about her, to describe her perfect strength and get them to agree that she had the most perfect brown eyes. He caught himself daydreaming about the slow smile she gave him, and the velvet softness of her skin.

But customers, especially the women, didn't want to hear about his perfect mate. They wanted to think his eyes were only for them and as long as Tex was trying to get information out of them, he was willing to indulge them in that delusion.

"Masterfully done," Breck told him, after watching him get Mr.

Canada's assistant to tell him all about Mr. Canada's failed hockey career. There was a lull in the traffic at the bar for a moment, while Mr. Ireland demonstrated a fireman's carry at the other end of the deck, to his American wife's laughing dismay. Breck was helping serve drinks while the restaurant was between meals; as busy as things were, none of the staff were enjoying much downtime.

"I'm no closer to finding a motive for poisoning Laura than when I started," Tex said mournfully. "And these people drink like fishes; our stock is never going to last through the closing cere—"

A scream from behind the bar interrupted him.

"This is getting to be a habit," Tex said, grabbing his baseball bat and rounding the bar at a run. Breck followed, grabbing a bottle off the bar as a makeshift weapon.

As girly as the scream had been, it came from Juan Lopez, the photographer.

Graham, teeth bared, was holding Juan's throat in one hand, hedge clippers in the other.

"I didn't mean to," Juan was stuttering, clutching his camera. "It was just, the leaves were in the shot, you know, and they were casting shadows I didn't want, and it was just a plant, and you have to frame the shot just so, and I'm famous in Europe, you know..."

He trailed off to a squeak as Tex handed his bat to Breck and strode forward to lay a careful hand on Graham's arm.

"It's okay Graham, he didn't mean any harm. We can't hurt the guests, come on, let him go." He wasn't foolish enough to say that they were only plants. You never said that to Graham.

With a predatory snarl, Graham abruptly let go of the struggling man, leaving him gasping and staggering.

He gave one angry snap of the hedge clippers that made Juan give a thin little shriek, then turned on his heel and left, white gravel crunching under his feet.

Breck actually laughed and offered Juan the bottle he was holding. "Don't ever cut Graham's plants," he told the gasping Juan. "It's right in the resort contract."

"Is it?" Tex asked, surprised. He wasn't sure if he'd seen a copy of a guest contract.

Juan took a deep slug of the liquor.

Breck nodded. "Next thing after 'No predation.'"

"It'll grow back," Juan protested. "This is the jungle!"

"Other things might not," Breck warned him with another chuckle. "I heard Graham killed a shifter with his bare human hands, so I wouldn't so much as step off the paths the rest of this week if you want to get out of here alive."

Cowed, Juan checked his camera for damage and slunk down the path away from the bar.

"There is no end to the crazy here," Tex said, shaking his head. "I'd better get back to the bar before someone decides to go all Tom Cruise with one of the single malts."

"How's it going with your sweetheart?" Breck asked, as they walked in through the back entrance of the bar. "Is she admitting she's your mate now that you saved her so dramatically?"

Tex could only smile foolishly at him, then he had to go mix drinks for Mr. Austria's ditzy assistant.

CHAPTER 15

Dinners with Fred were agony.

When the restaurant was quiet and the wind was just right, Laura could hear the low thrum of Tex's laugh from the bar below and the chatter of the people enjoying his drinks and showmanship. She had to assume his antics were particularly good when there were scattered cheers and laughter.

"What do you think?" Fred asked.

Laura looked up, totally derailed on their conversation. "About?"

"I said, you should go to the swimsuit competition tonight," Fred said. "I have some paperwork I need to work on, but you should go enjoy it."

Laura pictured Tex in one of the tiny, glittery swimsuits, and had to hide her sudden flush of heat with a bite of her exquisite roasted chicken in grapes and herb sauce. She had never heard of their chef before coming to Shifting Sands, but was sure he could give any cook in the fashionable LA restaurant district a run for his money.

It suddenly occurred to Laura that if there was a big competition tonight, maybe the bar would be slow. Slow enough for Tex to duck out.

"I think, ah, that I will turn in early tonight," she said, wondering if she could get away with feigning a yawn. "I was up really early, you know, and it was an exciting day."

Fred would think she meant the poisoning attempt, but Laura's thoughts were much more carnal, remembering the feeling of Tex's hands on her waist, the pressure of his—she stuffed another forkful of chicken in her mouth and smiled apologetically.

Two tables over, the little blonde event hostess, Jessica Linn, was protesting that her chicken was dry and tough, sending it back so stridently that conversation for several tables around her died to nothing.

"Honestly, as much as I'm paying to be here, I can't believe they don't give you more options for dinners. Seriously, the service here is deplorable."

Knowing the type, Laura suspected she was coming down off a good drunk.

"No, I don't want a replacement. If you can't cook chicken correctly, I don't want any castoffs from the buffet. I'll just hope I don't get faint from low blood sugar halfway through the swimsuit contest." She brushed Breck off with a wave of her napkin. "It's not like this is the most important event of the contest or anything. I'll just go see if anyone at the spa isn't incompetent."

She huffed away, tossing her long, bottle-blonde hair over her shoulder as she went.

Amused but hushed conversation sprang up in her wake.

"Give my regards to Chef for the meal," Laura told Breck when he checked in on them next. "I really enjoyed this."

She wondered if Chef would remember her undignified exit from his office earlier and had to smother a giggle.

Fred made one more weak attempt to convince her to watch the show, but Laura was already waving off dessert. She knew what she wanted for dessert and it wasn't any of the choices on the platter making the rounds of the dining room.

For the next hour, she paced her small hotel room. She tried concentrating on Jenny's laptop, but her mind was not up for unraveling any mysteries. She listened to the sounds of the resort through her open window instead—a note at the door of the hotel apologized for the air conditioning being under repair. Her heart lifted after a stampede of chattering traffic made its way to the theater, and the noises stilled to muffled music and distant applause.

When Tex finally knocked at the door, Laura was somehow not surprised that she knew it was him before she opened it.

It wasn't just a guess, she knew it somewhere behind her breastbone. Her wolf whined in anticipation.

She flung the door open, just as she realized that she should probably have changed into something more inviting during her wait.

Tex, holding a guitar in one hand and a cut flower in the other, looked at her as if she were wearing something that wasn't even an option from Jenny's limited wardrobe.

"I hoped you'd come," she said, breathlessly, wondering if it sounded as foolish as her smile felt.

"The bar was dead," Tex said, with a slow, appreciative smile. "I got Bastian to agree to serve drinks when the swimsuit contest breaks up and the losers need consolation drinks."

Laura grinned. "Would you like to host your own swimsuit competition privately here this evening? I've got four designs to choose from…"

They didn't even make it to the first, as Tex put his guitar in the corner and kicked the door closed behind him, reaching for her.

Laura tipped her head back and opened her mouth, sliding her arms up around his strong neck.

This wasn't the same kind of lovemaking that they'd desperately snuck in Chef's tiny locked office. This was slower, less urgent, more controlled.

He explored her body without removing her clothing, kissing where cloth revealed her skin, but making no move to tear it off. Laura followed suit, running her hands over his chest over the staff polo shirt. She let a fingernail trace his big belt buckle and ran her hands back to squeeze his fine ass through his khaki staff pants.

They kissed and discovered each other, rising to a fever pitch of desire that Laura had never felt before.

"May I?" Tex finally asked, fingers at the bottom of her tank top.

"Oh, hell yes," Laura managed, almost past speech with craving.

He peeled her tank top off so slowly that Laura actually whimpered. Then, when her hands were tangled in the garment above her head, he held her there for a long moment, his other hand following the curve of her side with worshipful slowness.

Laura didn't exactly struggle, but gave a whine and needy wiggle, and Tex finished pulling the tanktop off of her and threw it across the room.

Laura saved him the trouble of fumbling with her bra and unclipped the back, but relished the way he pulled the straps off her shoulders and released her breasts to the cooling night air as if in slow motion.

The bra joined the tanktop across the room.

Tex stepped back. The loss of his touch was delicious torture, and Laura swayed in place.

He drank her in, all appreciation and awe, then looked her in the eyes, expression overflowing with desire.

Laura had a sudden urge to prolong this, to wind him up and make him lose control, so when he moved to touch her again, she put up a hand and drew back to sit on the bed without him.

"Let's see your moves, cowboy," she told him, and she gestured with his hand.

He gave that slow, boyish smile and reached for his hat.

"No," Laura stopped him with a word. "Leave the hat for last."

Tex tipped it at her, then proceeded to reach for his belt buckle. He flipped it open in one smooth motion, but paused, and made a show out of pulling his belt from the loops of his khakis. The cowboy boots went next, and he turned away from her so that his reach for them showed off his ass.

In one smooth move, he managed to flip off his hat, pull his shirt off over his head, and drop the hat back on. Shirtless, now wearing only a hat and his pants, he faced her again to unbutton his pants, already bulging with promise.

Laura could not believe how hot she was getting. Her nipples were hard in the evening air, and she had to shift on the bed because her pussy was hot and demanding stimulation.

He teased her with the pants, flipping them open then covering up again, in time to the distant strains of the show music. He finally unbuttoned them entirely and managed to time the release of his barely-clad cock with a distant roar of applause from the Mr. Shifter's pageant.

They had no idea what kind of a show they were missing, Laura thought.

She lifted a finger and beckoned him nearer.

He sashayed over to her obligingly, and Laura put a finger into the band of his taut briefs.

He hissed and shuddered.

"You're quite the showman," Laura said, voice warm with appreciation.

"It's not all show," Tex promised. He drew a finger of his own down Laura's shoulder and she had to suck in her breath and shiver at his touch.

Waiting was suddenly not the best option.

Laura stood and let Tex unbutton her shorts with one hand while he caressed her shoulder and side, pausing to cup her breast.

He slipped both shorts and panties down together over her ass, pausing for a squeeze. They were still for just a moment, standing close together and breathing in each other's air before he kissed her roughly and tipped her down on the bed to pull them smoothly down her legs and toss them across the room.

His weight on the bed on either side of her made it creak and if Laura could have had any thought that wasn't of his touch and his smell and his skin, it would have been gratitude that the hotel was currently deserted.

Then he was touching her eager folds and she could feel the slick wetness that had gathered during his striptease against his big fingers. He stroked into her, once with one finger, again with two, and she arched up and cried out in a crest of pleasure and need.

Before she could come down from it, he was stripping off his briefs and entering her. His cock filled her impossibly, then filled her more at the next stroke, each thrust feeling deeper and wider.

Laura came again, moaning and writhing in his arms, and he slowed his thrusts to ease her fall from pleasure.

When she could breathe again, she kissed him, and they were a tangle of arms and touches and mouths in waves of sensation.

When he pulled out of her, Laura felt like she'd lost something, even though she was already feeling pounded sore and had found her bliss several times. She gave a little cry, but he kissed her, then turned her on the bed and mounted her from behind.

It was a whole new range of sensation, his cock pressing in new places of joy as he slid deeper into her.

She felt it when he began to lose control, his careful thrusts becoming frantic and his hands on her arms tightening. It excited her as much as it did him and she gave a scream of release as her final orgasm outdid any of the previous, matching his own moment of climax.

His last erratic thrusts died off slowly and Laura enjoyed the spiral down as much as she had the ride up, aware again of the squeaking bed and the sounds of the evening outside the open window.

As their heartbeats finally slowed, they lay together on the bed and Tex stroked her arms and hips and sides as if he was lost in wonder.

CHAPTER 16

The hotel was not well insulated for sound and a few hours later, a stream of noisy chatter and stomping feet went by. Tex woke briefly, marveled at Laura, blissfully still in his arms, and went back to sleep himself.

When he woke later, the hotel was still again, but Laura was stirring in his arms and the feeling of her curves under his hands was more appealing than more sleep.

He stroked the line of her hip, the sway of her side, the cup of her breast, kissing the line of her neck as she woke.

"Well, hello Cowboy," she murmured and Tex pressed his determined member at the small of her back. They were both still naked, tangled in a single sheet together. Outside, it was raining, as it often did at night.

In darkness, they were reduced to other senses. He reveled in the silky dream of her skin, the smell of rain mixed with the heady, hot scent of her desire, and the little sounds she made when he touched her. A hand at her thigh slipped higher, curving around to appeal at more intimate places.

She moved against him, rising like a goddess over him and he could just make out the curve of her breasts in what light there was.

She encased him in one smooth move, descending on his member and raising him to some new level of sensation.

He growled in need and lust, but let her set the pace, hands on her waist, enraptured by the feeling of the curve of her hips and the way her ass met her back.

She rode him carefully, like she was testing his paces, slow, then fast, then slow in tantalizing waves.

He obliged her, meeting every stroke with a thrust of his own, until she was gasping and groaning and the cheap hotel bed was creaking like a door from a bad horror movie being played in fast forward.

Using every inch of his control, Tex saved his climax until she had gained hers, moaning and writhing on top of him.

It wasn't until he was unwinding from his own coiled knot of orgasm that he heard the pounding on the hotel wall.

Laura collapsed on him, giggling and giddy.

"Oops!" she stage-whispered near his ear.

The bed gave a last wheeze of protest as she settled beside him.

"I hope you don't get fired for disrupting the peace," she teased him.

"It would be worth it," Tex laughed back at her. "Did you really think that you could deny being my mate?" The words were out before he could stop them.

It was the first time either of them had said it aloud, and Laura's laughter stilled as her body stiffened.

"I thought I had to," she told him quietly. "I thought it was the only way to keep my cover. You'd already met Jenny, and she might have thought you were cute, but you were definitely not her mate."

"You about drove me out of my mind," Tex had to confess. "I wasn't sure which end was up."

"I'm sorry," Laura said, but Tex felt like it was rather chilly and she was stiff in his arms.

"It couldn't have been easy," he tried to comfort her.

She sighed. "It was so hard," she confessed. "She was always the good sister, I was always the bad one who made terrible choices."

Tex pulled her closer. "You aren't *bad*," he said fiercely, his bear agreeing vehemently in his head.

"Everyone always thought I was," Laura said quietly. "If Jenny suggested something, everyone agreed. If I suggested the very same thing, my motives were always questioned, and everyone did the opposite."

"It's hard, being in the shadow of someone who seemed better," Tex agreed.

"Do you have siblings?"

Tex laughed. "An older brother who hung the moon. And probably invented sliced bread."

Tex felt Laura's laugh through his arms, rather than hearing it.

"It was pretty funny watching you trying to make sense of me," she chuckled.

"Funny?" Tex rolled over and growled near her ear. "I'll show you funny."

And he proceeded to tickle her until she was wheezing through her laughter for mercy, squirming and wiggling and jiggling in a most distracting way.

"Are you actually ready for another round?" Laura asked admiringly when she could breath again. A lazy finger traced around his erect member, getting all of his attention. "They might knock on the wall again."

"Let them," Tex said, kissing her deeply. "They can get complimentary earplugs at the spa if they want to sleep."

"I can think of better things than sleep," Laura agreed. "But I might be too sore to sit tomorrow..."

CHAPTER 17

Laura's plan to go swimming after lunch the next day was thwarted by a photo session at the pool.

A dozen nearly naked men were being oiled and posed, while Juan Lopez snapped orders and complained about the lighting.

"No, no! They squint, they get wrinkles! Get a shade over there!"

His mousy assistant leapt forward to scramble up on one of the tables with a gigantic white sunshade and nearly unbalanced onto the heap of men.

Mr. Canada, a brilliant red maple leaf swim brief barely covering his intimate parts, broke out of the crowd to catch the edge of the shade before it hit someone and then he paused to flex his muscles while Juan snapped a dozen extra shots, white teeth gleaming in his tanned face.

Laura was not sure her eyes could roll any harder.

Instead of joining the appreciative gawkers along the deck railing to watch the photoshoot, she wandered in through the empty bar and up the steps to the dining level. She wasn't particularly hungry—though Tex had assured her there was no remaining poison anywhere near the kitchen, she continued to eye food with some suspicion. But having the buffet to herself was a luxury that was hard to turn down after several days of having to hold her own with her elbows to get a plate of food.

She wasn't the only one taking advantage of the brief respite from crowds.

She recognized Tex at once, more by the shape of his shoulder muscles under the staff shirt even than by the distinctive (ridiculous, she reminded herself) cowboy hat. He was filling his tray along with a collection of other staff-uniformed figures that could have given the over-groomed Mr. Shifter flock a run for their money.

She recognized Graham, the landscaper that she had witnessed frightening off a shrieking assistant with a pair of giant clippers, and Breck, the waiter who had served her the poisoned latte, as well as the lifeguard, Bastian, and another staff member whose name Laura didn't know, an exhausted-looking native man who was muddy to the knees and juggling a toolbox along with his heaping tray of food.

"Goddamn air conditioning unit for the hotel is on its last legs," he was complaining. "There's only so long I can hold it together with duct tape and bailing wire. Breck, you've got to take a look at it for me."

"If we all survive the next week, we'll have enough to get a new one," Bastian said encouragingly.

Laura was struck by the observation that he spoke as if the resort belonged to them, as if they were invested in its success. She had worked in hospitality, and she knew that it was more common for staff to be a distant subclass to the ownership. Certainly, she had never felt any kind of loyalty for her employers.

Tex turned then and Laura's full attention was caught by the way he moved, as if he instinctively knew she was behind him, and he couldn't wait to see her. A smile was already blooming on his face, widening into a full grin at the sight of her.

Grateful that a blush wouldn't show on her brown skin, Laura strode forward boldly with her tray in hand.

The rest of the staff turned to see what Tex was looking at and gave her long, appraising looks.

What would they see? she wondered. A plump Black woman in Jenny's conservative sundress, wearing low wedge sandals? Did they believe her lawyer facade, or could they see the lies across her face?

Tex was just staring, a big smile and a slight flush on his face, so Breck stepped in. "Would you join us, Miss Smith? We'll be dining in the staff room while we have a chance and you are welcome to come eat with us."

To her surprise, the rest of the staff chimed encouragement. Even the gruff landscaper grunted and nodded at her in a fashion Laura guessed was meant to be inviting and not as terrifying as it came off.

Laura agreed, feeling uncharacteristically shy as she piled cold shrimp and fruit onto her plate. She snagged a roll so fresh it was still warm and even indulged in a rich slice of chocolate cake.

Out of sight over the railing, there was a wild cheer and appreciative hoots from the pool deck as the Mr. Shifters were cycled through their paces.

The staff room proved to be a very small room off the back of the restaurant, a round conference table in the center with a handful of chairs around it. Open windows looking out into greenery and a ceiling fan kept it from being stuffy. Tex held a chair for Laura, and she took it gingerly.

She expected to be the center of their attention, but they all concentrated on their own trays of food and carried on easily, as if she were one of their own.

"Did you have to use the pink duct tape, Travis?" Breck asked the repairman.

"It lacks dignity," Travis replied dryly. "But it holds it together, so I'll use it."

"We're going to have to get a different distributor," Bastian said, shaking his head. "They messed up a bunch of the orders this time!"

"I think Breck ordered the pink on purpose," the landscaper

said gruffly, and Laura nearly choked on her shrimp when he winked at her.

"As much as I appreciate the entire visual spectrum," Breck said severely, "I believe that duct tape should be like the force. Plain silver, dark on one side, light on the other. And it should hold the universe together."

"Geek," Bastian said, but he clearly got the reference, so Laura thought it said as much about him as it did about Breck.

They talked a little about where they were from, the invitation for Laura to join them on the table, but not full of pressure. Breck was from the midwest, Bastian was from the east coast. She was surprised to find that Travis was from a tiny town in Alaska that Laura couldn't pronounce. "Texas is cute," he said with a grin at Tex.

Tex had been gazing at Laura as he ate, and paused to glare back in good nature. Laura got the feeling that this was an old joke between them.

"What made you move to Costa Rica?" she asked Travis.

"After twenty-five Alaskan winters, you have to ask that?" he teased her easily. "I came for a winter job, but this place—Shifting Sands particularly, not just this country—gets under your skin."

Laura nodded. After only a few days, she couldn't imagine living anywhere else. She didn't think it was just Tex. She felt like this place fit her, like she clicked into a place that had been open just for her. There was something in the scent and the breeze and the way the sun hit her that felt like coming home. When she thought about fleeing further, it left an empty aching feeling, even when she fantasized about bringing Tex with her and finding another tropical place.

Her wolf, unexpectedly, agreed with her. *This is our home,* she told her firmly. *Here, with him.*

She glanced at Tex, who was trying not to be obvious about watching her while he ate.

"They're wrapping up the photoshoot." Scarlet stood in the doorway and Laura was surprised to see that she was holding her own tray of food. Scarlet felt supernatural, in a resort already full of non-human shifters, and Laura felt that it was reassuringly common of her to be eating. There was even a slice of the same chocolate cake that Laura had snagged on her tray.

The rest of the staff grumbled as they shoveled the rest of their food down as quickly as they could. Scarlet took the seat next to Laura and put down a small pile of flyers, passing one out to each of the staff. "I'd appreciate your feedback," she said, and Laura thought it sounded sincere. To her surprise, Scarlet put one in front of her.

"Looks good to me," Tex said, after a cursory look.

"Smashing," Breck agreed.

"It's glossy," Travis said, with questionable helpfulness.

The landscaper, Graham, shrugged and grunted.

Scarlet's eyes turned to her and Laura shivered at the weight of her gaze. It felt like a moment of judgment. She glanced at the flyer critically. It would be easy to say that it was fine and maybe compliment the gorgeous photographs that Scarlet had chosen.

But Laura had tasted the challenge in Scarlet's look. She read the carefully coded advertising through. A place like Shifting Sands couldn't be outright about catering to shifters—some countries gave them privileges, but more treated them like second-class citizens, others actively hunted them, and a few countries, like the US, continued to pretend they were a fairy tale. The brochure was clear that their guest-list was exclusive and only alluded to the fact that it was based on being a shifter if you read between the lines. The photograph with romping jaguars on the beach was a good clue, but it was the sort of thing that might have been just a reference to the wild jungle on the rest of the island. The flyer was all neatly deniable if it should get picked up by the wrong person.

"The kerning in the section headers is a little off. You might want to pick a different font for that," Laura said hesitantly. "And use the same one over here. You don't want to have more than two fonts in the whole thing if you can help it, one fancy, and one plain. Find a synonym for luxury or luxurious—you use it too many times in a row."

"You have some design experience," Scarlet said approvingly.

"I worked in an advertising agency for a while," Laura said. It was one of the few jobs she'd had more than a few weeks.

"They're going to be hitting the beaches soon," Bastian grumbled, draining his cup and standing.

"And the restaurant," Breck agreed with a sigh as he swallowed the last of his sandwich.

"And the bar," Tex said longingly.

Laura stood with him, glancing at the food still left on her plate, but Scarlet said to her, "There's no need for you to rush off. Please join me to finish your lunch." Despite the 'please', it was more of a command than a request.

"Of—of course," Laura said, sitting back down. She felt automatically defensive; this was too much like being in a principal's office and she was waiting for expulsion if she said the wrong thing.

Tex hovered for a moment, clearly not sure if she needed saving or not. "I'll be working until late," he said hesitantly. "If you need anything, I'll be at the bar."

"Go on, cowboy," Laura told him with bravado. "I'll let you know if anyone tries to poison me."

His crooked smile suggested that he wasn't sure if that was a joking matter, a sentiment that Laura could agree with.

After a moment of hesitation, he bent down and put a swift kiss on her cheek. Laura only just resisted the temptation to turn and catch it on her lips. The scent of him, that close, was musky and intoxicating. Laura felt her breath catch and her heart hammer in her chest.

She watched him walk out with her appreciation for his ass tempered by the fact that Scarlet was watching both of them.

"I'd love to hear any other ideas about the resort you might have," Scarlet said, once the door had clicked behind Tex and they were alone.

Laura took another bite of mango to delay her response, savoring the fresh tang of the fruit as if it were her last. It could be. "Have you thought about allowing non-shifters in?"

Scarlet raised an eyebrow at her, but nodded at her to continue as she took a nibble of her sandwich.

"I understand you've done that for the Mr. Shifter's competition on a temporary basis, just for the event, but you might get good business if you continued to allow shifters and their guests, whether those guests are shifters or not."

"An interesting prospect," Scarlet said, clearly considering the idea. It surprised Laura until she recalled that Scarlet thought she was Jenny; people listened to Jenny. "You are a shifter, are you not?"

"I am," Laura said automatically, then hesitated to remember that she had filled out her application stating that she wasn't. She was Jenny, she reminded herself. The *good* sister. "My father was, too, but not my mother."

"Or your sister."

Laura tried not to panic. Out of habit, she reached carefully for the nearest possible weapon, in this case a fork, and curled her fingers around it. She ignored Scarlet's words and said, as mildly as possible, "This is also the kind of place a shifter might like to have a wedding, if they could invite their human friends, too. Or kids."

"No kids," Scarlet said firmly, putting her sandwich down. "Laura, you don't need to have any fear here."

Hearing her real name from Scarlet's lips made Laura want to bolt, but she wasn't stupid enough to outright attack her with the fork now clenched in her hand. Whatever shifter animal Scarlet had within her, Laura doubted that four skinny, one-inch tines would even slow her down.

I could protect you, her wolf told her, but she didn't seem as sure as she usually was.

"Just imagine the gorgeous beach-side ceremony, and the sunset photos you could get afterwards," she babbled.

"Tex told me about your trouble."

Laura's fear transformed to fury. He'd told Scarlet? He'd jeopardized her cover by blabbing to this woman about her deepest secrets? Just like everyone else, he thought he could make better decisions for herself than she could. How *dare* he.

Scarlet continued, either oblivious to Laura's anger or assuming it was just a symptom of her fright. "I'm doubtful that your former, unsavory associates could have followed you here. We've been booked in full with a waitlist for weeks now and your visit was only just confirmed a few days prior to your arrival. I'd like to talk about the possibility that someone may have had designs on your sister and see if we can figure out any details about who this could be and how to catch them.

With effort, Laura unclenched her jaw. "I appreciate your help in this matter," she said, aware that it sounded as icy and insincere are she felt. "I don't know anyone who didn't like my sister, and I don't know anything about her work."

Scarlet gave her a long, thoughtful look, but didn't question her. "You are, of course, welcome to stay here as long as you wish, and your safety is one of our first priorities. I can arrange a room with Tex as soon as—"

"No!"

There was a moment of silence, and Scarlet cleared her throat. "Forgive me," she said formally. "I presumed that because he was your mate…"

"Being a mate apparently doesn't mean he isn't a class A jackass and I will have nothing more to do with him," Laura said without thinking. "A mate isn't a mandate."

"Very well," Scarlet said neutrally, after a heartbeat. "Your invitation to remain at Shifting Sands stands regardless of that. I will expect civility. You can come by my office and have a look at my standard contract at any time. It's room and board with profit share instead of tips and you would be expected to pull your weight; no one is too good for laundry duty or cleaning when it's needed."

Laura wondered if she imagined the skepticism in her voice, but it only hardened her resolve.

Don't fall for cowboys, she told herself. *You knew better.*

She always knew better and fell anyway.

CHAPTER 18

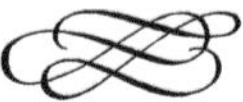

Tex flipped the bottle in one hand, a grin the size of Texas on his face while he tossed the shaker in the other hand. He poured the concoction out with a flourish and added the garnish with a spin.

The scattered applause warmed his heart, but not as much as the memory of Laura in his arms. It was her smile that he remembered the best. Her curves, yes, and oh little green gods, the way she rose to meet him… but it was the relaxed, easy smile that lit up her face afterwards that made him feel like he'd just turned a stampede.

"A gin and tonic, Cowboy! And a Libertas!"

Tex tipped his hat at the bikini-clad guest, putting the beer glass under the tap while he selected the gin from the glass display behind him and put ice in a tumbler. A generous splash and a squirt from the tonic tap and he had both drinks out on napkins.

He turned to take the next order and found himself looking at Laura's face.

It was not smiling. It was neither relaxed, nor easy.

His bear actually quailed at that face, filled with anger and looking for a fight.

Tex immediately cast back to try to figure out what on earth he had done wrong. They had parted amicably, as far as he knew. She'd joked about an attempt to poison her again. Had someone actually tried to? Had he failed to protect her?

We would not fail, his bear insisted.

"What's wrong?" Tex blurted. "You look…" angry probably assumed too much "...upset?" He had a feeling careful word choice was going to be important here.

"Upset?" Laura said, with icy tones. "I look upset?"

It's a trap, his bear helpfully told him.

Tex swallowed. "Yes?"

"What an amazing coincidence," Laura said sarcastically. "I am upset," she continued. "I am livid. I am furious. I just came by to tell you not to bother coming by tonight. Or any night."

She turned on her heel and stalked away, heels clicking on the tiled floor. Tex watched her go with his jaw hanging, divided between his instincts telling him to follow her and his duty to stay at the bar.

"Can I get a beer?" a guest asked from the end of the bar.

"Margarita!" someone called.

Bastian, still in his lifeguard gear, saved him from the dilemma by walking up at that moment. It was just getting dark and he was getting off his watch.

"Go get her," the dragon shifter said in a resigned voice, coming behind the bar. Clearly, he had heard Laura's departure. A gaggle of guests already nursing their drinks were staring and murmuring about it as well. "I can mix up some sidecars and spill some beer in a cup with the best of them."

"Thank you," Tex said, heartfelt. "I owe you one."

"You and everyone," Bastian said, rolling his eyes. He wasn't as cranky as he had been, now that they had settled into the new house, but he wasn't entirely back to his usual cheerful self, either.

Tex didn't pause, but took off after Laura, who had left through the back entrance towards the hotel.

He caught her almost at the hotel door and took her arm.

"Laura, Laura, love…" he said, glancing around to make sure no one was in obvious earshot.

"Don't you Laura, Laura, love me," she snapped back, shaking her arm free. "*That* is why I am *upset.* You can't keep your mouth shut with the one secret I give you. You betrayed me. You told, well at least Scarlet, and probably half the big-mouthed staff."

Tex stood his ground, but relinquished her arm. "I had to tell Scarlet," he protested. He hadn't really thought about the fact that he was betraying her trust, but he'd known that Scarlet could help protect her and that knowing the truth would help her do that. His mate's safety was his first, driving priority.

"You don't get to choose for me," Laura spat. "I make my own choices, Tex."

"This isn't a choice," Tex said firmly.

"Everything is a choice," Laura retorted. "And I can choose not to be with someone who can't respect my secrets."

"You're my mate," Tex insisted.

"And what, being my mate makes you my owner? You get to make my decisions for me?" Laura scoffed. "I pick my path and that may not include you, Cowboy, so don't get too settled."

The idea cut to the center of Tex's chest and he was suddenly, desperately afraid that he'd screwed this up and had no idea how to fix it.

She was turning to walk away into the hotel when there was suddenly a muffled bang above them, followed by a very familiar panicked woman's scream and the wail of the smoke alarm.

"That sounded like it came from my hotel room," Laura said in a small voice, casting Tex a wide-eyed look.

Laying aside their argument, they ran for the stairs.

CHAPTER 19

The hallway at the top floor had a little smoke that smelled to Laura like plastic but there didn't appear to be any fire. Laura's hotel door was open and several guests were milling about outside of it, peering in. She wondered briefly what the smoke smelled like to Tex's keen nose, then elbowed her way into her hazy room past the housekeeping cart.

Marie was sobbing in the arms of Juan Lopez, who was trying to comfort her.

"I barely touched it," Marie wailed. "I was just dusting up, and bang!"

Her desk was blackened, along with the curtains nearby and the ceiling above. The mangled wreck of Jenny's precious laptop was shattered plastic and warped, exposed circuit boards. The paper stationery on the desk had burned away and the cover of the 3-ring binder of resort details had melted into a grotesque puddle. The scene was smothered in a fine pale dust and there was a fire extinguisher on its side by Juan's feet. The fire alarm continued to wail.

"What is going on here?"

Laura wasn't even sure how Scarlet had gotten there; she hadn't been in the stairwell with them, but now she was right behind Tex, edging past the housekeeping cart into the room.

"We just got here," Tex told her, as Marie protested, "I barely touched it!"

"My laptop," Laura said weakly, and Juan scoffed, "I don't know what kind of place this is!"

The fire alarm was still shrieking.

"Enough!" Scarlet said, holding up her hand.

Marie buried her face in Juan's chest with a squeak but the fire alarm, to Laura's wry surprise, did not silence at her command.

"Tex, go turn off the alarm."

Tex, beside Laura, stiffened and Laura thought he was going to protest, then he agreed, "Can't hear yourself think this way." To Laura he said, "I'll be right back."

Laura didn't have time to tell him it was irrelevant to her. For such a big man, he certainly moved quickly.

Scarlet pointed at Juan. "You, explain."

Juan drew himself up, facing the challenge in Scarlet's voice. "I was walking past when I heard the explosion and the scream. The door was open and I went in to find the desk on fire. I used the fire extinguisher to put out the flames just as the smoke detector went off."

"He saved my life!" Marie added at that point.

"Are you hurt?" Scarlet asked Marie briskly.

Marie shook her head vigorously, remaining in the protective circle of Juan's arms. "No," she said in a trembling voice. "I barely touched it," she repeated. "I was just dusting."

Scarlet frowned at the desk and picked up a sooty pen that had rolled to the ground. "This isn't how laptops usually fail," she said dryly.

The fire alarm abruptly went still and the silence seemed remarkable.

"Clearly this is another attempt on Miss Smith's life," Juan announced into the space it left.

Laura had been looking in despair at the black disaster of the laptop. All of her memories of Jenny were there.

But at Juan's statement, she looked up and the enormity of the situation crashed down on her.

Someone really was trying to kill her. And it was more the cartel's style to slit throats in sleep, not poison lattes and blow up laptops. Someone else was after her. Or after Jenny.

"Jenny? Jenny?" Fred pushed into the room through the growing crowd, panting and sweating. "Are you okay? Oh, Jenny, what happened?"

Juan was happy to repeat his tale of heroics for him while Scarlet thoughtfully took pictures on her phone of the mess. Tex returned during the tale, to find there was no space in the tiny hotel room for him to squeeze in. Laura was equal parts glad to see him sulk at the doorway and sorry not to have him at her side; Fred was a disappointing replacement and, even though she was furious with Tex, she felt safer with him at her side than with Fred.

"What were you doing cleaning the hotel room so late?" Fred asked Marie suspiciously.

Marie, who had finally stopped crying, burst into tears again. "I couldn't get all the rooms done any earlier!"

Scarlet swooped to her defense at once. "We are all working odd shifts right now. The Mr. Shifter event has left us spread thin."

Juan sniffed and muttered something barely audible about being under-staffed and unprepared. Scarlet shot him an unappreciative look and he snapped his mouth shut.

"Are you okay?" Fred asked Laura again. He was rubbing her arm in a familiar way, and even though she knew that Jenny wouldn't have, Laura pushed him away with a growl.

"I'm fine," she insisted. "I wasn't even here."

"Your poor laptop," Fred said. "Did you have much that wasn't backed up?"

"No," Laura lied. "I have *everything* I need on the cloud."

Jenny would do that.

Scarlet turned to Laura decisively. "You can't stay here tonight," she said firmly. "Tex..."

Laura was about to stop her, but Scarlet only told him, "Get

Travis and find every free fan that you can to get the smoke in the hallway cleared out."

Tex looked at Laura, who ignored him, before agreeing. "Yes, Ma'am." He vanished back into the audience.

Scarlet turned her scowl to them next. "There's nothing more to see here, people." They scattered obediently, chattering excitedly as they went.

To Juan she said, "Thank you for your quick thinking."

"He's my hero," Marie said, still tangled around him.

He looked pleased, if not quite sure what to do with the housekeeper clinging to him. "It was my pleasure," he finally said, and took Scarlet's hint to leave, Marie trailing alongside him.

The door shut behind them and Laura and Scarlet were alone in the little room, which felt much larger with everyone gone.

"Pack up your personal items, but leave your clothing," Scarlet commanded. "We'll launder everything to get the smoke smell out and bring it to the cottage I'll put you up in. It's on the rustic side, the shower is outside and only has cold water, but it's the last unoccupied room we have and it will do in a pinch. I'll see about replacing the laptop, of course, and I'll be placing a guard on you at all times."

Scarlet did not so much as hint that Laura room with Tex, which she was grateful for, and Laura knew better than to argue about a guard at this point.

"Thank you," she said weakly.

"I'll wait in the hallway while you get your things together," Scarlet said gently.

Alone in the hotel room, Laura wandered about aimlessly for a moment, putting things randomly in her carry-on bag. She stared at the burnt-up laptop and tried to imagine what she was going to do next. Most of her wanted to sit down on the extinguisher-dusted bed and sob her eyes out, but she was afraid that if she started, she would never stop.

So she shouldered her bag and went out to let Scarlet lead her on.

CHAPTER 20

Tex finished out the night at the bar in a stupor. He didn't have the energy for any stunts and had to ask people to repeat their orders more times than he had ever had to in his life.

Laura's flashing eyes and bared teeth were burned into his brain. His bear, always a blustery, self-confident brute he had to restrain, was as shocked and dismayed as he was and offered no help.

She doesn't want us? His bear was crushed.

Had he done what she accused him of? Had he betrayed her trust? It simply hadn't occurred to him *not* to tell Scarlet the truth. At the best of times, he was a miserable liar and there was something about Scarlet that made falsehood feel pointless. Besides, his first priority was Laura's protection and Scarlet was her best hope of that, next to him.

Not that he'd been able to help her today.

"I asked for a beer like ten minutes ago," Mr. Canada groused. Tex stared at him stupidly while the girl hanging on his arm tittered drunkenly.

"Sorry, sir," Tex said automatically. "What kind was that?"

"A pilsner," Mr. Canada scoffed. The girl giggled again.

Tex looked at the clock, which seemed to be crawling towards closing time too slowly and poured the beer more sloppily than he usually did, requiring him to mop up the counter afterwards.

Mr. Canada was unimpressed. "Americans," he said scornfully to his armcandy as they moved away from the bar to one of the tables overlooking the pool.

Her silly laugh made Tex long for Laura's intelligent, warm chuckle.

But… she doesn't want us? Tex sometimes thought that his bear was not the swiftest animal that could have shared his head.

She will, Tex replied to him, not entirely convinced himself. *She has to.*

He tried not to think too hard about the fact that he'd always considered himself unlucky in love… and that maybe that really was the truth.

The cottage that Travis had put Laura up in was at the very edge of the jungle, nearly swallowed in vines and flowers. The path was an obstacle course of old concrete fractured by roots, not yet replaced with white gravel like the rest of the updated paths.

Tex wandered there directly following last call and nearly lost his hat to one of the overhanging branches.

Graham was sitting on the lowest front step, a menacing shadow with a machete, but when Tex approached, he stood up. They exchanged a look that didn't require words and Graham shrugged and left Tex to take his vigil.

Tex mauled his hat in his hands as he stood at the doorstep, but didn't knock.

Finally, he simply sat where Graham had been.

He could no more push himself on her than he could leave her unprotected. Her doorstep was the best place for him, for now.

CHAPTER 21

Laura didn't sleep until Tex arrived.

She sensed him changing places with the surly landscaper and spent several long moments anticipating the knock on the door before she realized he wasn't going to.

It was strange to be courted by someone who listened to her refusals, who treated her with respect.

Once she figured out that he planned to stay the night on her doorstep, she fell easily into a deep, restful sleep. Her dreams were of a strange field of tall grass, brightly lit as if by daylight, but the sky had no sun.

The cottage had not been fitted with curtains or blinds, so the rising sun woke her early. She looked at it curiously for several moments, trying to recall the details of the fleeting dream.

Laura dressed in the same sundress she had been wearing the night before and went out onto the front porch to find a gigantic brown bear that took up not a step, but all the steps, head laying on crossed paws next to a tidy pile of Tex's clothing topped by his ridiculous hat. He sat up when she came out, moving aside so she could get down the stairs.

He is a fine bear, her wolf told her suggestively.

He is a fine man, she responded with a sigh.

Instead of walking past, she sat down beside him. She ought to be afraid, she thought. Each of his paws was the size of her head, fringed with sharp claws as long as her fingers.

"My secrets are mine to keep," she said severely. "I choose who to share them with, not you. I get to decide how to keep myself safe."

The bear gave a whine, then shifted gracefully down to the form of a man sitting beside her. A gorgeous man.

A gorgeous, very naked man.

And to Laura's surprise, the gorgeous, naked man did not offer a single excuse. He could have pointed out, rightfully, that Scarlet would probably have figured it out anyway, or that he needed her help to protect her.

All he said was, "It was wrong of me. I am sorry."

Laura waited, too experienced with men not to expect the 'but…'

It didn't come.

"You won't always be able to protect me," Laura pointed out.

His sorrowful look cut her to the heart. "I can always try," he said fiercely. "I couldn't rest if you weren't safe."

Laura picked up his hat, running a finger along the band before setting it on her head. It was big on her, but she had enough hair to hold it up from her eyes.

"I know you meant well," she conceded. "I'm not used to having someone willing to run to my rescue," she confessed. "I'm not sure what to do with it."

"I like you in that hat," Tex said shyly, with a crooked smile.

Laura tipped it at him, an echo of his own habits. "Pleased ta meetcha," she drawled.

"I am so glad I met you," Tex said, all sincerity and chivalry.

Laura gave a laugh that was more snort. "Me, with all of my baggage."

"Ma'am," Tex said seriously, "I'm happy to carry all of your baggage."

Laura tipped forward to kiss him, forgetting that his hat was still on her head. It hit him in the forehead and he lifted it off her head in one smooth motion, cupping her face with his big, gentle hands.

She had not forgotten that he was naked, however hard she was trying to ignore it. Her whole body tingled to be so close to him, and she put one of her hands on his chest. Fine hair curled over her sepia fingers. He felt like the softest leather imaginable, warm in the early sun.

He shivered at her touch and drew her in for another, deeper kiss.

They kissed until they had to break apart for breath, hands exploring over muscles and the planes of their bodies. Tex had his hand up under her sundress, barely touching the wet heat of her entrance, while she just accidentally brushed the attentive member that Tex was sporting. And kept accidentally brushing it.

"Scarlet wants you to take the boat to the mainland, Tex. Travis can't go because he is fixing the toilet in cottage eight."

The voice that interrupted them was matter-of-fact and Laura and Tex scrambled apart hastily to find a woman standing in the overgrown path, looking at them with open curiosity. Her salt-and-pepper hair was wild around her face and her feet were bare beneath a short, flowing sundress.

"Gizelle," Tex said, strangled. He pulled his hat over his lap. "This is Laura."

Gizelle stared at Laura. "Your skin is much browner than mine," she said candidly.

Laura blinked at her unexpected statement, and slowly agreed, "Yes, it is." Gizelle had pale, freckled skin and Laura couldn't decide if she looked very young, with her straight, innocent gaze, or very old, with the white that streaked her hair and the unexpected wariness in her expression.

Tex coughed. "Gizelle hasn't been in human form very long," he explained, hinting at a deeper story.

Gizelle finally turned her intense stare from Laura to Tex and she felt like she could breathe again. "Scarlet says we need more things before the bonfire tonight and Travis wants duct tape that isn't pink. I like the pink duct tape. Chef wants kiwis, twenty pounds if you can get them. What were you doing when I walked up?"

Laura blessed the brown skin that kept the heat of embarrassment from showing. Tex, not so lucky, was scarlet-faced. The blush extended down to his chest, Laura was amused to see.

"I'll explain it to you later," Tex promised. He stood up and grabbed his pile of clothing, keeping the hat in place in front of him. "I'll just go grab a quick shower…"

He paused just a few strides down the path. "Do you want to come to the mainland with me?"

Laura had to consider only a moment—escape from the crowded resort in a boat with only Tex?—and she said, "Yes!" exactly as Gizelle primly said, "No, thank you."

The two women looked at each other and Gizelle explained, "Scarlet says I shouldn't, until I stay human when I get frightened. You'll have a nice trip. The sunlight will be pouring before the ocean gets in."

"How long will it take you to get ready?" Tex asked Laura.

Laura shrugged. It wasn't like she spent a lot of time on makeup and the shower was too chilly to tempt her to stay in it long. She did want a quick bite first, though. "Thirty minutes?"

"You know the staff house by the cliffs? The one closest to the beach?" At Laura's nod, Tex said, "Meet me there when you're ready to go."

Then he left and once his adorable bare buttcheeks had vanished around the corner, Gizelle turned to Laura.

"Will *you* explain what you were doing?" she asked directly.

Laura felt her cheeks heat again. "He's my mate," she finally said, simply.

"Ah," Gizelle said knowingly.

Laura braced herself to explain further, but Gizelle tossed her head as if she were scenting the air and said, "He likes you," before she turned and scampered off.

Probably, her befuddled look was similar to the look Fred gave her when she caught him leaving the buffet. "I'm headed to the mainland on the boat today," she told him. "So don't worry if you don't see me around!" Then she was off to grab the quickest food available at the buffet before she went to meet Tex.

Laura wasn't sure what to expect when she tapped at the door to the staff house, but it definitely wasn't the cheerful roar of welcome that the staff gave her.

"Come in!" Breck hollered from the kitchen. "*Mi* castle, *es so* castle, or something! Can I get you a breakfast beer? Some juice?"

Travis stood at the bottom of the stairs and shouted up, "Tex, your *girlfriend* is here!" He wandered back into the kitchen to take a plate of eggs from Breck. "It's supposed to be *mi casa*, my *house*."

"Compared to our last place, this is totally a castle," Breck retorted. "It's also one of the only buildings in the place with its own kitchen. Do you want some eggs Miss Smith?"

Bastian, who had answered the door, smiled down at her. "We're watching last night's speeches, join us?" He was already wearing his lifeguard's uniform, the first aid kit strapped to his waist.

Even Graham thawed enough to smile and stand up to remove a pile of questionable literature from the end of the loveseat so she could sit.

Laura did sit, gingerly, and accepted the juice Breck brought her with a flourish.

The Mr. Shifter competition being streamed on the big TV was returning from a promotional break and the little blonde hostess was standing in front of the red curtains of the little theatre, all her charm turned on. If Laura hadn't watched her stridently return a perfectly good meal at the restaurant two nights before, she might have believed the charismatic little act.

Mr. India took the stage and flashed a perfect white smile before launching into a well-rehearsed tirade about responsibility to the environment.

"Keep it down," Breck told Tex, as he stomped down the stairs in his cowboy boots. "This one's actually coherent."

"Unlike Mr. Canada, who might have written his speech from a Tim Hortons menu. Maple syrup and donuts, eh?" Travis was clearly unimpressed.

The bachelor banter faded to Laura's ears at the sight of Tex. Mr. India, in his crisp white shirt, was forgotten.

Cowboys had never done it for her, but there was something about Tex, something that made Mr. India look inconsequential. It was something that made Laura forgive the foolish boots and the big buckle. And the hat was perfect.

"Bring me back some double A batteries, will you, Tex?" Travis indicated an ancient personal tape player.

"I need a new pair of socks," Breck showed off the hole in his stockinged toe. "And can you grab me copy of the latest People magazine?"

"A new septic system would be great," Travis quipped. "I don't know how this one hasn't failed yet."

"We've only got a few more days," Tex reminded them calmly. "Tonight are the final awards, we just have to get through them and then the beach party, and almost everyone will be leaving tomorrow on the charter."

"I don't know if the water system is going to last that long," Travis said. His golden skin couldn't hide the dark circles under his eyes. As early as it was, Laura suspected he had been up late the night before and already been hard at work that morning.

"I wish I was going," he added longingly. "But I know if I step foot off the island, there won't be a working generator in the place."

"I could probably fix a generator," Breck told him. "But I am not touching the toilets, so you aren't allowed to go."

"If people wouldn't keep flushing whatever the hell they are flushing, they'd all work just fine," Travis stormed. "Seriously, who flushes paper towels?"

"Let's get out of here before Travis goes off on a rant about the crappy electrical system that the original builders put in," Tex suggested at Laura's elbow.

"Lucky dog!" Breck called after them.

The dock at the south end of the beach was simple and old, which also described the boat that waited for them. It had two outboards, one tipped up out of the water. While the boat was still moored and Laura was getting comfortable in her seat, Tex drew the other up and put the dry one into service. "Travis says to switch them every time we use them," he explained to Laura's quizzical look. "Says it prolongs their life."

"Why are there two?" Laura asked.

"Emergency, mostly, but also speed. It's a good hour to get to the mainland, a good hour back, and it's open water. You can run both if you're in a hurry, but it's really loud that way, and we're in no rush."

One engine sounded plenty loud to Laura; it drowned out easy conversation as it was.

The day was beautiful; Gizelle's lyrical description of pouring sunshine seemed incredibly accurate. The ocean glittered under the rays and twice they saw pods of whales in the distance, flipping tails and blowing spouts. Laura would not have wanted to see them closer.

"Otter!" Tex pointed out. A small dark head swam beside them for a short while, but they quickly outstripped it. "You don't often see just one of them," Tex observed.

Laura let her hand trail in the sparkling waves and marveled at the ocean. It was incredibly clear. At first, they could see down through turquoise layers to the sand and reef below, but it fell away to unspeakably dark depths very quickly.

There was something comfortable about the journey; the rocking of the boat was initially alarming, but it settled into a soothing, mesmerizing pattern. They felt like a part of it, like they fit together into an interlocking destiny.

Turning to look behind them, Laura watch the island shrink. Roofs and landmarks that already felt like home disappeared into the dark emerald jungle that surrounded it and eventually even that dissolved into the waves of the ocean. It was an odd feeling of loss when it was finally impossible to make out. But by that time, the mainland was in sight, stretching across the eastern horizon like an invitation.

Tex took the boat into a protected little jetty, to a dock so rickety it made the Shifting Sands dock look new and modern. The mix of boats already there ranged from shining yachts to tiny rowboats with ancient outboards bungee-corded onto them.

"Can we just leave the boat here?" Laura asked, looking around. The village they'd landed at was a curious mix, the kind of abject poverty she'd expect from a third world nation directly next to a shiny new tourist cart with a menu in English, German, and Japanese.

"It's perfectly safe," Tex assured her. "They know us here, and no one will risk Scarlet's wrath by stealing anything. That's the sort of thing that only happens once..."

He helped her up onto the dock, which swayed under their steps, and laughed and held her up when Laura's sea legs caught her by surprise. "It didn't feel like that long of a ride," she laughed.

"We'll put our order in at Lee's and go have lunch and a cold drink while they get it together," Tex suggested, tucking her arm into his and strolling to solid ground.

Lee's seemed to be a poorly marked shack from the outside, but was a modern grocery on the inside, stacked to the low ceiling with Spanish-marked goods and more bottled water than Laura had seen in her life. Tex went straight to the back, where a grizzled little Asian man took their order.

"Not sure I can get that many bottles together," Lee said, shaking his head over the wine order. "But I'll ask Lita to run up to the In and Out and see what they have."

Tex tipped his hat to him. "My thanks, sir."

"Anytime, Cowboy. Take your beautiful young lady here over to the market for a while and come back late afternoon. We'll have your boat loaded by four."

Tex shook his hand.

"Give my regards to Ms. Scarlet," Lee added with a wink.

"Always," Tex agreed.

"They know Scarlet here?" Laura observed. "I didn't think she left the island."

"I've stopped being surprised by anything to do with Scarlet," Tex said.

"Will we be able to get back before dark?" Laura asked with sudden concern. She didn't like the idea of boating out into darkness without being able to see where they were going. She was honestly a little unnerved by the thought of boating on the open ocean altogether, but she didn't want to admit that to Tex.

"When Lee says four, that means four on the dot, so we'll have a little over an hour to get back before sunset. Should be fine."

The reassurance was all Laura needed to enjoy herself.

They ate lunch at a place on the outskirts of the village that was mostly a leaning porch and a hut, but it served ice cold colas in glass bottles and plates piled with rice, beans, plantains, a salsa Tex introduced as *picadillo*, something that was almost coleslaw but not quite, and a thigh of spicy grilled chicken.

A skinny stray dog made itself at home underneath their table, and Laura fed it the last of her rice when she was too full for the last few mouthfuls.

There was something about the hum of the ocean and the insects, the cries of toucans in the treetops. The fruity smell of warm jungle was comfortable, and the hum of conversation that Laura didn't understand somehow didn't make her feel excluded. Everyone flashed wide, sincere smiles at her, eyes almost crinkled shut in their enthusiasm.

Laura had stuffed herself full and the stray dog was thumping its grateful tail on her foot when Tex stood up and took her hand. "Let's go see the market."

The market proved to be a crooked row just off the beach of tents and cars with their back hatches open, an informal collection of local merchants selling an array of colorful goods. Scarves fluttered in the breeze and opportunistic sellers offered overpriced suntan lotion and bottled water next to hand-carved masks and sculptures.

Tex stepped knowingly into a slightly more permanent booth, built of weathered plywood on two sides, with a metal roof over tables heaped with open bins of spices.

"I've got a shopping list from Chef," he said apologetically. "I thought I'd get it out of the way first."

"Don't mind me," Laura said, and Tex entered heated negotiations for quantities of spice in the pounds.

Laura wandered away to let him haggle, stroking silky sarongs hung in wild-colored clusters at the edge of the next booth.

"Real silk," the vendor tried to tempt her.

Laura stopped touching them and moved on with an apologetic smile and shrug. The vendor moved on to the tourist behind her, launching at once into a friendly explanation of the dying technique.

Laura glanced to find that Tex and the spice seller were still deep in discussion and wandered to the next booth.

It had a collection of carnival masks, brilliantly painted and finely detailed. She was used to masks that relied on the natural color of the wood, but these were entirely covered in a rainbow of paint, bright animal markings, with tiny toucans and many-hued parrots added in relief along the edges. An empty-eyed wildcat with a tiny emerald island painted on its forehead caught Laura's attention.

"Hand-carved by my uncle, painted by my sister," the seller said with an ingratiating smile. "A special price for you."

Laura touched it gingerly, drawn to it but skeptical of the sales pitch. The price tag was on the high end of reasonable, but even reasonable was out of her price range.

She pulled her fingers back, sobering to remember that she was going to need every penny she had in the event she needed to flee further. The idea of staying at Shifting Sands was undeniably appealing, but part of her still doubted her safety there. There had been two attempts on her life, and although Scarlet was skeptical that it was the mob, Laura couldn't imagine what else it might be.

And she couldn't fathom the idea of someone wanting to hurt Jenny.

She shook her head at the hopeful seller, and walked on, past rows of magnets and souvenirs that had COSTA RICA written in all caps, and, almost as frequently, "*Pura Vida*," the Costa Rican motto that meant "pure life."

She was looking at carved wooden keychains when she glanced around and saw a fit, dark-haired young man in obviously American clothing talking to the seller in the next booth. He looked shifty, with his close-mouthed smile and mirrored sunglasses. Did she imagine the words "Shifting Sands" at the edge of her hearing? She ducked her head and turned away from them. How far would she have to run to get away from the cartel? And how would she do it with the paltry money she had?

She hurried back to where Tex, a heavy bag of spices already purchased, was haggling for socks and double A batteries with a seller out of the back of his car.

A glance back showed the young man buying a keychain, laughing easily. He looked like a tourist, not like a hitman. Laura shook her head and steadied her breath.

There was no point in becoming paranoid.

She greeted Tex with a smile that was first forced, then irresistible in return for his delighted grin. Something about his boyish charm drove away her dark musings, and she resolved not to return to them until they were back on the island. She would enjoy this excursion.

The vendor, having lost Tex's attention, made a valiant effort to get it back. "Both for twenty-five hundred colon, perhaps?"

Tex looked back at him blankly, their negotiations clearly forgotten. "Sure," he laughed with a shrug.

Laura hoped she hadn't distracted him into a terrible price.

Money exchanged, Tex took Laura's hand and they walked on, pausing to look at the items for sale.

Tex convinced her to model ridiculous gemstone sunglasses from one table. Laura got him back by convincing him to try on a rainbow sombrero.

"I love it," she teased, hiding his cowboy hat behind her back. "It's your fabulous new look. Much better than the cowboy hat!"

Tex laughed at her, reaching for his own hat, but Laura giggled and held it away.

Tex tossed the sombrero back onto the display and made a

tackle for Laura, tickling her until she released the hat, and then refused to let go of her without a kiss, which she willingly gave him.

When she glanced back towards the market, she thought she saw the man with the mirrored sunglasses, but he disappeared back into the crowd before she could be sure.

CHAPTER 22

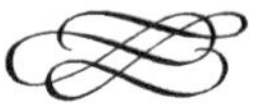

"Are you going to want dinner before we head back?" Tex asked Laura.

"After that lunch? I don't want a whole meal," Laura laughed.

Tex loved the way her eyes sparkled when she wasn't worrying about her future. He would have done anything the in world to keep that stress from her beautiful face. He vowed to make it his life's goal to make her laugh whenever she wasn't.

He introduced her to *queso palmito*, the mild string cheese ball that peeled into delicious layers, and paired it with roadside strawberries.

"Oh," Laura said with delight, putting a second berry to her lips. "These are the best strawberries I've ever had."

She tried to pay the vendor, but there was no way Tex was going to let her open her wallet. "My mother raised me right," he told her firmly.

The stubborn flash in her eyes told him he was in for a fight, but a moment of darkness passed over her face and she put her wallet back in her purse instead.

They walked in silence down to the edge of the beach. A downed tree made the perfect bench, and they sat with feet in the sand, watching the wild brown children playing in the waves. A few tourists in designer chairs sat with a big cooler between them. Laughter and chatter made a lovely soundtrack to their little snack and Tex snuck his hand into Laura's. It lightened his heart when she squeezed it and leaned into him.

Putting his arms around her was the most natural, perfect way to sit.

"I love you," he said, so quietly that he wasn't sure if she heard him. She didn't respond.

After they had licked their hands clean, Tex glanced at his cracked phone display. "They've probably got our order packed up at the boat," he said reluctantly. "We'll want to get out soon to make it back before dark."

He stood and offered a hand to Laura. She looked at it skeptically for a moment, then gave him a slow smile and let him help her up. Tex shouldered the dense spice package and settled his hat on his head, tucking Laura's hand into the crook of his elbow.

They walked back over the sand, laughing at the tiny crabs that scuttled away from their steps, and peering up into the sun at the calling seabirds.

Their steps slowed as they reached the pier and they found that the boat was indeed ready to go. The delivery boy, hauling an empty wagon bigger than he was, presented them with a receipt that Tex signed off on. He put the carbon copy into his wallet and then turned to help Laura step down into the boat, to find that she had already scrambled into her seat.

They putted out of the little bay slowly, then Tex kicked the motor into high gear and the boat skipped over the little waves easily. The sun only just seemed to be dipping down from the zenith, but Tex knew how fast it could set. He squinted out onto the horizon, but the island was still invisible. After a moment of consideration, he crawled back into the stern of the boat and went through the steps to put the second engine into service.

At Laura's quizzical look, he explained, "We want to get back before dark and we're just cutting it a little close."

The engine tipped easily down into the water and Tex pulled

out the choke and yanked on the starter cord until it caught. The motor thrummed to life, coughed, and then caught in earnest.

He was happier with the speed they were making after that.

"Here!" he told Laura, pulling her into his lap. He showed her how to steer the ship, and let her find the right combination of throttle to use against the wave, and how to point the compass.

She grinned and squeaked when she mistimed her charge against a wave, sending shattered saltwater over them. Tex held a protective arm around her, enjoying the way she reacted to the ocean by moving in his lap.

He kissed the back of her neck, and she responded with a throaty purr. "You'll make me drive the boat off course," she scolded him.

Tex was giving her another kiss, followed by an irresistible nibble, when the second engine gave a sudden, unexpected sputter and roar. He only had time to turn and look at it curiously before it exploded.

CHAPTER 23

Laura was trying to focus on keeping the tiny jumping compass line on track with the distraction of Tex's mouth at the back of her neck. She barely heard the noise of the explosion over the roar of the ocean and the engine and she was caught by surprise when Tex's arms wrapped around her and pulled her out of the chair and over the side of the boat.

The water was shocking, even if it wasn't exactly cold, and Laura thrashed reactively when she came up again—until a chunk of railing flew over her head and she realized that Tex was trying to pull her away from the sinking, burning boat, one of his arms around her. For a moment, she went limp, and Tex's strong strokes drew her away from the blaze. Then she added her own strength to their retreat, as the fire hit the water and turned to explosive steam. The boat gave a death gurgle as it sank, and the sound of it was lost to the endless ebb and splash of the ocean around them.

Laura kicked off her shoes and tread water beside Tex, who had only reluctantly let her go to remove his own boots.

"What the hell was that?" she demanded.

Tex shook his head in confusion. "I have no idea what happened!"

His hat was gone, Laura realized with a pang, and she never expected that she would miss it so badly.

Debris surrounded them: chunks of decking, engine molding, a large piece of the awning. Her purse had probably sunk like a stone, but Laura suddenly remembered Jenny's phone, still in her shorts pocket. She'd bought one of those ridiculous waterproof cases for it, but she'd only hoped to save it from being splashed at the beach; she wasn't sure if it was going to work for a full-body salt-water soak.

She must have looked awkward, treading water with one arm and reaching for it with the other. A wave hit her square in the mouth while her attention was divided and she spat and sputtered.

The swells that seemed insignificant in a boat were far more malevolent when Laura barely had her head above water.

While she struggled with her soaking pocket underwater, Tex swam into the debris, testing various pieces with his weight. They weren't going to be able to tread water until someone found them, and swimming back to the mainland seemed as impossible as swimming to the island—both were tiny on the horizon.

Laura was alarmed to see that the sky was beginning to tint red as the sun began its madcap decent for the ocean.

"What the tarnation?!" It was as close to swearing as Laura had heard from Tex, and she looked up from her successful retrieval of the phone to see a small whiskered face poking from the water between them, not even an arms length away.

The otter chittered at her anxiously while Laura backpedaled in alarm.

As quickly as it appeared, it dove down again out of sight, little tail flipping behind it on the choppy water.

It came up a stone's throw away, chattered noisily, and then dove again, to reappear further out.

"It's probably scared of us," Laura guessed.

It scolded them, then made an unmistakable gesture with its diminutive paw, almost capsizing itself with the effort.

"It... wants us to follow it?"

Lacking any other guidance, Laura and Tex exchanged a helpless look and kicked out after it.

It led them unerringly to a chunk from the bow of the boat.

"I thought dolphins were the ones that were supposed to do deep sea saving," Laura said. "I've never heard of otters doing anything like this."

"I think we could sit on that," Tex said, testing its buoyancy by pulling on the edge.

He helped Laura clamber aboard first, a strong hand on her rear nothing but professional.

Laura still found it incredibly sexy.

She moved carefully to the far side of the wreckage to balance it as Tex pulled himself up.

It was tippy and water sloshed up over it regularly, but they could huddle together near the center and catch their breath, at least. Tex's strong arm around her helped Laura calm her racing heart and she let her head rest at his shoulder.

"Couldn't ask for a more romantic view," Tex said, in his dear drawl.

The sun was plunging for the water and all of the waves around them were crimson and gold, glittering with a million facets in every direction. The sky above them was a tapestry of color, rich purple scattered with puffy orange and magenta clouds.

"I think I'd prefer the view from the beach," Laura laughed, but she had to appreciate the incredible hues.

She was acutely aware that they had just survived something awful, that they were stranded on a shard of a boat that could tip them out into the unforgiving ocean at a moment's notice, and that darkness was impending. But all she could think about was Tex's warmth and the feeling of his muscles through his soaked clothing. She tipped her head back to find that he was bending to kiss her, and captured his mouth with her own.

His hands slid over her salty skin, over her collarbones and down to cup her breasts and pull her closer. He nibbled her neck and caressed her back. If Laura hadn't already been soaked to the skin, she would have become immediately wet.

Tex kissed her again, more demandingly, and one of his hands drifted down her thigh, touching her lightly between the legs.

Laura shifted, inviting him in, and the decking they were on plunged and rocked. Laura clutched at his arm and fumbled her hard-won phone, pulling away with a squeak as she recovered it with a lucky catch.

Bless your reflexes, she told her wolf.

One of us has to be useful, her wolf responded, but it was tinged with affection.

"We should, ah, probably save this thought for later," Laura said breathlessly. "For some time when a good orgasm won't swamp our precarious boat and send us both into the salt."

Tex agreed reluctantly, promising, "I'll save knocking your socks off for when it won't drown us."

Then he noticed, "You have a phone? You brilliant angel!"

"Here's hoping it works," Laura said, touching the button. How she had hated that water proof case when she first put it on.

The screen was so bright it lit them up like a torch, making Laura aware of how quickly that darkness was descending.

"Come on, signal," she said, biting her lip.

"There's a bar! There's a bar!" Tex squeezed her shoulders and they bounced in excitement until the slosh of cool saltwater reminded them how precarious their vessel was. "Can you call your friend at the resort? I don't know the resort's number by memory, but having Bastian come get us will be faster than trying to get the Civil Guard out here to find us. Bastian can tow us back."

With shaking hands, Laura pulled Fred from the contacts and dialed.

It rang, while the sun finished its swandive and its last rays faded at last.

It disconnected without giving Laura a chance to leave a voicemail, and she looked in distress at the low battery warning that popped up. "Let me text him," she said desperately, putting the phone into battery saving mode.

She stalled, looking at the text window. "Lost at sea," she finally typed. "Boat exploded. Contact Bastian."

Her life had certainly taken a surreal turn.

After a moment of thought, she added, "He's the lifeguard." She added the emoticon of a dragon impulsively.

The phone registered the text as sent, then viewed, and Laura waited, tensely, for the reply.

Nothing happened.

The bar of signal flickered out and then returned.

She let the screen go to sleep to save the battery life and settled into Tex's careful embrace. The dark water lapped around them, and the bow of the boat dipped and ebbed in the swells that even Laura's night vision could barely make out.

CHAPTER 24

As far as being lost at sea went, Tex thought that things could have been worse.

It was a warm night and they seemed fairly stable on the shard of decking that had survived the explosion. After a short time, the moon, half full, rose to cast a silver-blue sheen over everything.

"I don't think Fred is going to answer," Laura said, puzzled. "I… guess I should call the… what are they called here? Is it 9-1-1?"

"It's 9-1-1," Tex assured her. "And they have an English support line. It's the Civil Guard, they have a coast guard division. Are you sure he saw it? The Mr. Shifter final awards are tonight, so maybe he didn't hear the phone ring."

Laura shrugged under his arm. "The phone says he did. I don't know why it would say he had, if he hadn't." She opened the phone to show him and nearly dropped it as the sliver of boat took an unexpected lurch.

She squeaked and grabbed it hard. Tex watched the line of texts spin backwards as her finger slid across the touchscreen. She started to scroll forward again and slowed down, reading the backchat.

"What is it?" Tex asked, feeling her stiffen.

"This… this conversation. Fred and Jenny." Laura's voice caught in her throat.

Tex tried to guess why it was making her sound so strangled. "Were they having an affair?"

"Ew, no! He was a friend of our dad's! But…"

She let her breath out in a rush and sucked it back in. "He knew that Jenny was planning to use my car and that she wouldn't be at work that morning. She texted and let him know, and he even said he'd be by to pick up a package before she left. I slept through all that… but… he knew. He *knew* I wasn't Jenny. This whole time, he's known I wasn't Jenny."

"That's a little… odd," Tex agreed.

"He could have tampered with my car," Laura said softly. "He's good with electronics, I bet he could have done something to make it go off that curve and look like an accident. He could have rigged at bomb on my laptop, too. And the boat."

Tex had to unclench his fists, consumed with protective rage. "Why would he want you dead?"

Laura gave a hiccup of laughter and shrugged. "He's the closest thing to family we have. Had. I thought we could trust him. I was *this* close to telling him who I was, about a hundred times on this trip. The only reason I hadn't is that I was afraid he would be terrible about keeping a secret, he's so trusting and honest." She snorted. "I guess he was better at keeping secrets than I gave him credit for."

She went rigid again. "My parents… my parents died in a car crash. He was up for the partnership my dad got just a few weeks earlier. You don't think he could have done that?" She sounded shaken to the core.

"I'll find out, if I have to rip off his face to make him talk," Tex snarled, hearing how ridiculous it sounded.

Laura's answering laugh was strained. "Right now, I will settle for solid land under my feet again," she said plaintively. "Gory revenge can wait."

The phone, even though it declared a few percent battery

remaining, gave a chirp of protest and shut down. The sudden darkness was stark.

Laura shivered, and Tex wrapped his arms around her, willing more of his warmth into her. He couldn't imagine how it felt, finding out someone she'd trusted had betrayed her.

"I wonder where the otter went," Laura said softly.

"I guess it figured it had done its duty by saving us," Tex shrugged.

There was a streak of light at the horizon and just as Tex was wondering if he'd imagined it, a star of light exploded in the sky above it, followed by a distant boom.

"We're missing the fireworks!" Laura said with a little laugh.

"You kidding?" Tex said, determined to maintain morale. "We have the best seats in the house. From the resort, there'd be palm trees marring up the view. Everyone fighting over the best chairs."

"Jessica Linn would be drunk and bitchy," Laura chuckled. "I'd be sorely tempted to tip her into the pool."

"I think that's an excellent idea," Tex agreed. "Wish I thought of it sooner."

The first fireworks were swiftly followed by more. It was a great show, with swirling white candles and trailing golden globes. A series of red crackers looked a little like a dragon before fading into smoke.

"They'll be having a bonfire on the beach now," Laura said wistfully. "It must be past midnight."

"I'd be set up at the beach bar," Tex said. "And no one would be able to understand that no, I don't have anything on tap there. And no, I didn't haul down the entire collection of single malt scotches. Bastian is probably already out of tiny umbrellas."

"Who do you think won the Mr. World Shifter competition?"

"Mr. Brazil," Tex guessed. "He took the Mr. Speed contest without trouble, and his speech was lovely."

"Nah," Laura said. "He just didn't have the same charisma as some of the others. And Mr. India was a better speaker."

A green shower of sparkles lit up the water in reflections,

followed by a rainbow of explosions and a coil of white, sizzling lights.

"Mr. Ireland got the most popular votes," Tex said thoughtfully.

"That will get him the Mr. Internet title, but it won't win him the Mr. Shifter title," Laura said decisively. "His speech went over on the time, so he probably lost points for it. I desperately hope Mr. Canada goes away without placing. I can't believe he won the swimsuit portion."

An amethyst waterfall of spinning lights sparkled off of the waves.

"I wouldn't discount Mr. South Africa," Tex said. "He was in second for the race."

"You were keeping pretty close tabs on these standings," Laura observed wryly.

"It was a little hard to miss what was going on, even if I was being distracted by the hottest thing I'd ever seen in my life," Tex told her.

Laura waited a beat, then teased, "You mean Mr. Brazil, right?"

"I mean, you, you sexy vixen," Tex told her, managing to goose her with one quick arm.

She squeaked and giggled, nearly capsizing them.

They stilled, watching the fireworks continue to dazzle the sky and Laura poked him. "Why haven't you ever sung to me?"

Tex blinked. "Sung to you?"

"Everyone tells me you're a great singer and guitar player, but you've never played me anything." Tex could tell that the whine to her voice was for mostly for show, but he wondered if there wasn't a little real hurt down underneath it.

"I thought you didn't like country music," he said, not entirely truthfully. Really, he cared what she thought and didn't want to be a disappointment to her.

She poked him again. "So sing me something that doesn't have stolen pickups and run-over dogs in it."

Tex cleared his throat, feeling suddenly vulnerable. It was odd not to have his guitar under his fingers. He wracked his brain for an appropriate song, something not too sad or depressing. Finally he chuckled and set a beat on the fiberglass beneath them with his fingers before opening his mouth and singing Johnny Cash's Ring of Fire.

They may not ever be contenders for a reality talent show, Tex thought, but after watching the backstage of the Mr. World Shifter contest, he wasn't sure he'd ever do that kind of thing anyway.

For the moment, this was perfect, singing only for his mate. Laura was finally relaxed next to him and Tex was singing the last few repeats of the ring of fire, not wanting to break the spell, before he recognized that one of the blaze of fireworks… wasn't fireworks at all.

"That's Bastian," he said, with sudden relief, pointing.

Something dark was flying near the surface of the water, periodically lighting the area with flame. The finale of the fireworks, a chaotic, brilliant, flower garden of light, lit up the top of its wings. It was obviously a dragon, skimming just above the water in a search pattern.

CHAPTER 25

She was adrift on an unsteady piece of a blown-up boat, in a dark ocean with non-sequitur fireworks exploding overhead and Tex was singing Johnny Cash to her. Laura felt like she was caught up in a crazy analogy of her own crazy life.

When Tex stood up, waving his hands and shouting to attract Bastian's attention, the shard of boat jerked alarmingly. Laura squeaked and tried to flatten herself further, stabilizing their makeshift craft. Warm water splashed over the surface of the decking, soaking parts of her clothing that had only just gotten dry.

But it worked. Within a few moments, Bastian caught sight of Tex, or heard his ridiculous cowboy yodeling, and circled around to fly straight for them. He dove into the water just in front of their craft and came out of the water in human form, pulling himself partway up and asking flippantly, "Hey, you guys need some help?"

Swamped in the water that rushed up over the decking due to his extra weight, Laura could only laugh weakly. "I'd love a drink."

Bastian tsked. "What kind of bartender are you, Tex, coming out all this way on a romantic excursion with no drinks?"

Tex, crouching again to keep them from capsizing, mock

laughed. "Very funny, Bastian. All the booze sank with the boat. Can you tow us home?"

Bastian was already inspecting what was left of the railing and nodded in approval. "Shouldn't be a problem." He had a little coil of rope unclipped from his belt and began tying a sturdy knot. "The real problem," he added, "is what Scarlet it going to say when she sees what you did to her boat."

"It won't compare to what she'll say when she realizes the entire shipment of wine is at the bottom of the drink," Tex said.

"How did you know to come looking for us?" Laura had to ask. "Did Fred tell you?" Something was very wrong with the entire situation with Fred and she had a bone-deep need to understand it, as badly as she didn't want to believe it.

"Fred? That balding fellow with the nervous twitch? No, he hasn't had anything to say beyond asking for more drinks at the bar. Which by the way, Tex, I don't think Scarlet is ever going to let you leave again. No one can keep the natives from getting restless like you can. No, it was an otter that clued me in."

"An otter?" said Tex and Laura together in astonishment.

"We were just talking about whether I should go out after you when it came right up on the beach looking utterly wiped out, dragging what was left of your hat. Must have swum it's little heart out, poor thing."

Twice that otter had saved them, Laura realized, and she felt unsettled.

"Now, speaking of swimming a heart out, you two hold on. I can move a little faster than an otter."

Bastian shifted as he dove back into the water, jeweled scales cutting through the waves in the pale moonlight like diamonds. He had the other end of the rope in his mouth, and Laura was glad that she'd taken his advice to heart and wrapped both arms around a piece of railing.

The rope went taut with a jerk and they were gliding across the water like a poor attempt at a water skate, every other wave cresting over and drenching them. Laura was pathetically grateful when Tex wiggled his way over to her and reached around so he was cradling her between his arms as he held them both on.

She even felt safe enough to take some enjoyment out of the wild ride; the water seemed to be going past as fast as it did on the boat, but they were down at the surface of it. It felt like they were part of it, like they were somehow connected to the ocean's fierce energy.

It was difficult to look up, as that meant a faceful of water periodically, but glances showed Laura first a glimmer of light on the horizon, then it resolved into the familiar terraces of Shifting Sands, the pool deck lit like a beacon. There was a dying bonfire on the beach.

Over the reef, the water was suddenly much more still, and Laura could look up and see all the gorgeous levels of the resort. It felt like home and she suspected that not all of the saltwater on her face was from the ocean.

Bastian remained in dragon shape as they got to the beach and pulled the boat fragment far up onto the sand. A few remaining guests and tired staff reached hands to help them up from the fiberglass shard.

Laura was wrapped in a thick towel and handed a bottle of water.

She was stiff from the long wait in the cool night air and her whole body protested the workout that had come from holding herself in place while being dragged back to shore.

Everyone had questions and Laura truthfully answered what she could, not bringing Fred into the conversation but keeping a wary eye out for him in the crowd.

Tex was never far from her side and she was glad to lean on him.

"Your hat," Bastian said, handing Tex what was left of it.

"It's all chewed up," he said mournfully. "I've had that hat for fifteen years!"

"Give the otter a break," Laura said, feeling defensive of the creature who had been so good to them. "What happened to it? The otter, I mean."

"Gizelle wrapped it up in a towel and took it up to the pool deck," Bastian said. "Muttering about her human being scared, too, and something about long swims and water that wasn't wet. You know Gizelle. About half of it is nonsense."

"And half of it isn't," Tex said thoughtfully, fingering the hole in his hat.

Laura swayed on her feet as a wave of exhaustion broke over her and Bastian immediately noticed. "You guys have been through a lot. Do you want some dinner?"

"Breakfast, actually," said Breck, indicating the dawn breaking on the horizon.

Laura's stomach rumbled distinctly, but she said, "A shower. I'd really like a shower first."

The crowd dispersed, back to their drinks and what was left of the bonfire, and let Tex and Laura climb the stairs from the beach up to the pool deck alone.

CHAPTER 26

Tex was not surprised to find Scarlet waiting for them at the top of the stairs, her critical gaze taking careful stock of their condition. Gizelle was sitting cross-legged on one of the lounge chairs, a towel cradled in her arms. The sunrise was gaining strength and casting glowing orange light over the white deck.

"I presume the boat was lost," Scarlet said without preamble.

"Bastian dragged the biggest piece back, but I'm afraid it's not terribly seaworthy," Tex told her, too tired to be intimidated by her non-nonsense air. "Everything was lost."

"Except you, I'm glad to see" Scarlet said gently, her nod including Laura. "Insurance will cover the rest. I presume it was not merely an… accident."

At Tex's side, Laura suddenly went stiff and Tex looked around to see Fred, standing at the foot of the stairs from the bar deck.

They were both watching him when he caught sight of them and the expression of disbelief and anger was so brief that Tex actually doubted he'd seen it.

Laura had no such doubts.

"If you want answers," she told Scarlet furiously, "ask him!"

Fred managed to look innocent and slightly offended at the same time. "What do you mean, Jenny? Are you okay? What happened?"

"What I don't understand," Laura said, voice heartbroken, "is why. Why would you try to hurt Jenny? Why would you try to hurt *me*? What did we ever do to you?"

Tex was still watching Fred's face, held back from roaring across the tile to smash the man into the ground only by Laura's hand on his arm.

For just a moment, Fred looked shocked and angry, but it was so swiftly masked in hurt innocence that Tex might have been fooled if he hadn't been watching for any sign of guilt.

Before he could do more than growl, there was a streak of fur and the otter that Gizelle had been holding bolted towards Fred, shrieking in fury.

Fred stepped back, nearly tripping on the first step up to the bar deck.

The otter chittered and growled and seemed bigger than an otter ought to be.

Gizelle dashed after the creature and knelt a short space away from it, gazing intently at it. "Use your words," she scolded gently. "Remember yourself!" She ignored Fred completely.

Tex was still trying to figure out how to attack Fred without stepping on the otter or mauling Gizelle on his way when the otter shimmered, seemed to hiccup in form.

It was the most painful shift that Tex had ever witnessed, as if otter and human were fighting for control of the form. Fur stretched, limbs took unnatural shapes and lengths one at a time. Finally, it became...

"Laura?"

He had to check to see that Laura was still standing at his side, mouth open in shock.

"Jenny!"

Then his mate was leaping into the chaos, weeping and throwing her arms around a mirror image of herself.

"You're not dead, I couldn't feel you anymore, I thought you were gone."

"Couldn't," Jenny said, awkwardly. She was swaying, as if exhausted and not sure how her own limbs worked. She picked up a hand, which Tex realized still had short webbed fingers and claws and inspected it thoughtfully. "Lost."

Gizelle looked at Laura warningly. "She's not very found yet," she said.

Tex was not looking at Fred anymore, captured by the drama unfolding.

"I'm not sure if this simplifies or complicates matters," Scarlet said mildly at his elbow.

Fred turned as if to flee and Tex caught the motion out of the corner of his eye. He moved without thinking, crossing the space between them and grabbing him by the back of the neck. His bear wanted to crush the loathsome man, bite his windpipe, and maul his smug face, but Tex reined him back, satisfying his blood lust with a simple shake that left Fred gasping for breath.

Laura wrapped her towel around Jenny's naked shoulders and drew her to one of the lounge chairs. "What happened?"

"She needed help," Jenny answered, in a sing-song voice that Tex knew wasn't hers. "I saw a place for me."

"Was it Fred?" Laura asked, desperately. "Did he booby-trap my car so that you got hurt?"

Jenny cocked her head at her. "Booby-trap?" She considered. "Yes. And another car, long ago."

Laura sucked her breath in. "Our parents?"

"They had things he want. Things he valued. Mo-ney?"

"There was no money," Laura scoffed. "We were paupers."

"There was!" Jenny said, more strongly now, more like Laura would have, Tex thought.

It was very disconcerting, seeing two of them together, features so familiar and dear. It was even more disconcerting watching Jenny struggle with her otter companion.

"What happened to it?" Laura asked, incredulously.

Jenny seemed to rally herself. "Fred very carefully managed it away for us, so it looked like it was just bled away on the market, or lost to taxes, but it was really going into his accounts. And he didn't tell us about the life insurance at all. But I caught him and I figured out what he'd done."

"Your laptop. He blew up your laptop after he saw that I'd accessed your accounts."

Laura's mirror nodded firmly. "He'd do that," she agreed.

"And the boat," Laura said, "He blew up the boat after I told him that I had everything I needed on the cloud. I was just talking nonsense, but he thought I'd figured out what you had figured out and was going to expose him."

"I had enough on him to send him jail for a very long time and we would have been very rich indeed. Mom and Dad's life insurance policy alone would have set us both up for life. We were millionaires, Laura. We just didn't know it."

With a moan, Jenny's eyes rolled up into her head and she slowly shifted into an otter who took two wobbly steps and fell at Laura's feet.

CHAPTER 27

Jenny was alive! She was real, and whole, at least in body, and she was somehow now a shifter. What's more, they were apparently much richer than Laura had ever realized was possible. She gathered the dazed little otter up and cradled her gently. "Are you okay?" she asked plaintively. How cruel would it be to get her sister back, just to lose her so soon?

Gizelle stepped forward with the towel she had the otter wrapped in previously. "There isn't much room in one mind," she said cryptically. "But your sister is still there."

"I won't let him get away with any of it," Laura promised her armful of unconscious otter, wrapping the towel gently around it.

Tex gave Fred another shake, only needing one arm and a grip at the back of his neck to make him plead for mercy.

"Enough!" Fred croaked.

Laura could only imagine the restraint that Tex was showing, given the fury on his expressive face.

She could relate!

"I loved your Dad like a brother," Fred explained to Tex sullenly. "But he got everything that should have been mine. He was a shifter, I wasn't. He got your Mom. He got two beautiful daughters. He got the partnership at the firm. Sure, I got rid of them, but I raised you two like you were my own after that, or I would have, if you hadn't gone haring off after high school. I set Jenny up at our firm when she graduated, and her thanks for that was getting a partnership offer that should have been mine."

"If they offered her a partnership, Jenny earned it," Laura snarled.

Fred ignored her, continuing his confession. "I knew that she was onto the insurance money before I got her text that she was going to be bailing you out again. I thought I could get her out of the way, and do with Laura what I'd failed to do with Jenny. She would confess her masquerade once it got hard to maintain, and I'd protect her and *she'd* be the grateful daughter I deserved."

"Then why did you try to poison me with rattlesnake venom?" Laura demanded. "This is not the way to earn a daughter's love, not that any of this was."

Fred spread his hands innocently, and this innocence was more believable than his earlier show. "I had nothing to do with that. I didn't try to hurt you until you gave me no choice."

Laura didn't want to believe him, but the latte was such a different attempt than the others that Fred had confessed to. And however twisted his motives, he had followed them.

"Where would I even get rattlesnake venom?" he asked. "It's not like they sell it in the gift shop!"

"Then who did?" Tex growled. Laura could tell that it was taking all of his self-control not to flatten the odious man.

"It was probably my cousin," said a new voice. Laura turned to see the man in sunglasses from the mainland bazaar she'd overheard mentioning Shifting Sands. He was walking up the steps from the beach with Bastian.

"Who are you?" Scarlet, Tex, and Laura asked together.

"I saw you on the mainland asking questions about the resort," Laura added suspiciously.

Bastion explained, "He pulled up in a boat and demanded to see Scarlet."

"My name is Sid," the stranger explained, and his smile showed fangs that were just a little sharper and longer than they should have been. "My cousin Maryanne works here. I've come to bring her home."

"Who the hell is Maryanne?" Laura asked incredulously. "And why should she want to poison *me*?"

"We don't have a Maryanne on the staff," Scarlet said with a frown.

Sid ran tired fingers through his hair. "She's probably under an assumed name. She's... not entirely right in the head. She has a habit of lying about who she is, fabricating these involved personas to be, fixating on people who are kind to her. She's a rattlesnake shifter, which makes her little fantasies especially dangerous if they get disturbed."

"Marie," Tex said, in a strangled voice. "Marie thought I was her hero." It was hard for Laura to blame her. He was the best-looking guy at the resort, during a world male beauty pageant, and he was sweet and gentle and perfect.

Scarlet frowned. "She said she was a genet. From France."

"We're from Arizona. She's been missing from the home she's supposed to be in for about six weeks and needs to be on her medication again," Sid said apologetically. "I'm really sorry for the trouble, I hope you weren't hurt, ma'am."

"I wasn't," Laura assured him, still mystified.

"You have some kind of proof of this?" Scarlet asked. "I am unlikely to release a member of my staff to a stranger on the weight of one person's word."

"I have paperwork from her doctor," Sid assured her. "I can give you the number of her facility."

"Please take her," a familiar voice begged.

Laura looked at the side entrance of the pool deck to find that Juan Lopez was approaching, looking wild-eyed and nervous as he came through the arch of greenery. "She's completely nuts! I can't get her to leave me alone! Ever since I put that damned fire out, she's following me around with goo-goo eyes, talking about destiny and heroes."

Laura smirked. It couldn't have happened to a more deserving jerk.

Scarlet was rubbing the bridge of her nose. "Well, this certainly explains everything, even if it does introduce some new complications." She gave Sid a hard look. "Presuming your paperwork checks out, I will release Marie—Maryanne—to your custody."

"Thank you, ma'am," Sid said humbly. "I would, ah, appreciate it if we could leave the authorities out of things. She forgets that she's venomous, sometimes, and doesn't understand consequences."

"There is a report on file with the civil guard for the initial incident," Scarlet said candidly. "But they tend to turn a blind eye to what happens out here. If they pursue an investigation, I shall simply tell them that it turned out to be a… misunderstanding."

Sid nodded. "I think that's an accurate summary," he said wryly. "She really doesn't understand what she's doing."

Scarlet was already turning away from him. "You, on the other hand," she said in icy tones to Fred. "You are a problem."

Fred was glaring sullenly at the ground. Tex helpfully tipped his head up. "It's good manners to look at a lady who's talking to you. I could escort him off the resort," he offered suggestively.

"As tempting as it is to walk him off the cliffs, we *will* let the civil guard deal with *him*. I'm sure he'll be extradited to the US for his crimes there."

Tex looked disappointed, but brightened when Scarlet suggested, "Truss him up in the meantime. I don't take attempts on my staff's life lightly."

Laura wasn't sure when she had gone from guest to staff, but hearing Scarlet say it let a knot of tension unravel in her chest.

"Juan? Juan darling?" Marie's—Maryanne's—false French accent was light and airy above the island sounds of surf and rustling leaves. "Where aaaare you?"

Juan groaned and bolted for the stairs. "You haven't seen me!" he shouted as he fled.

Maryanne did a double-take when she walked through the side door. "Sid!" she cried.

"I'm here to take you home, Maryanne."

Maryanne pouted artistically. "But I was having so much fun!"

"You almost killed someone!" Sid protested. "Again!"

"She didn't get hurt," Maryanne whined. "It was all just pretend."

Sid rubbed the bridge of his nose, much as Scarlet had earlier. "I told you that you can't spit in people's coffee. It's bad! Let's go home, kitten. I'll help you pack up."

"Oo," said Maryanne. "I'll show you my room!" Her French accent was completely gone. She took Sid's hand willingly and tripped off with him towards the staff housing.

CHAPTER 28

Tex growled at Fred to stay and cowed him enough to obey while he ducked into the pool's mechanical room and found the duct tape. "I'm afraid all we have on hand is pink duct tape," he said without apology.

Fred gave a token struggle as Tex trussed up his wrists, thought about it, and did his ankles, too.

"Hey, I've got rights," Fred protested. "This isn't constitutional! You can't leave me like this!"

"We're not in the US," Tex reminded him. "But you're right, I can't leave you like that." Another piece of duct tape went over Fred's mouth and Laura laughed out loud.

"That will do," Scarlet said, not disapprovingly. "I'll send Graham down to watch him." She turned away from his wiggling protests to address Laura. "You are, of course, welcome to stay as long as you need. Your sister will need some time and help to come to terms with being a shifter and this is a safe place to do that."

"I can work," Laura said automatically. "I'm happy to help at the spa, or make beds, or do laundry."

"We can come to an arrangement in a day or two," Scarlet

suggested. "Get a good night's—a good morning's sleep. Eat and have a shower. Gizelle can watch over Jenny while you rest."

Gizelle bobbed her head up and down vigorously and stepped forward to take the little bundle. "I won't let the darkness burn her," she promised.

Laura gave her a quizzical look, then reluctantly passed her the towel-wrapped otter.

As Gizelle trotted off to… wherever it was that Gizelle stayed at night, Scarlet frowned at Tex. "You head to bed, too. We'll be seeing most of our guests off today and everyone will get a little well-deserved break." She strode off up the stairs towards the restaurant.

Tex suspected Scarlet would not be getting any immediate rest herself.

"Well, handsome," Laura told Tex, "Let's go to bed. You made certain suggestive promises on what was left of the boat that I expect you to make good on."

Tex tried to tip his hat to her and his fingers found the otter-chewed hole. "I could find the energy for that," he agreed as they slowly climbed the stairs, heading without consulting each other towards Tex's room in the staff house.

"We'll get you a new hat," Laura promised. "Jenny said we're millionaires, remember?"

"I thought you hated the hat," Tex said. "This would be your chance to get rid of it."

"It's grown on me," Laura decided. "And you wouldn't be you without it."

"I wouldn't be me without you," Tex told her, stopping on the stairs to look her earnestly in the face. "Everything else is just trappings."

"I love you, Tex," Laura told him solemnly. "I love all the parts that make you, even the big belt buckle and the beat up hat. I want you to sing me the saddest, countriest songs you know, because you love them and I love you."

Tex's slow, earthy smile was as brilliant as the sun in the tropical sky. "I love you, Laurelangelina Lily."

"Fancy you remembering that whole name," Laura said, clearly impressed.

Tex moved closer. "I also remember that promise I made you about knocking your socks off when we were safe on land."

"I'm not wearing socks," Laura told him suggestively.

"I'll improvise," Tex promised.

EPILOGUE

Laura tossed her sandals to one side and settled into the nearest beach chair. Tex was restocking the little self-serve beach cabana and cleaning up the ravages of the party from the night before. The late afternoon beach was all theirs, empty lounge chairs and beach umbrellas invitingly lonely. The piece of the boat they'd been stranded on still lay at one end near the dock, a few crabs enjoying the rare afternoon shade beneath it.

"Everything's sorted," Laura said with great relief.

Tex closed the little cooler and walked over to pick up one of her feet to rub. "Did you talk to Tony?"

Laura nodded, letting his clever fingers massage her toes. She'd been on the phone for nearly three hours with the operative of a mysterious government agency that represented shifter issues. It didn't sound like hard work, but she'd spent most of the call pacing nervously.

"He's got all the paperwork in motion for getting me declared not dead," she said. "We're going with the story that I was concussed, picked up by an illegal Central American fisher, and eventually left here at the resort. Fred has been transferred to American custody already. Our testimony might not have been enough, but he had rambled an insane confession before they even made the exchange with the Civil Guard. Tony says that it's going to take a while to unravel the paperwork regarding the inheritance, but signs are good that the money will be ours free and clear."

"And the cartel?"

"He took my testimony and got the slow grinding gears of the American legal system working on that, as well. He thinks it's a good idea that Jenny and I lay low here until they've gathered enough evidence, which is probably best for a while anyway."

"How *is* Jenny?" Tex asked, more seriously, switching feet.

"Oo," Laura said, as his fingers found the sorest spots. "She's… better. Shifting is still really painful for her, and she hasn't exactly sorted out how to deal with the otter in her head, but Gizelle says she can help her."

"I'm so glad you have her back," Tex said, in his sincere drawl.

"Me, too," Laura agreed. She took her feet back and sat up, looking up towards the pool deck. "The resort seems so peaceful today," she said wonderingly.

"This is a lot more normal for us," Tex assured her sitting beside her and putting an arm over her shoulders. "Last week was an anomaly, and while it looks like we've got more business than usual coming up, by comparison, it should be pretty quiet."

"I am going to love working here," Laura said with a sigh, letting Tex nibble at her neck.

"Scarlet would probably let you stay on credit," Tex told her.

Laura shook her head. "I don't want to," she said firmly. "Even if we're millionaires or whatever, I think I'd rather be part of something like this than sit on my ass paying people to wait on me."

"It's a fine ass," Tex said admiringly.

"Undeniably," Laura teased back. "I hope you'll have time to finally play that guitar you drag everywhere, now that it's quieter."

It was leaning in the beach cabana now, and it didn't take more than the suggestion for Tex to walk over and get it. He sat back down with it cradle in his hands, testing the tuning with a few bars of a Spanish love song.

Laura leaned back and let him start playing a sad song about death that took a bizarre turn halfway through and turned into a plea to prop his corpse up by the jukebox if he died.

Laura ended up in tears of laughter and clapped as he played the final lines. "All these years I thought I hated country music," she said, "and didn't realize what I was missing."

Then she sobered. "There is something terribly important I am still missing though."

Tex looked worried and his fingers, which had continued playing chords, stilled on the strings. "What is it? Anything you need, I'll get it for you."

"I never found out who won the Mr. Shifter competition," Laura told him with deadpan seriousness. "My life cannot be complete without this knowledge!"

The lines around Tex's eyes crinkled perfectly with his laugh. "Mr. India," he told her, when his guffaws let him. "Mr. Brazil was the first runner up and Mr. Ireland was the second runner up. Did you lose any bets?"

Laura shrugged. "I'm just tickled that Mr. Canada didn't place. That was my only desire."

"Your only desire?" Tex said suggestively. He kissed her neck again, letting teeth brush her skin.

"Well, maybe not my *only* desire," Laura agreed with a breathless laugh.

They made it back to Laura's little cottage in the jungle with their clothing barely intact; Tex had gotten his shirt off, and Laura's shorts were unbuttoned by the time the door was open. The remaining articles had been shed by the time they reached the bed.

Tex lowered her onto the mattress as if she were weightless, then joined her there, his skin like hot velvet against hers.

He paused, thick member at her entrance, but not pressing. "I'm yours," he told her, voice low and rough with emotion.

Wild with need and hunger, Laura pressed herself up and around him. "I'm yours," she agreed.

But Tex held back. "Do you mean it?" he asked.

Laura stilled. "I mean it completely," she said. "I'm *yours*."

Tex nuzzled her, then nibbled at the place where her shoulder met neck as he entered her.

Her cry was all pleasure, and she arched up to his strong thrust. “Oh, yes…”

Tex claimed his mate with every stroke and touch, bound to the lush woman as he’d never imagined was possible. “I’m yours,” he told her, between ragged breaths.

“I know,” she told him.

TEX'S COCKTAIL RECIPES

Shifter's Mate

Ingredients:
1 1/2 oz Light rum
1/2 oz cas juice (aka sour guava.)
1/2 oz Orange curaçao
1/2 oz Orgeat syrup
3/4 oz Dark rum (Centanario)

Preparation:

Shake first four items together in a cocktail shaker with ice. Strain into glass with fresh ice and float dark rum on top. Garnish with cubes of fruit and an umbrella, serve with a straw.

Rise and Shine

Ingredients:
8 oz Iced coffee
1/2 oz Orange curaçao

Whipped Cream

Preparation:

Mix first two ingredients, serve in tall mug over ice with garnish of orange and whipped cream.

~

The Hairy Martini

Ingredients:

1/2 oz dry vermouth
3 oz gin
1/2 oz kiwi syrup

Preparation:

Mix all ingredients in cocktail shaker with ice. Strain into glass (straight) or over ice (on the rocks). Garnish with a kiwi slice with the skin still on. Umbrella optional.

~

Magnolia's Mango Mojito

Ingredients:

2 oz Light rum
generous fistful of mint leaves
4 oz mango juice
1 teaspoon of superfine sugar

Preparation:

Bruise the mint leaves in the rum, stir in sugar and mango juice until sugar is dissolved. Serve over crushed ice and garnish with fresh mint and a wedge of lime.

~

Graham's Ginger Snap

Ingredients:

1 1/2 oz vodka
1 oz ginger liqueur
1 oz fresh lemon juice
1/4 teaspoon agave syrup
1/4 teaspoon grated fresh ginger
Pinch cinnamon
Pinch cloves
Pinch nutmeg

Preparation:

Shake all ingredients in a cocktail mixer. Serve over ice with a cinnamon stick.

A NOTE FROM ELVA BIRCH

Shifting Sands Resort has a very special place in my heart and I hope you enjoyed your introduction to this island full of secrets. This story continues in three more volumes, and I hope you'll join me on the journey!

I would love to know what you thought—you can leave a review at Amazon or Goodreads (I read every one, and they help other readers find me, too!) or email me at elvaherself@elvabirch.com. I really enjoy hearing from my readers and I especially love finding out what your guesses for what Scarlet's true nature were before you got to the big reveal!

If you'd like to be emailed when I release my next book, please visit my webpage and sign up to be added to my mailing list at elvabirch.com. You can also also follow me on Facebook or join my Reader's Retreat Group on Facebook for sneak previews and conversations!

SHIFTING SANDS RESORT COMPLETE TIMELINE

Shifting Sands Resort shares a world with Fire and Rescue Shifters, and Shifter Kingdom. This is a complete timeline of all three series, with short stories in their appropriate order. This is not at ***all*** *the order I would recommend reading them the first time, as many of the short stories spoil the subsequent books!*

Steps (Tropical Tails)
Roots (Tropical Tails)
Run (Tropical Tails)
Treasure Sense (Tropical Tails)
A Recipe for Happiness (Tropical Holiday Tails)
Firefighter Dragon
Firefighter Pegasus
Royal Guard Lion
Royal Guard Tiger
Firefighter Griffin
Tropical Tiger Spy
Other Duties as Assigned (Tropical Tails)
Locked (Shifting Sands Omnibus Vol 1)
Tropical Wounded Wolf
Unlocked (Shifting Sands Omnibus Vol 1)

Firefighter Sea Dragon
The Master Shark's Mate
Tropical Bartender Bear
Not Kitten Around (short story)
Detective Breck (short story)
Tropical Lynx's Lover
The Storm (Tropical Tails)
Tropical Dragon Diver
Tropical Panther's Penance
A ChristMOOSE Story (Tropical Holiday Tails)
Dance Lesson (Tropical Tails)
The Betting Pool (Tropical Tails)
Firefighter Unicorn
Tropical Christmas Stag
Scarlet and the Christmas Kittens (Tropical Holiday Tails)
(the epilogue of Tropical Christmas Stag)
Lift (Shifting Sands Omnibus Vol 3)
Firefighter Phoenix
Tropical Leopard's Longing
Her Hellhound Bodyguard (Tropical Tails)
(the epilogue of Tropical Leopard's Longing)
Pregnancy Knows (Shifting Sands Omnibus Vol 3)
Tropical Lion's Legacy
Fake Fur (Tropical Tails)
Reunion (Tropical Tails)
Pickled Magnolias (Tropical Tails)
(the epilogue of Tropical Lion's Legacy)
Tropical Dragon's Destiny
A Will and a Wedding (Tropical Tails)
A Hoard of the Their Own (Tropical Tails)
Of Course (Tropical Tails)
Perfect Match (Tropical Tails)
All in the Timing (Tropical Holiday Tails)
Thawing His Hart (a holiday novella)
(the epilogue of Tropical Dragon's Destiny)
Unreliable Senses (Tropical Tails)

OTHER BOOKS FROM ELVA BIRCH

The Royal Dragons of Alaska: A fascinating alternate world where Alaska is ruled by secret dragon shifters. Adventure, romance, and humor! Reluctant royalty, relentless enemies…dogs, camping, and magic! Start with *The Dragon Prince of Alaska*!

Fae Shifter Knights: A four-book fantasy portal romp, with cute pets and swoon-worthy knights stuck in a world of wonders like refrigerators and ham sandwiches. Start with *Dragon of Glass*!

A Day Care for Shifters: A hot new full-length series about adorable shifter kids and their struggling single parents in a town full of mystery and surprise. Start the series with *Wolf's Instinct*, when Addison comes to Nickel City to take a job at a very special day care and finds a family to belong to.

Lawn Ornament Shifters: The series that was only supposed to be a joke, this is a collection of short, ridiculous romances featuring unusual shifters, myths, and magic. Cross-your-legs funny and full of heart! Start with *The Flamingo's Fated Mate*!

Green Valley Shifters: A sweet, small town series with single dads, secret shifters, sweet kids, and spinsters. Standalone books where you can revisit your favorite characters. Start with *Dancing Barefoot*!

Suddenly Shifters: A hilarious series of novellas, serials, and shorts set in the small town of Anders Canyon, where something (in the water?) is making ordinary citizens turn into shifters. Start with *Something in the Water*!

Birch Hearts: An enchanting series of short stories and novellas. Unconstrained by theme or setting, each short read has romance, magic, and heart. And always, the impossible and irresistible. Start with *Prompted 2* for fourteen pieces of sizzling flash fiction.

Not sure where to start? Take the quiz at elvabirch.com to find your perfect book!

BEHIND THE SCENES

What is Patreon?

Patreon is a site where readers and fans can support creators with monthly subscriptions.

At my Patreon, I have tiers with early rough drafts of my books, flash fiction, coloring pages, signed and sketched paperbacks, exclusive swag, original artwork, photographs…and so much more! Every month is a little different, and there is a price for every budget. Patreon allows me to do projects that aren't very commercial and makes my income stream a little less unpredictable. It also gives me a place to connect with my fans!

Come find out what's going on behind the scenes and keep me creating at Patreon! patreon.com/ellenmillion

www.ingramcontent.com/pod-product-compliance
Lightning Source LLC
Chambersburg PA
CBHW070552310726
48982CB00011B/1553/J

* 9 7 8 1 9 3 3 6 0 3 6 7 4 *